VANDALS

THE PHOTOGRAPHY OF THE MOTION PICTURE

THE BIKERIDERS

VANDALS

THE PHOTOGRAPHY OF THE MOTION PICTURE THE BIKERIDERS

A FILM BY JEFF NICHOLS

CINEMATOGRAPHY BY ADAM STONE

PHOTOGRAPHS BY BRYAN SCHUTMAAT AND KYLE BONO KAPLAN

INSPIRED BY DANNY LYON

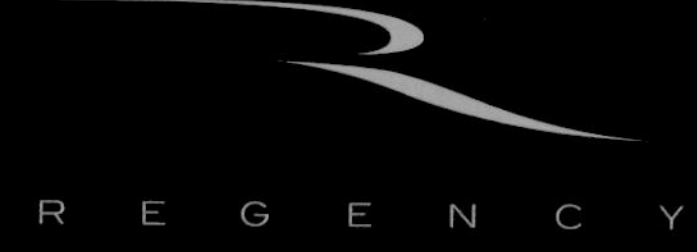

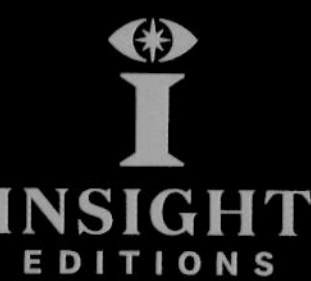

SAN RAFAEL • LOS ANGELES • LONDON

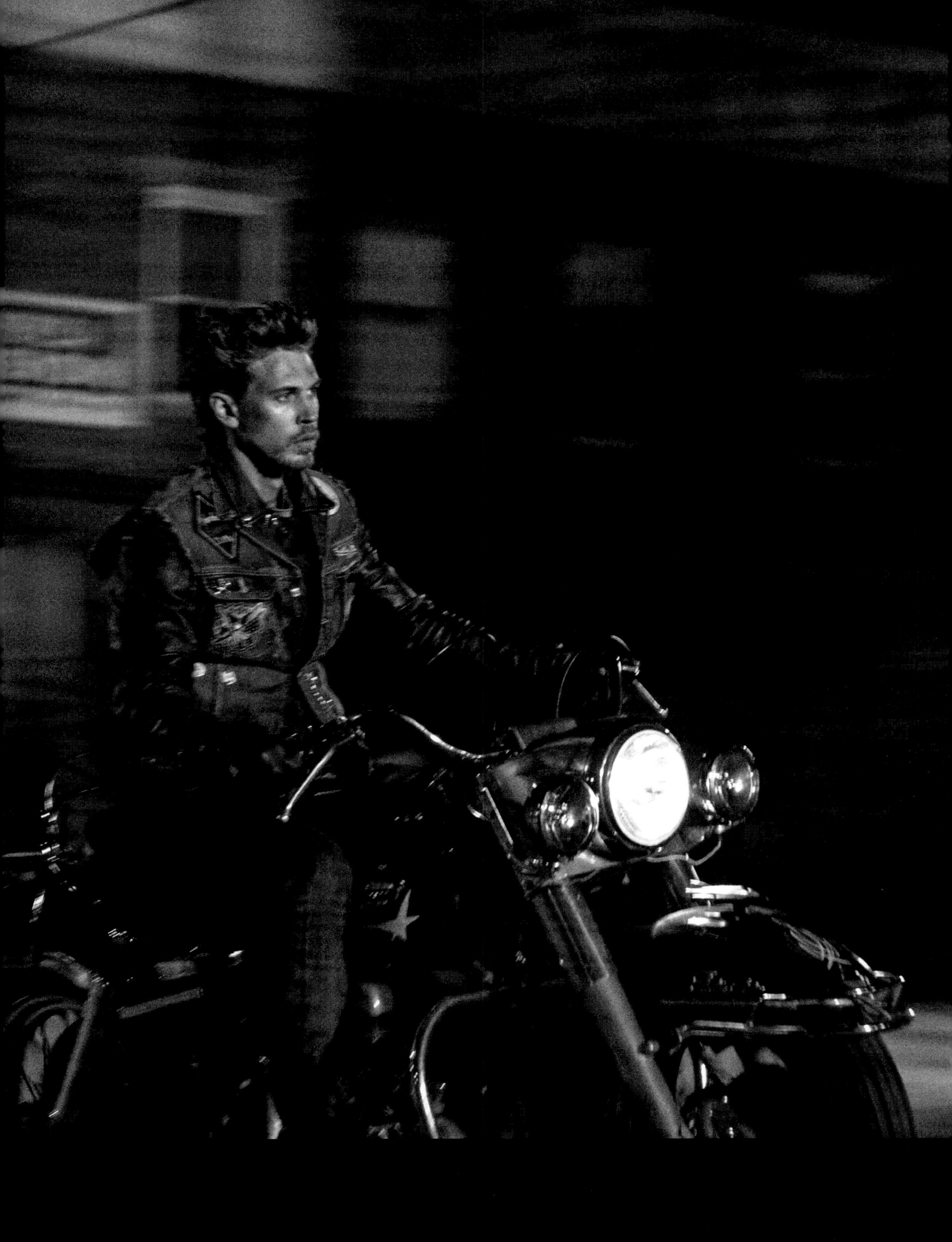

KATHY

I've had nothing but trouble since I met Benny. I've seen more jails, I been to more courts, and met more lawyers. I mean it can't be love, it must just be stupidity.

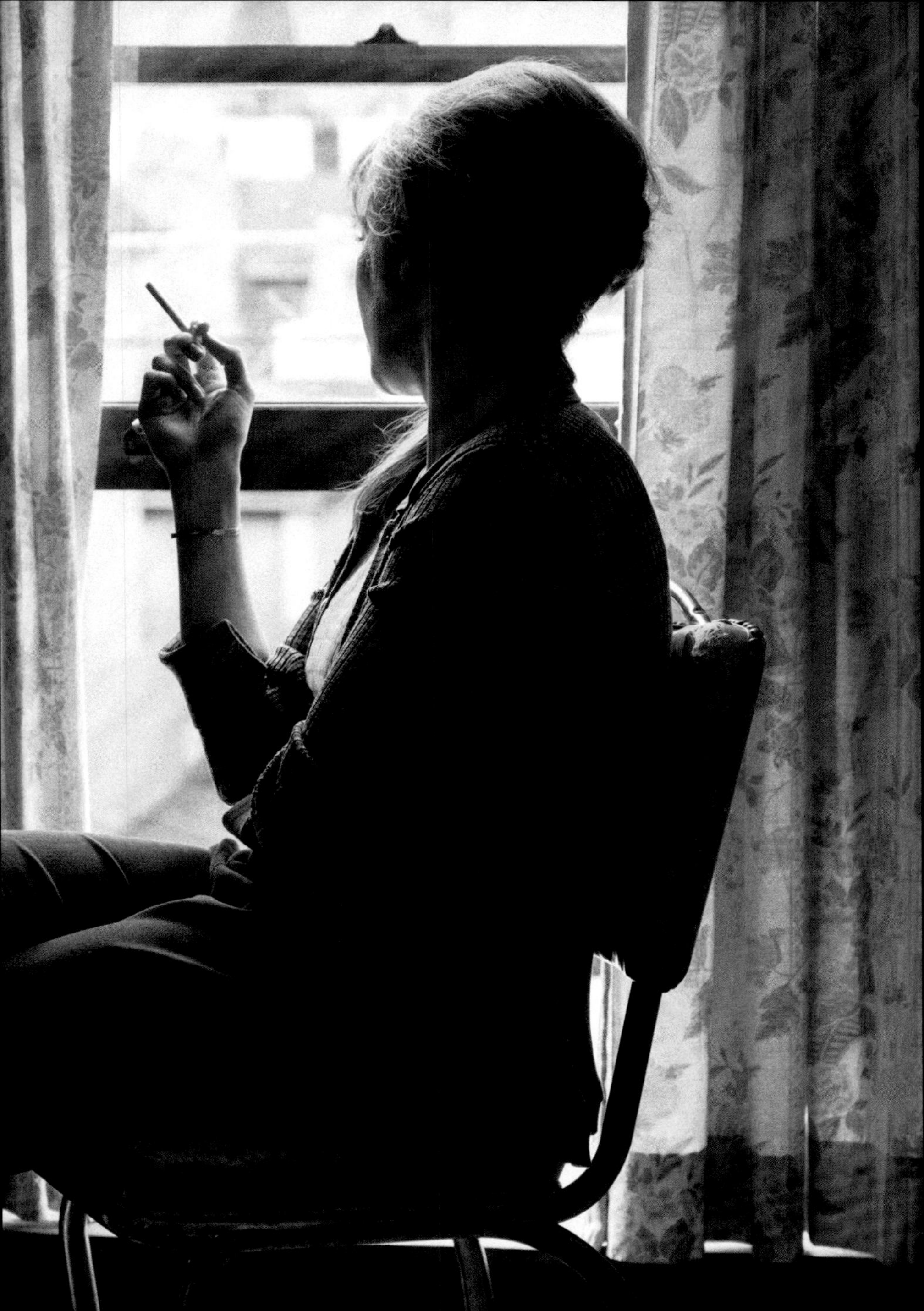

FOREWORD by Jeff Nichols

Around 2003, my brother Ben was living with his band, Lucero, in a Memphis warehouse that was once a dojo where Elvis did karate. I walked into his bedroom and saw a book sitting on the floor that would then become my obsession for two decades. It had a brilliant red cover with the words "THE BIKERIDERS" knocked out in bold, white text. Above this, was a black-and-white photograph showing the backs of five motorcycle riders cresting a rise on a rural highway in the 1960s. This cover is one of the most compelling things I have ever seen.

That copy was a re-issue of Danny Lyon's 1968 book, *The Bikeriders*, a landmark of photojournalism. Detailing his days riding with the Chicago Outlaws, Danny was able to capture images and the voices of people as they truly were. The photographs alone are enough to captivate and inspire, but when combined with the transcribed interviews Danny recorded, you got a portrait of the people who made up this subculture that was jarringly honest. In this re-issue, Danny wrote a new foreword that included a brief recounting of what happened to the people and the club that he rode with decades before.

When talking about the fate of the club's original leader, Danny wrote, "While a group of old and new members sat in their cars watching, Johnnie Davis walked out alone to fight for his leadership, and his young rival simply took out a gun and shot him. That was the end of the club I had joined and ridden with in 1966." With these words, the shape of what would become my screenplay took root. A prequel of sorts, I wanted to follow a small, regional motorcycle club that eventually grows into a proper gang over the course of a decade. I first reached out to Danny in 2014 to discuss the possibility of a film inspired by his book. At his home in New Mexico, I began, somewhat clumsily, to lay out my ideas for the film.

I've always tried to find a universal theme in my films. The idea being that if you have a universal thought at the core of your story, it is possible to make a very personal, regionally specific film that feels totally unique to a specific time and place but can still resonate with a broad and diverse audience. I think the film *The Bikeriders* is about our search for identity. It is very much about American masculine identity, but only thinking of it in those terms misses a bigger idea. We are all desperate to find and build an identity for ourselves. I think this is one of the greatest animating forces at work in our society right now. People no longer simply define themselves by their work or where they went to college. We are turning to our sex, race, culture, and history to help us find a deeper, more meaningful identity for ourselves.

What I find interesting, and what *The Bikeriders* film directly addresses, is that in our search for a unique identity, we very often turn to groups to help us define ourselves. It is human nature to want to belong, but that feeling is compounded when the group we choose to belong to is more unique. The more specific the group, the clearer the identity. In some instances, this can be a wonderful, powerful thing in our lives. In others, it can be terribly destructive. The film *The Bikeriders* represents both possibilities.

When you combine this universal idea, or truth, if you want to go that far, with a subculture as complicated, colorful, dangerous, and alluring as American motorcycle culture, I think you have the recipe for a film that will speak to a lot of people.

While Danny Lyon's book illuminated for me all the thoughts mentioned here, it was also, quite simply, the coolest book I'd ever come across. My hope was to make a film that captured, and more importantly transferred, that feeling to a moviegoing audience. Ultimately, that was my wish for *The Bikeriders*.

While in preproduction, our studio, New Regency, approached us with the idea of making a book about the filmmaking process for their publishing partners, Insight Editions. I'm a fan of the beautiful books they've published that detail the inner workings and thoughts behind some truly incredible films. However, given that the DNA of our film came from an art photobook, it felt interesting to us to attempt to make an art photobook of our own. Rather than capturing behind-the-scenes imagery supported by details that pull the curtain back on our production, what if we photographed our characters and scenes as if they were really happening? My cinematographer, Adam Stone, who has shot all six of my films and remains one of my most important collaborators, introduced us to the incredible work of Bryan Schutmaat and Kyle Kaplan. The idea of having photographers as accomplished as Bryan and Kyle helping photograph our film was thrilling, and I think this collection of photographs demonstrates that feeling.

It's important to note that the images created here are the result of an immense amount of work from a collection of very talented people. While Kyle and Bryan's talents captured these moments, the craftspeople that helped us bring the period and culture of *The Bikeriders* back to life deserve more credit than I can give them on this page. Our costume designer, Erin Benach, was responsible for creating and layering details into these clothes and styles. It's easy to look at all this work and think, "Yeah, they look like bikers." But know that every piece was thoughtfully considered, down to each patch and grease stain. Our production designer, Chad Keith, was responsible for overseeing the incredibly detailed and beautiful sets. Our hair and makeup departments, led by Tony Ward and Ashleigh Chavis, gave us greased hair, hands and faces covered with a myriad of tattoos, and an insane array of bouffants and pompadours. All of this was lit by our gaffer Michael Roy. I must also mention the efforts of our co-stunt coordinator and motorcycle guru, Jeff Milburn. Every bike you see here is period correct and was lovingly sourced by Jeff. Finally, I need to credit our incredible actors who carried the weight of these characters on their faces. You'll of course find movie stars in these pages. It is easy to understand why they are great actors by studying these faces, but you'll also find background characters and extras who faithfully filled out our sets with extraordinary attitudes and even better countenances. I owe a lot to everyone who helped bring these images to life, and I hope you enjoy them as much as I do. I'm incredibly proud to have been a part of this work.

Sincerely,
Jeff Nichols

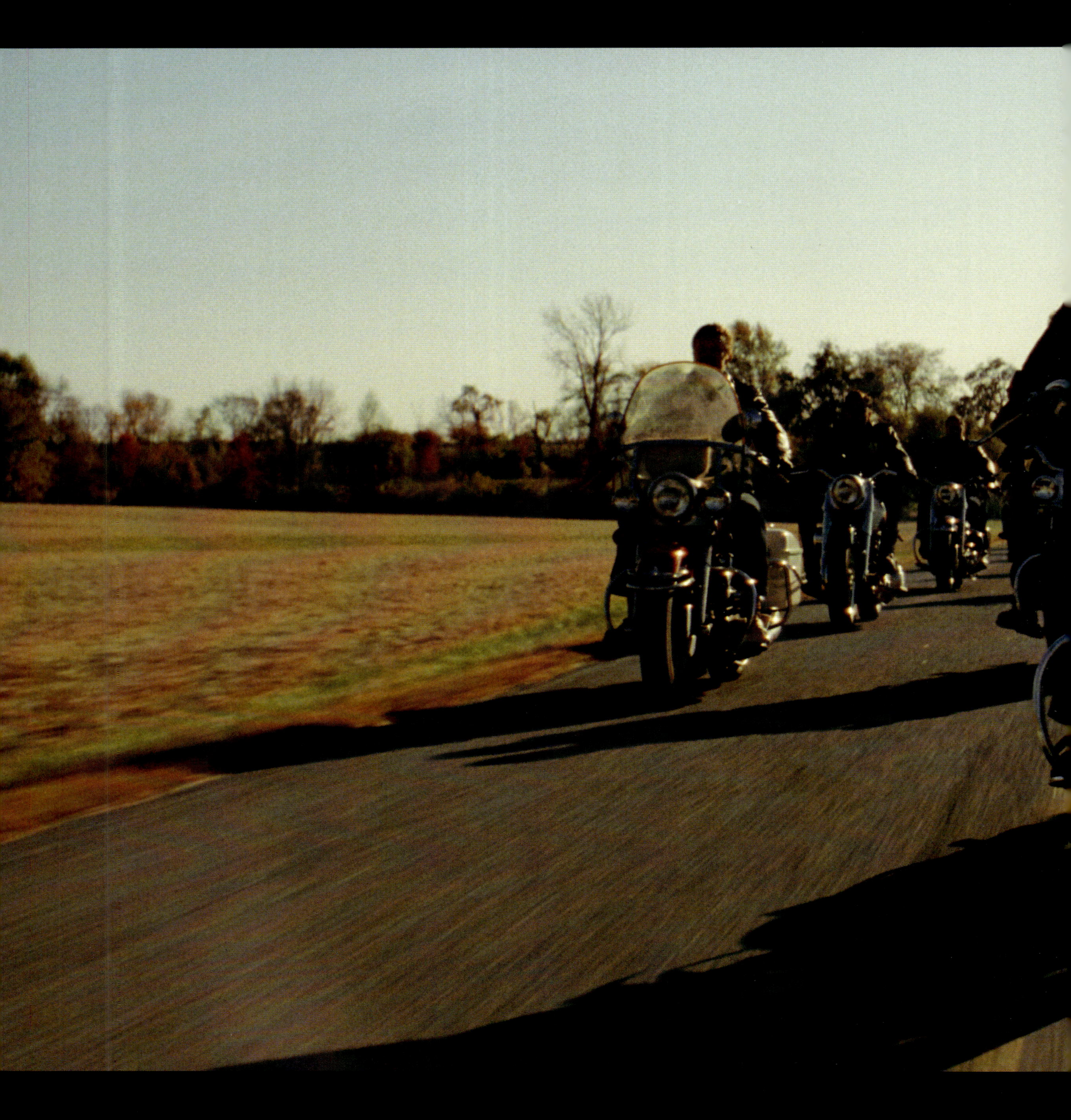

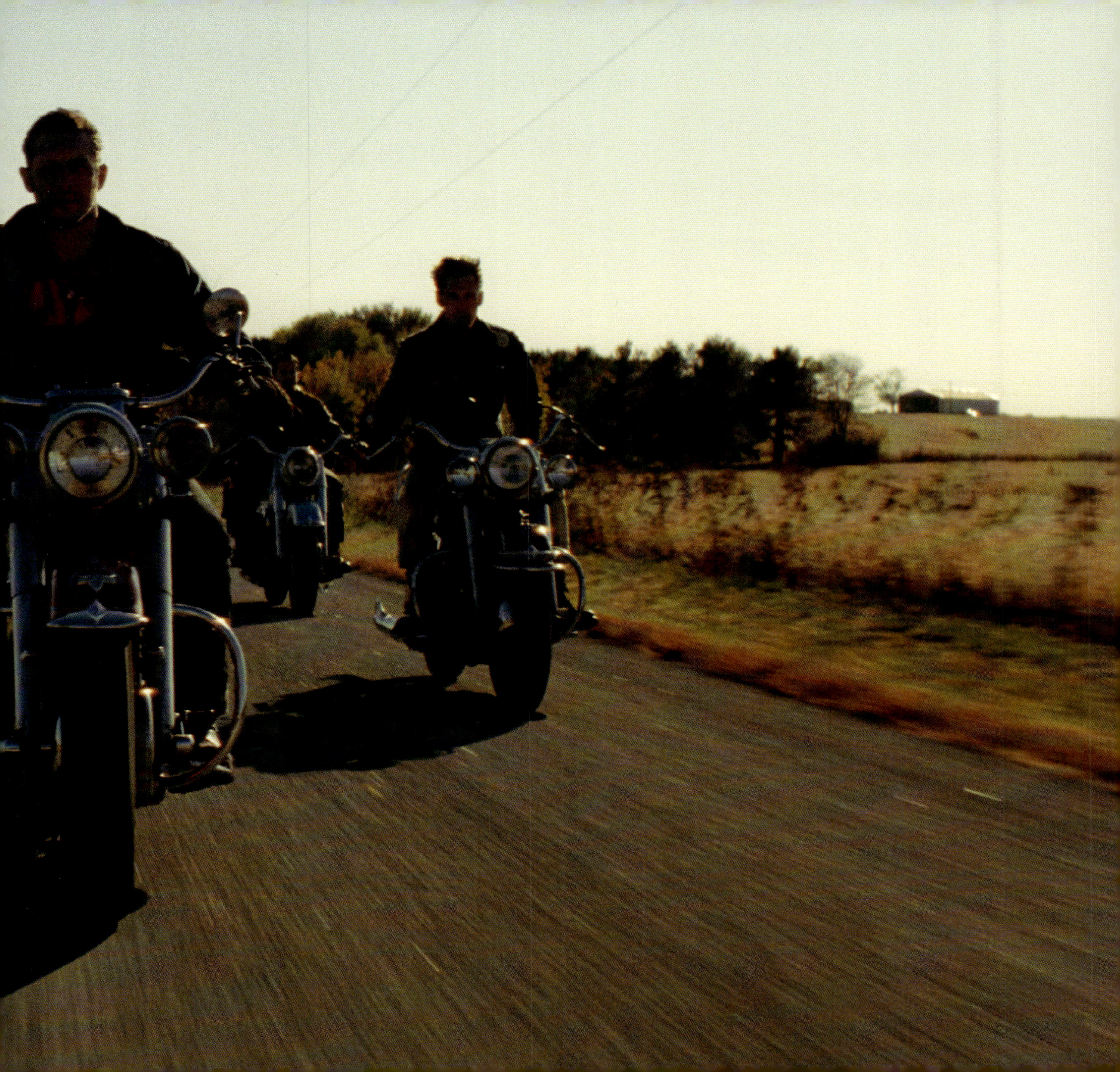

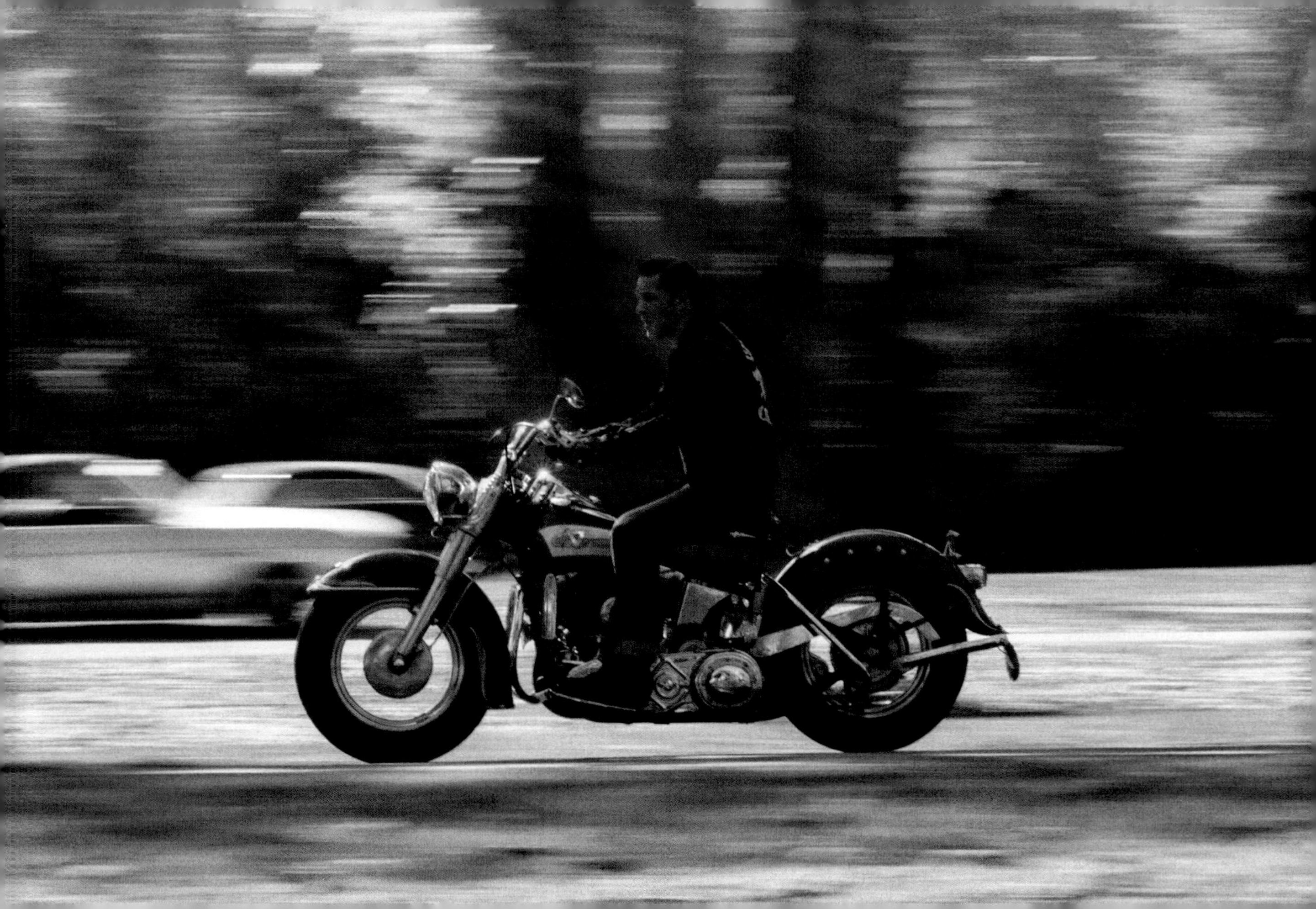

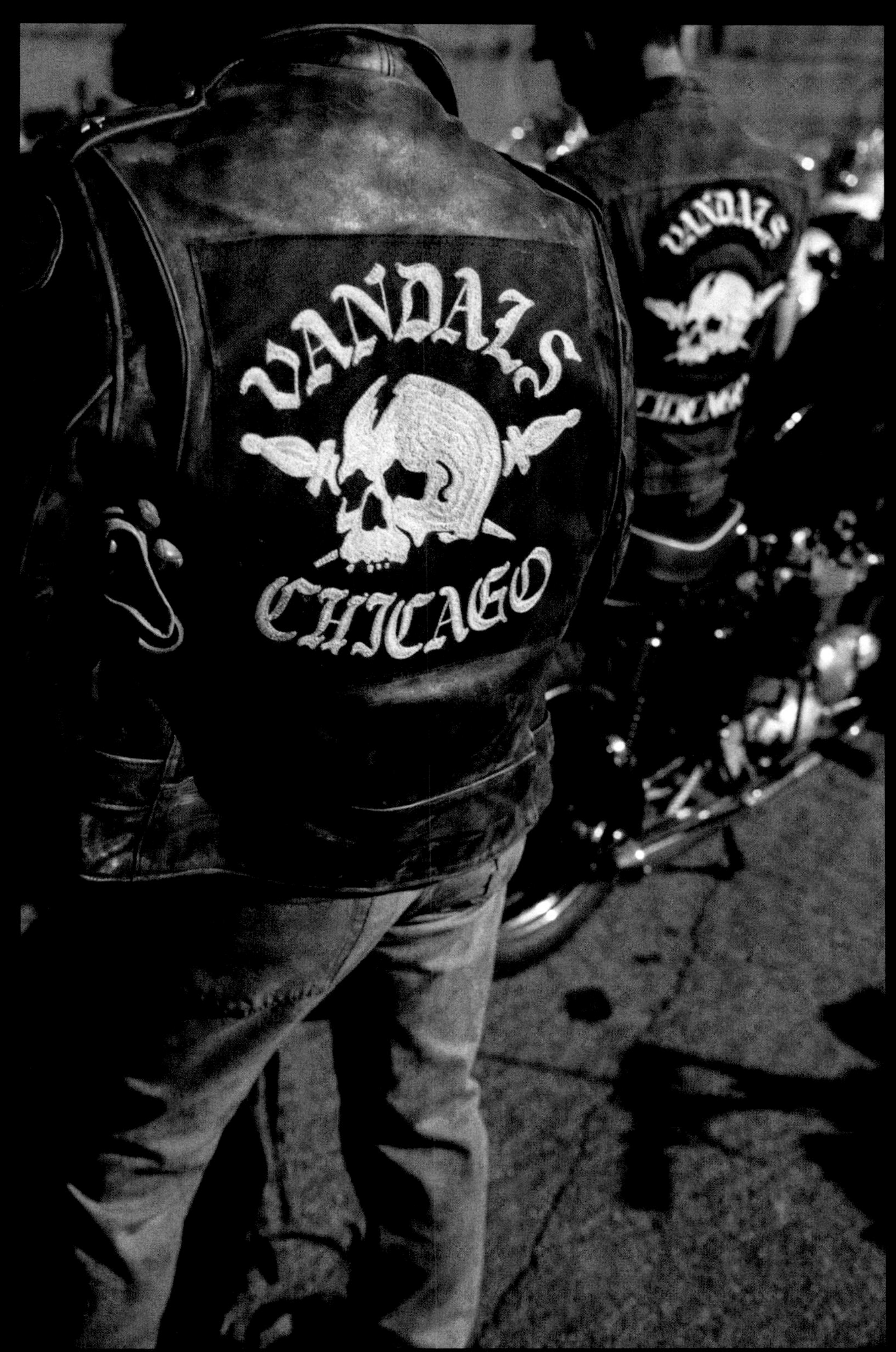
VANDALS
CHICAGO
VANDALS

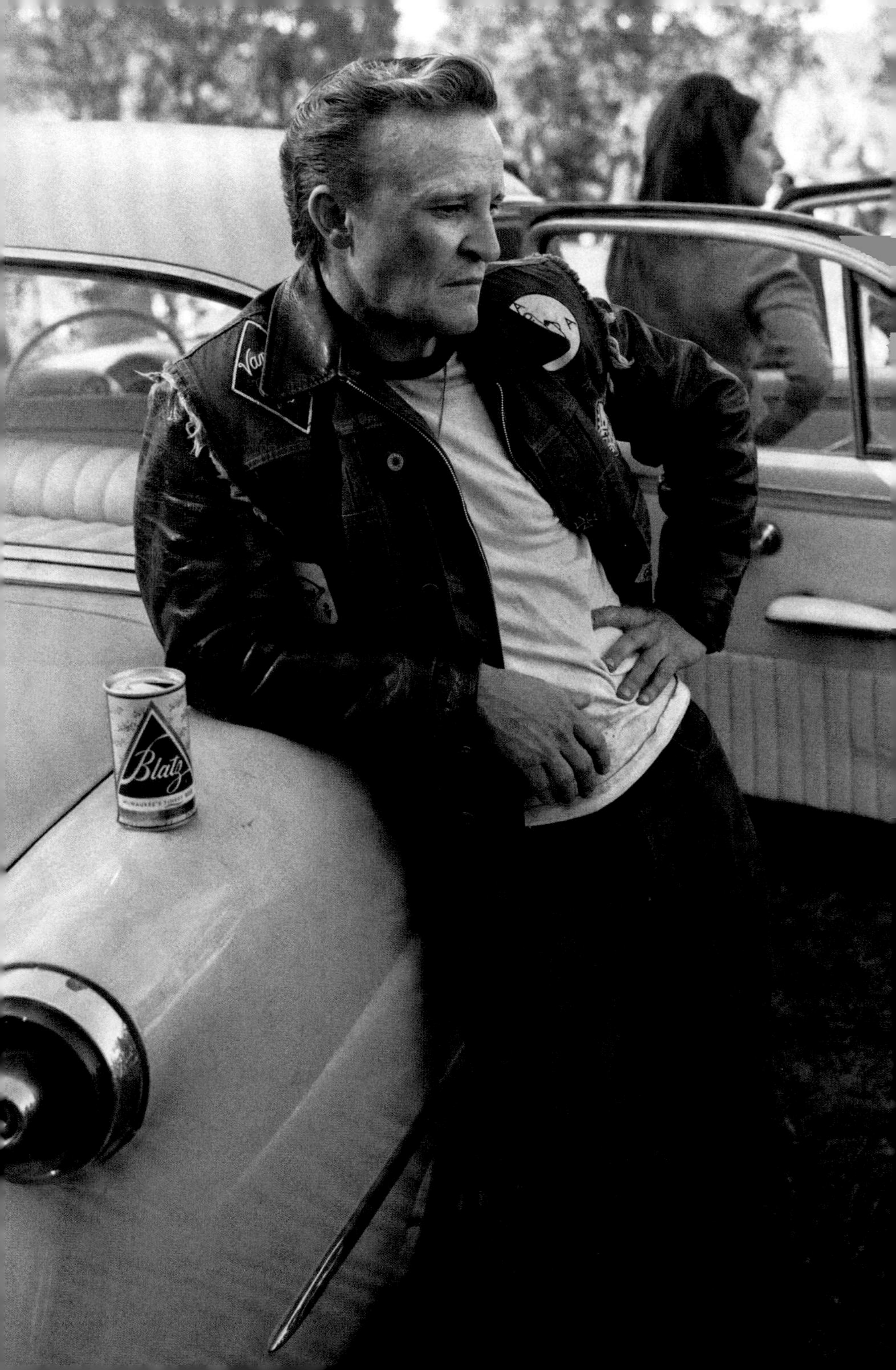
Blatz

BRUCIE

Everyone wants to be a part of somethin'. I mean that's what it really is. These guys don't belong nowhere else, so they belong together, you know.

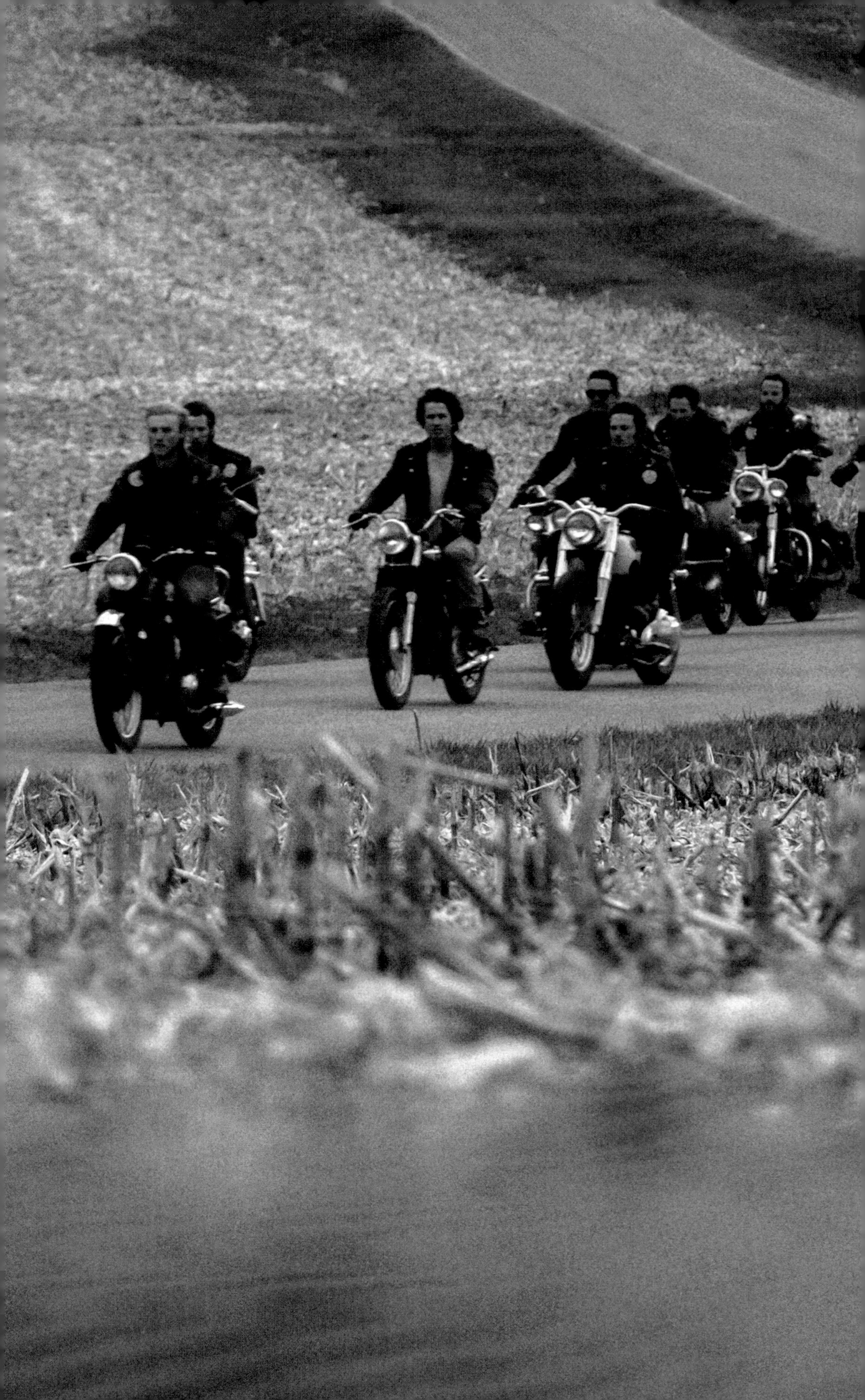

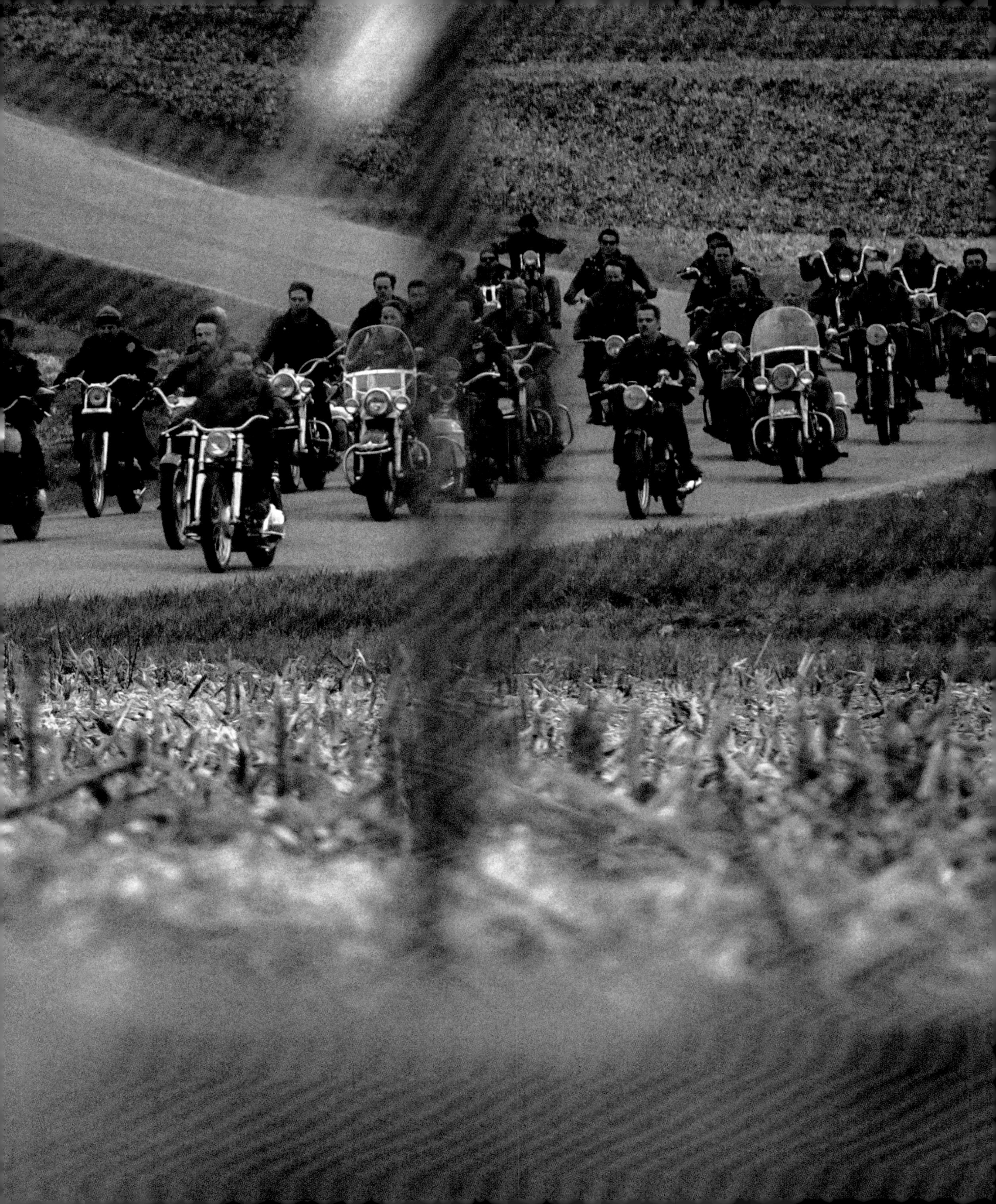

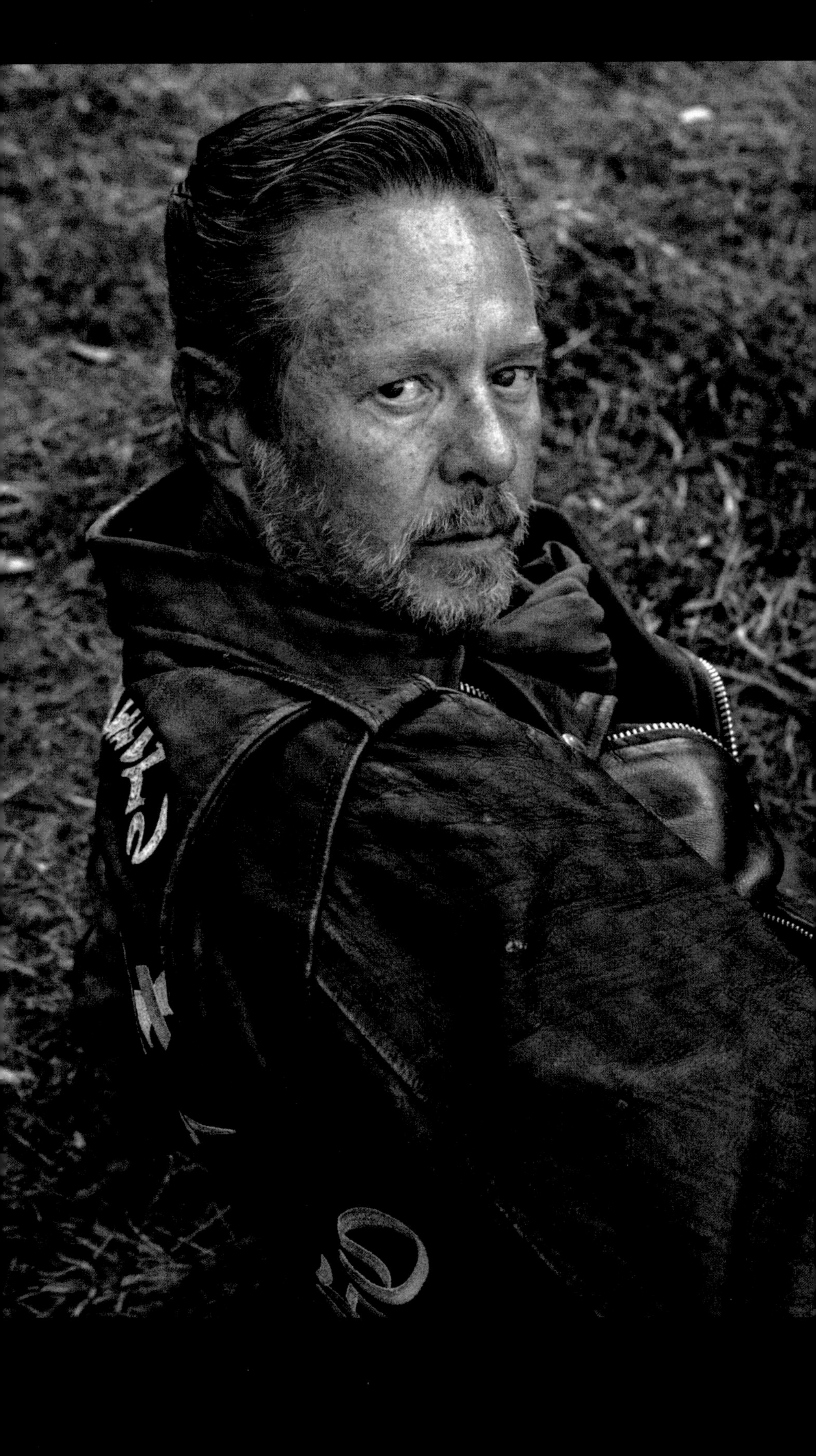

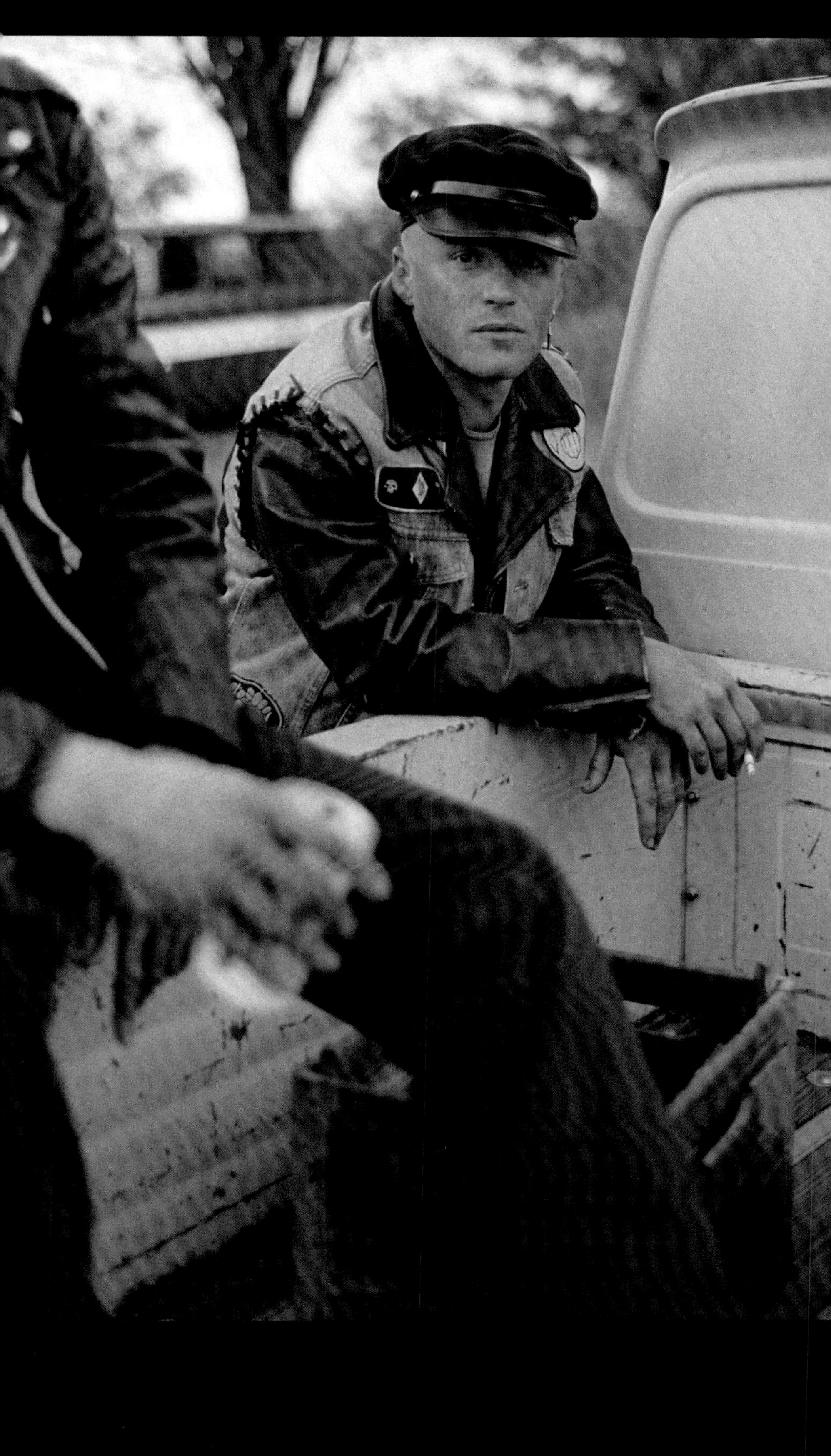

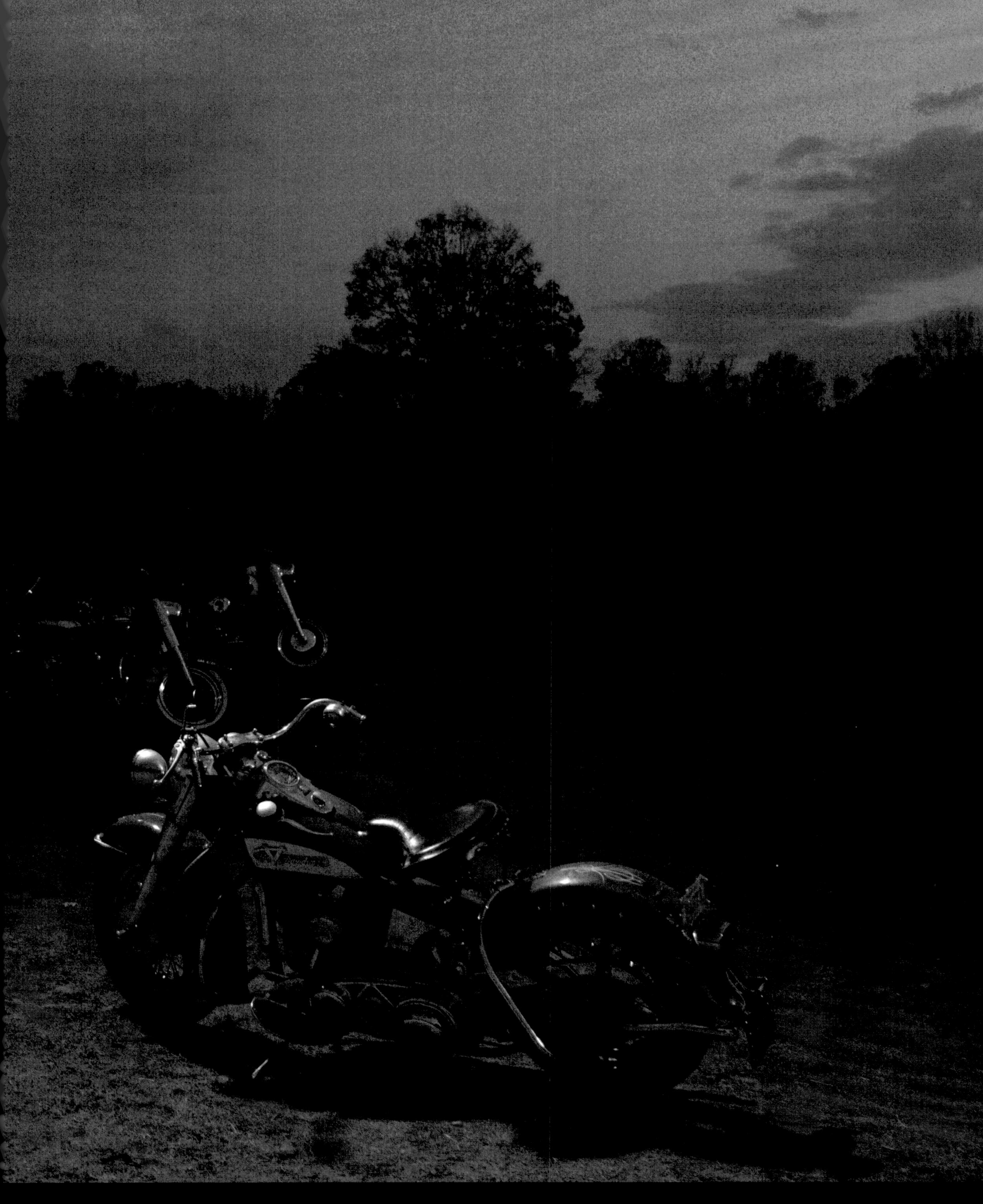

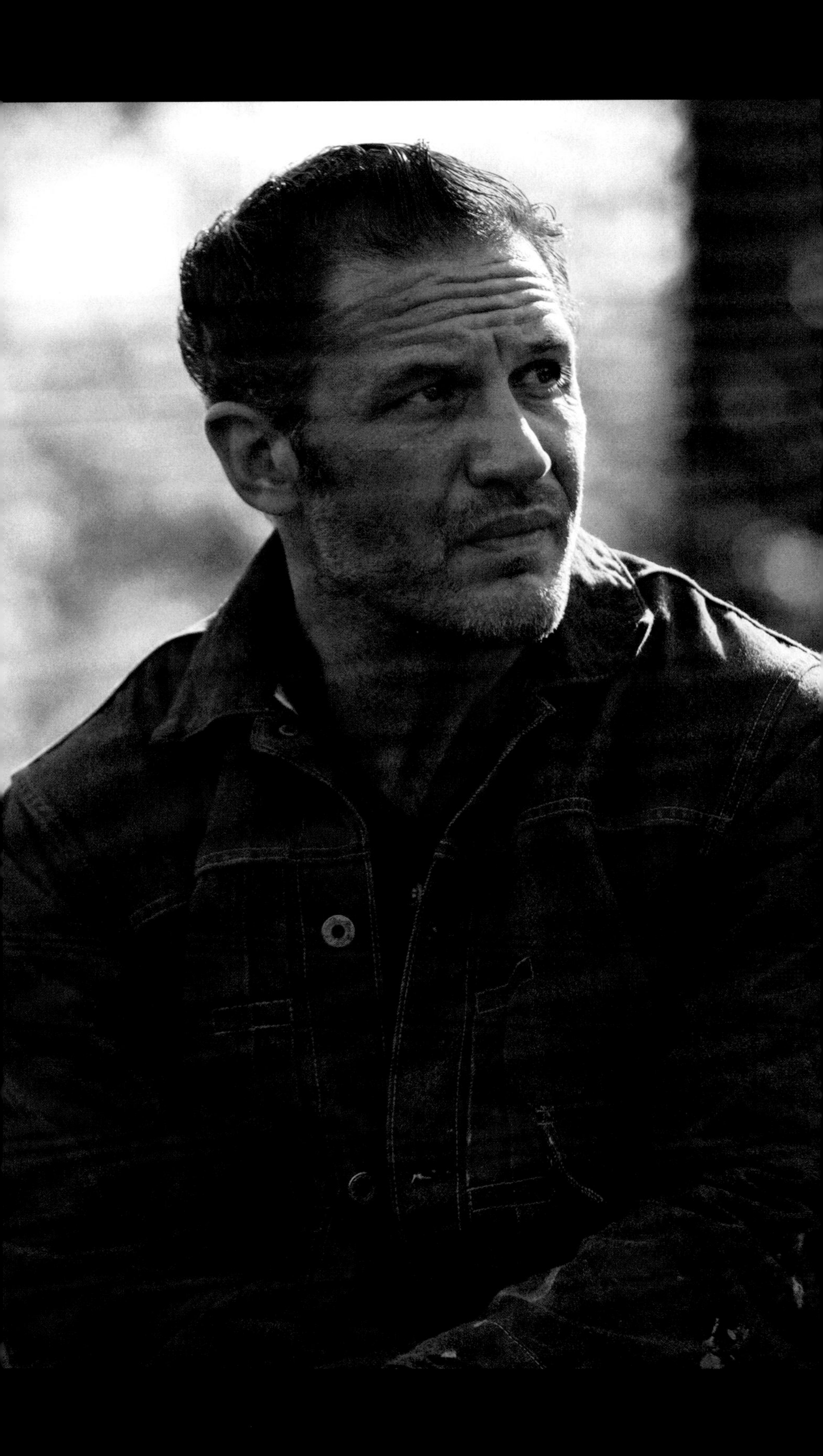

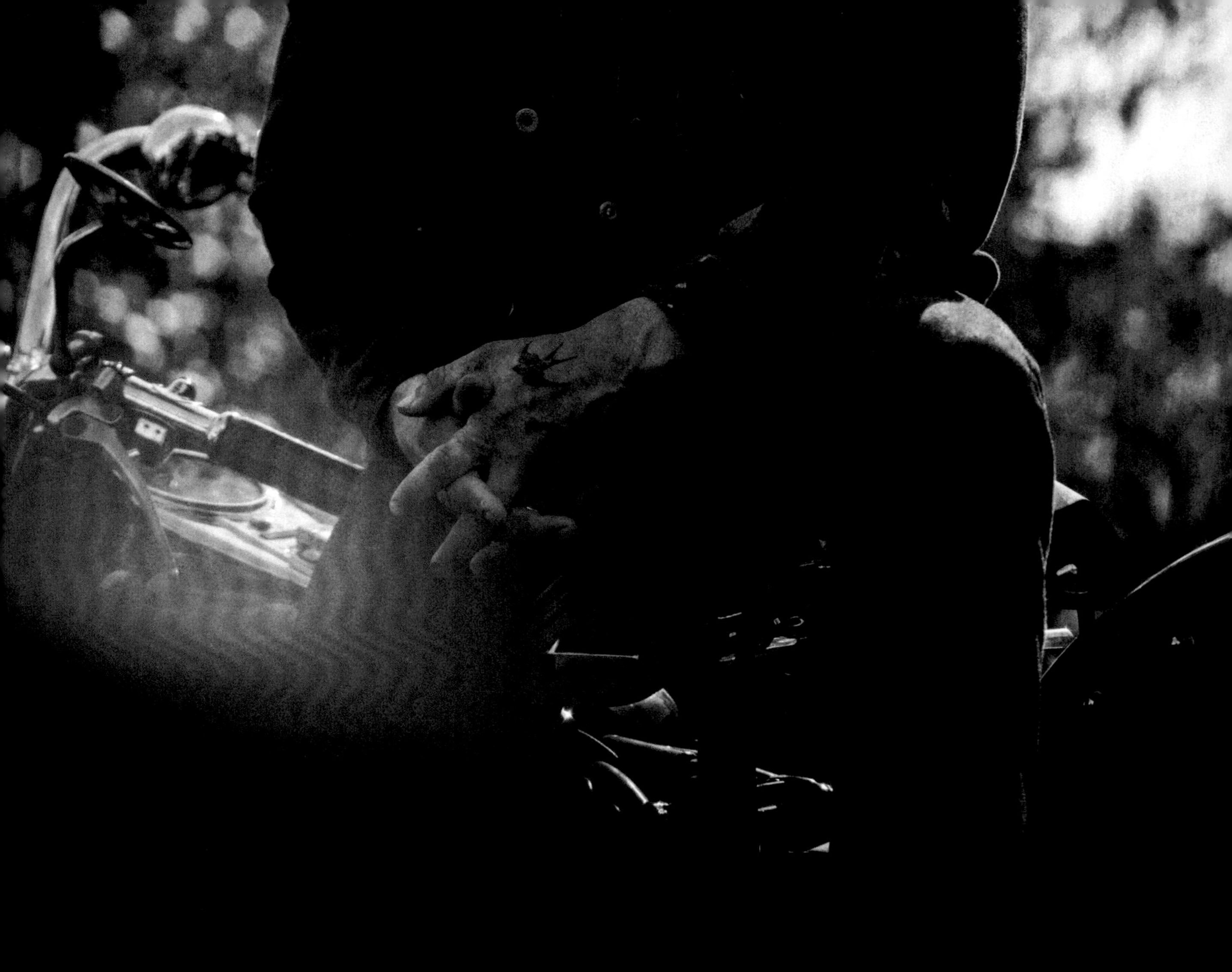

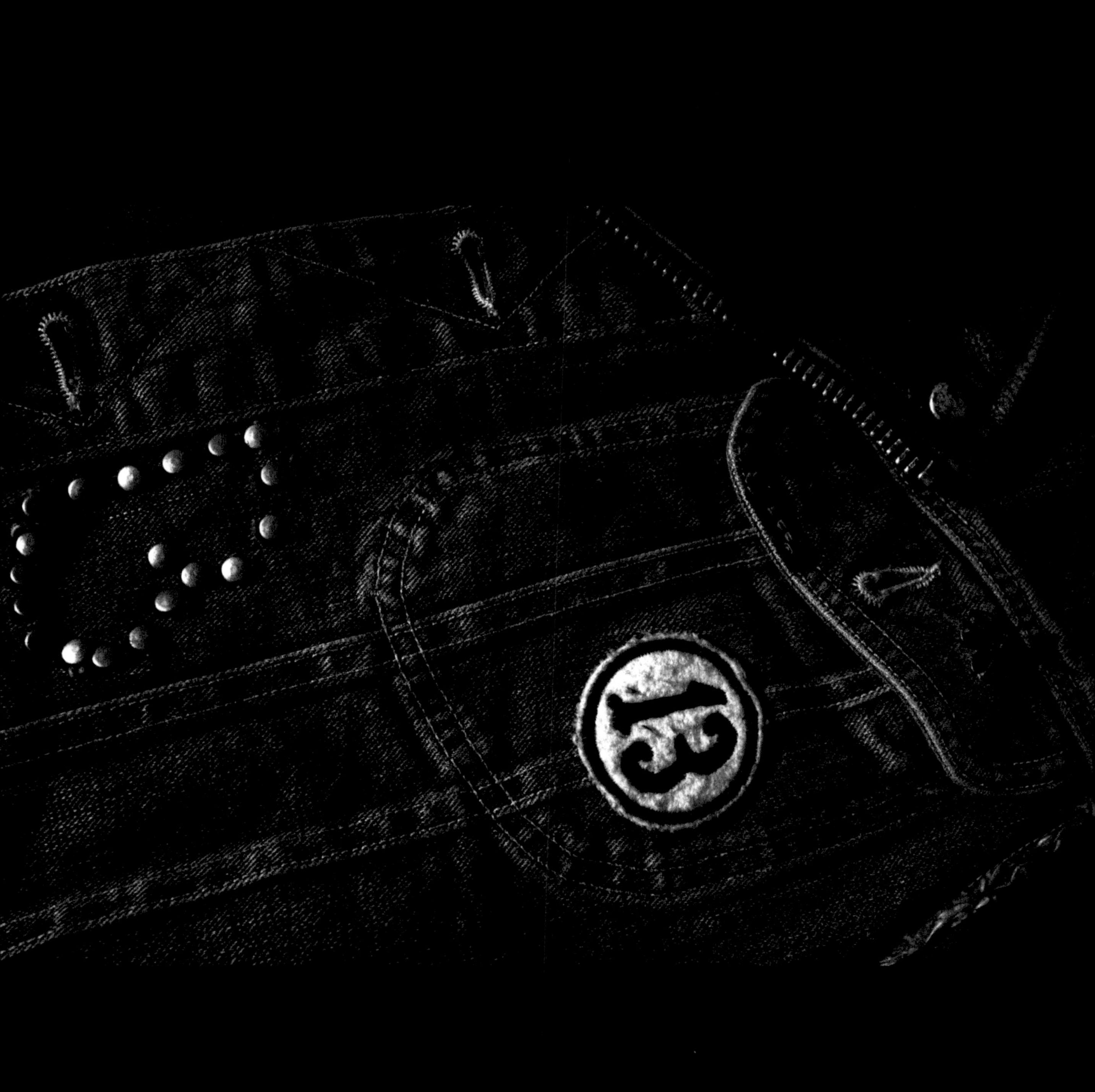

BRUCIE

But with a bikerider, an outlaw bikerider, a 1 percenter, you go anywhere in the United States, I don't give a shit where it's at, anywhere in the United States, his bike breaks down in any little town, that man won't be in that town no more than an hour before some type of bikerider will come along and offer him a roof over his head, will offer him a place to stay until he can get back on the road again, you know. It's somethin' people don't understand.

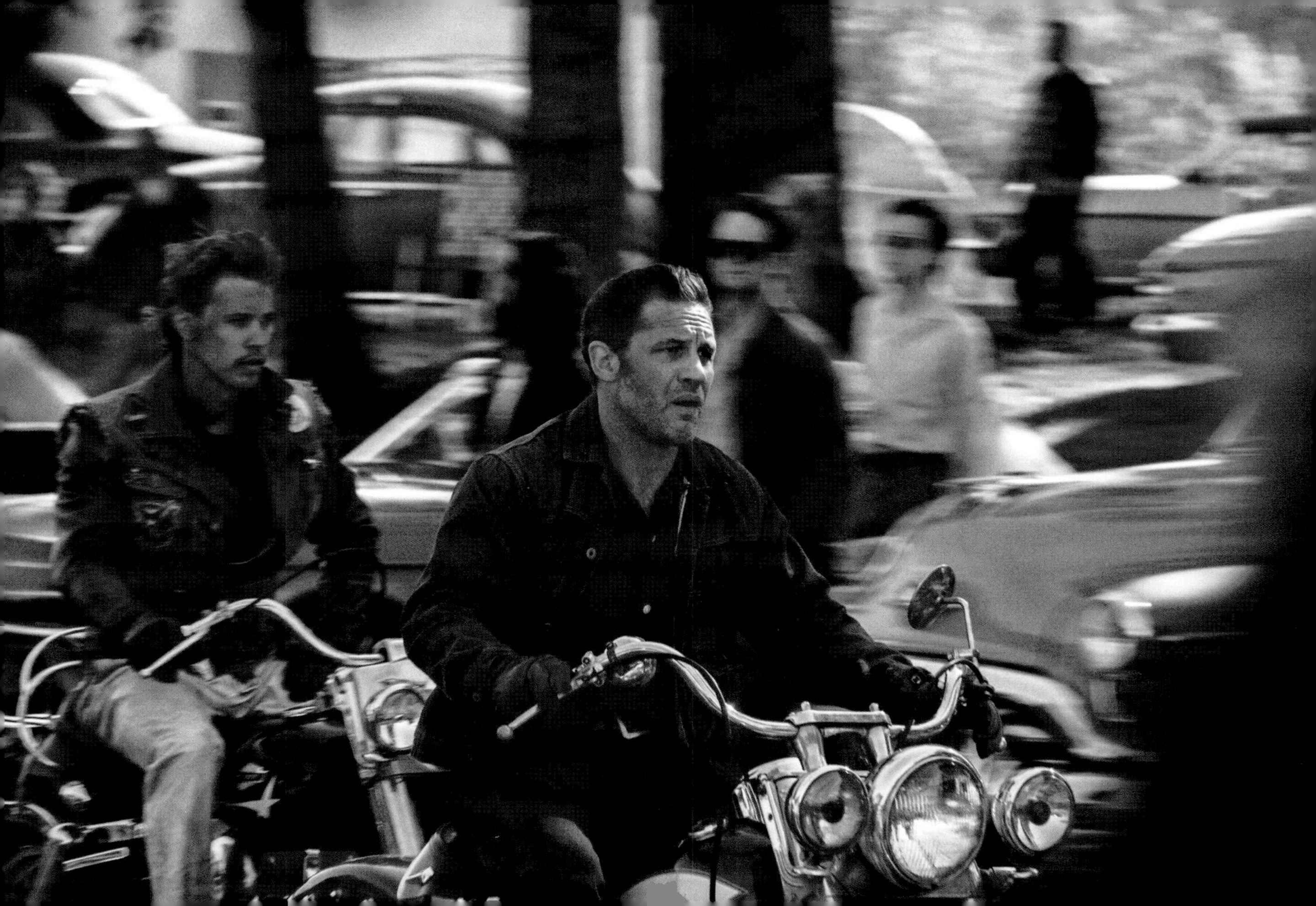

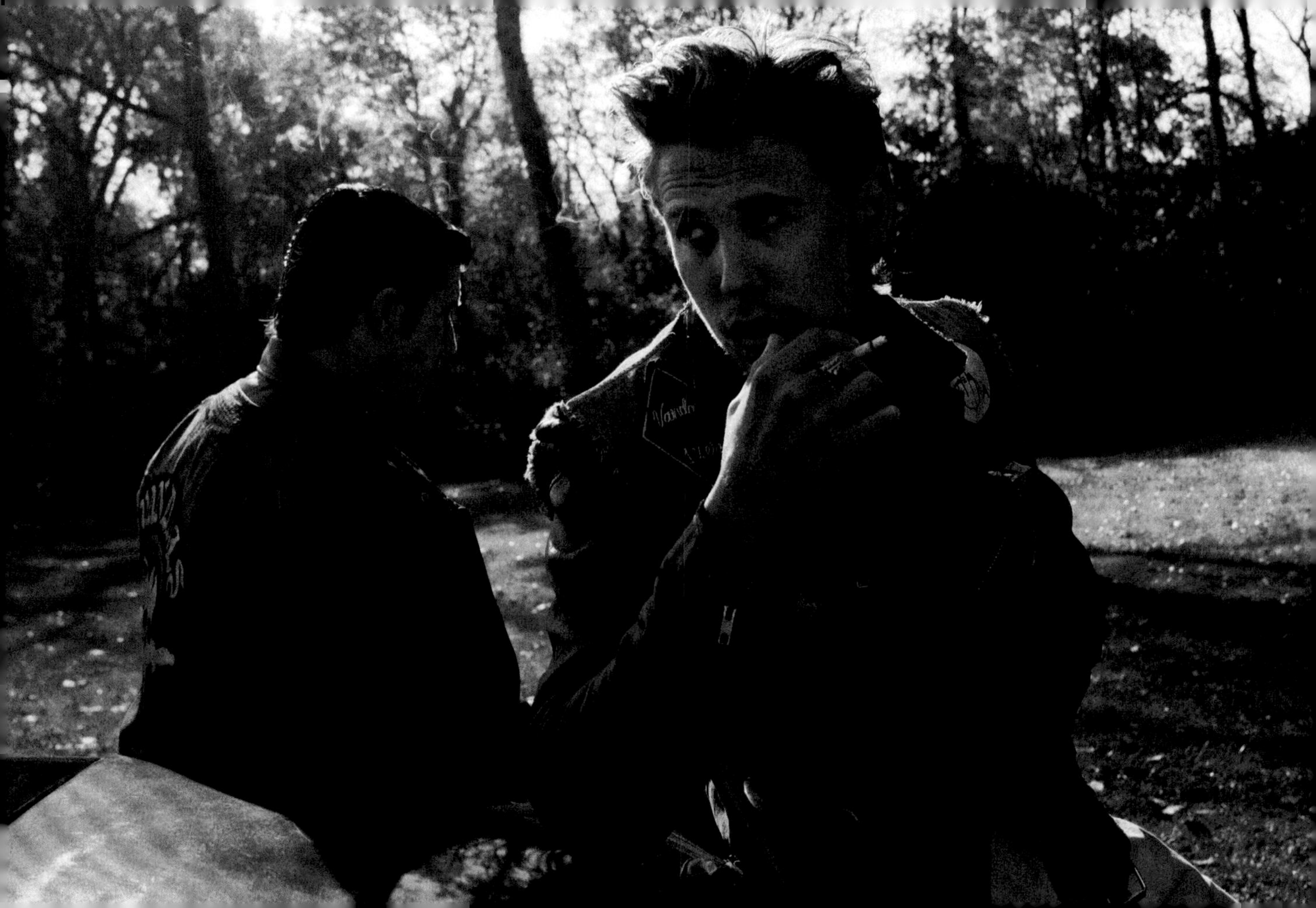

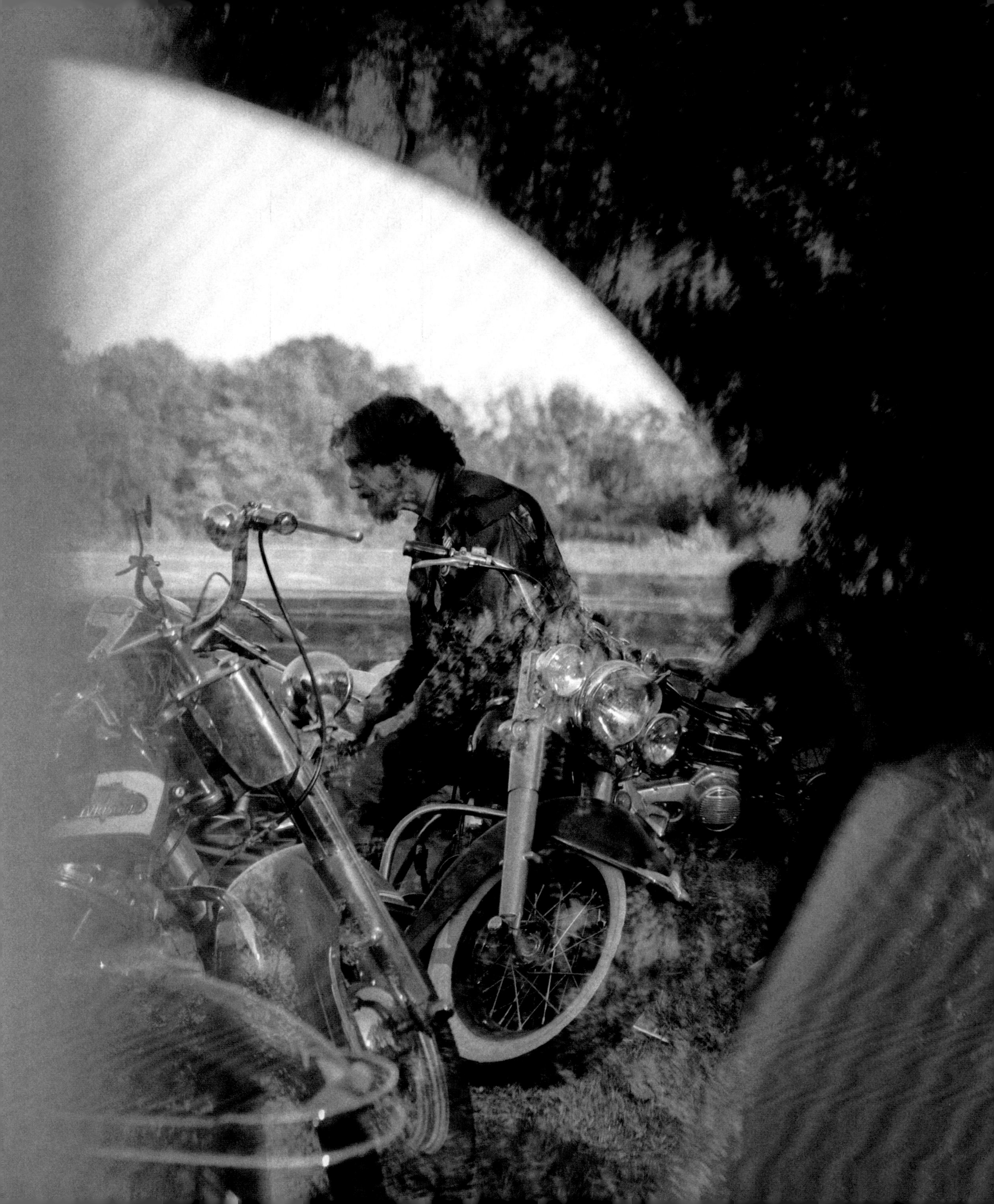

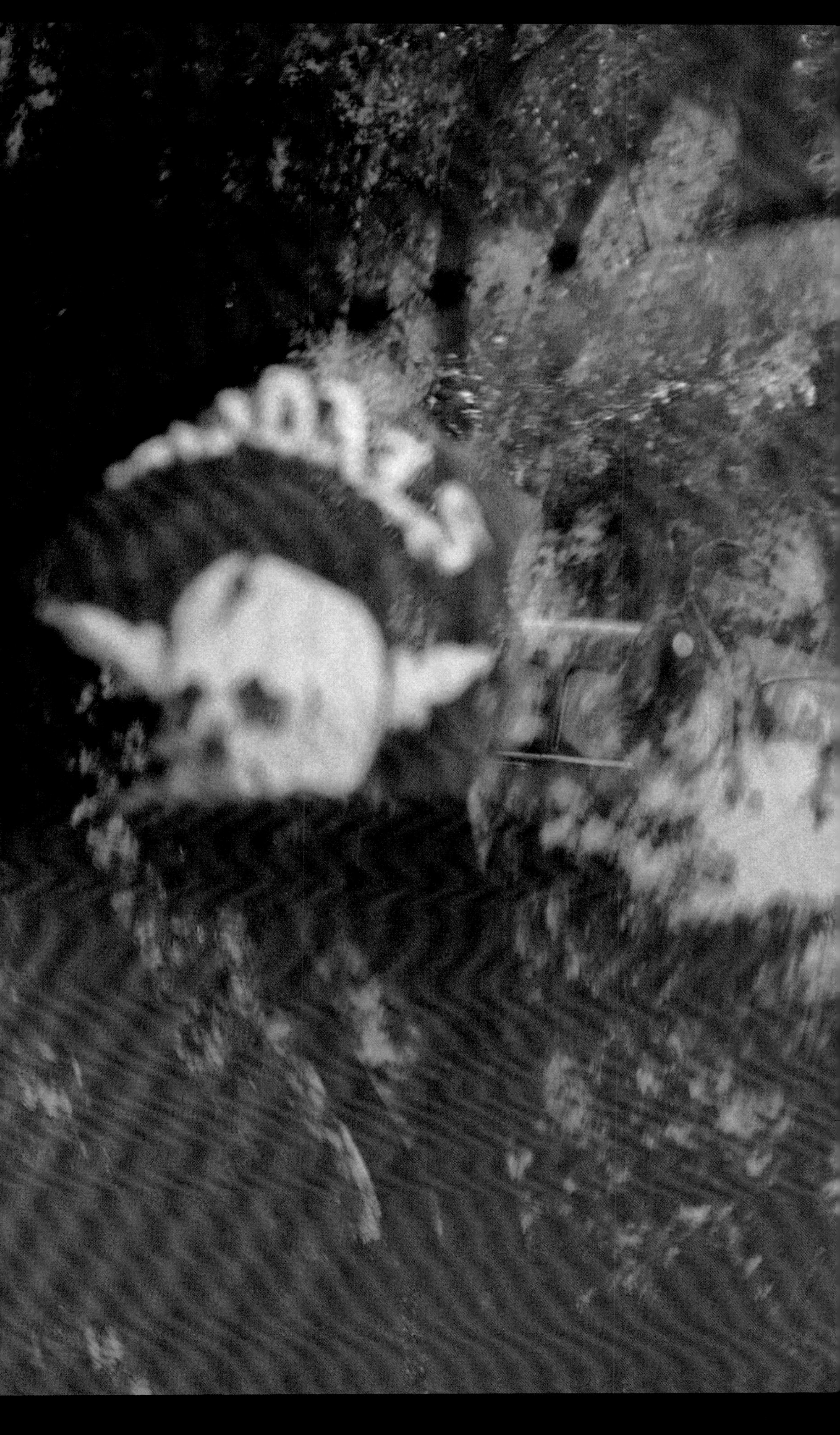

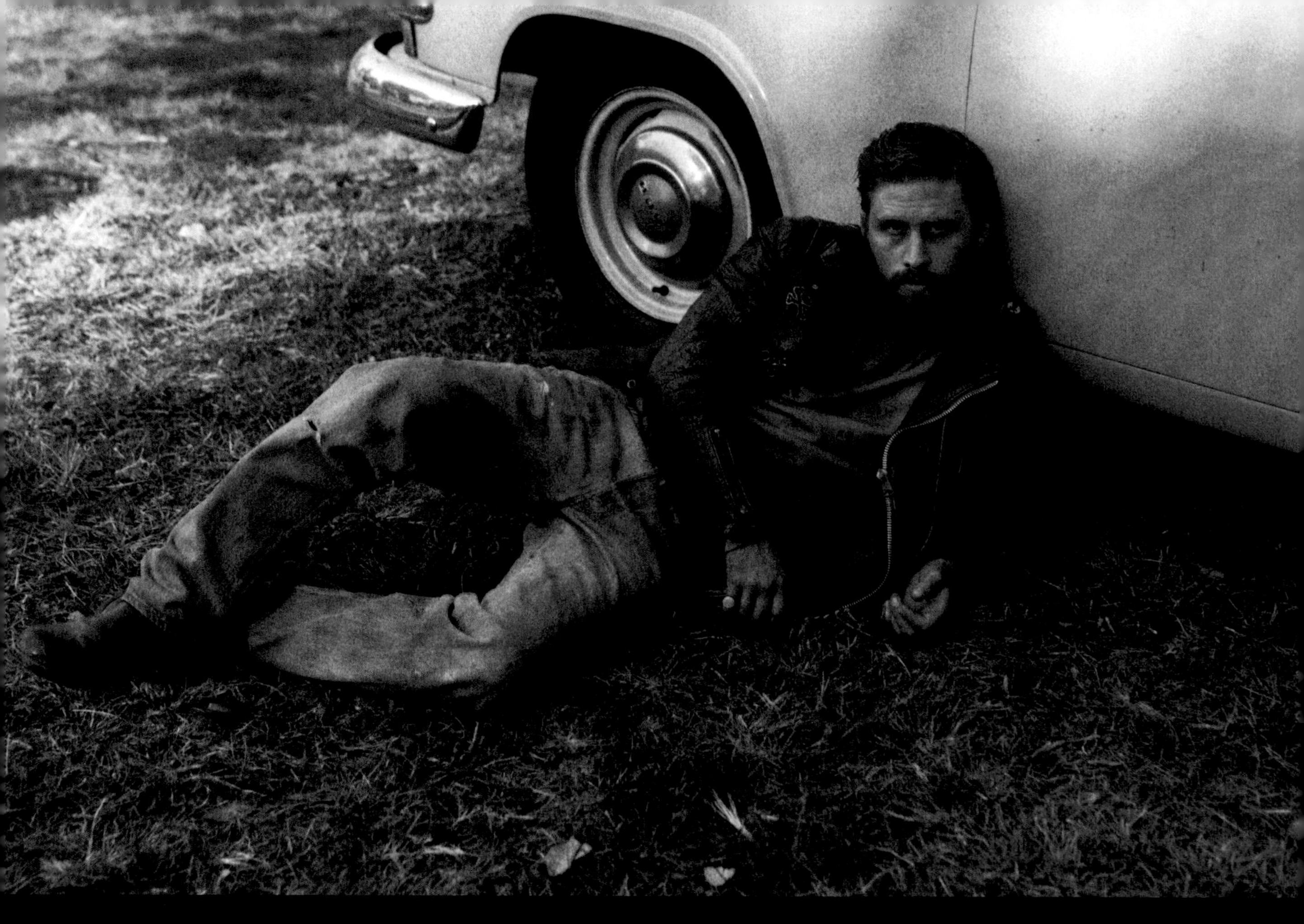

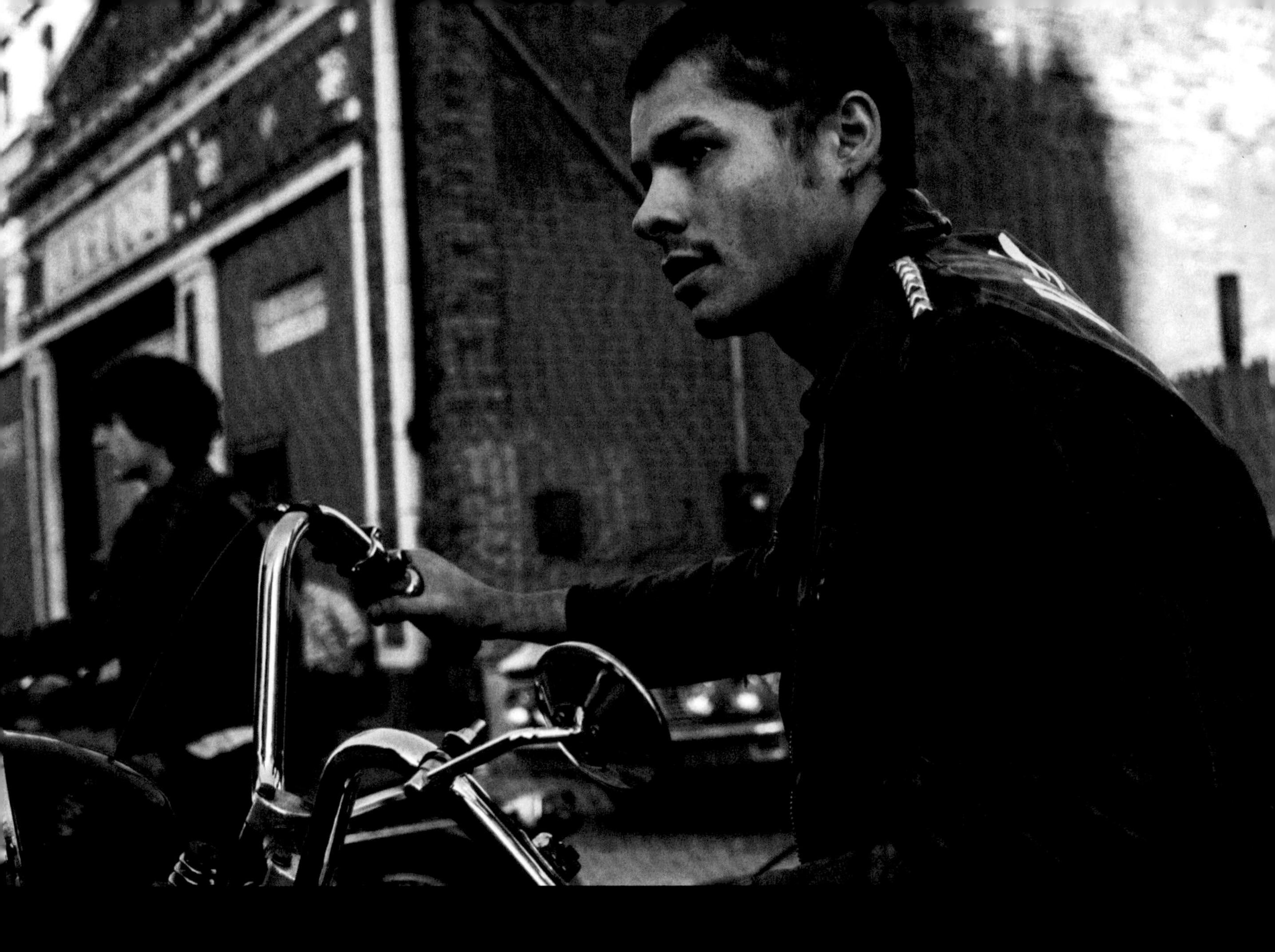

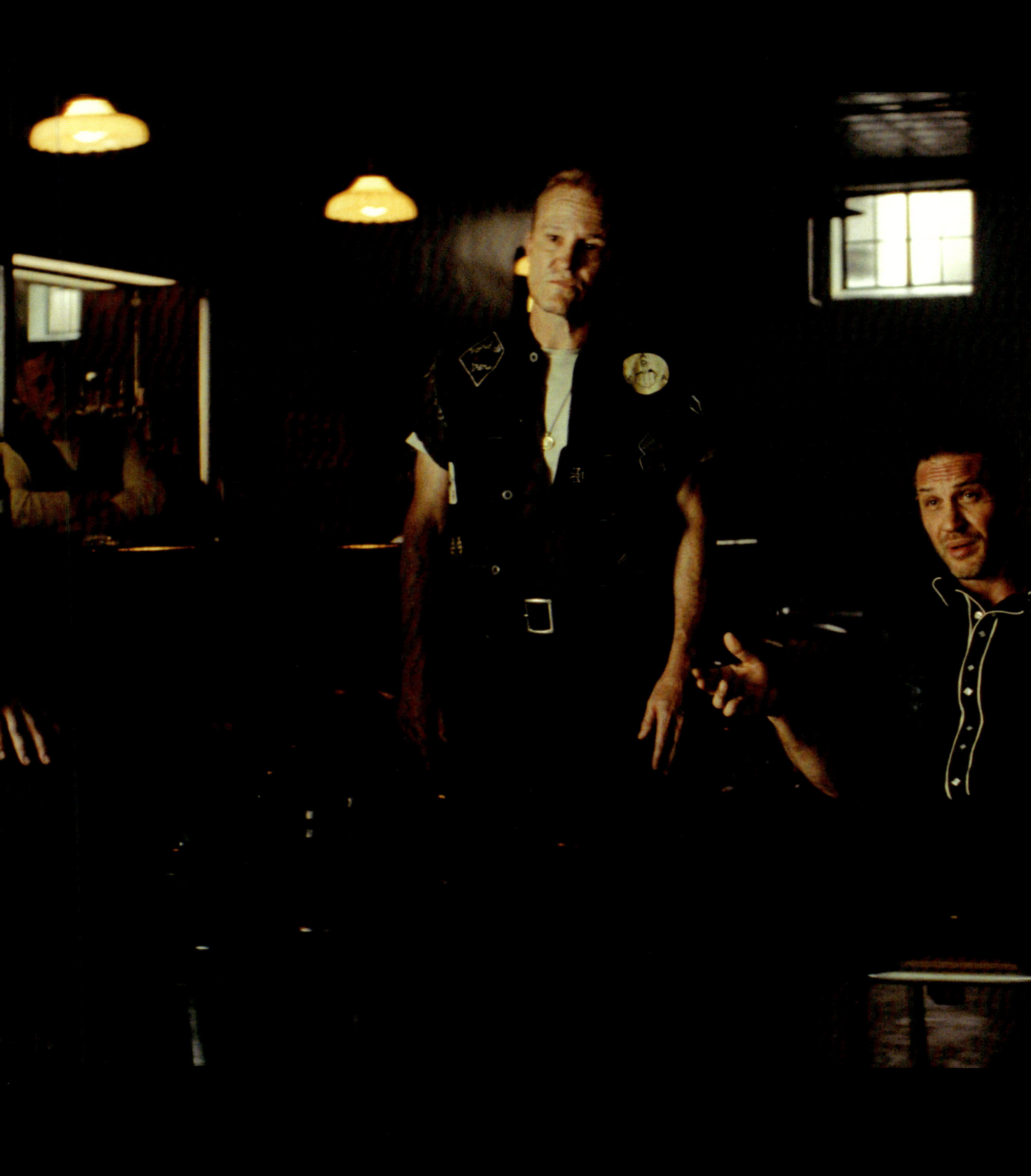

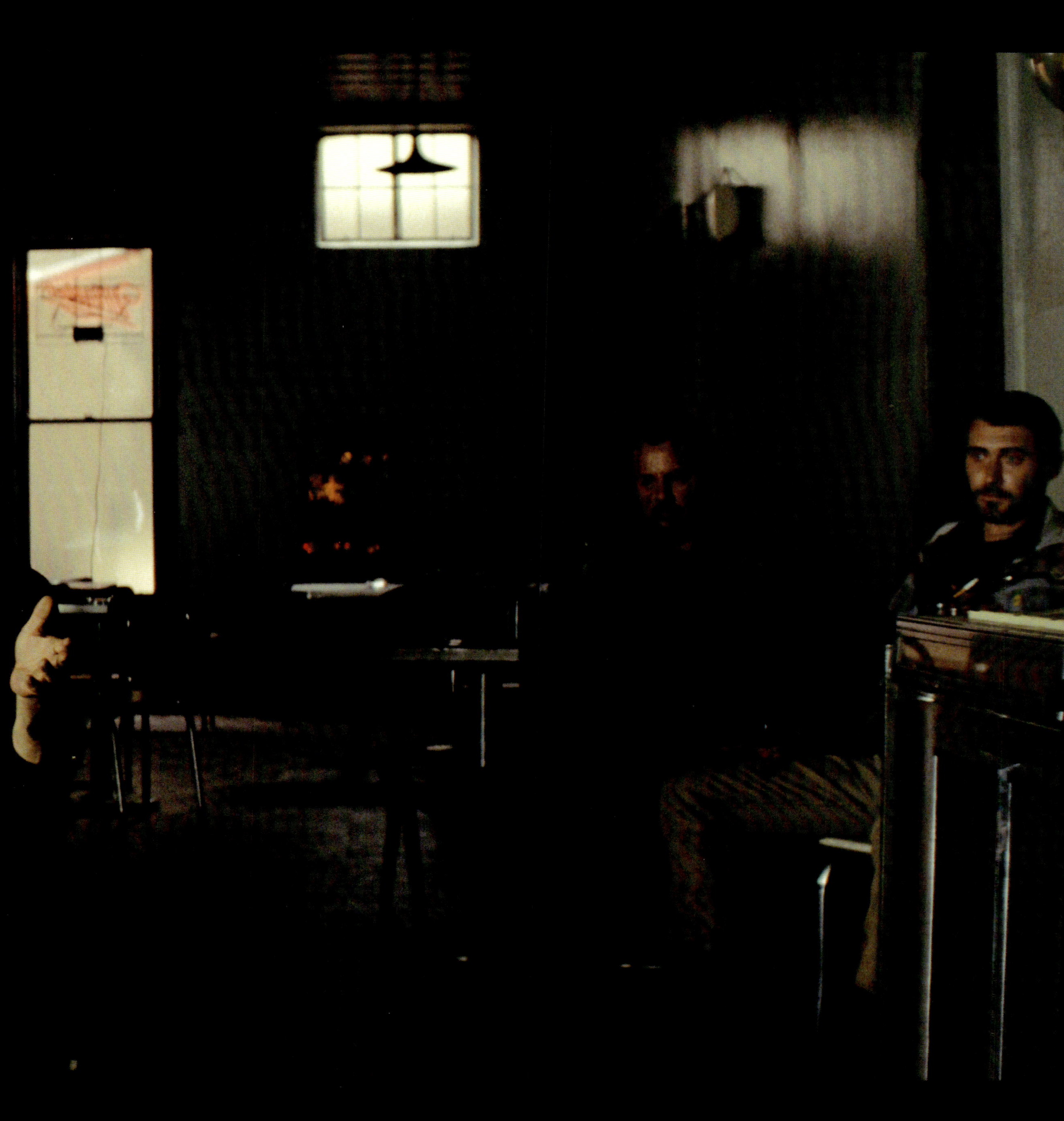

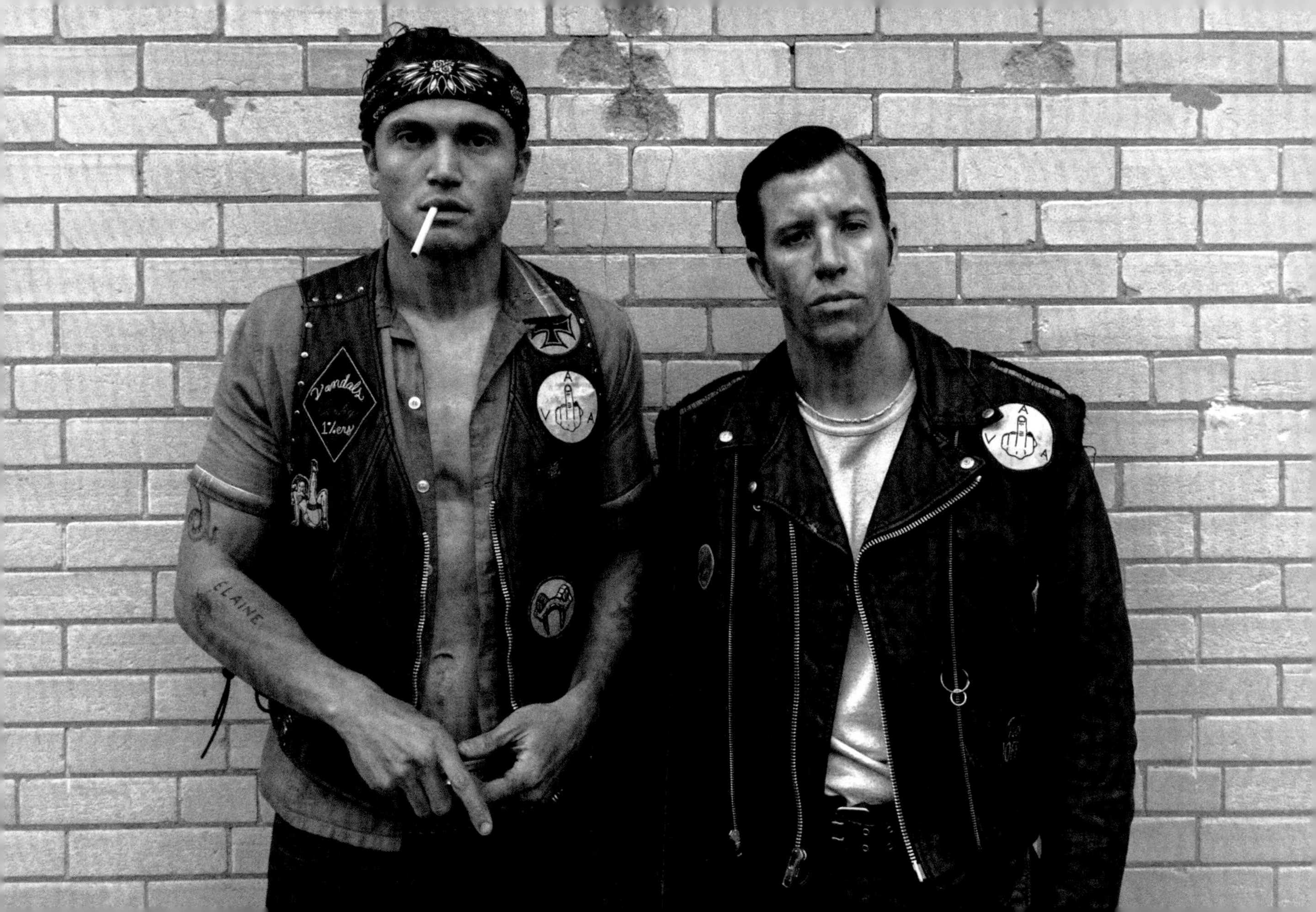
Vandals
1%ers

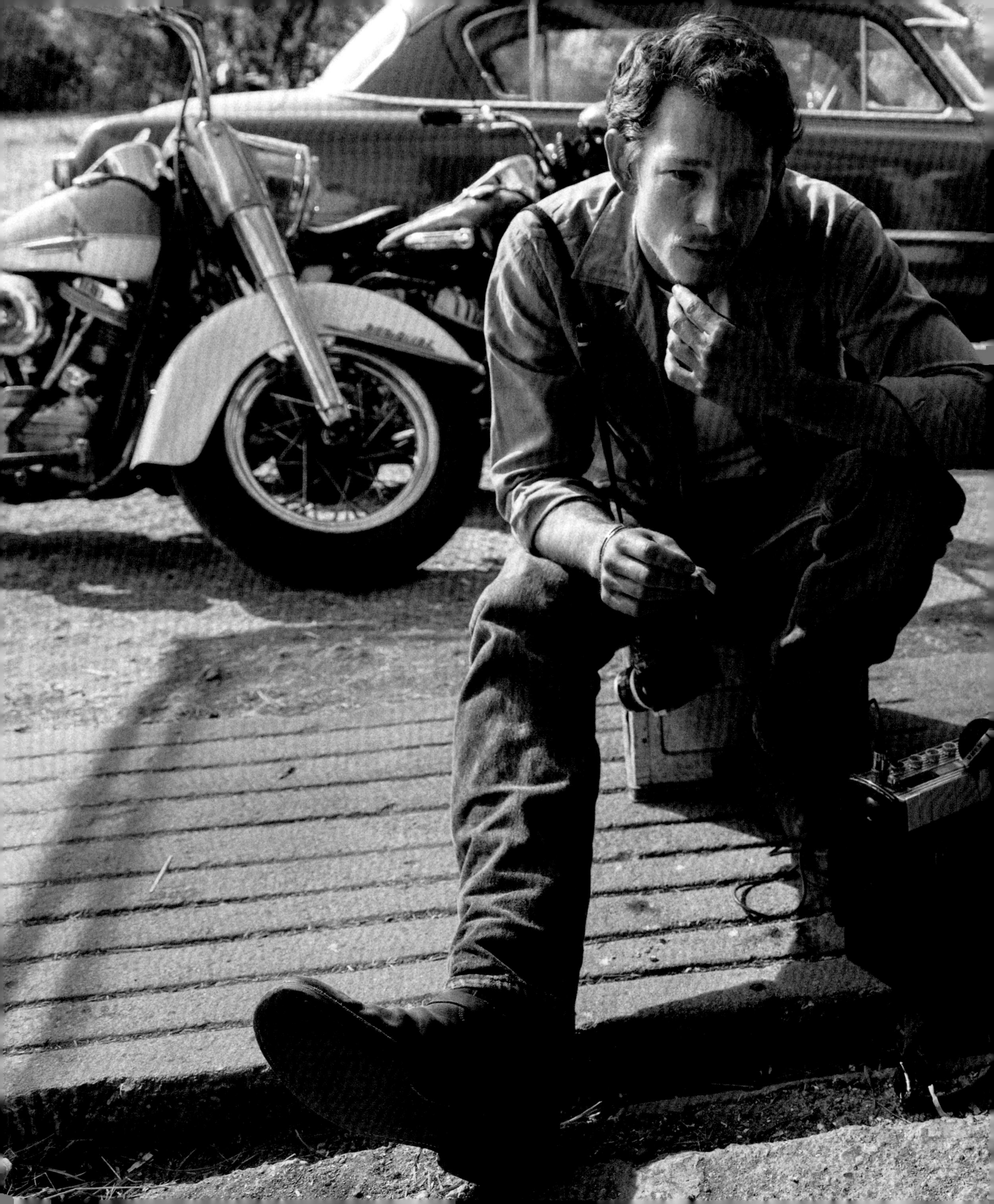

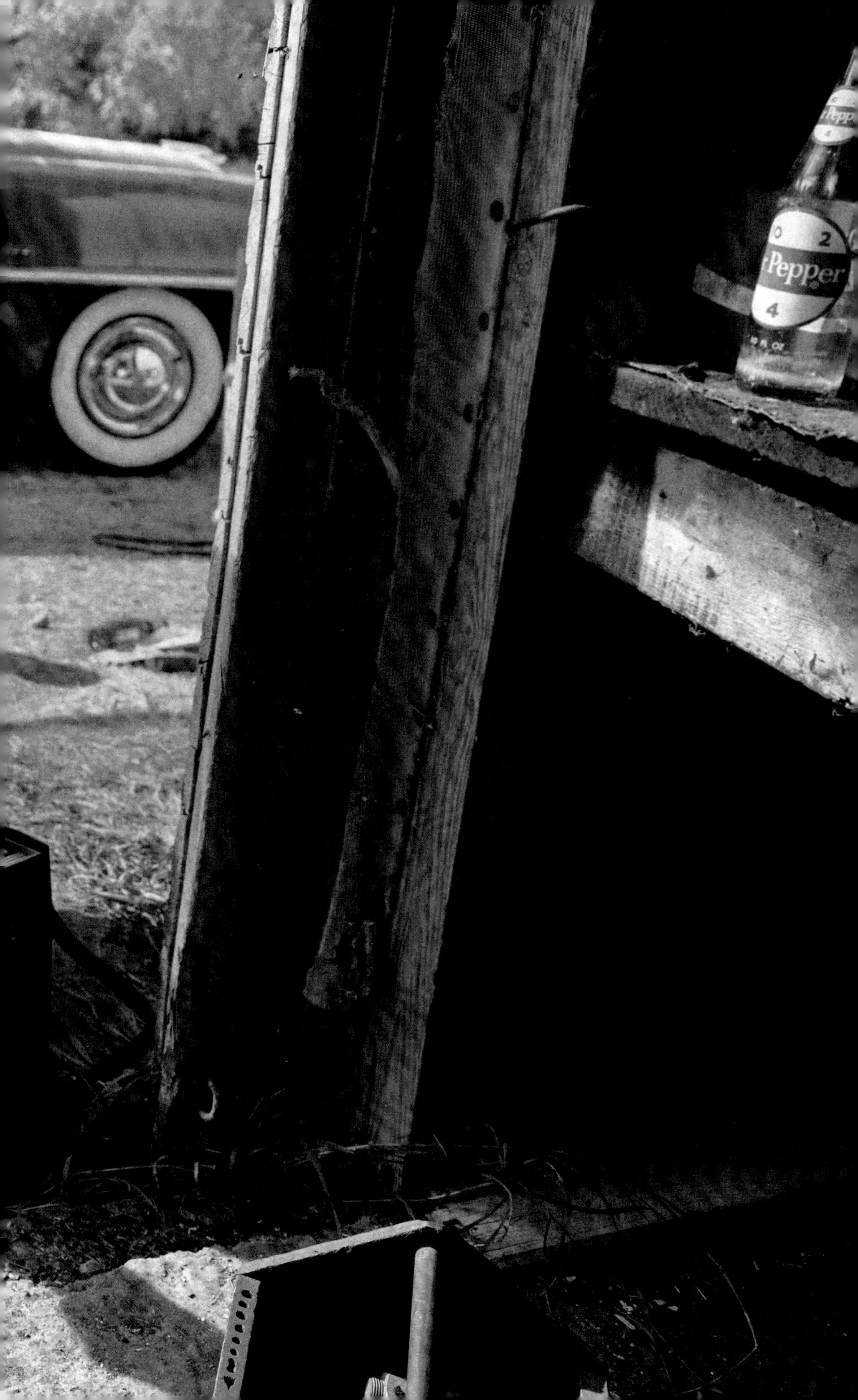
0 2
Pepper
4

CAL

I look at a scooter, man, that's completely chopped, man, and every part on it he either made himself, man, or bought special for it, you know. Now you look at that dude, man, and that dude's a Vandal, see. Say you take a guy that buys a brand-new Harley-Davidson, fully equipped. There'll always be a motherfucker that comes along and says, 'Well, I got one exactly like yours.' 'Cause he can get it exactly like his. But all choppers are different. Every one of 'em, different. No matter how much alike you build, you know what I mean? 'Cause everybody's melon's different.

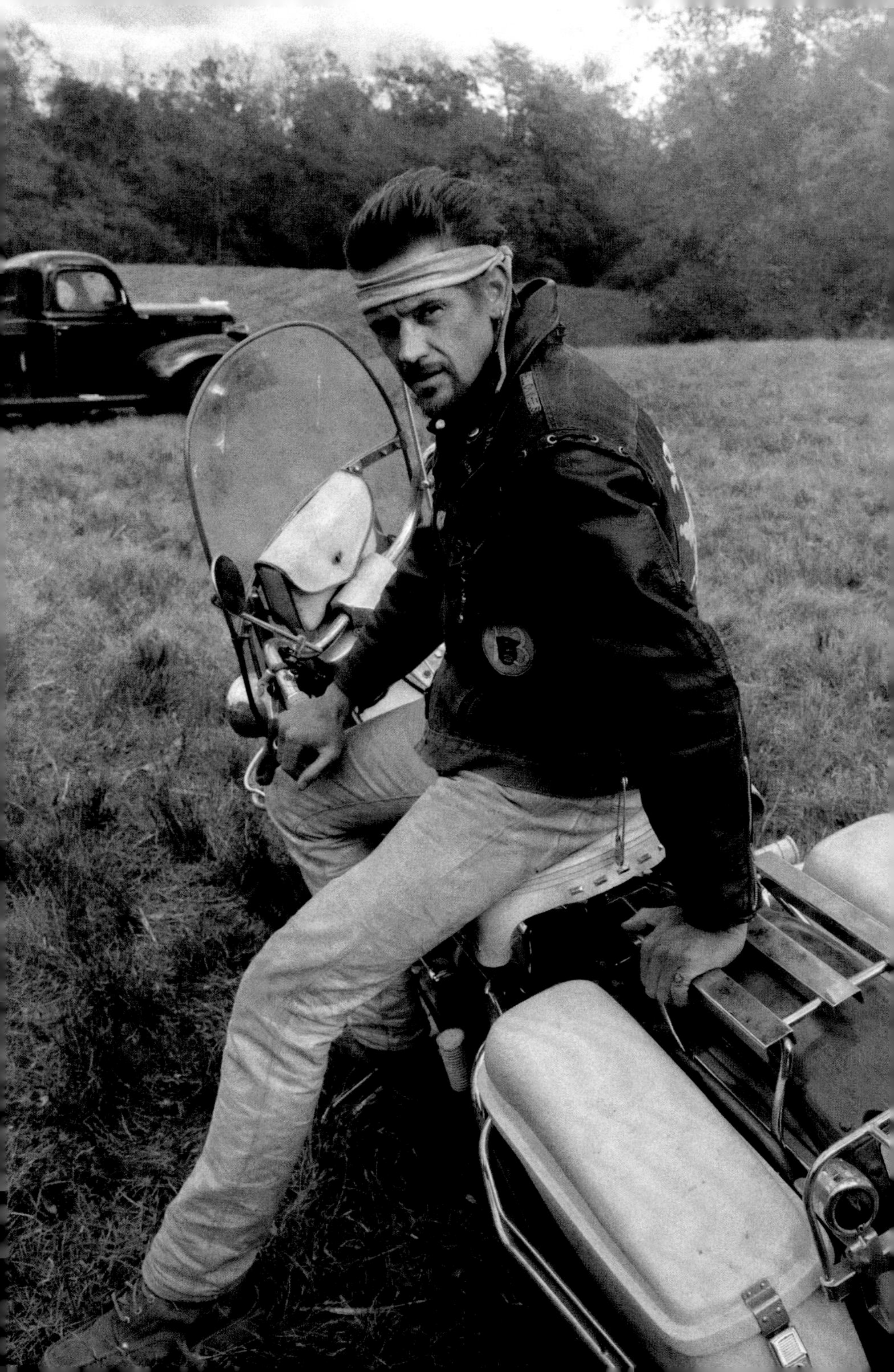

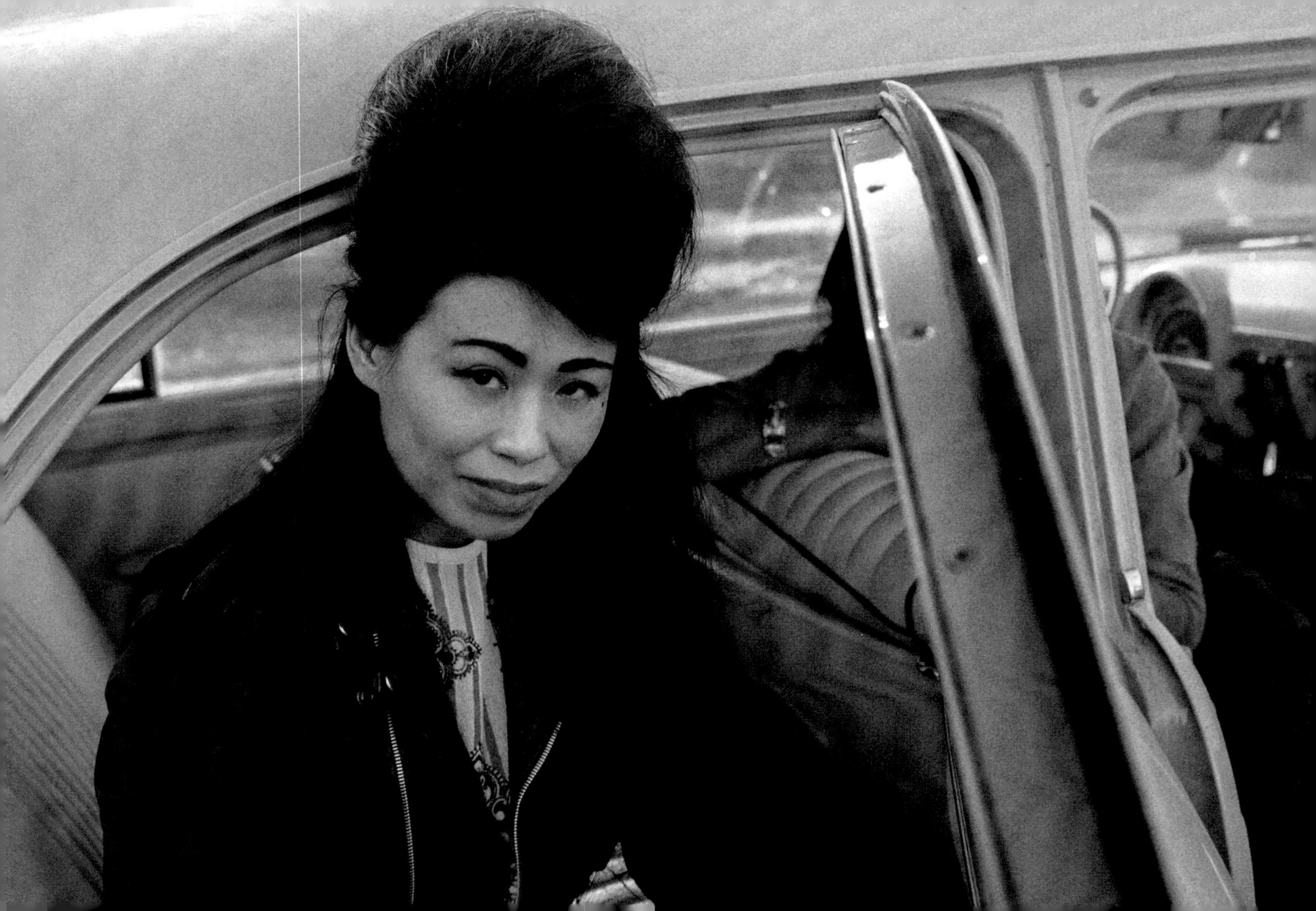

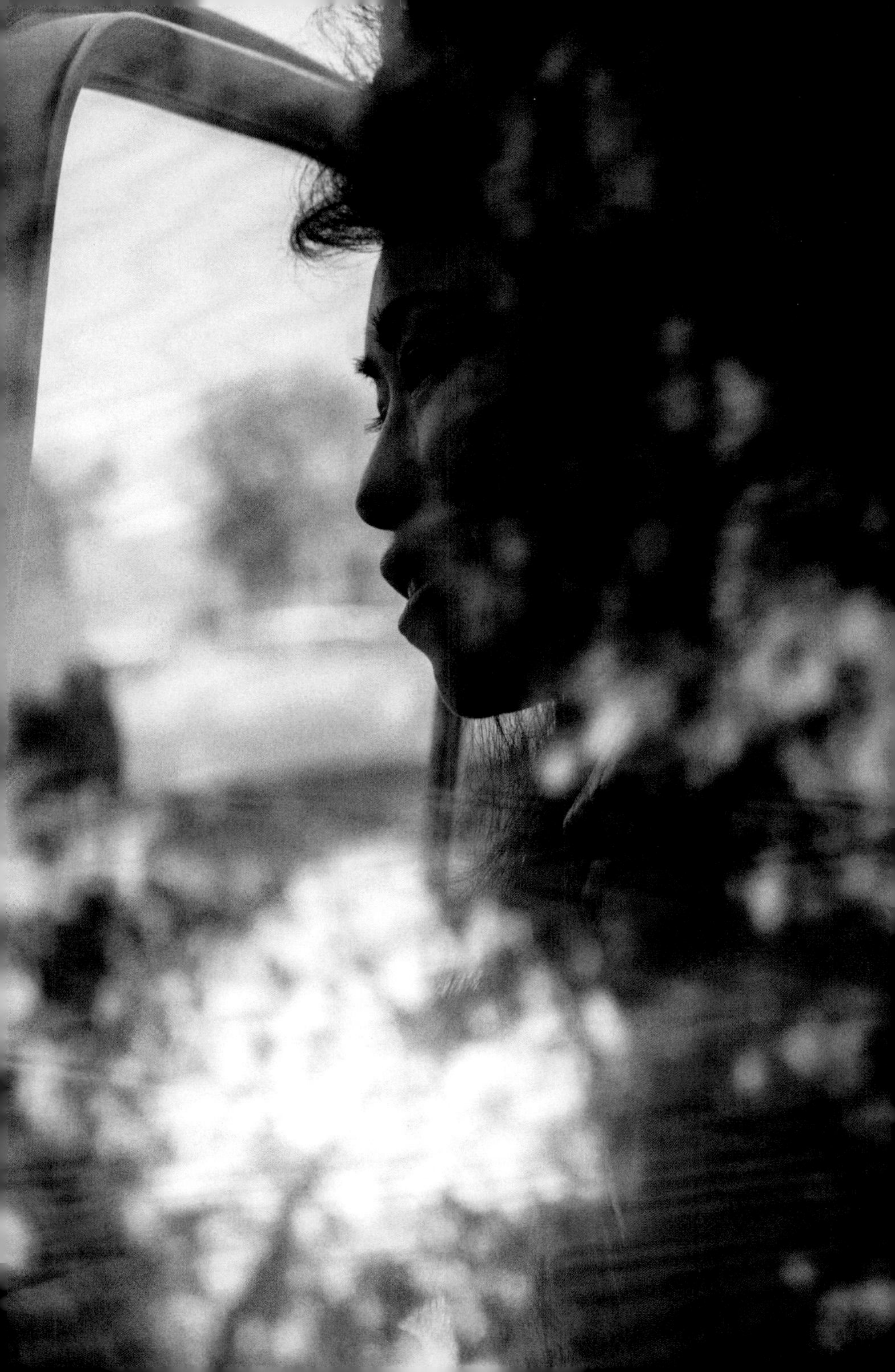

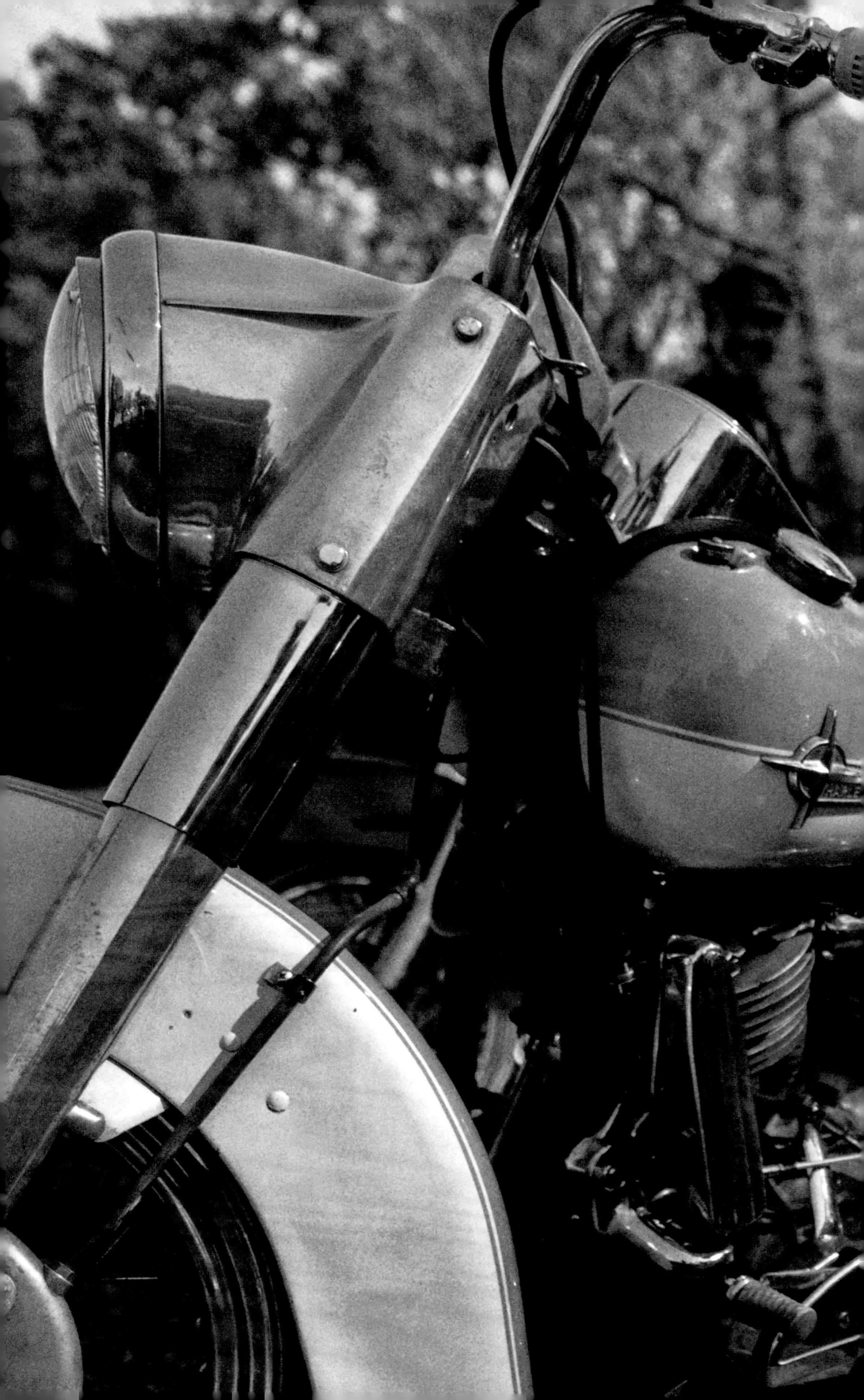

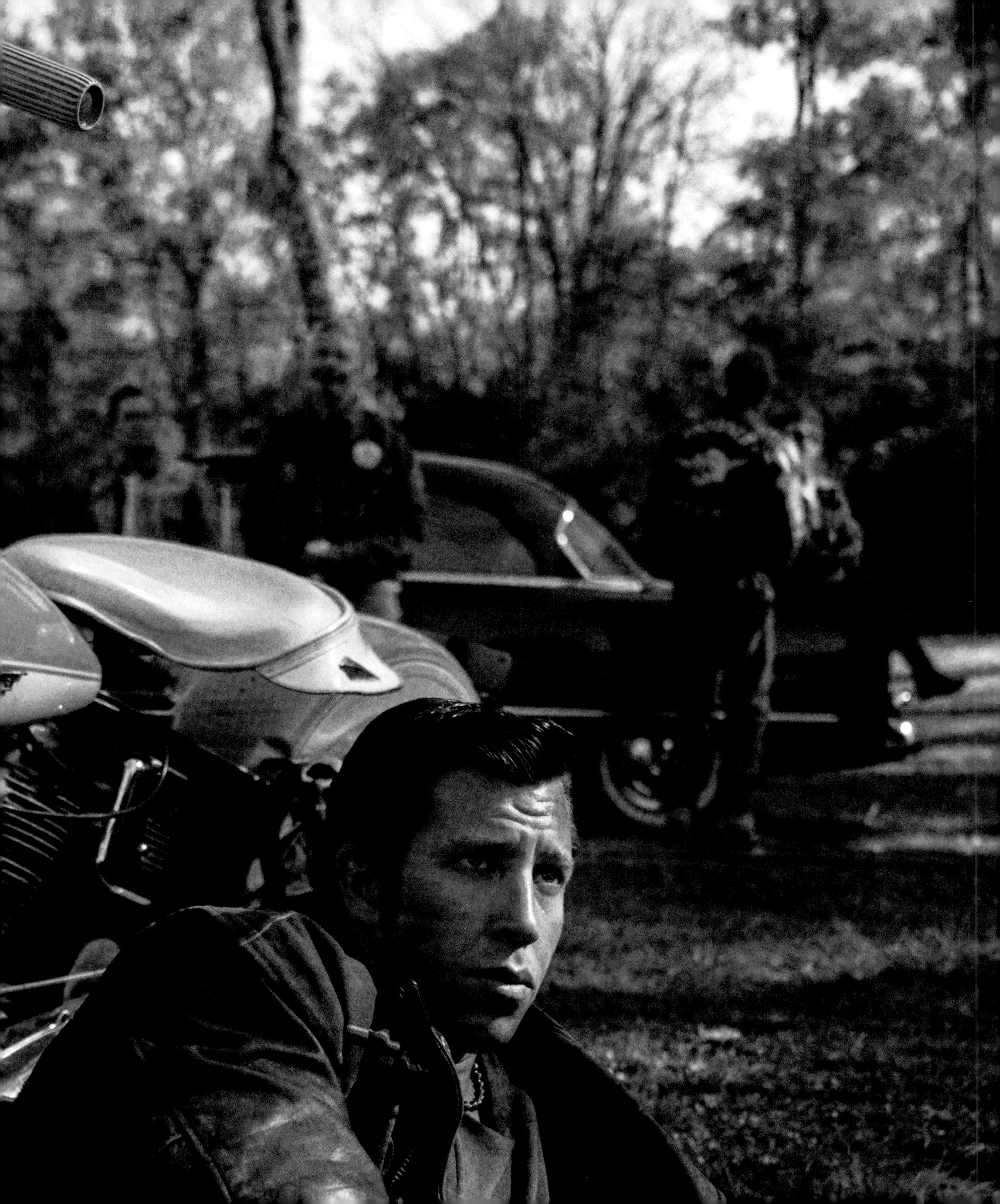

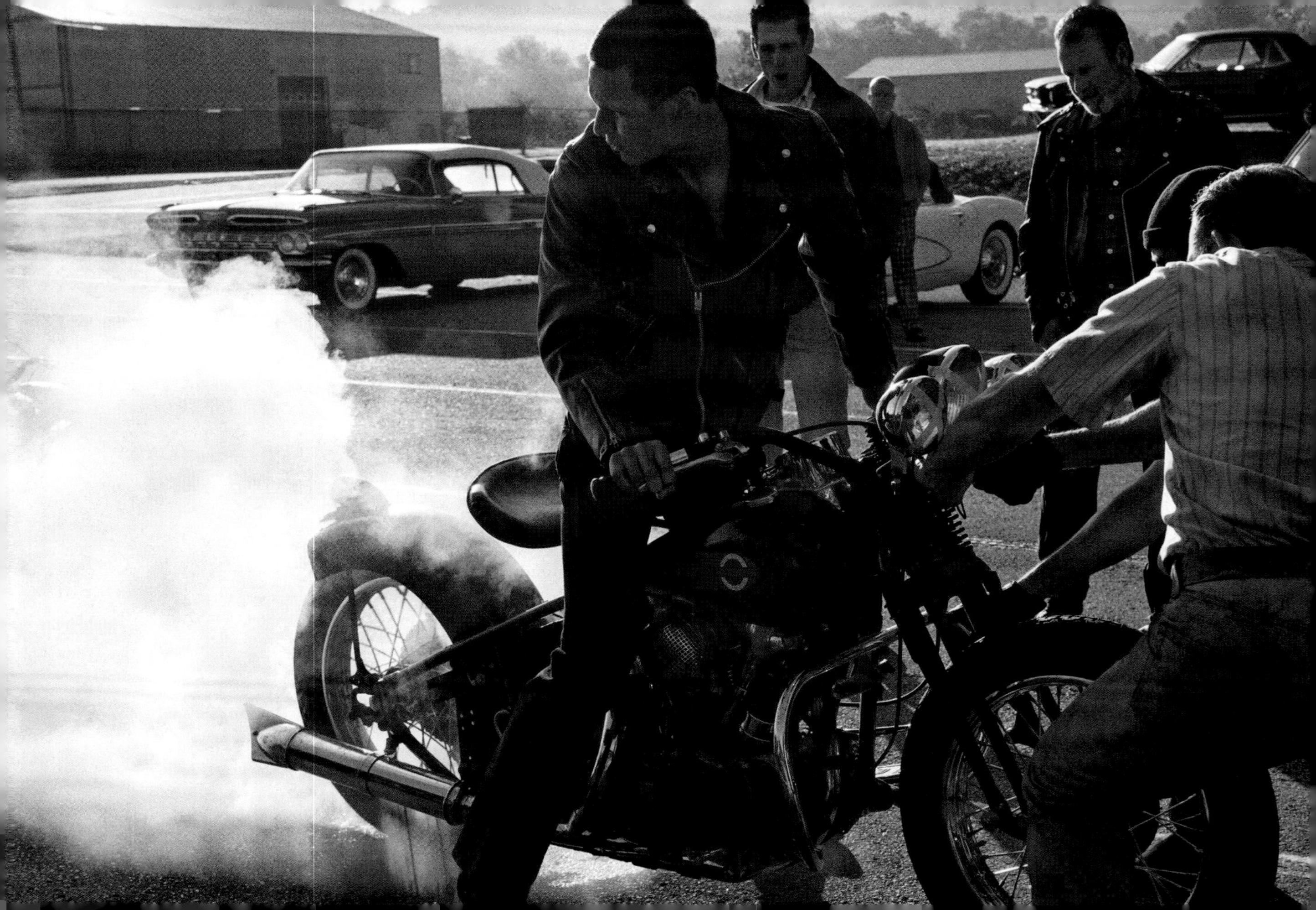

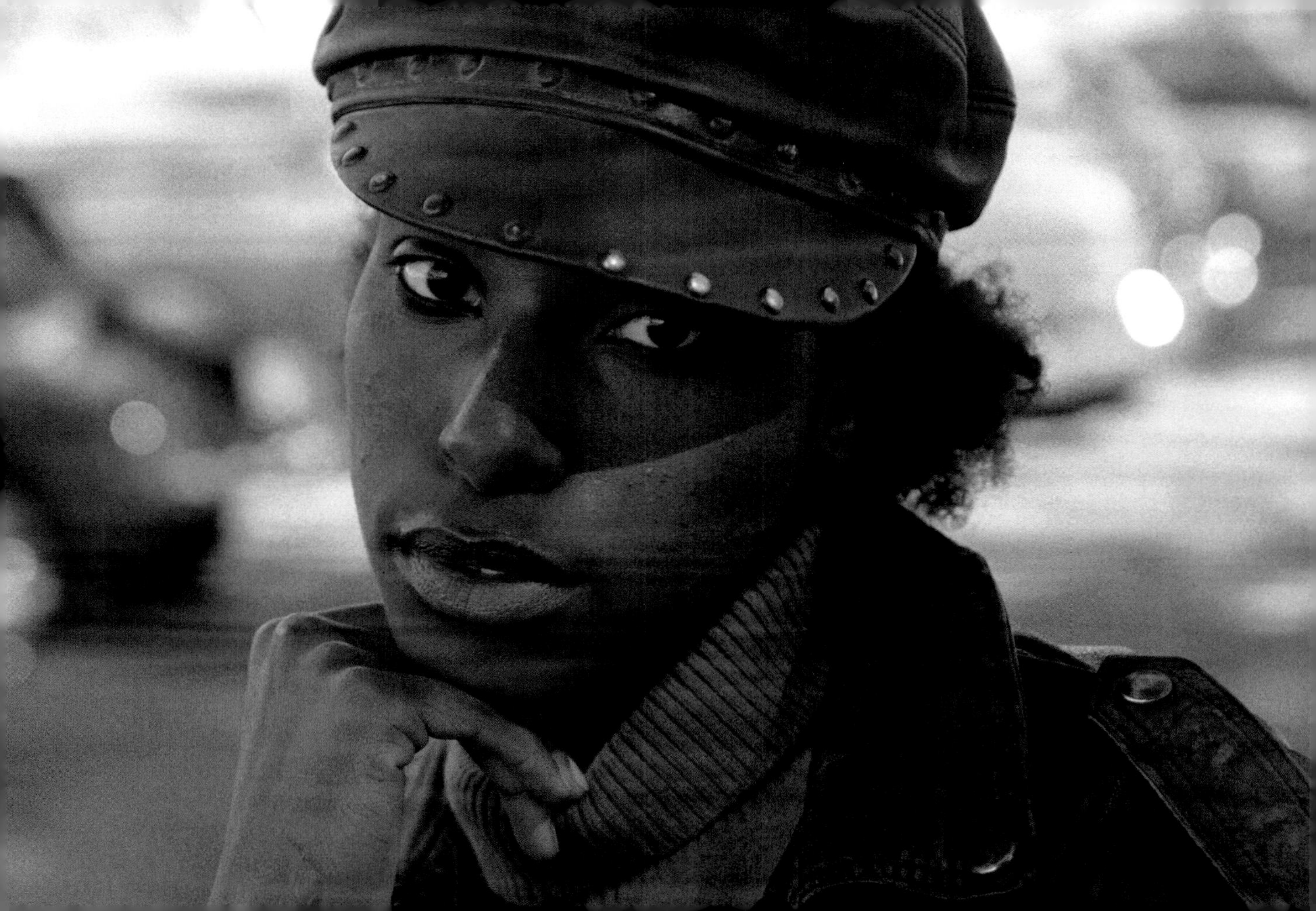

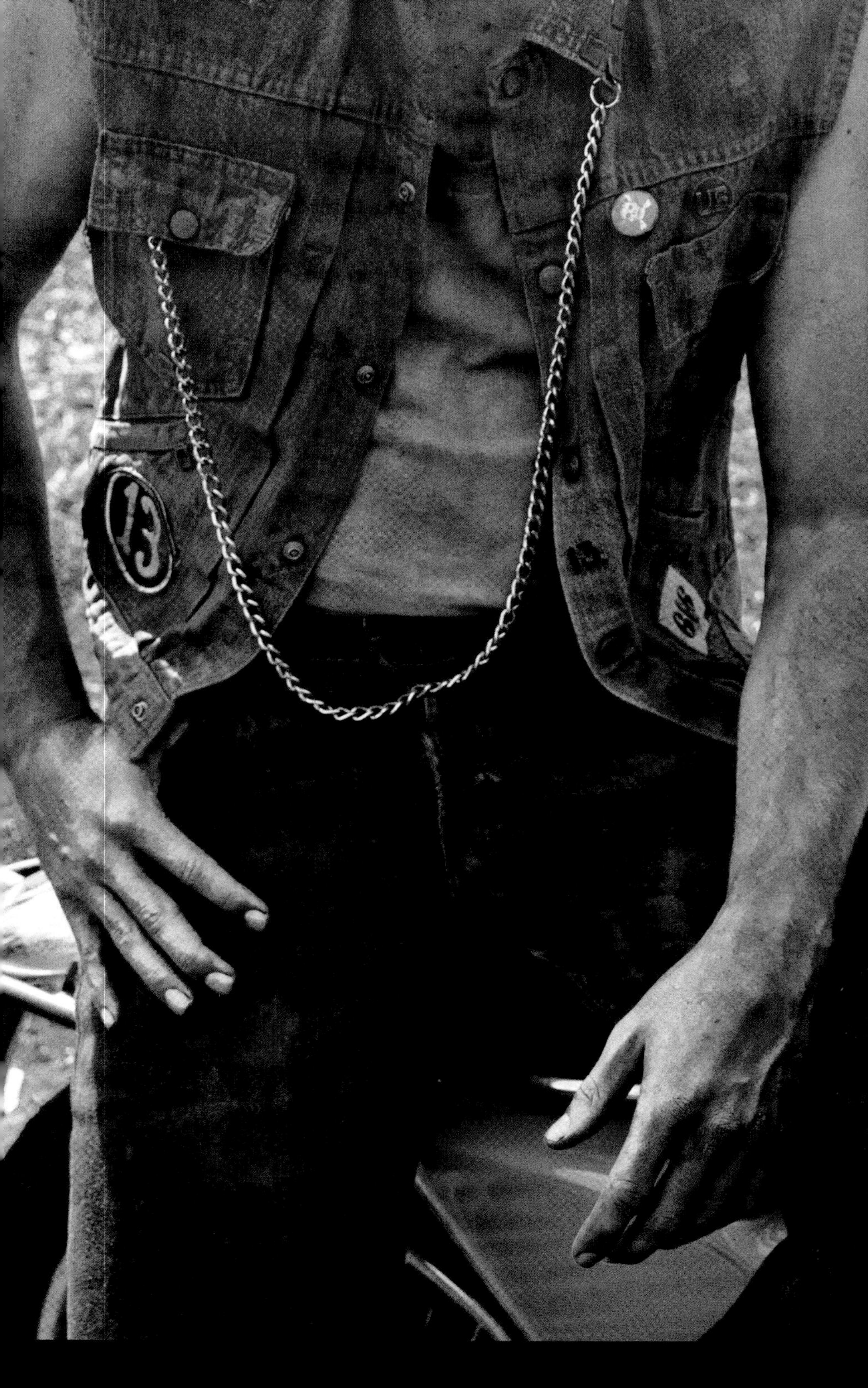

BRUCIE

I can't explain it to my parents, they don't understand the way I live, because bikeriders, a lot of people seem to think bikes lead to something negative, that's why they think guys ride 'em. They think it leads to something obscene. I don't know why, but obscenity and motorcycles travel hand in hand. That's what everybody thinks anyway.

DANNY

Why?

BRUCIE

I guess everybody needs someone to pick on. Can you think of anyone better than us?

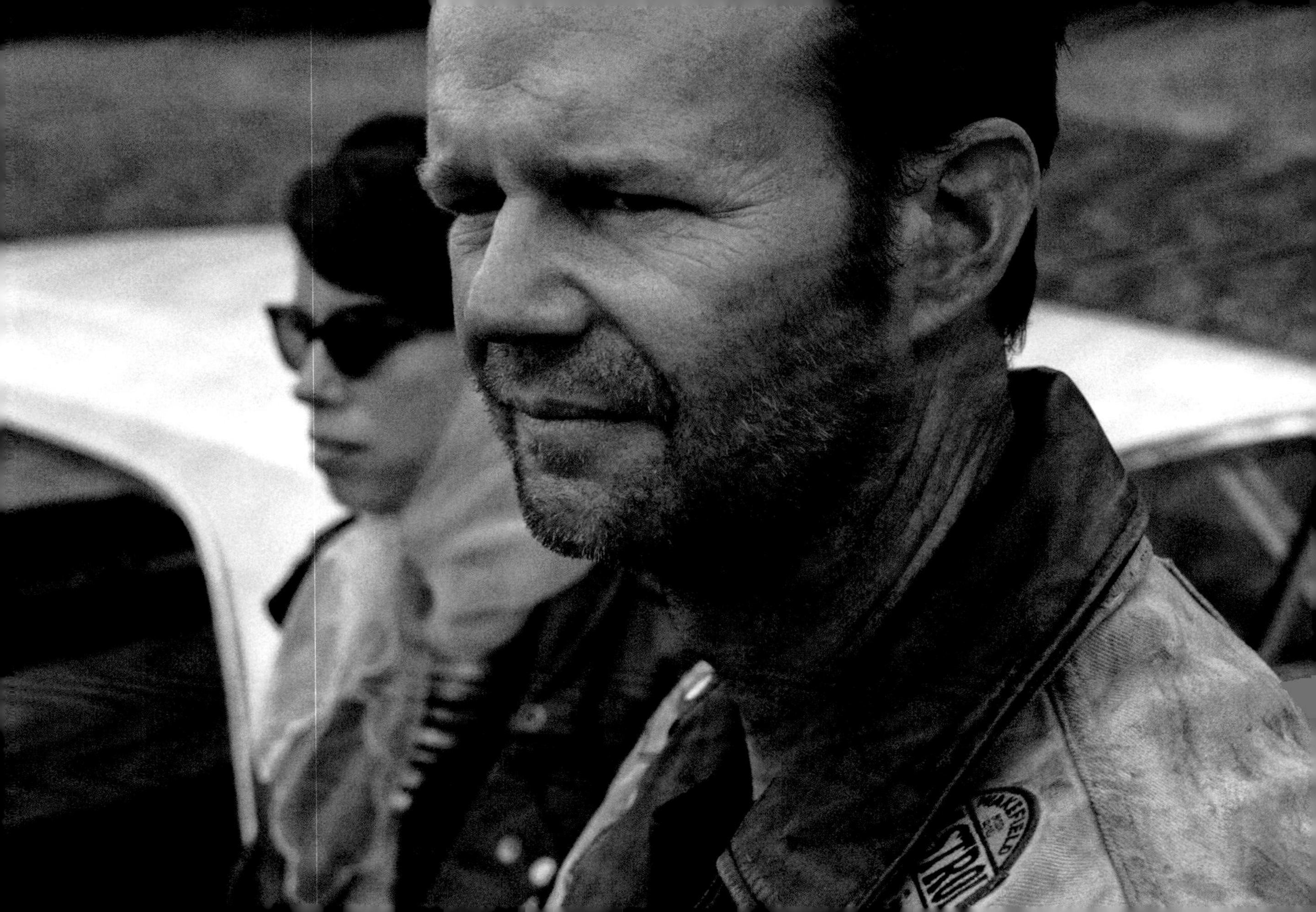

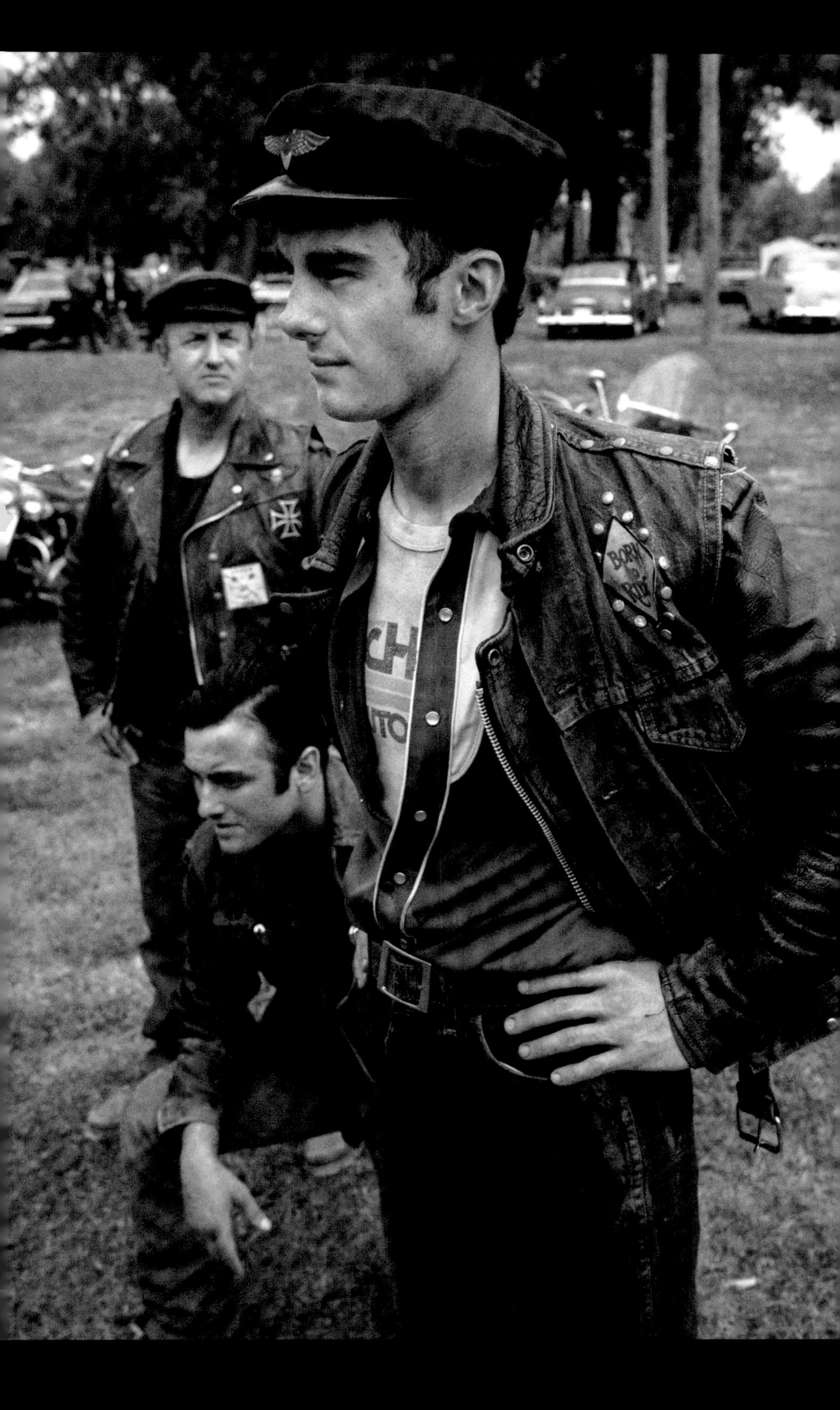

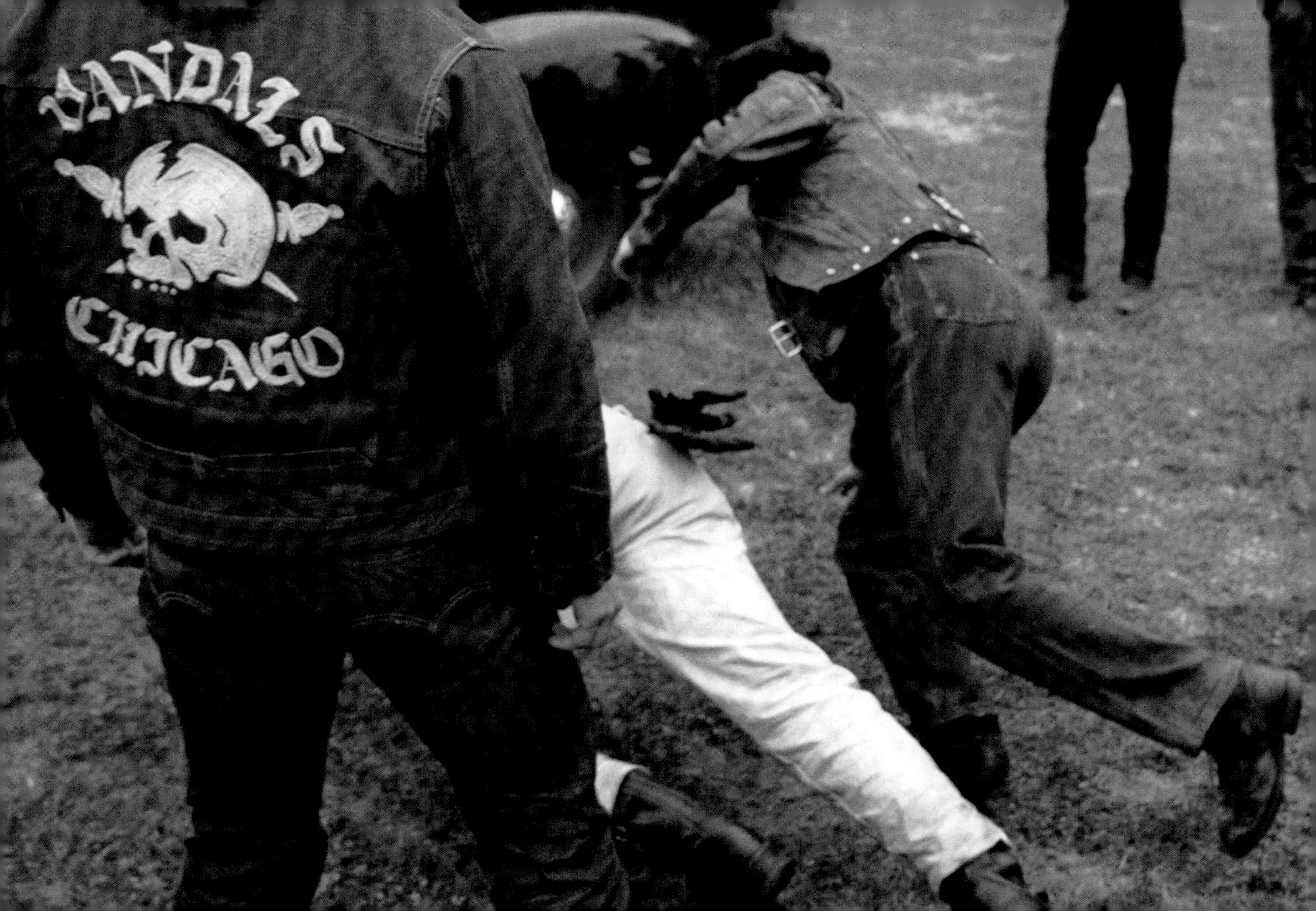
VANDALS
CHICAGO

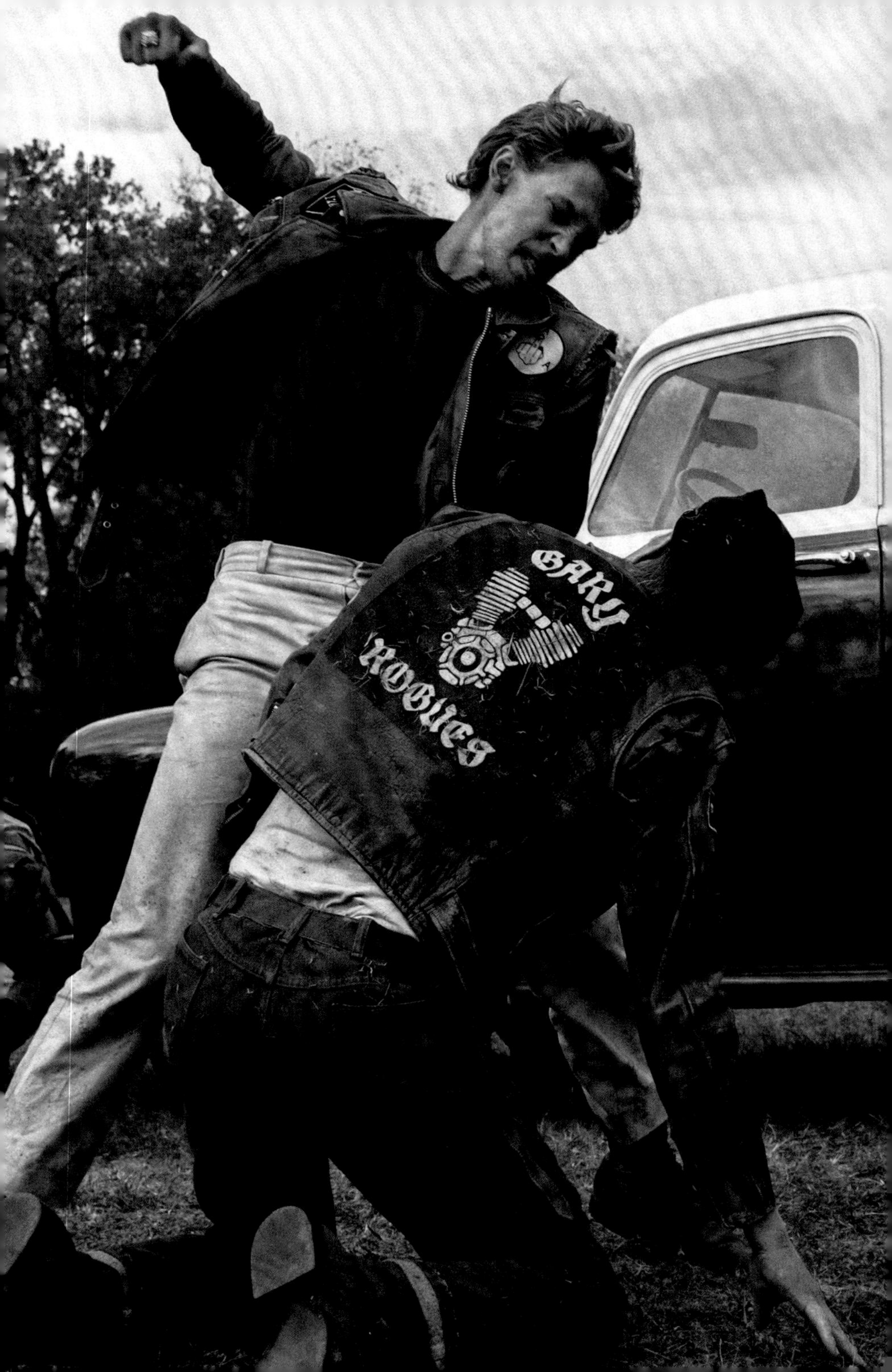
GARY
ROGUES

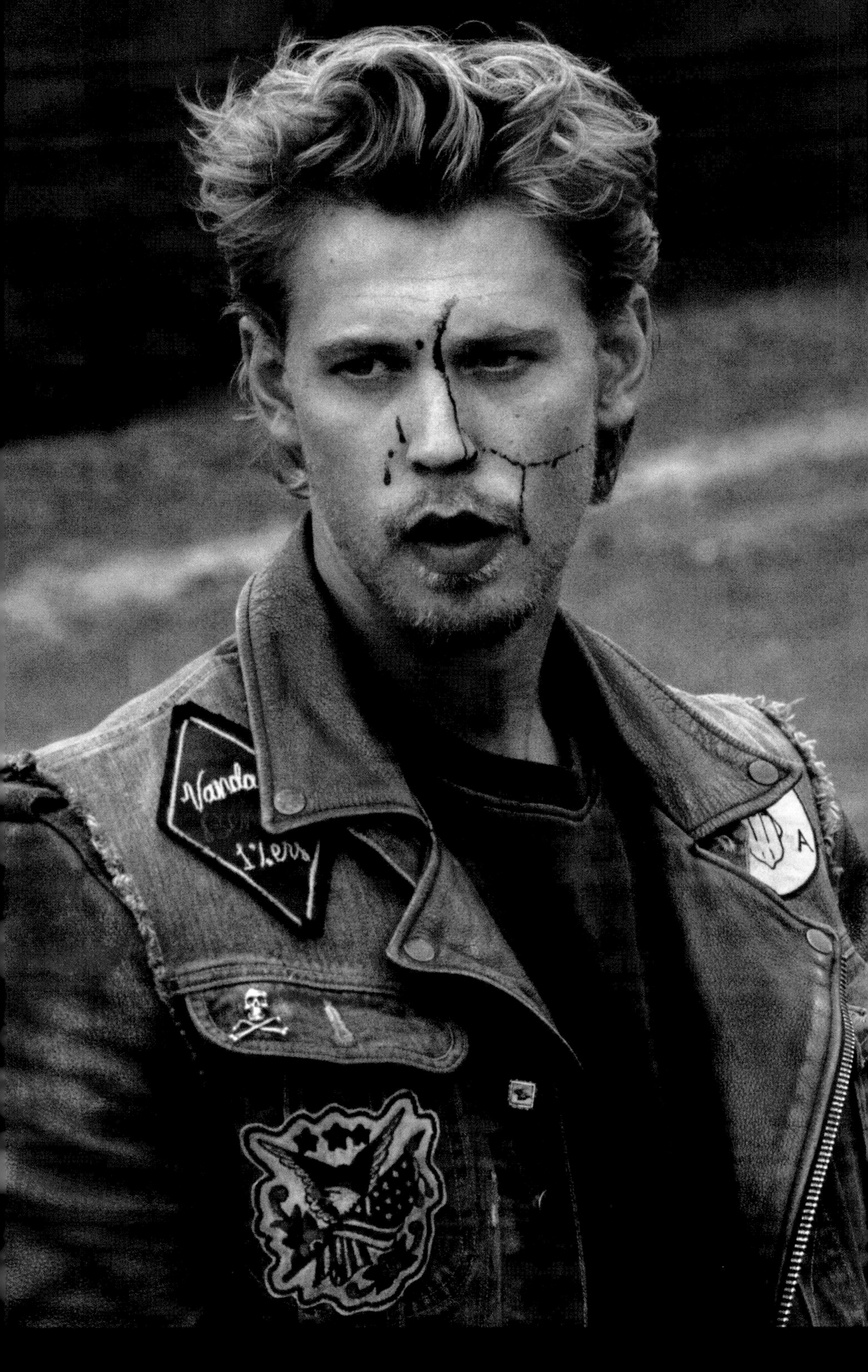

KATHY

Johnny always loved Benny.

DANNY

Why?

KATHY

Because Johnny always wanted what Benny had.

DANNY

. . . and what's that?

KATHY

To not care about nothin'.

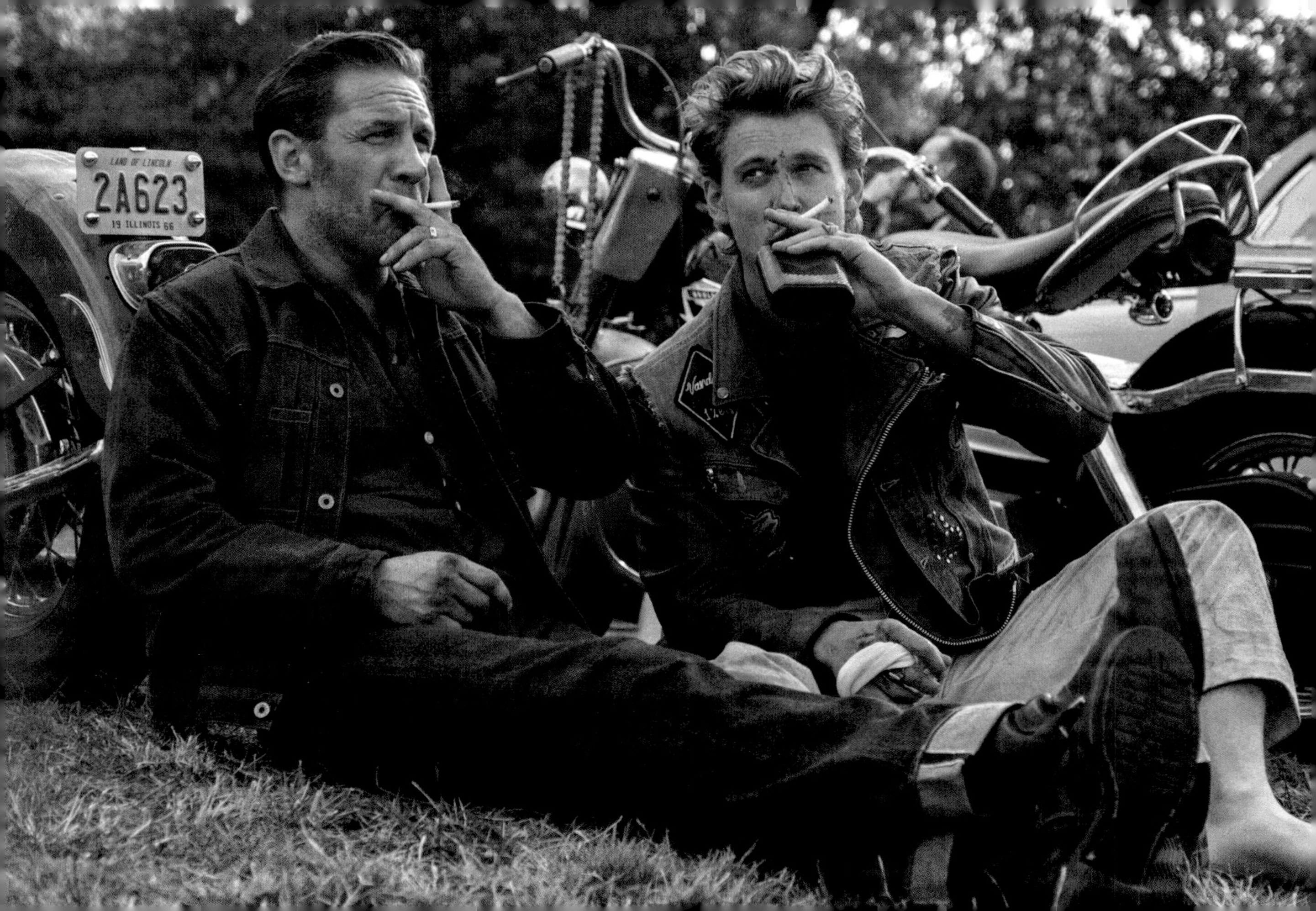
LAND OF LINCOLN
2A623
19 ILLINOIS 66

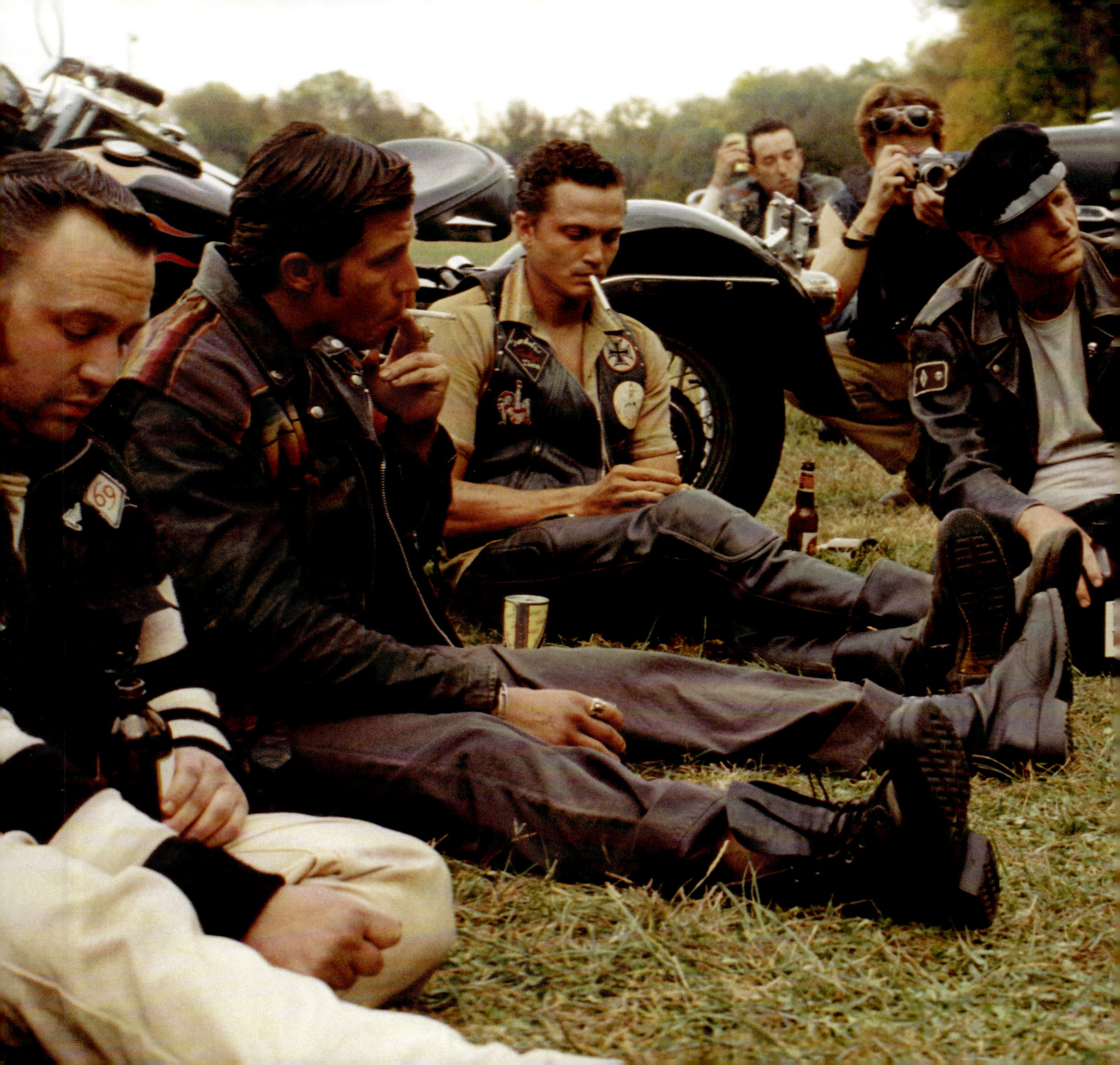

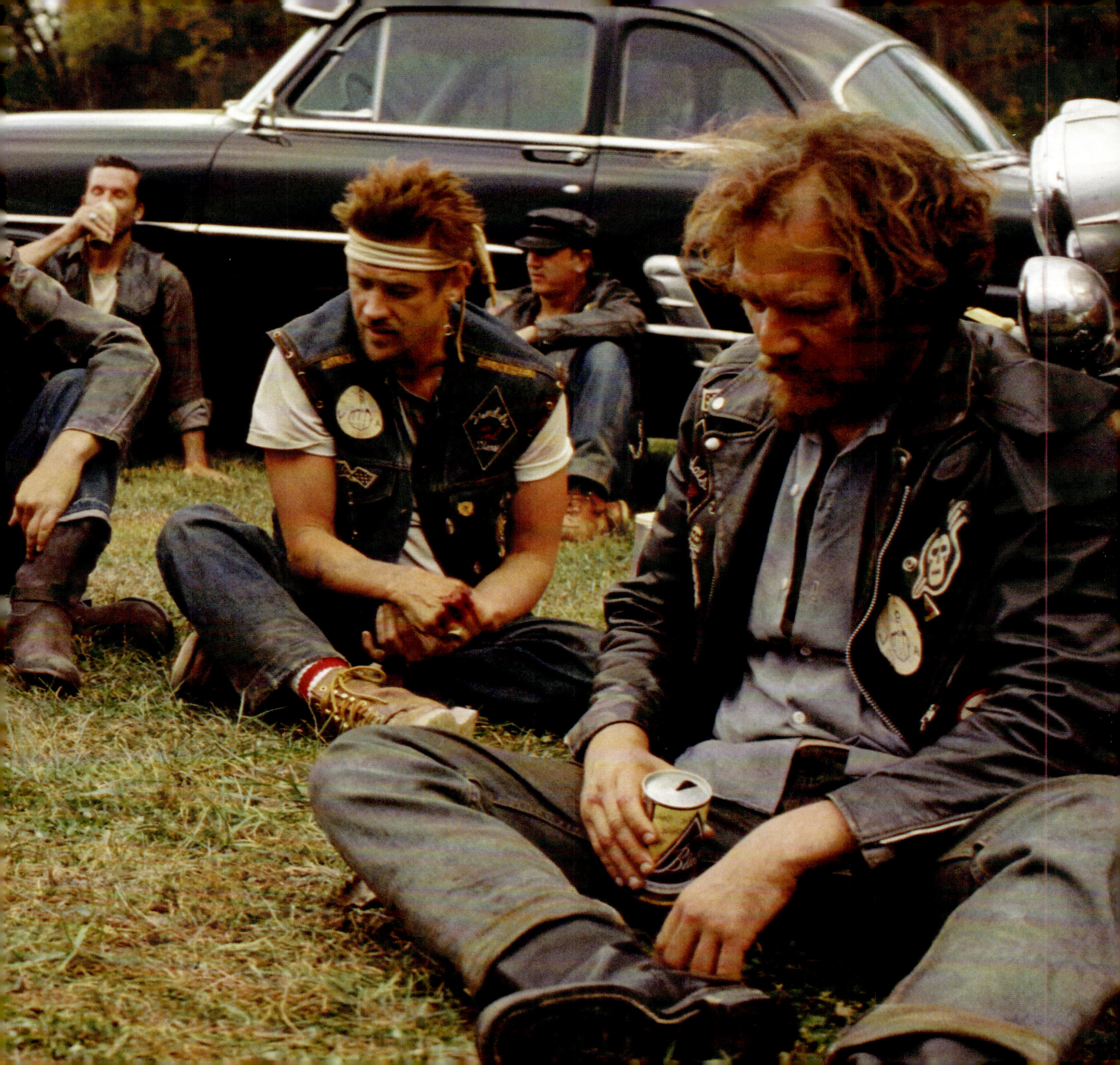

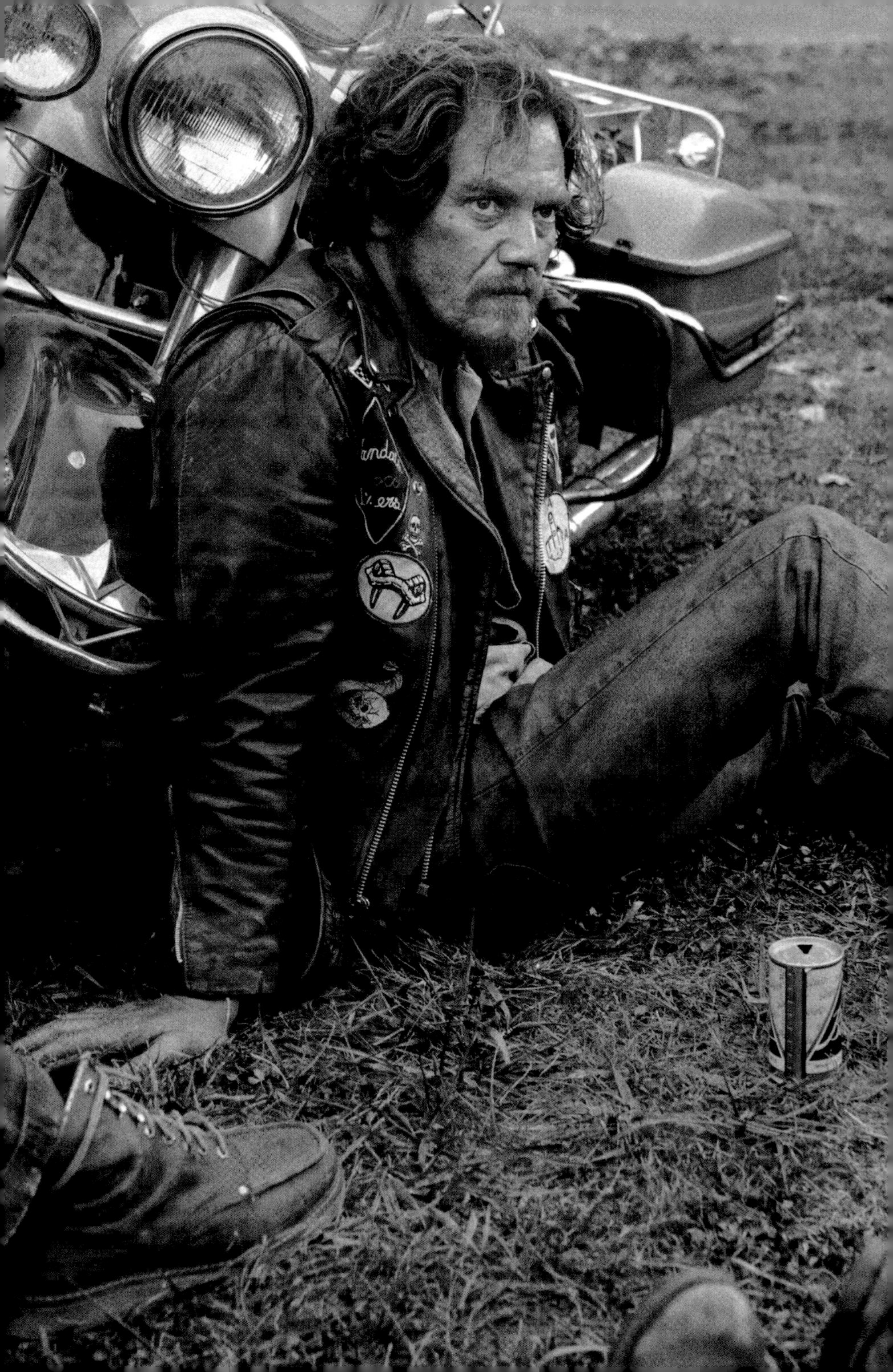

ZIPCO

I told my brudder, he went to college one year, I said fucker you don't quit that college, I'm a beat the shit outta you. And he quit, 'cause I told him I don't want no goddam pinkos in my family. 'Cause I can't stand that shit you know. 'Cause if you can't work with your fuckin' hands, you ain't no fuckin' good . . . I ain't ah, I like to work. I ain't a fuckin' prick. I like to work with my hands and shit. I work hard for my money, you know?

DANNY

Oh yeah . . . yeah.

ZIPCO

What do you do?

DANNY

I study photography. In college.

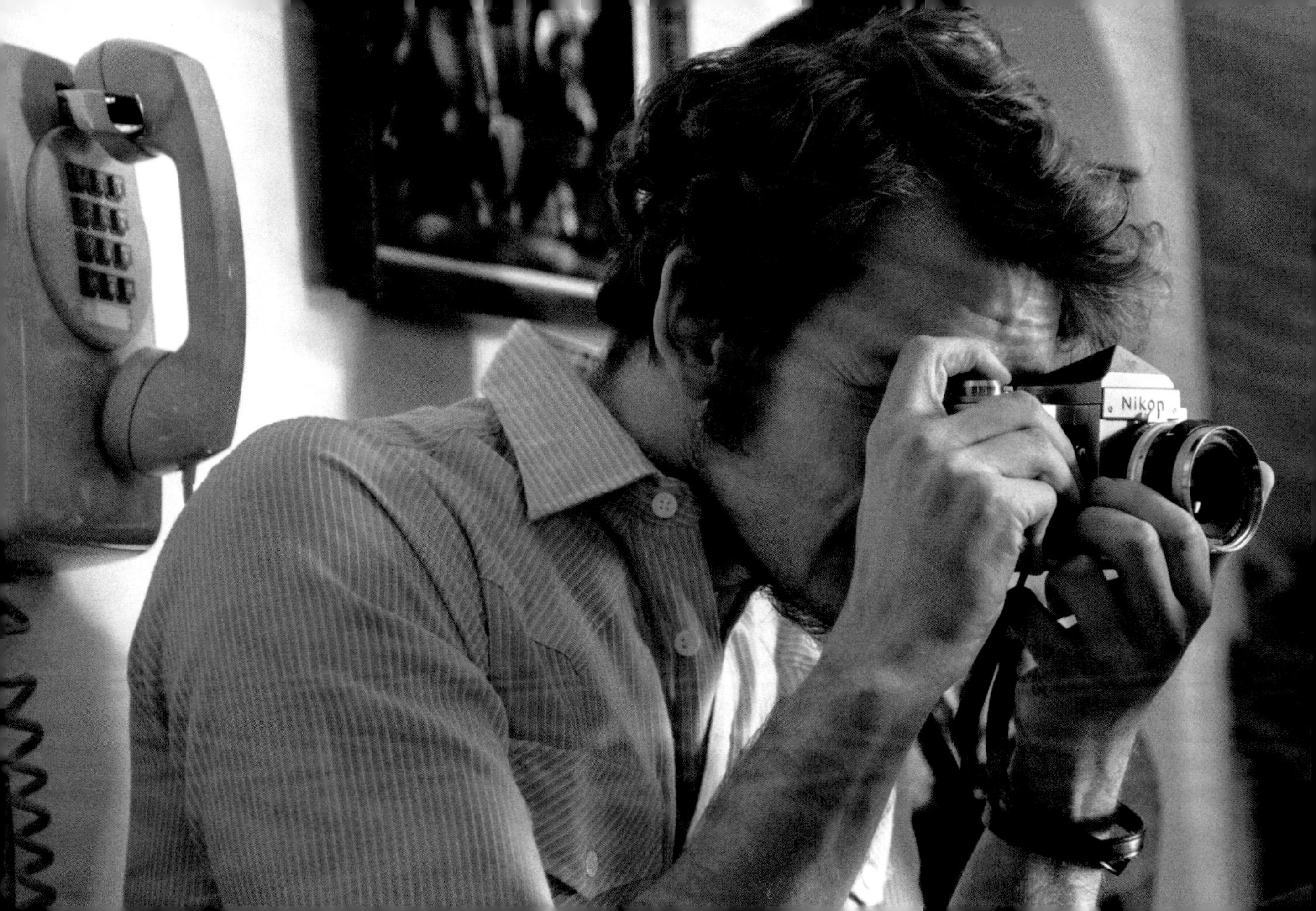
Nikon

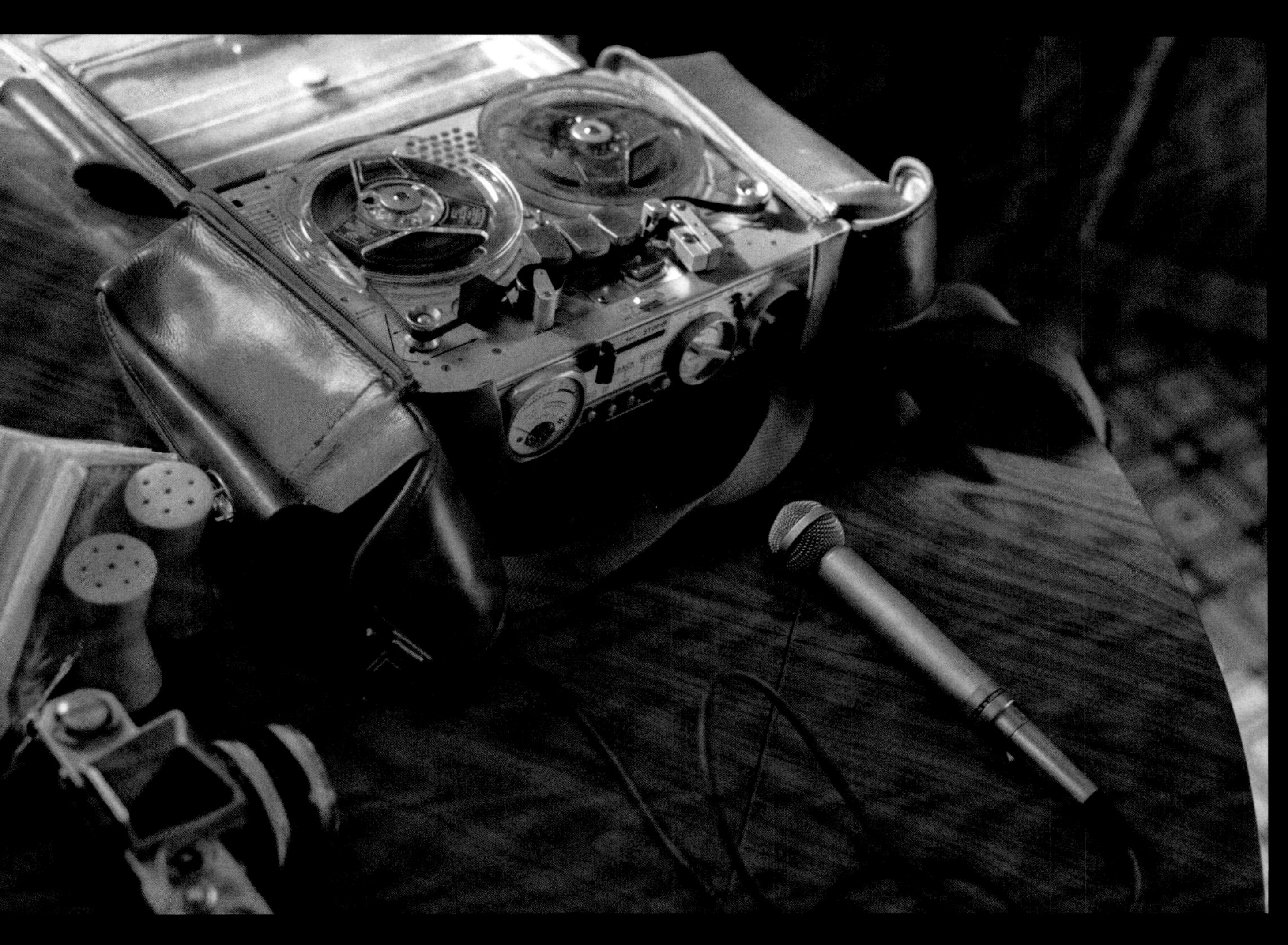

COCKROACH

When I was about fifteen years old my father bought me an Indian four-cylinder motorcycle. I like to be dirty. I'll go out of my way to put filth on my clothes, dirt on my pants, dirt on my face, mess up my hair, and eat bugs. A bug isn't really bad to eat, it's all in a person's mind. Now, if you will eat a raw beef sandwich, or you will eat a rare steak, a bug won't hurt you any more.

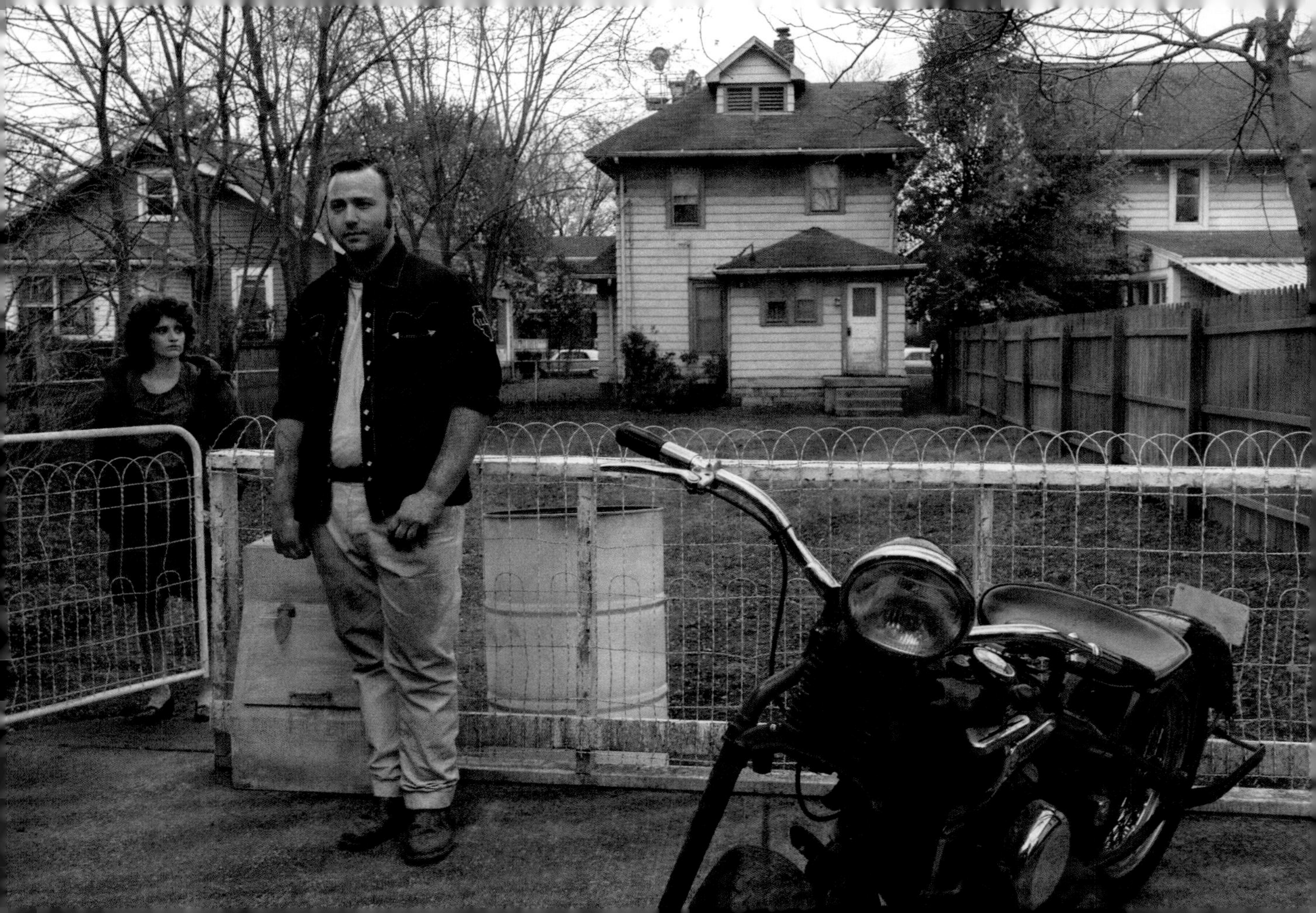

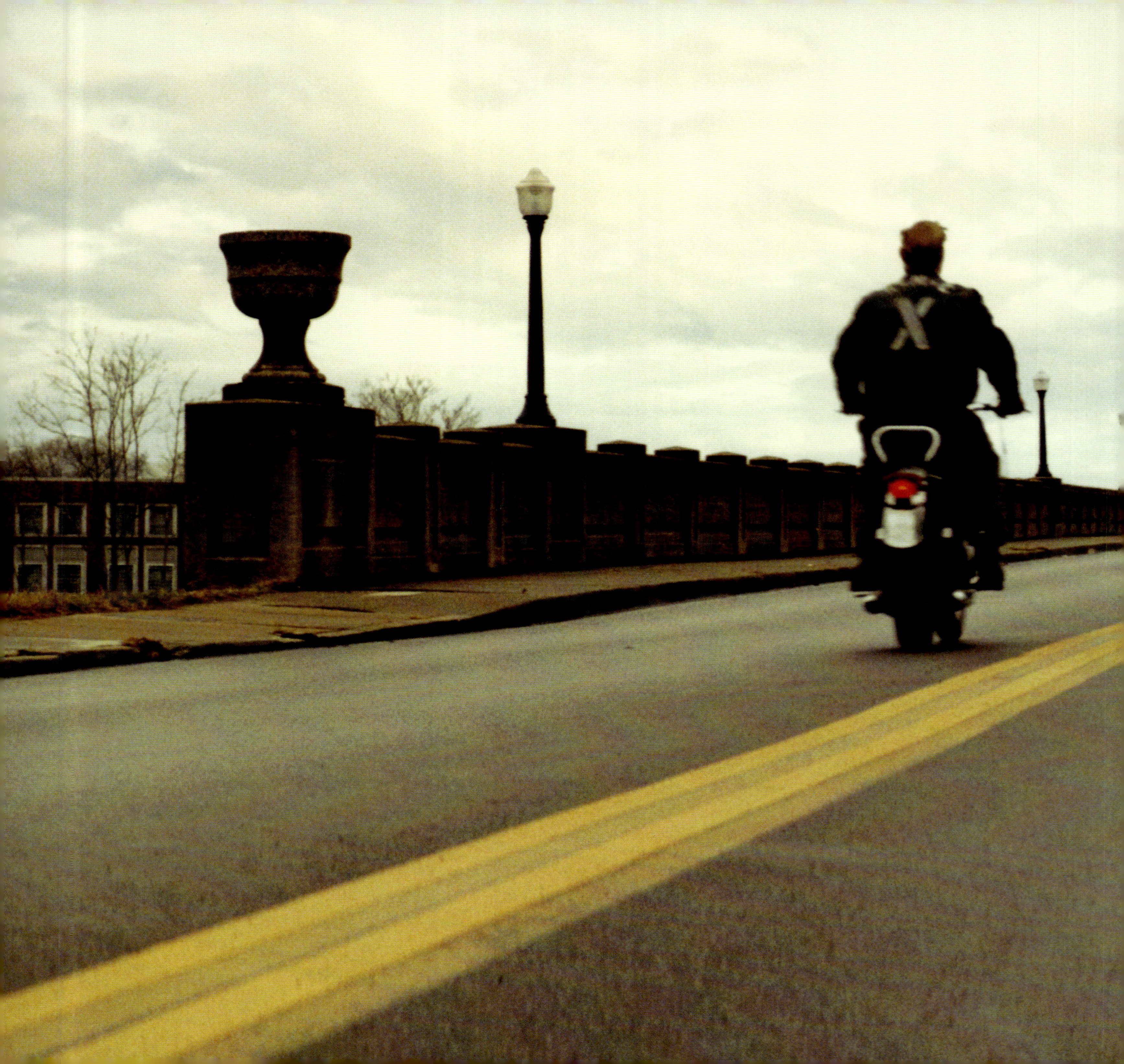

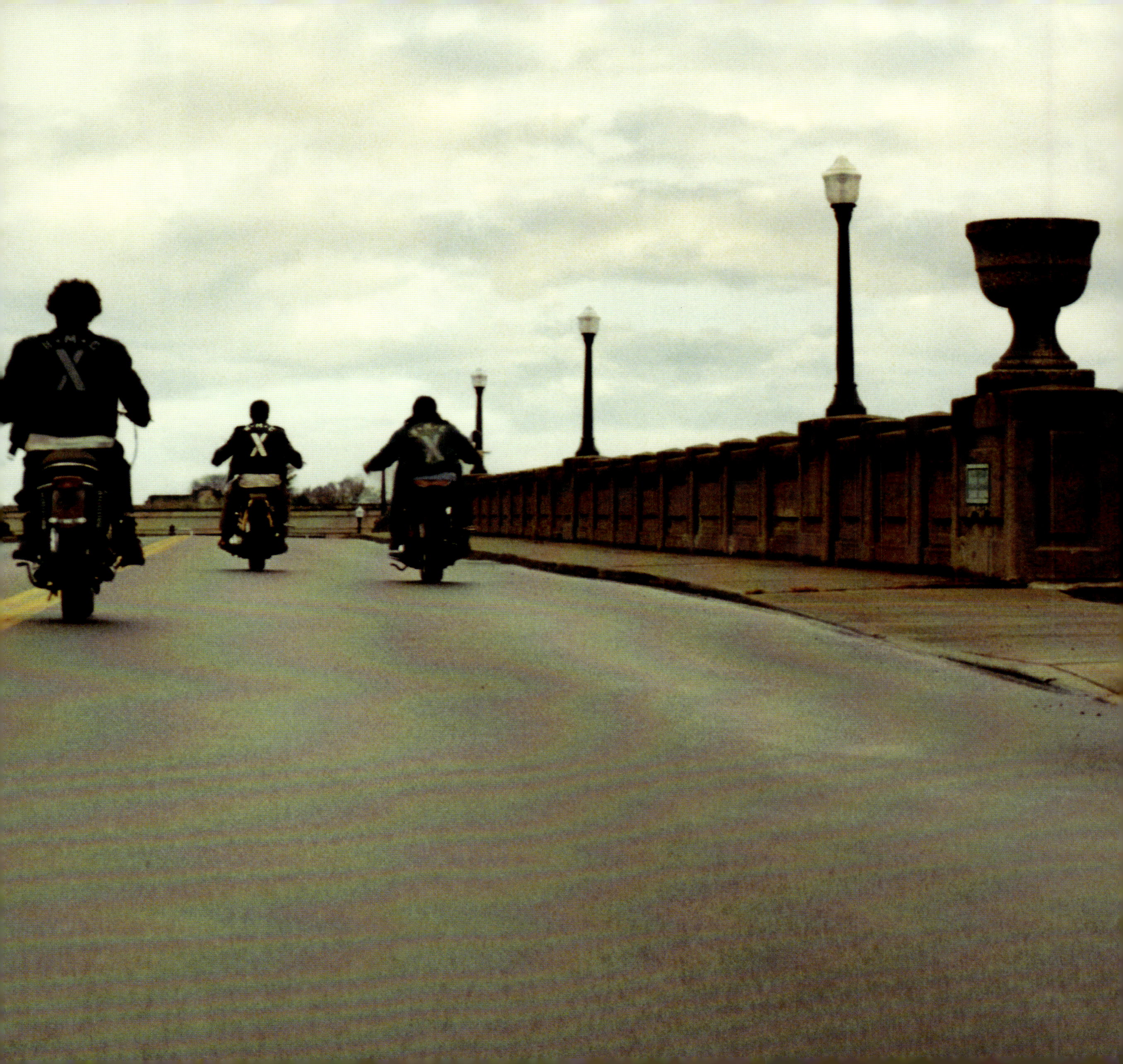
X

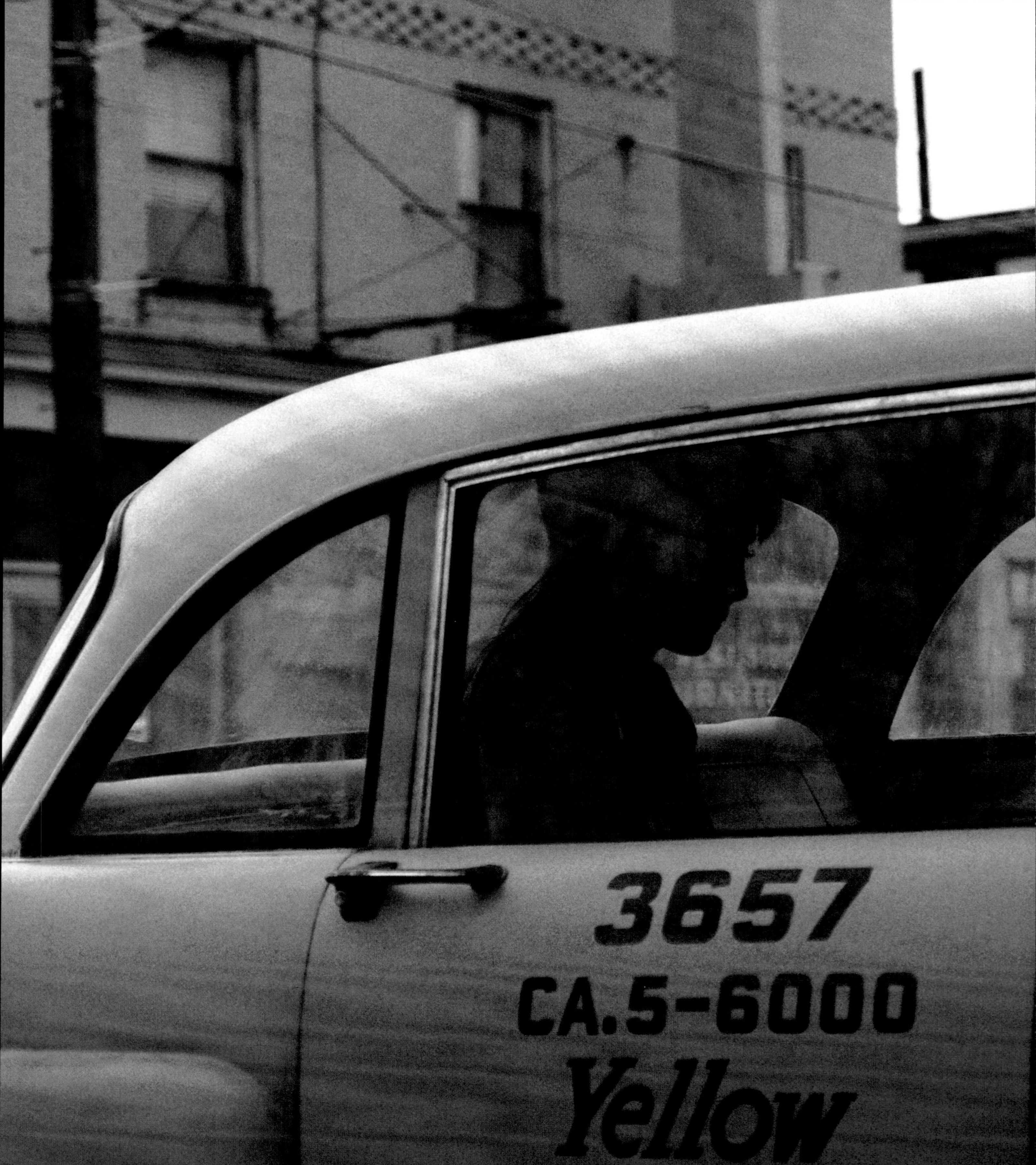
3657
CA.5-6000
Yellow

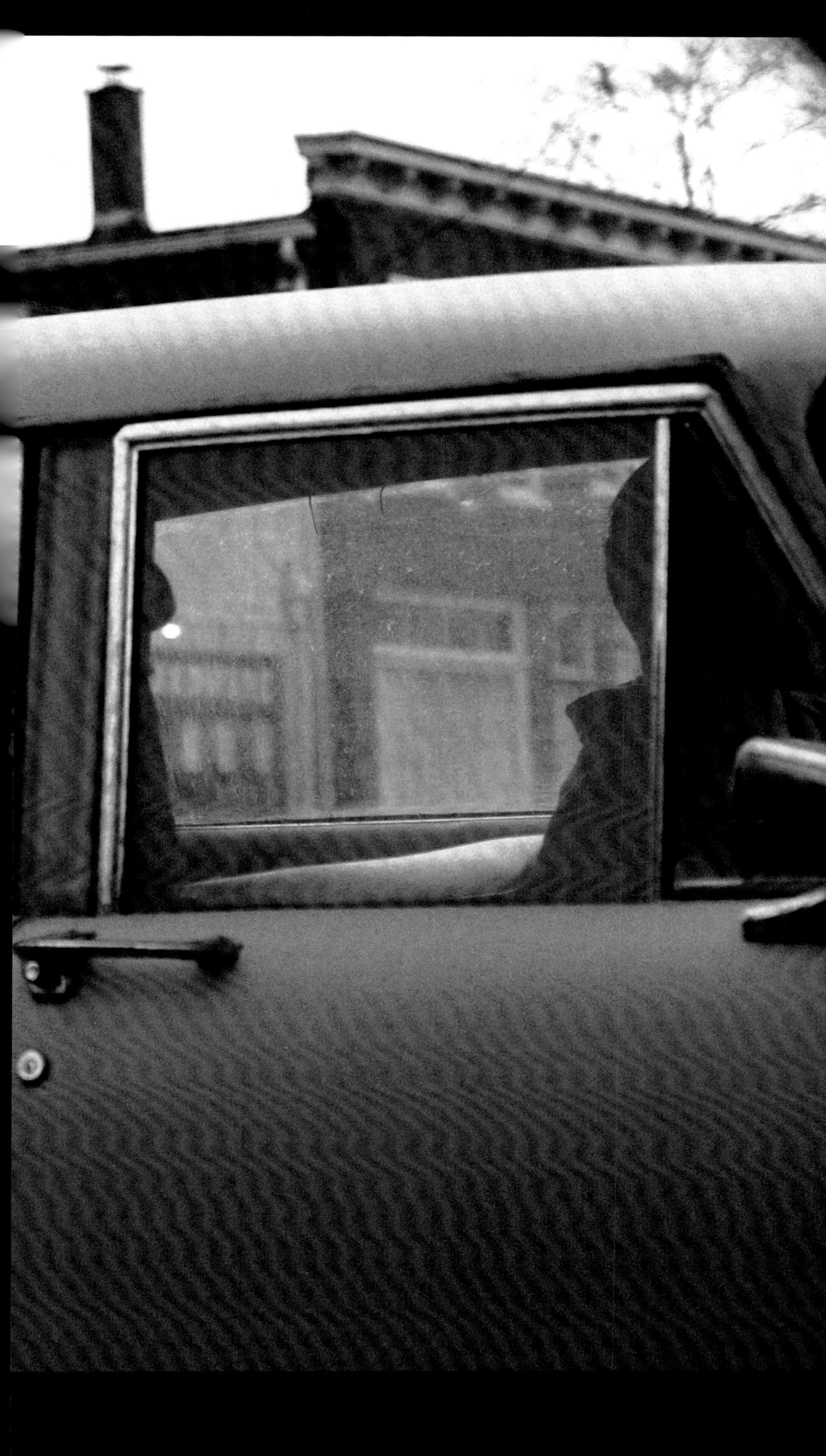

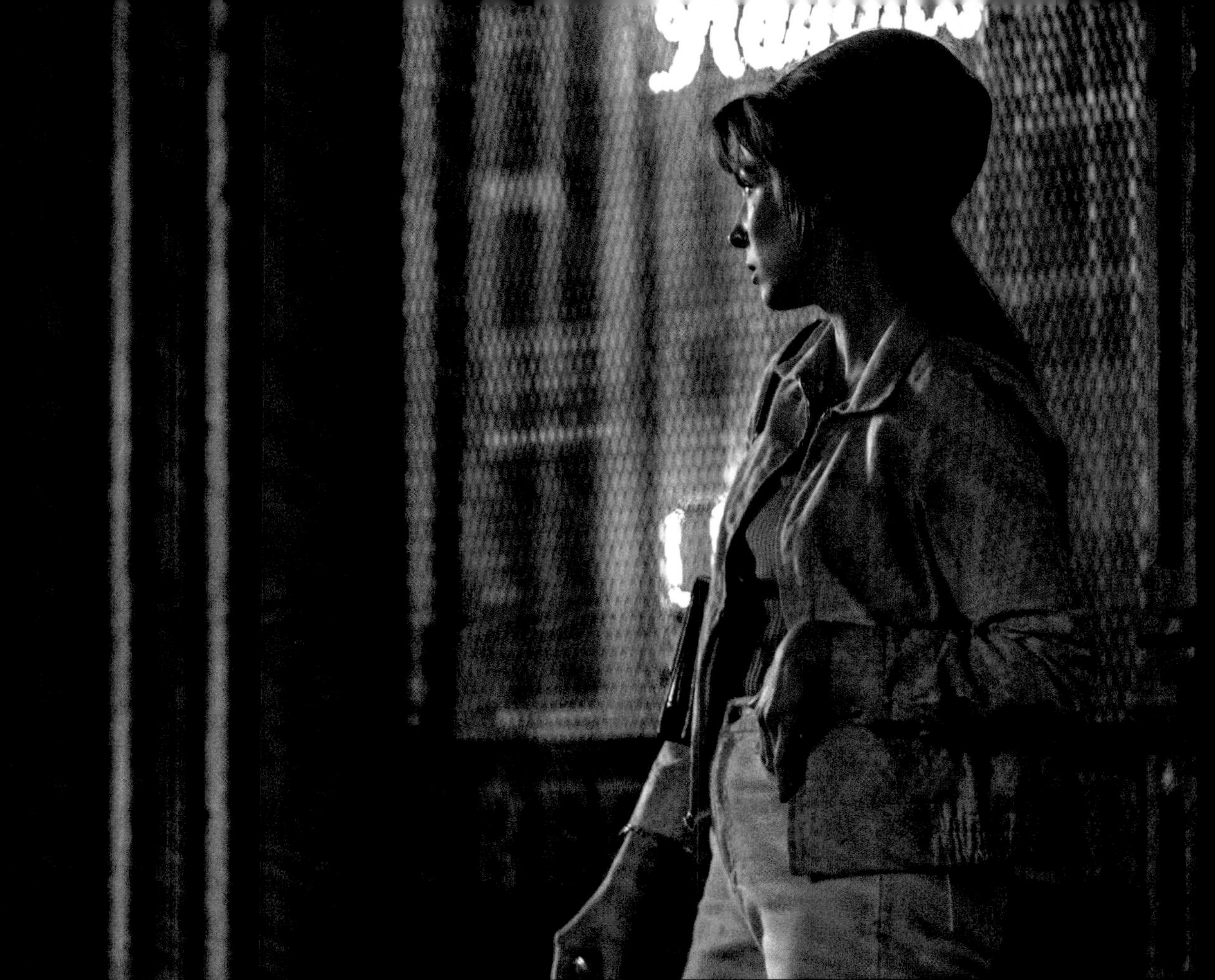

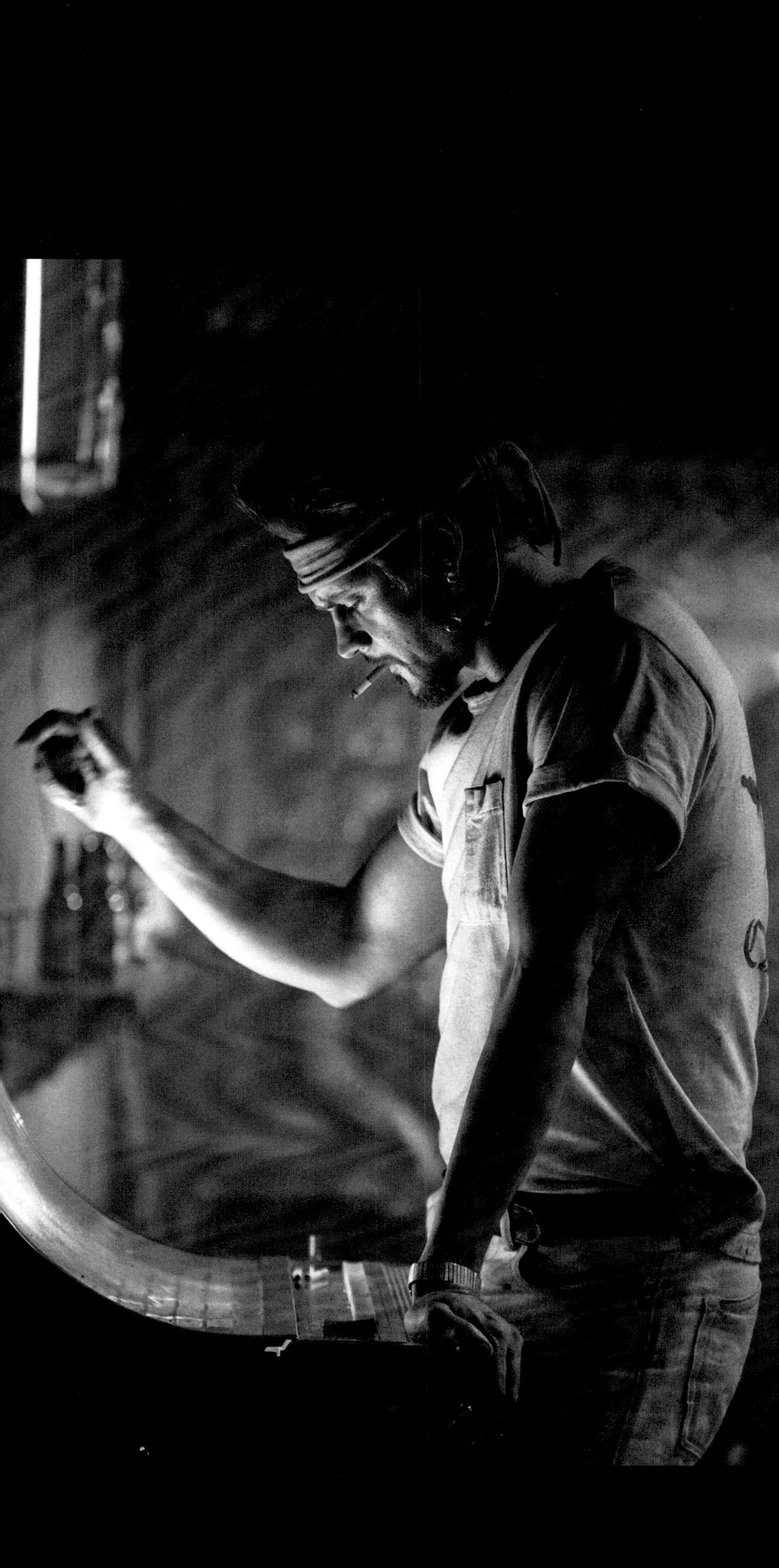

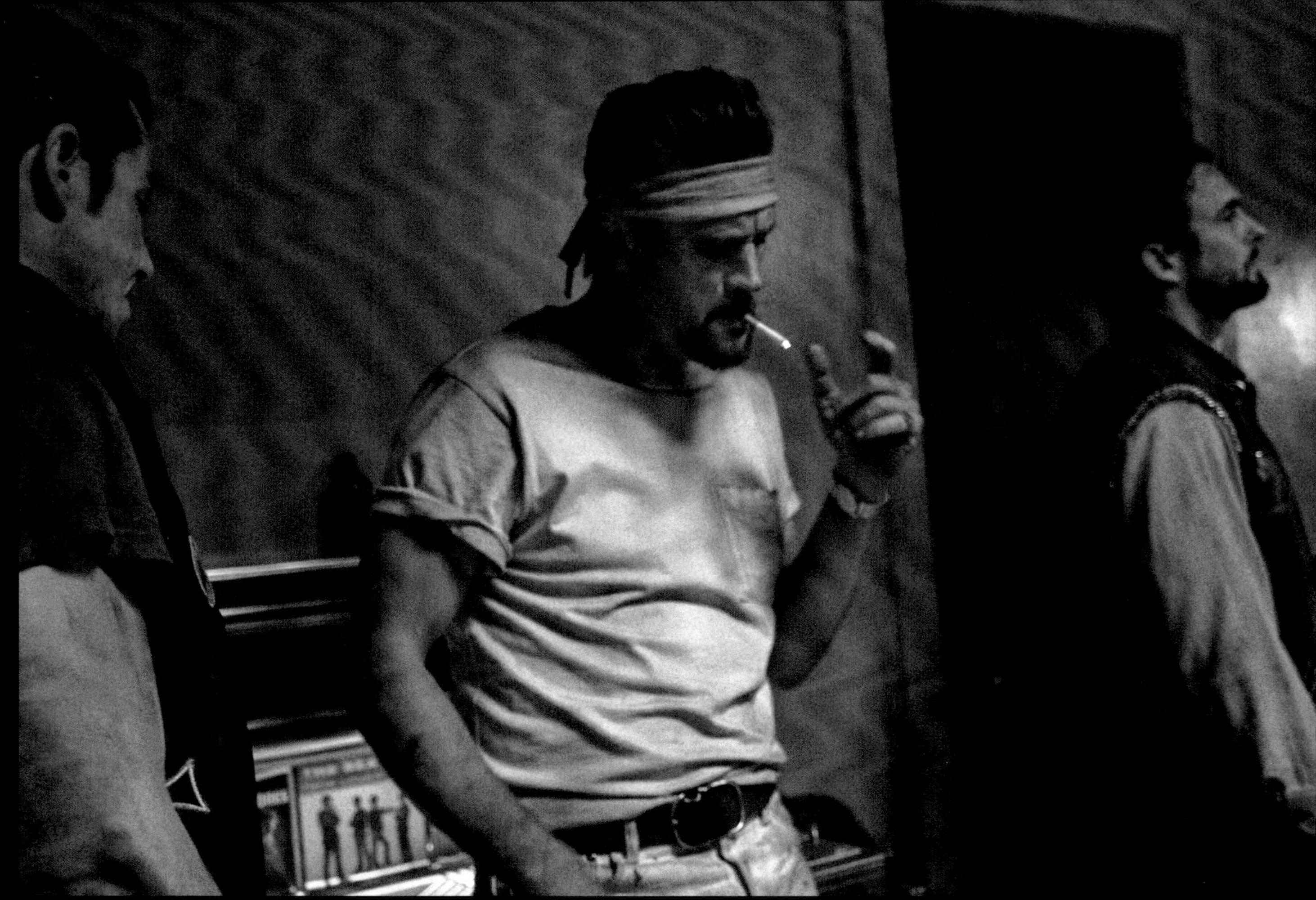

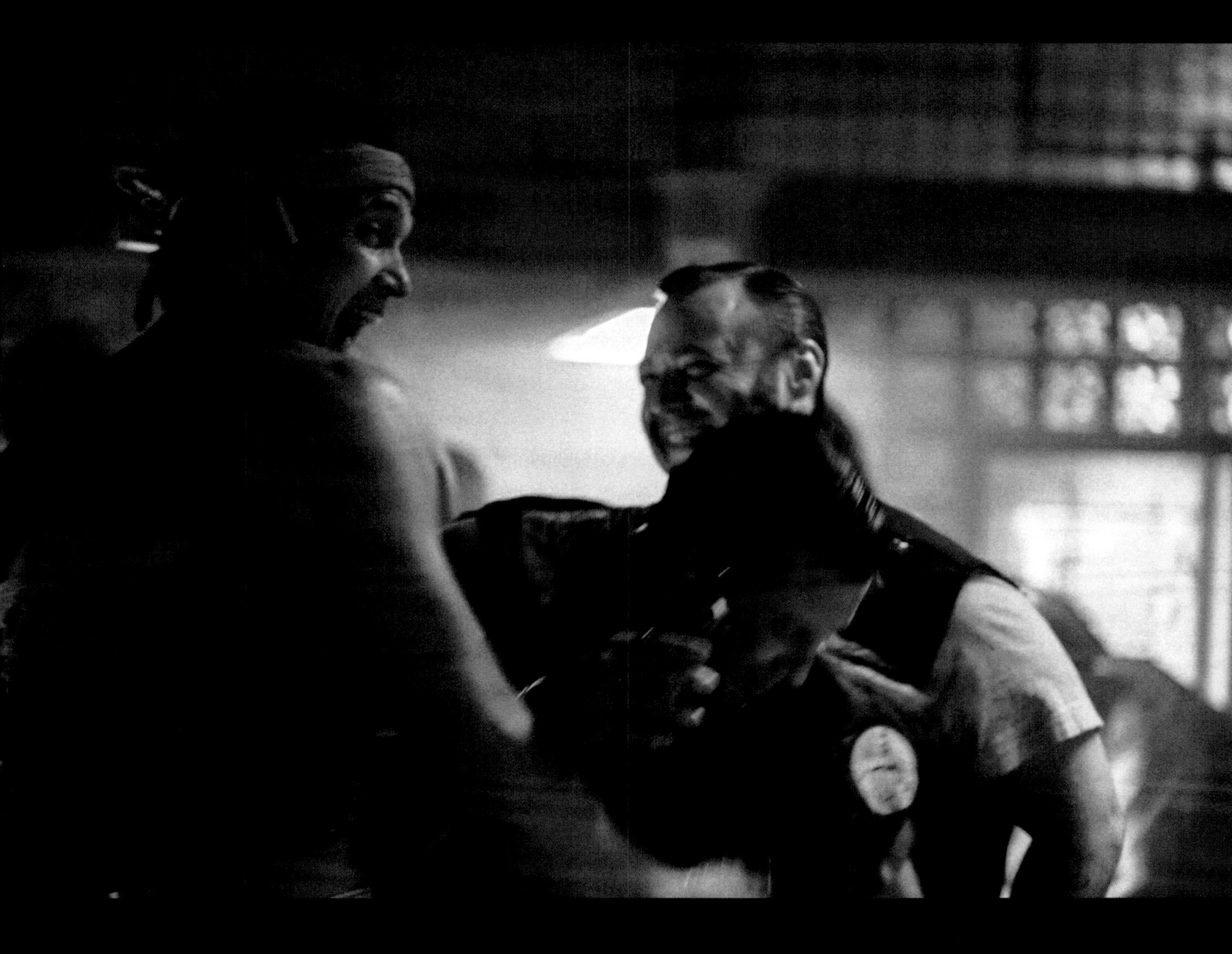

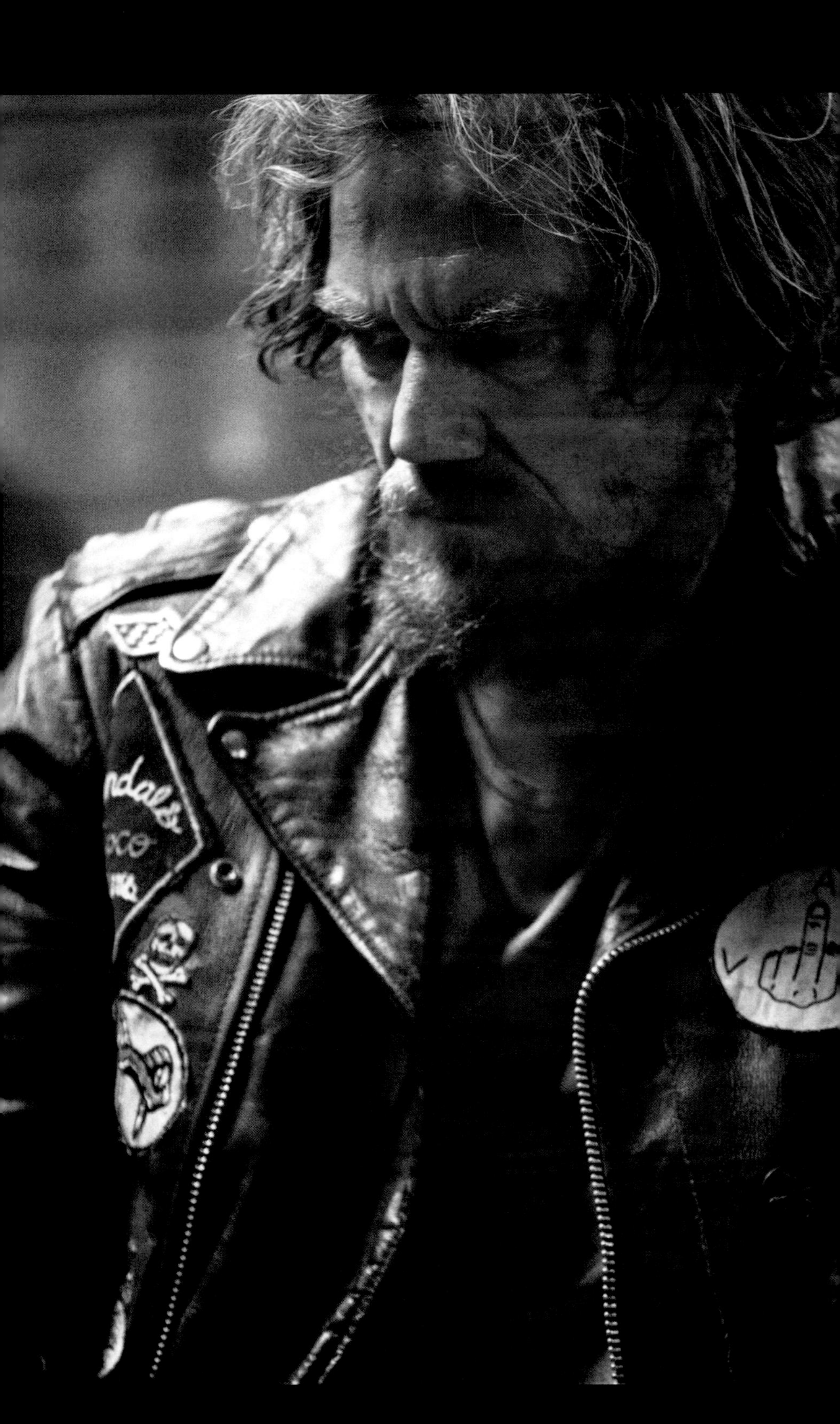

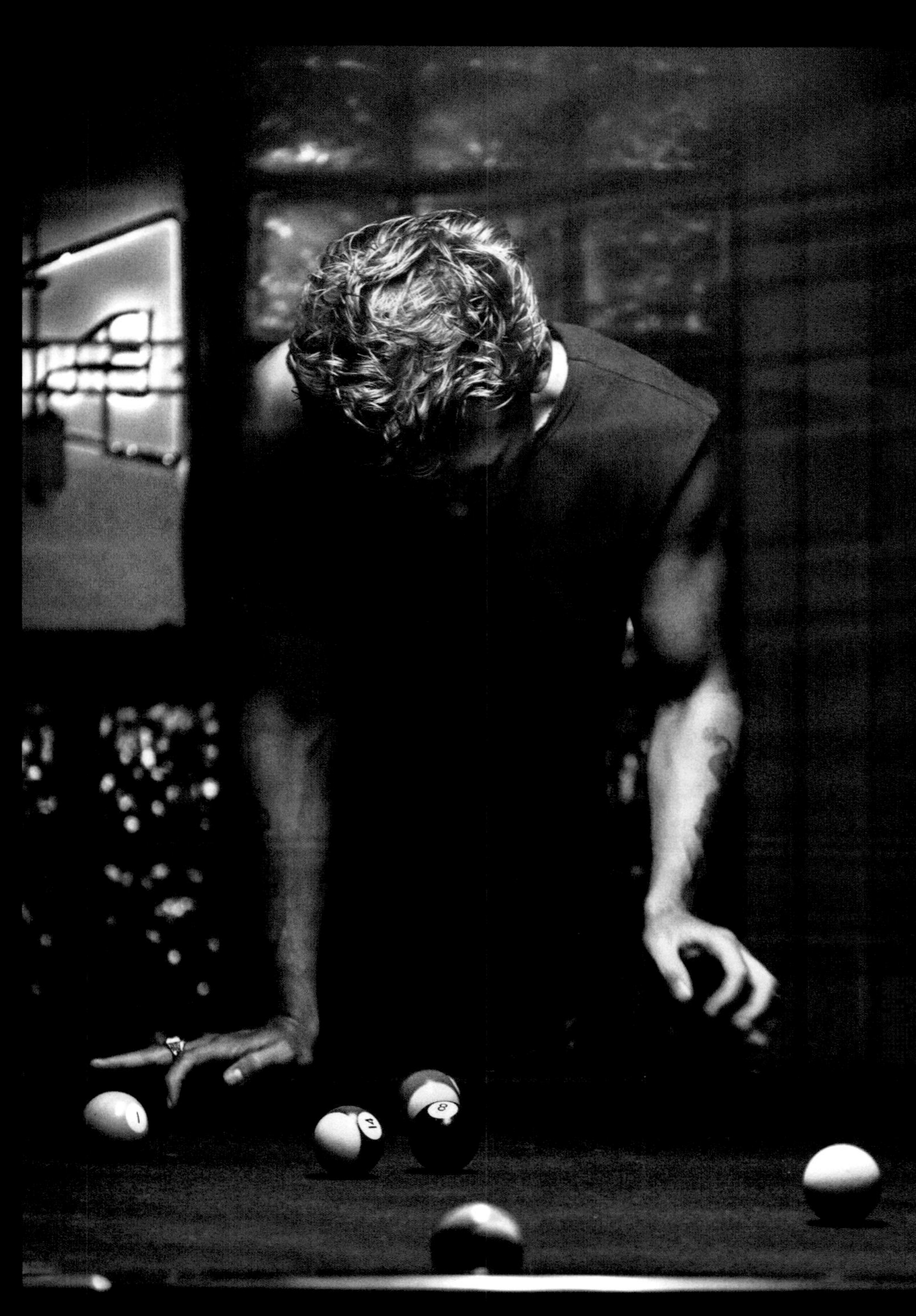

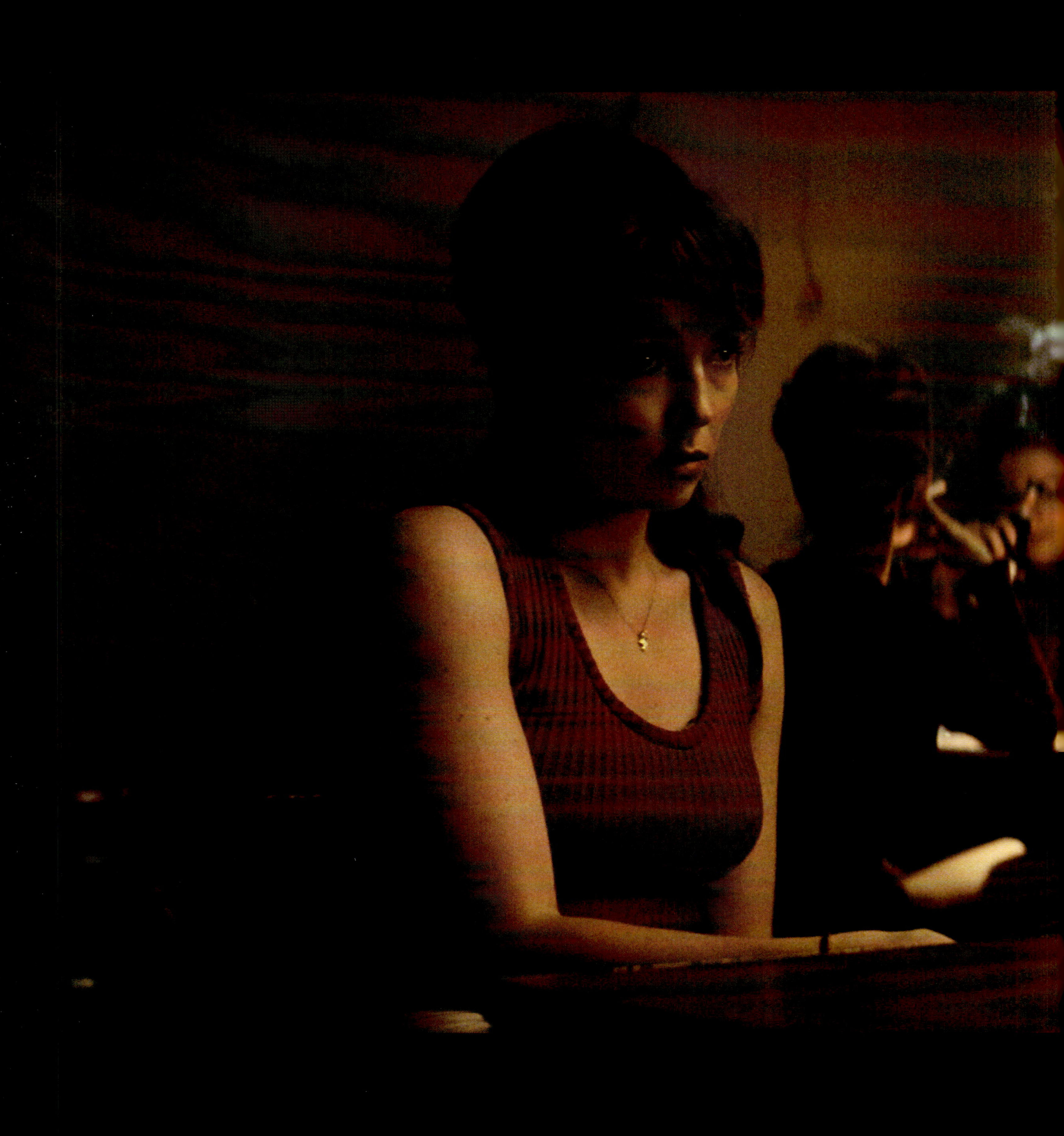

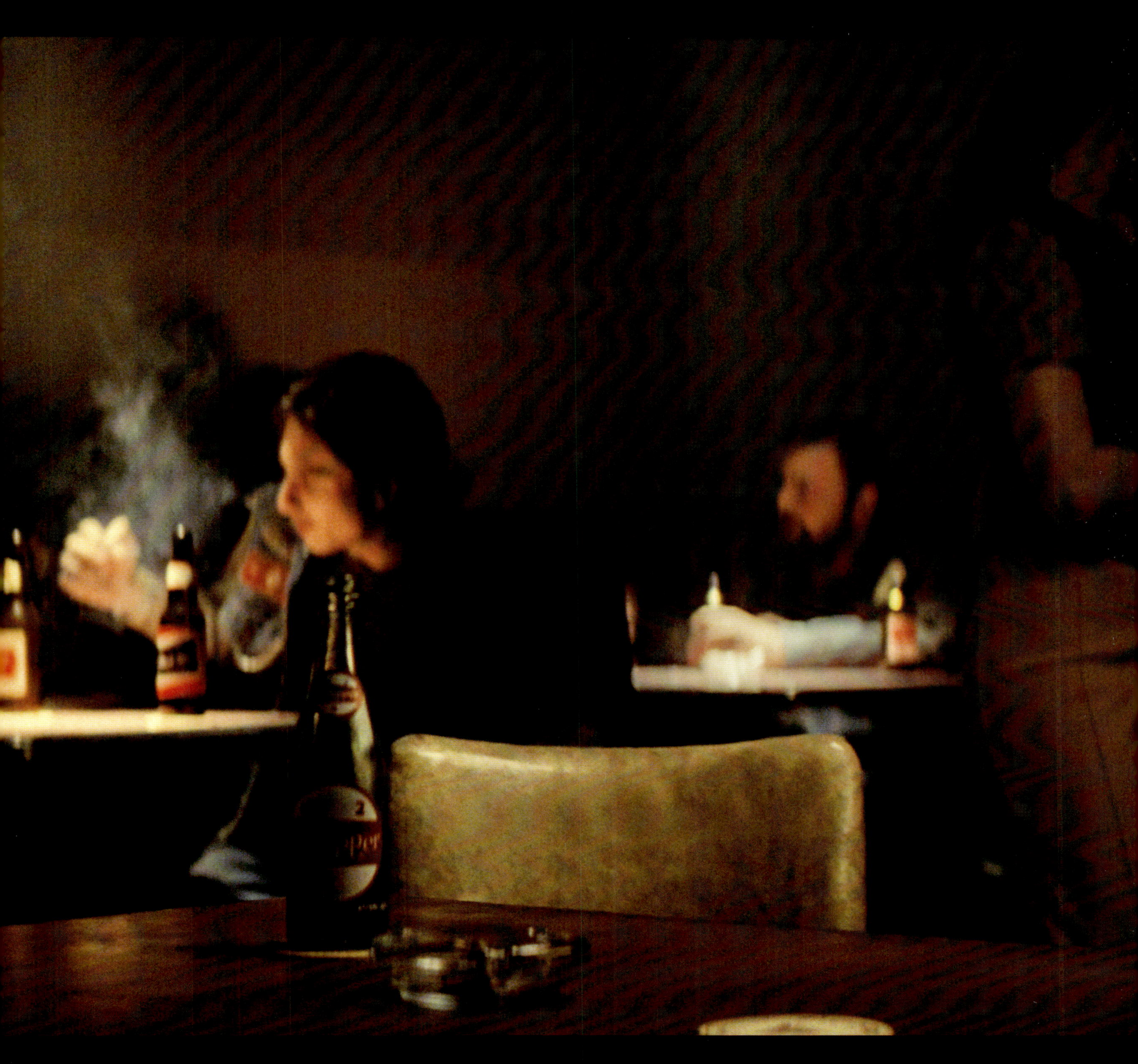

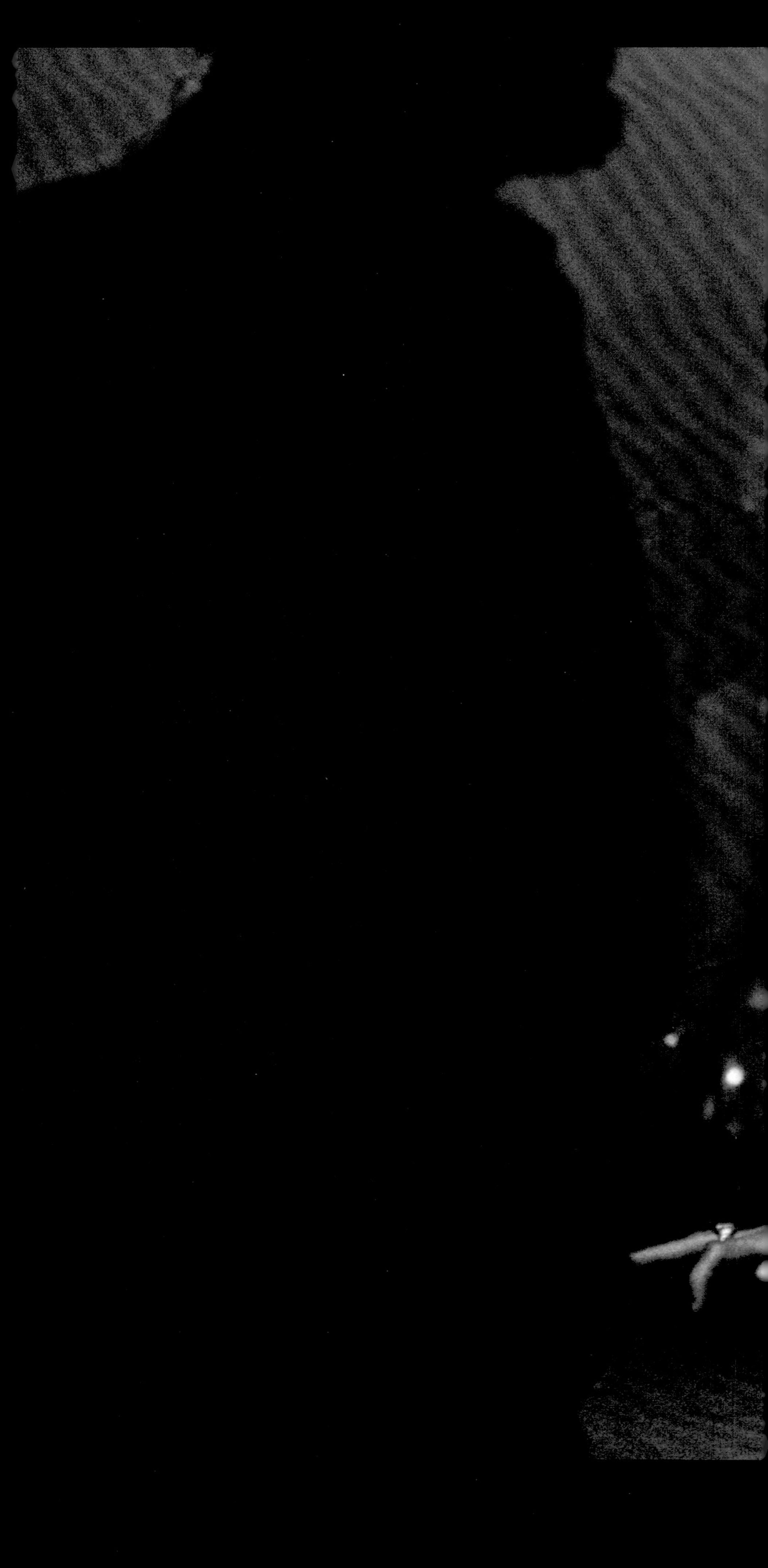

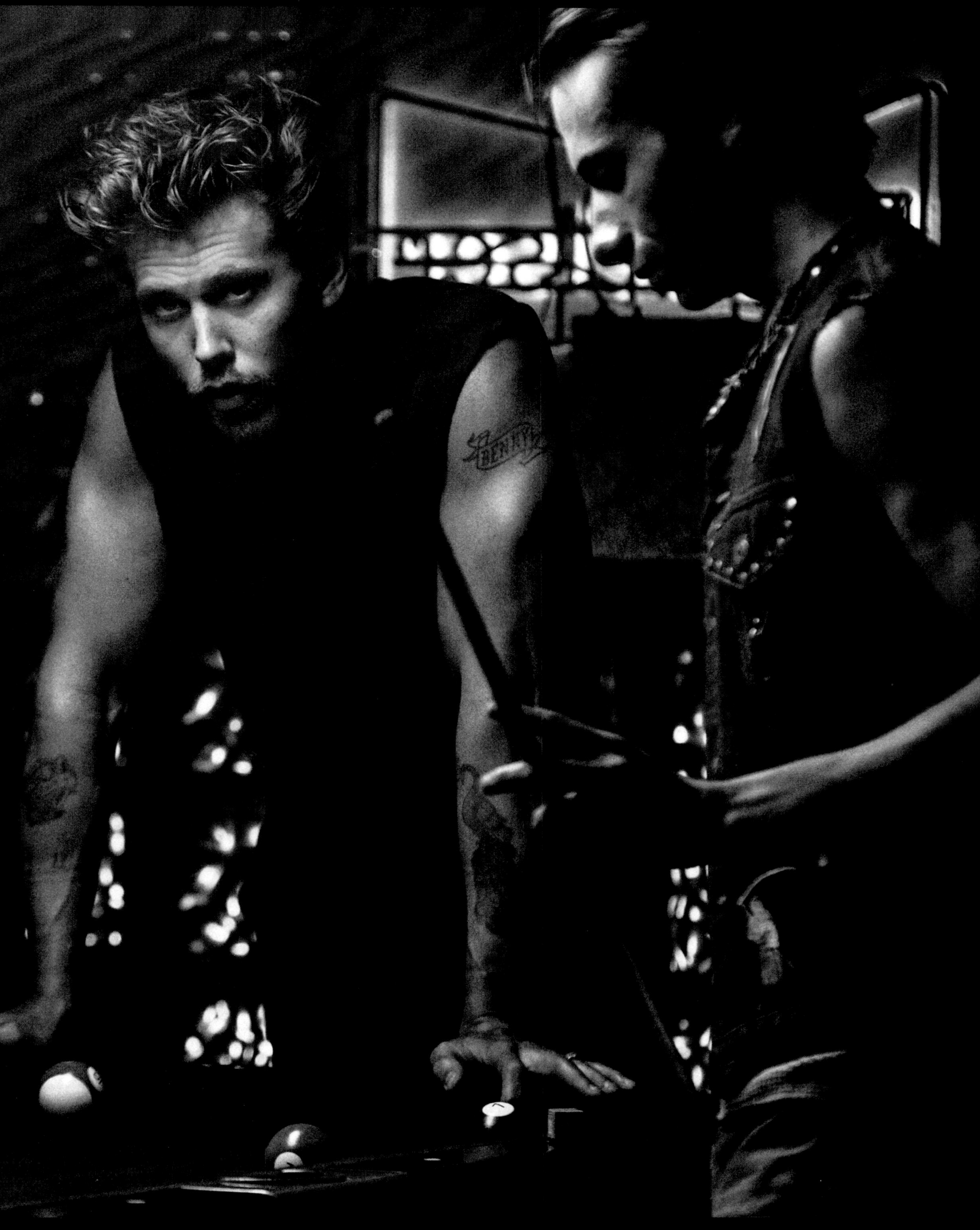

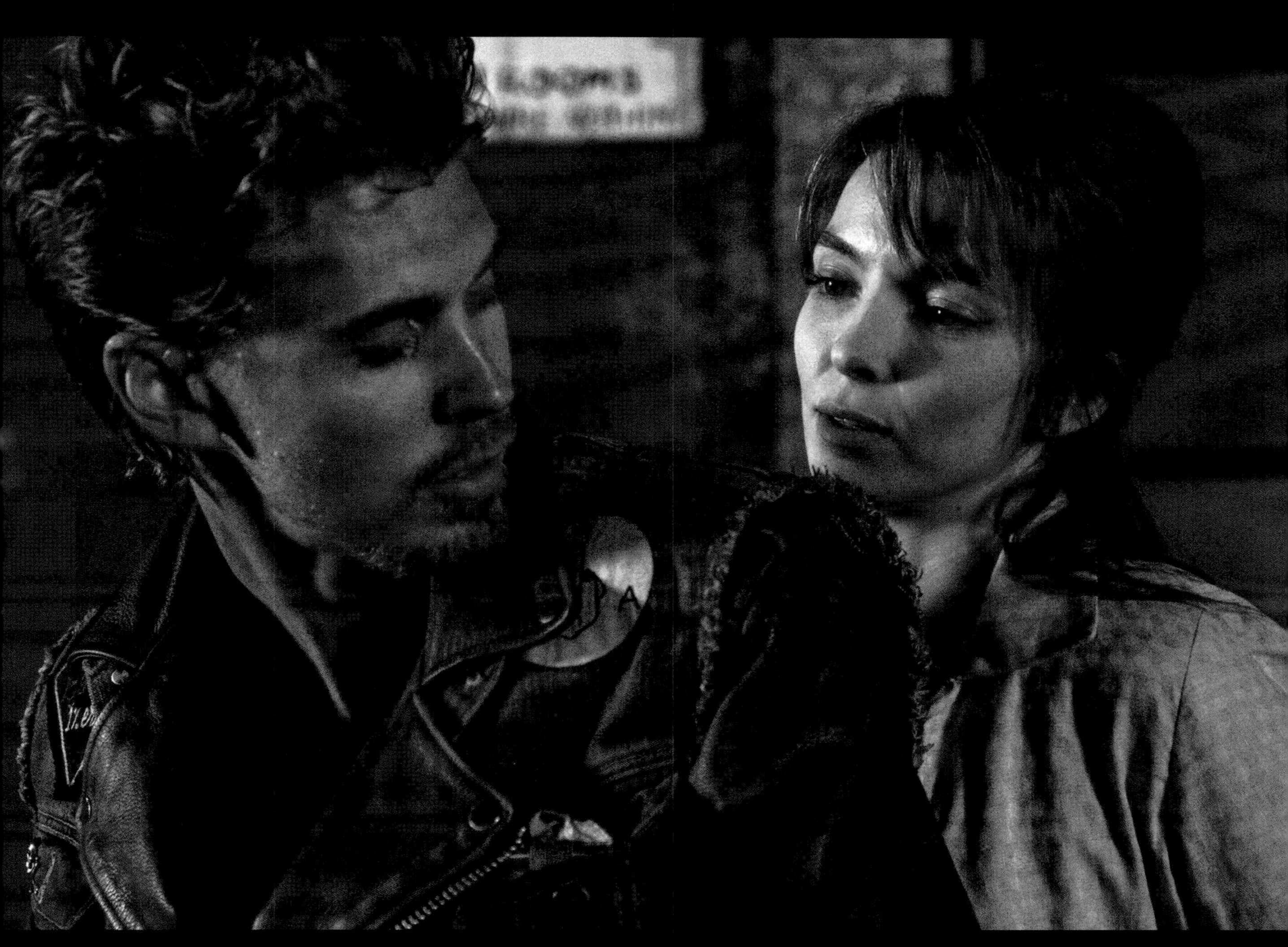

KATHY

Finally we get out on the expressway, and that's when it happened, ya know. That's when I saw 'em all for the first time, you know, really saw 'em. I mean, I have to admit, it took my breath away.

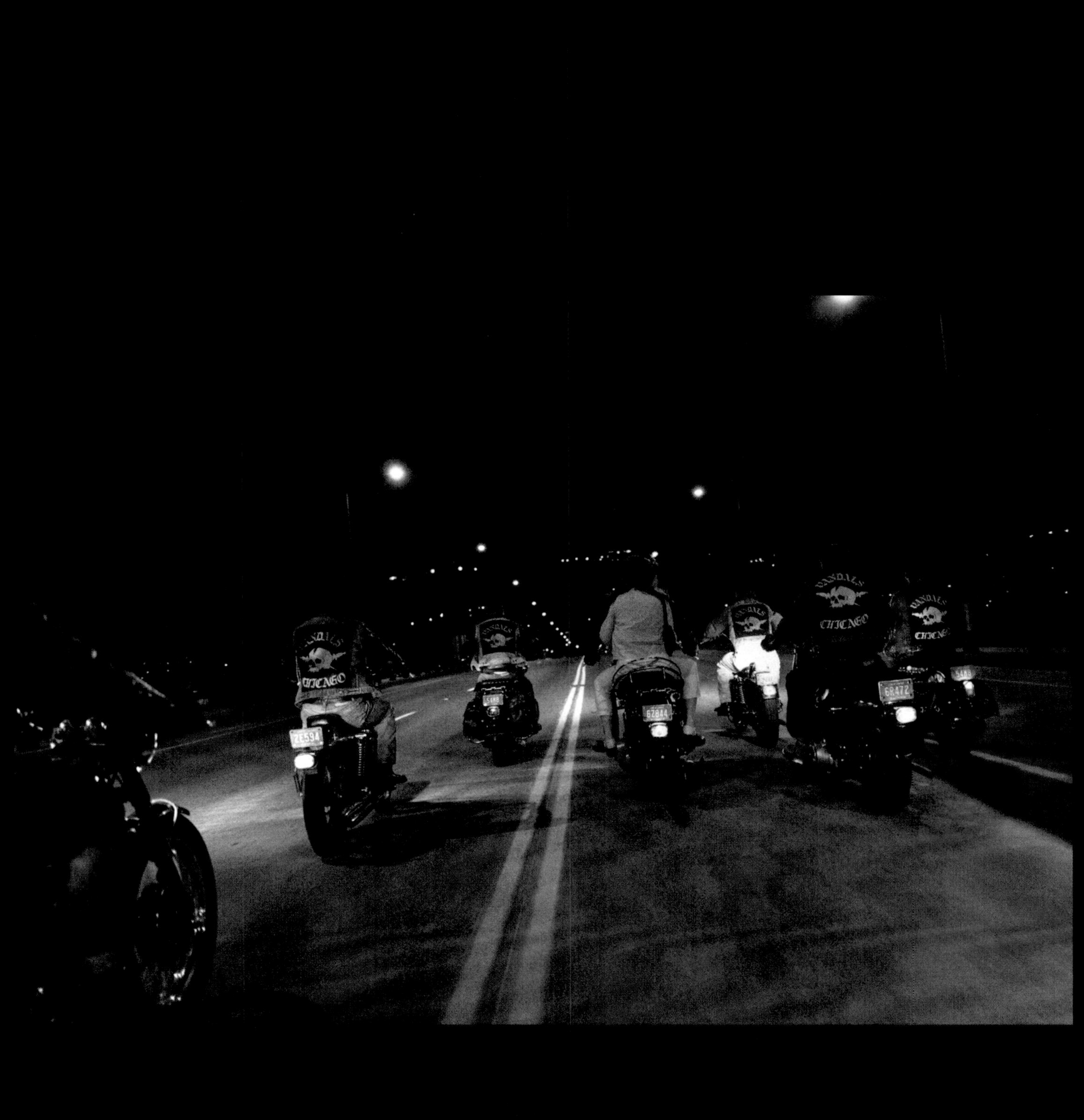
VANDALS
CHICAGO

KATHY

The only thing is I thought I could change him, you know?

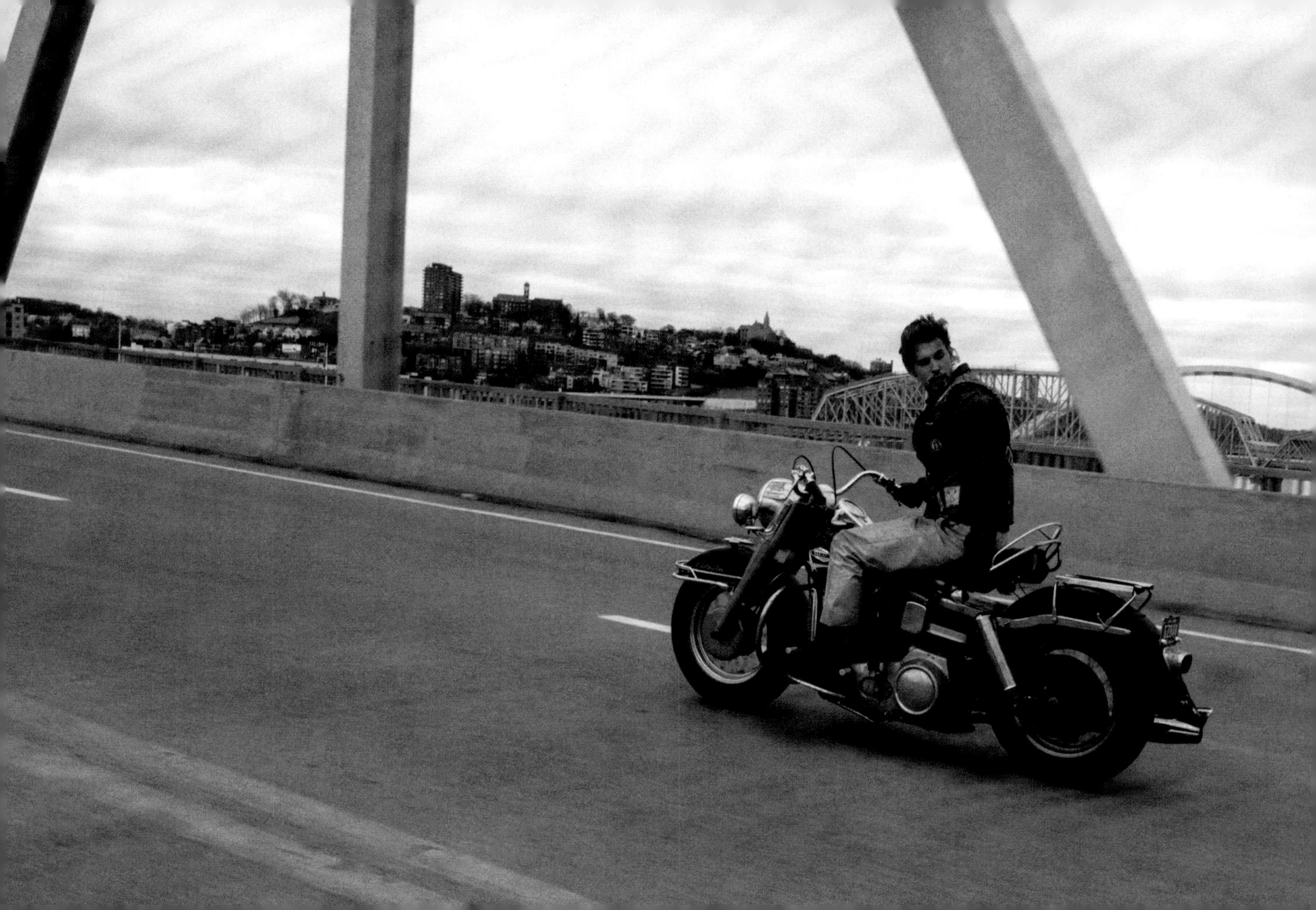

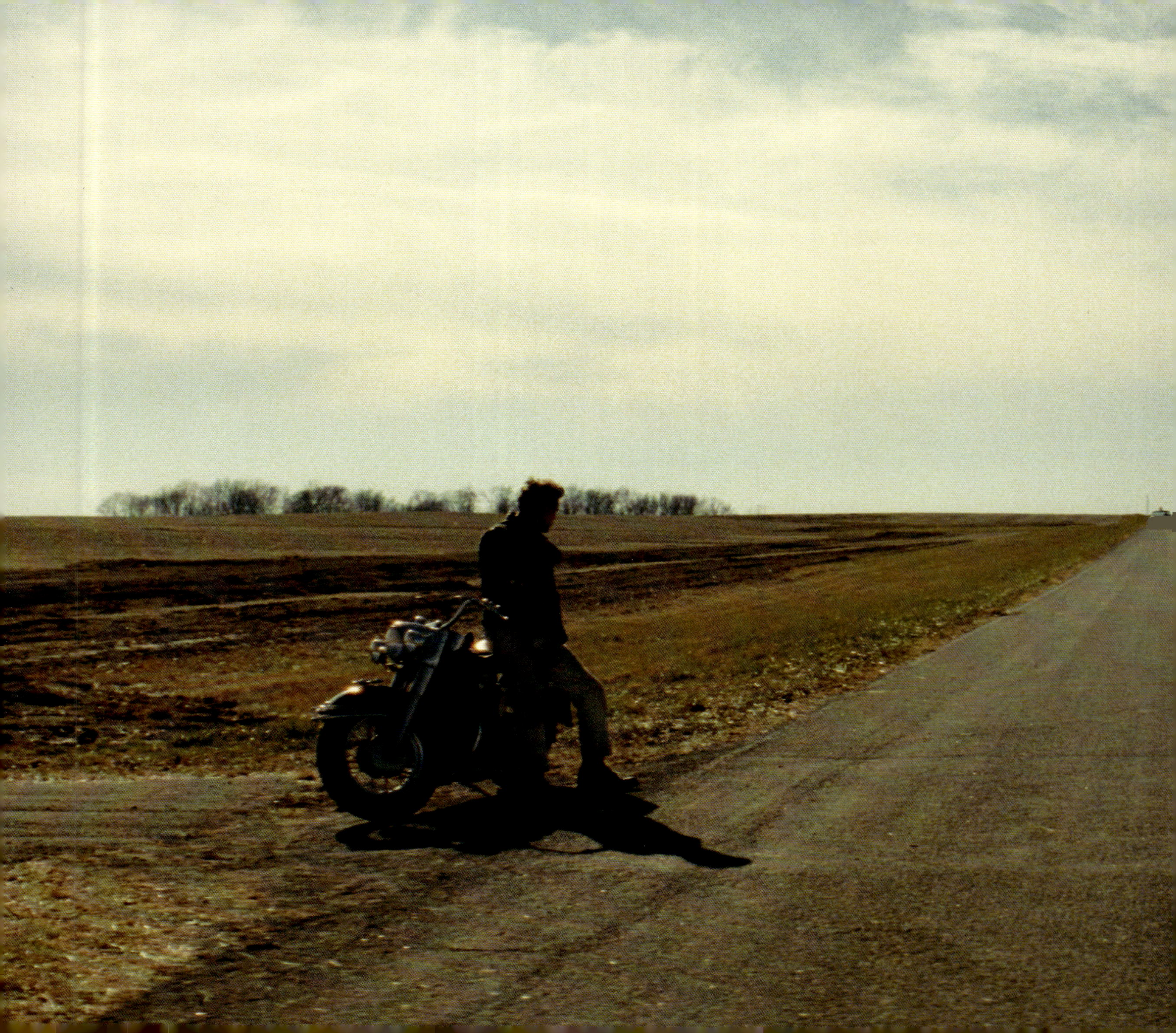

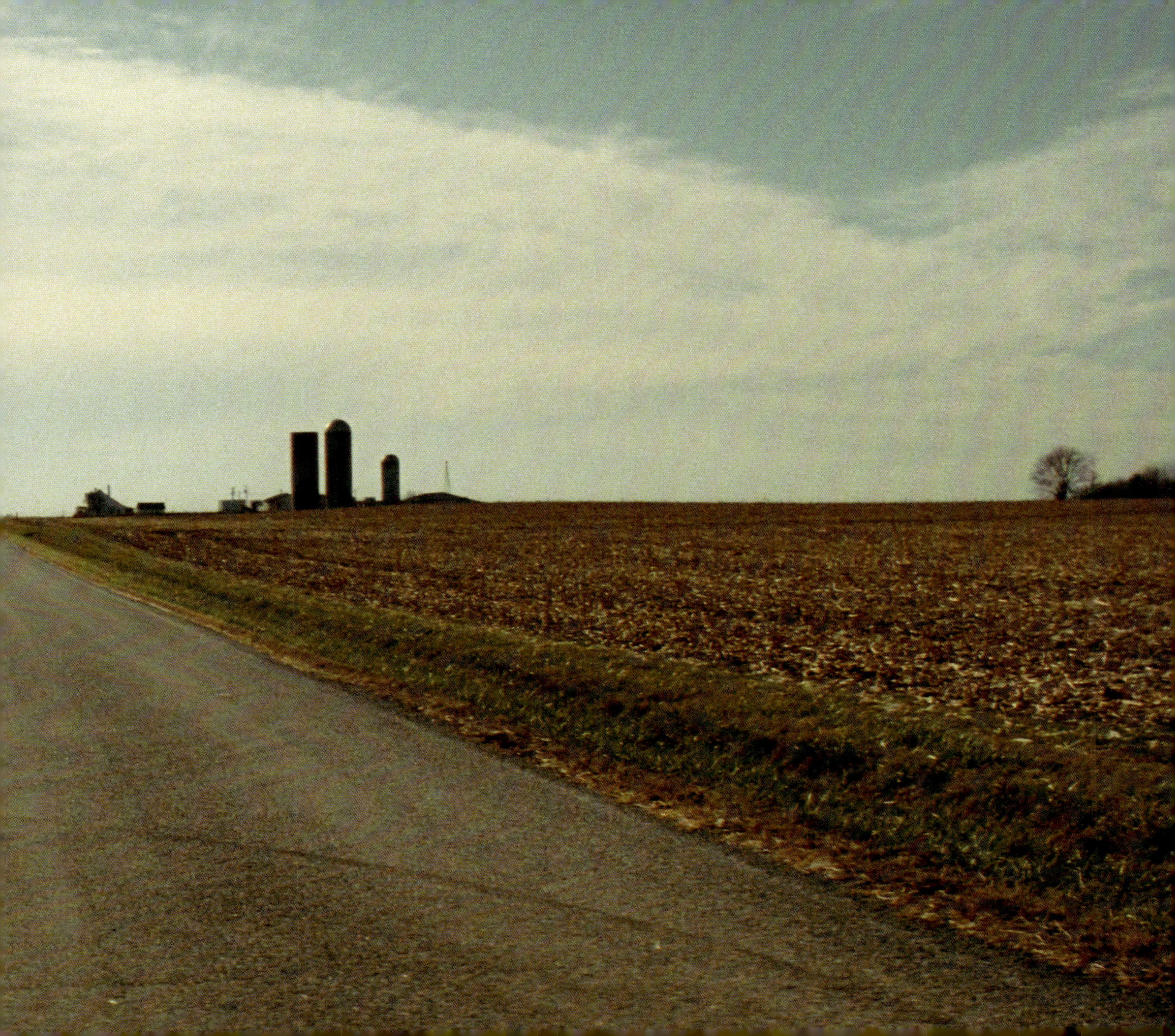

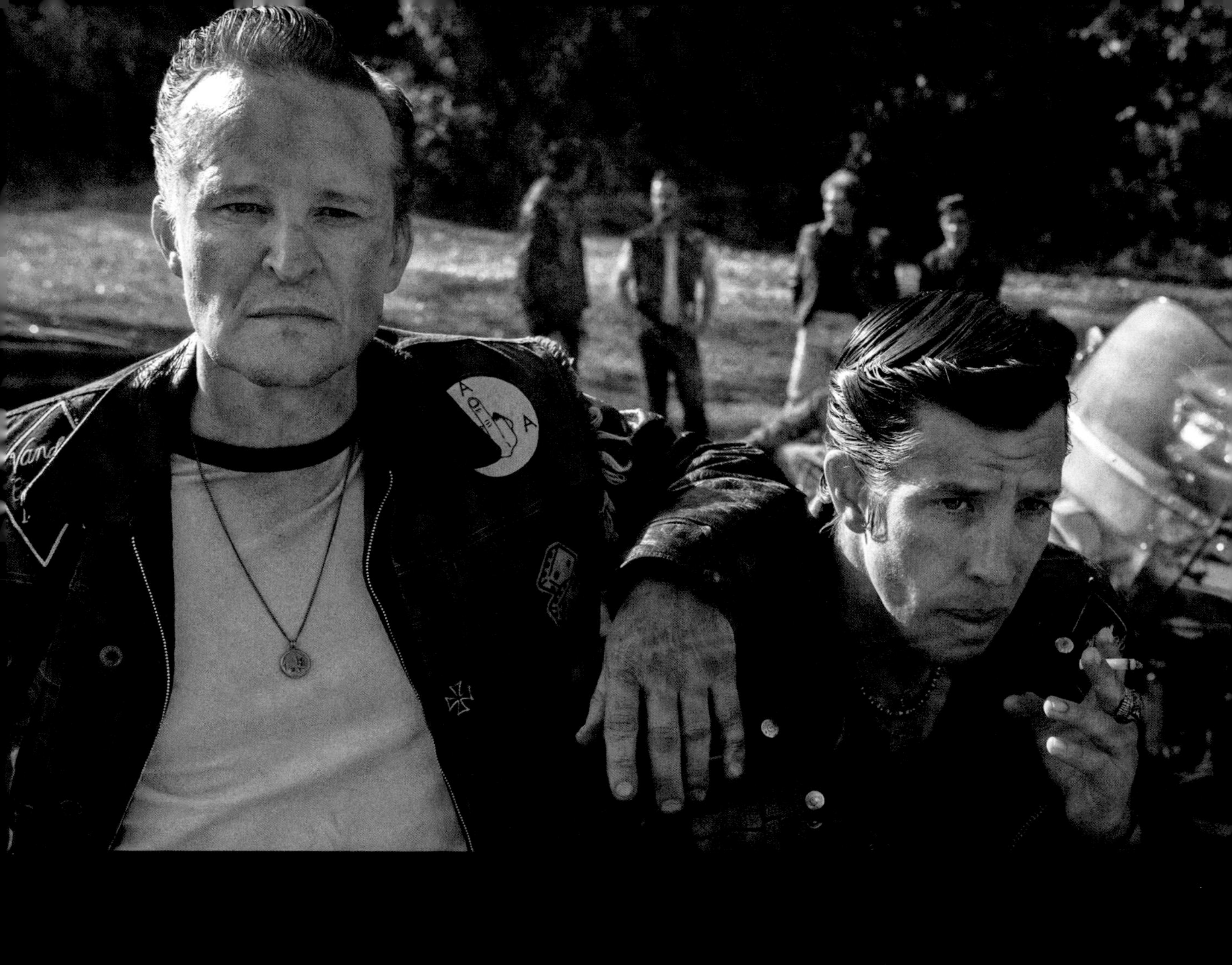

CORKY

I always wondered what riders out in California looked like.

BRUCIE

Can you imagine a thousand of those fucking guys?

KATHY

Somebody told me Funny Sonny got paid five bucks to sit on his bike outside the movie theater to try to get people in to watch Easy Rider.

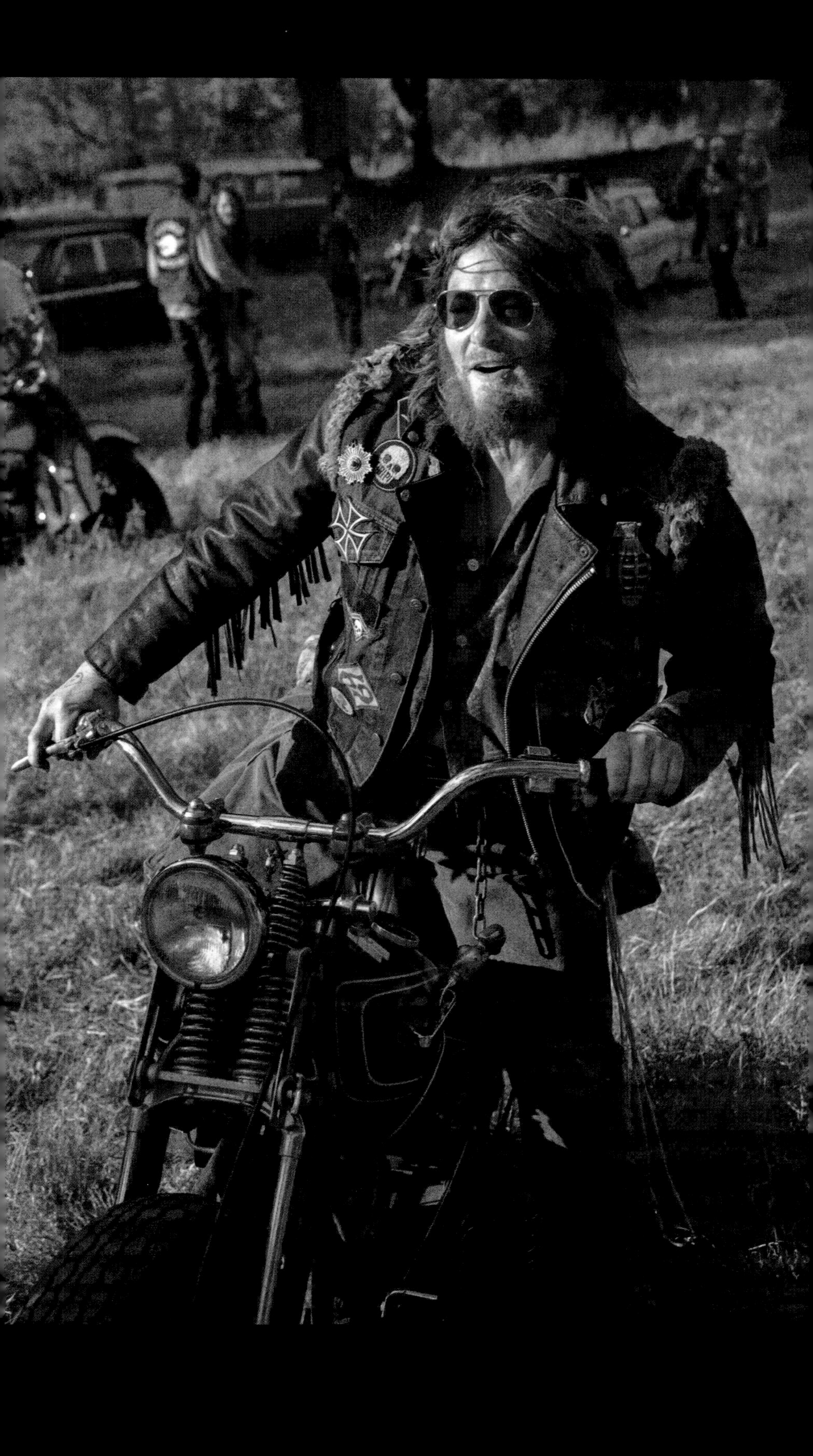

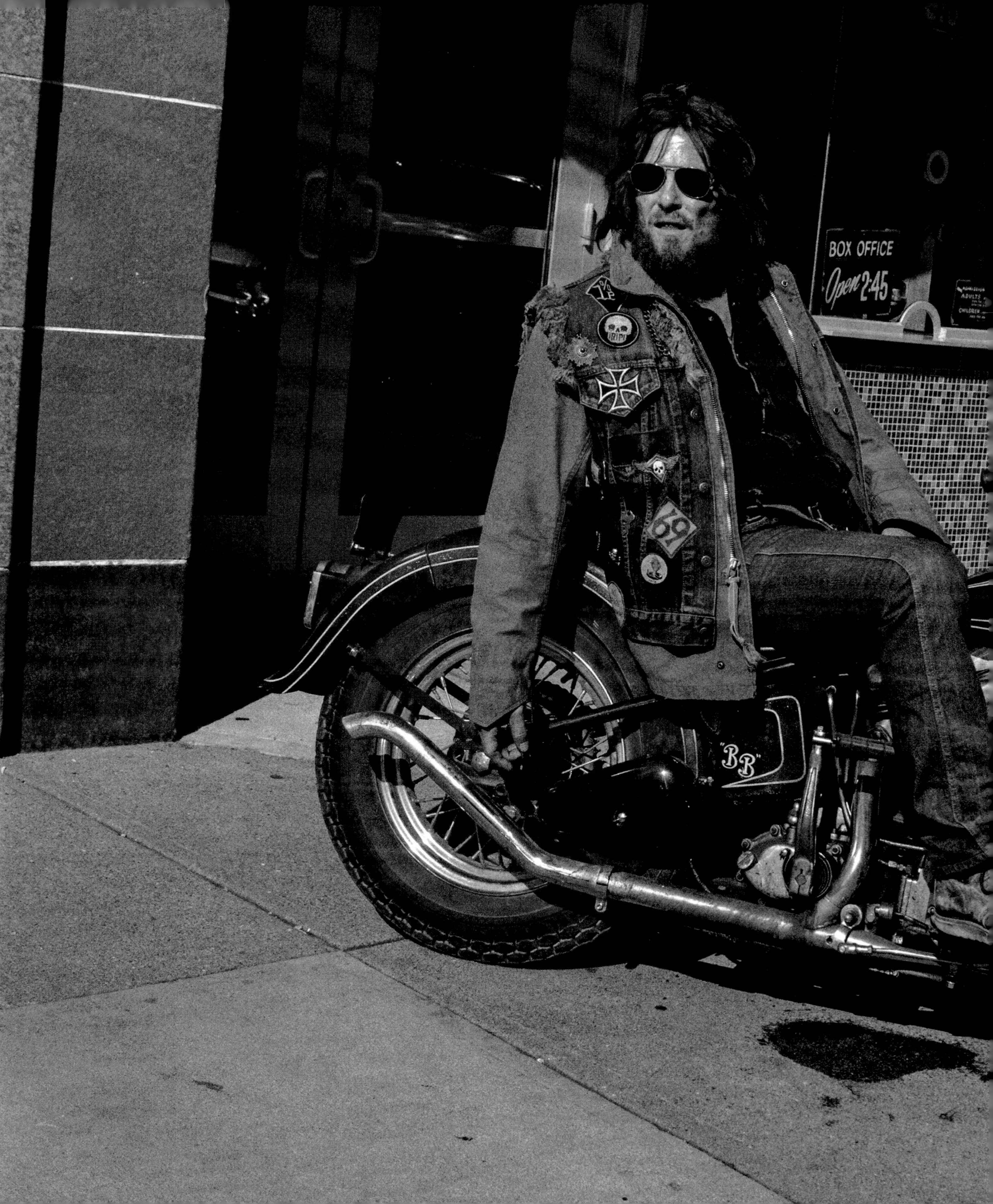
BOX OFFICE
Open 2:45

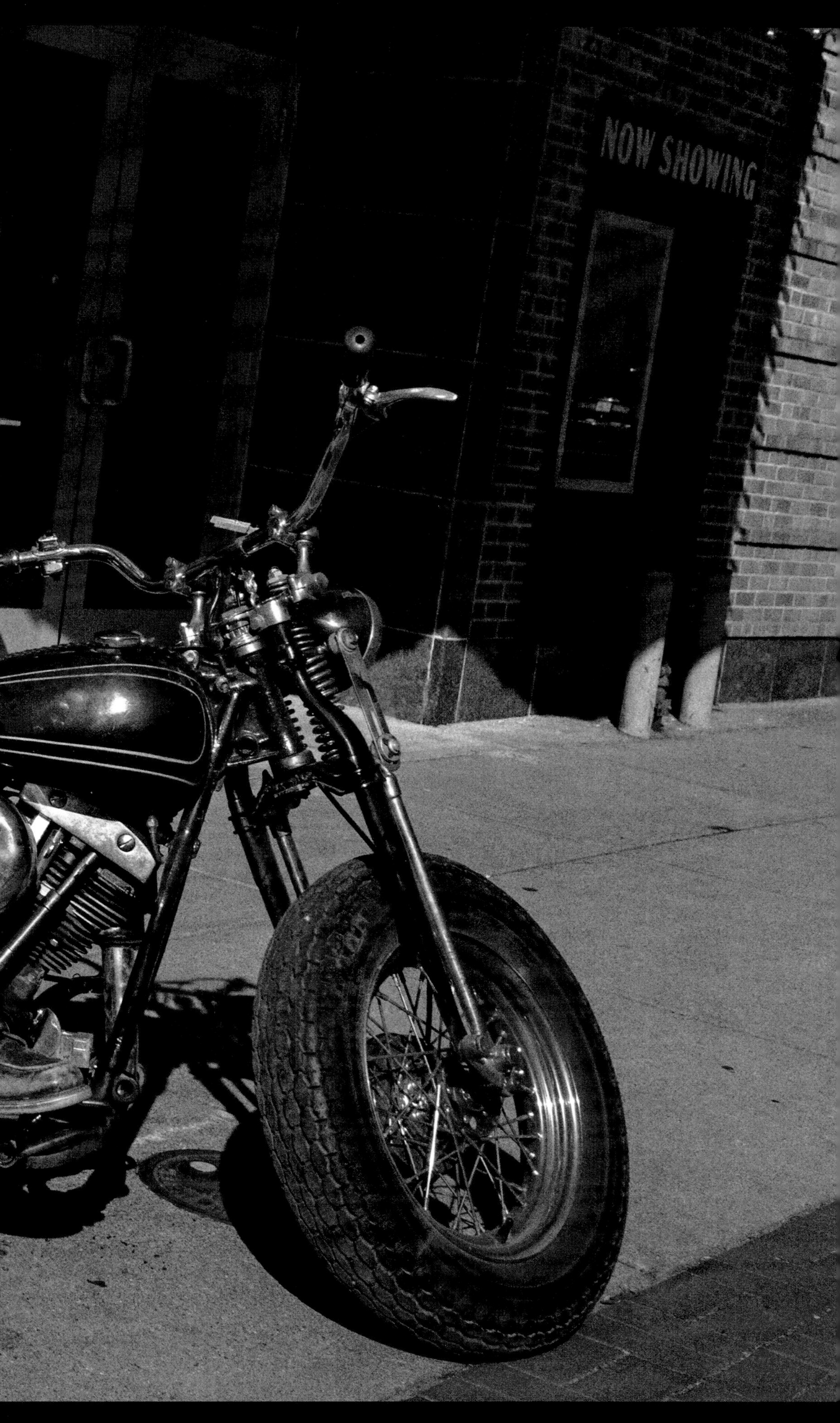
NOW SHOWING

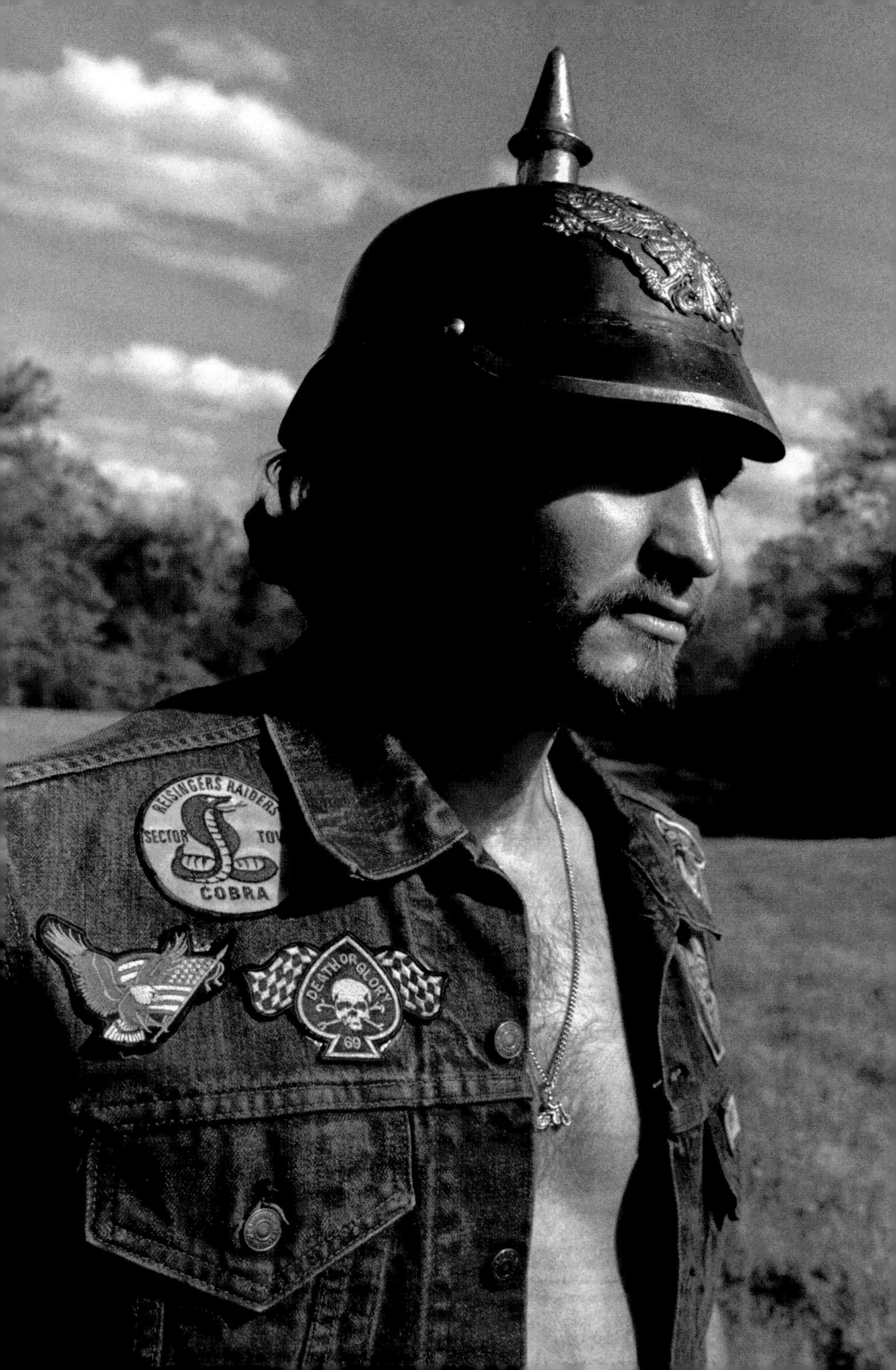
REISINGERS RAIDERS
SECTOR
COBRA
DEATH OR GLORY
69

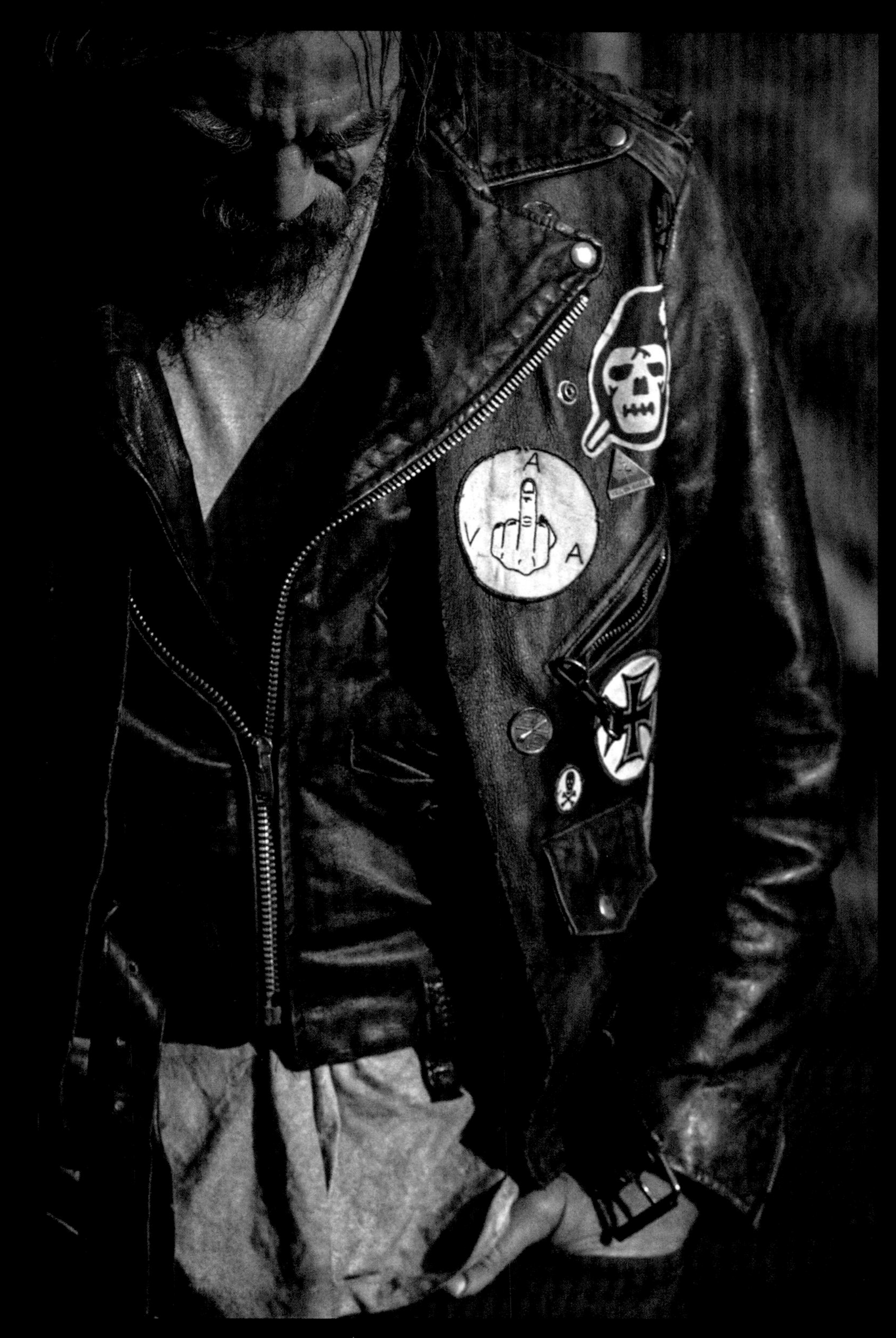

JOHNNY

Look. I built this club outta nothin', alright, I built it. I put more into this fuckin' club than my own family, right. This is my family.

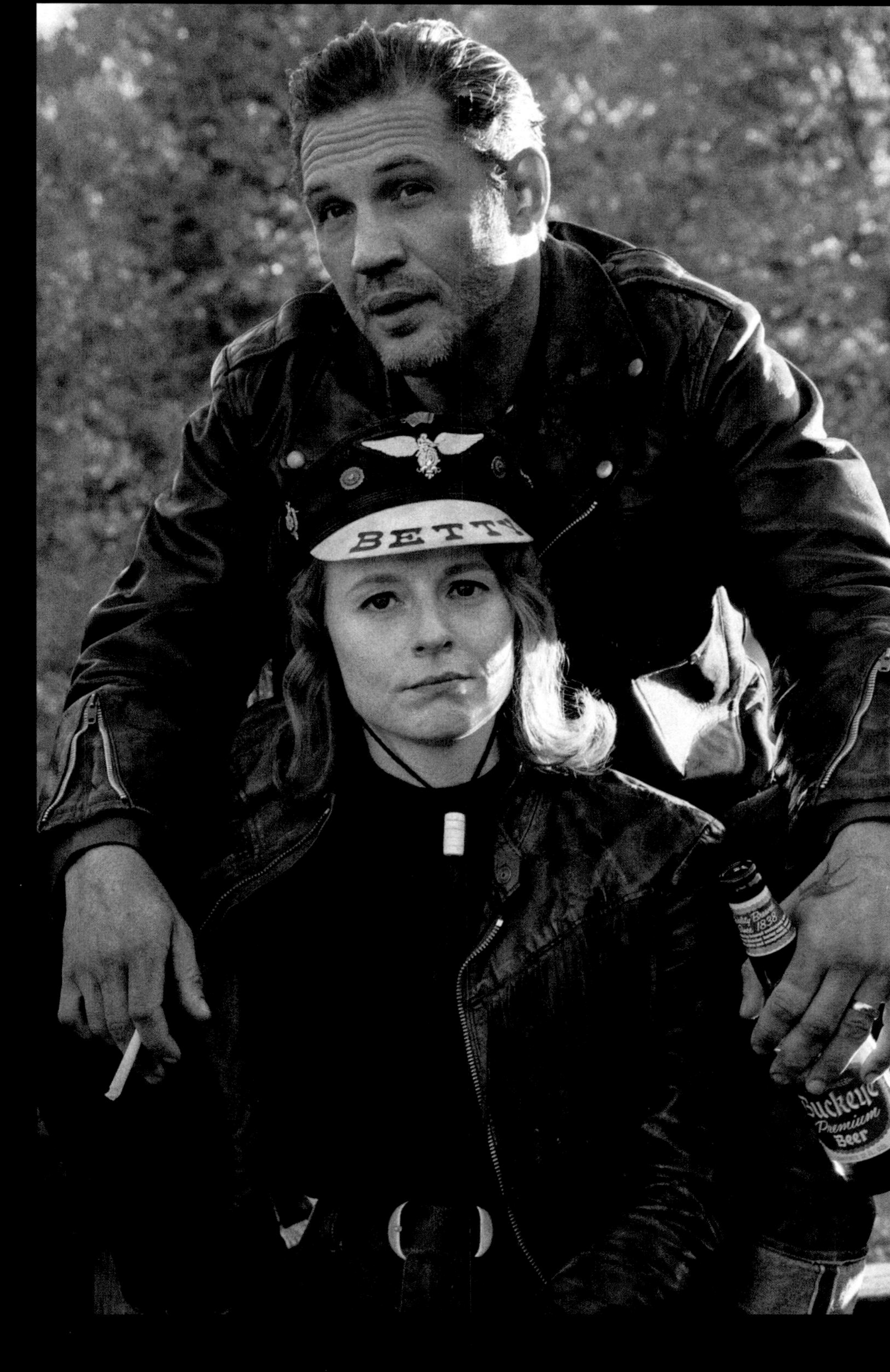
BETTY
Premium
Beer

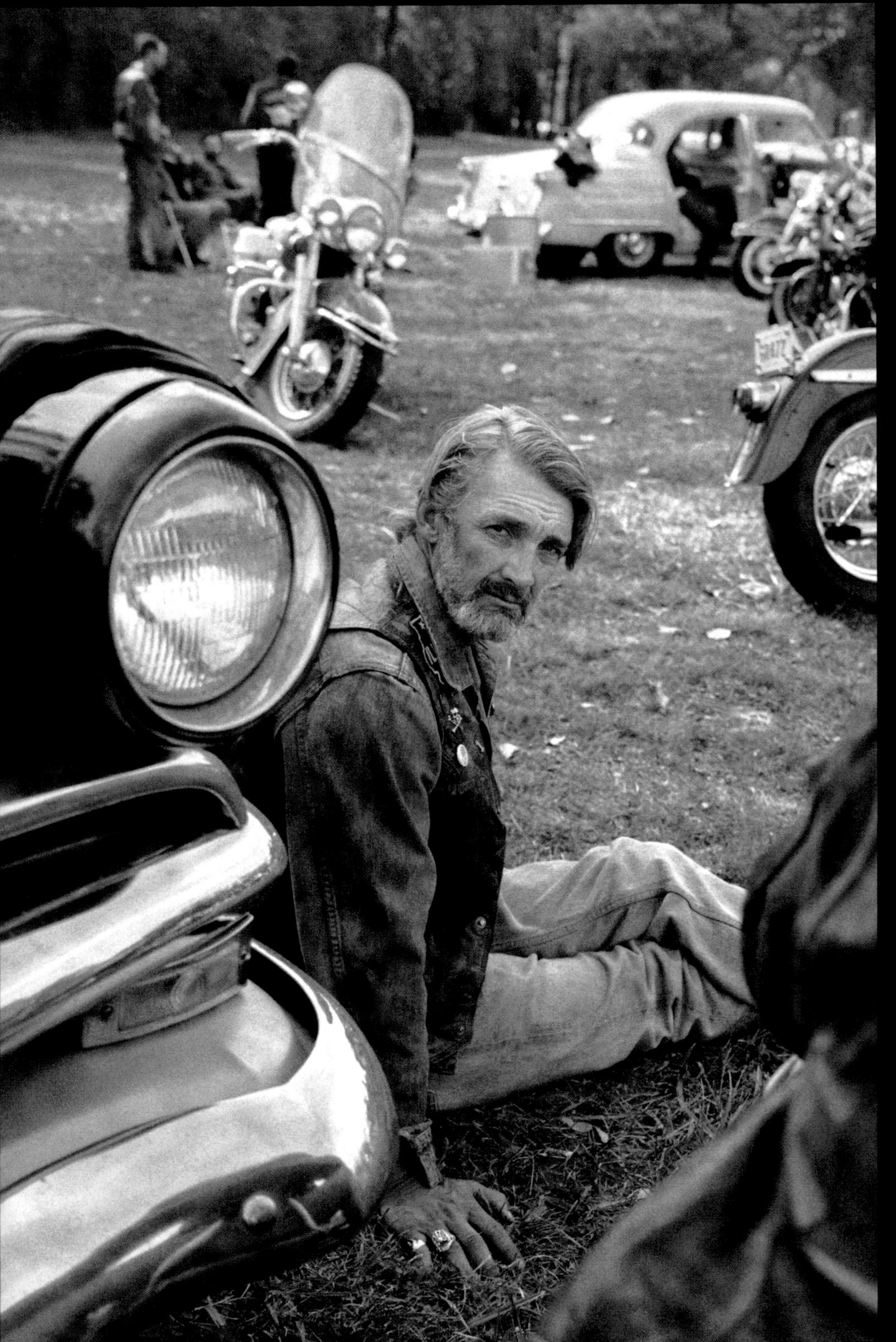

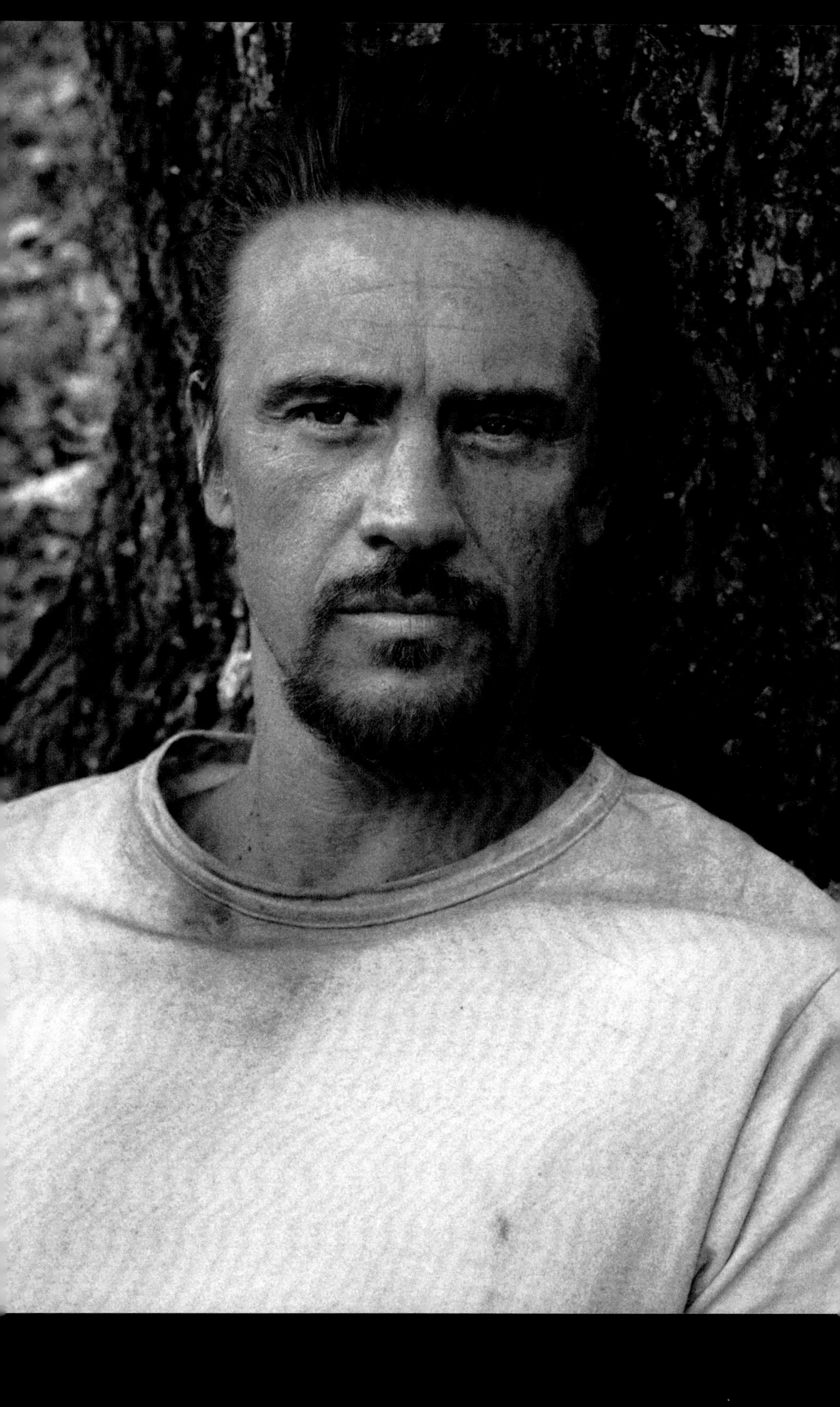

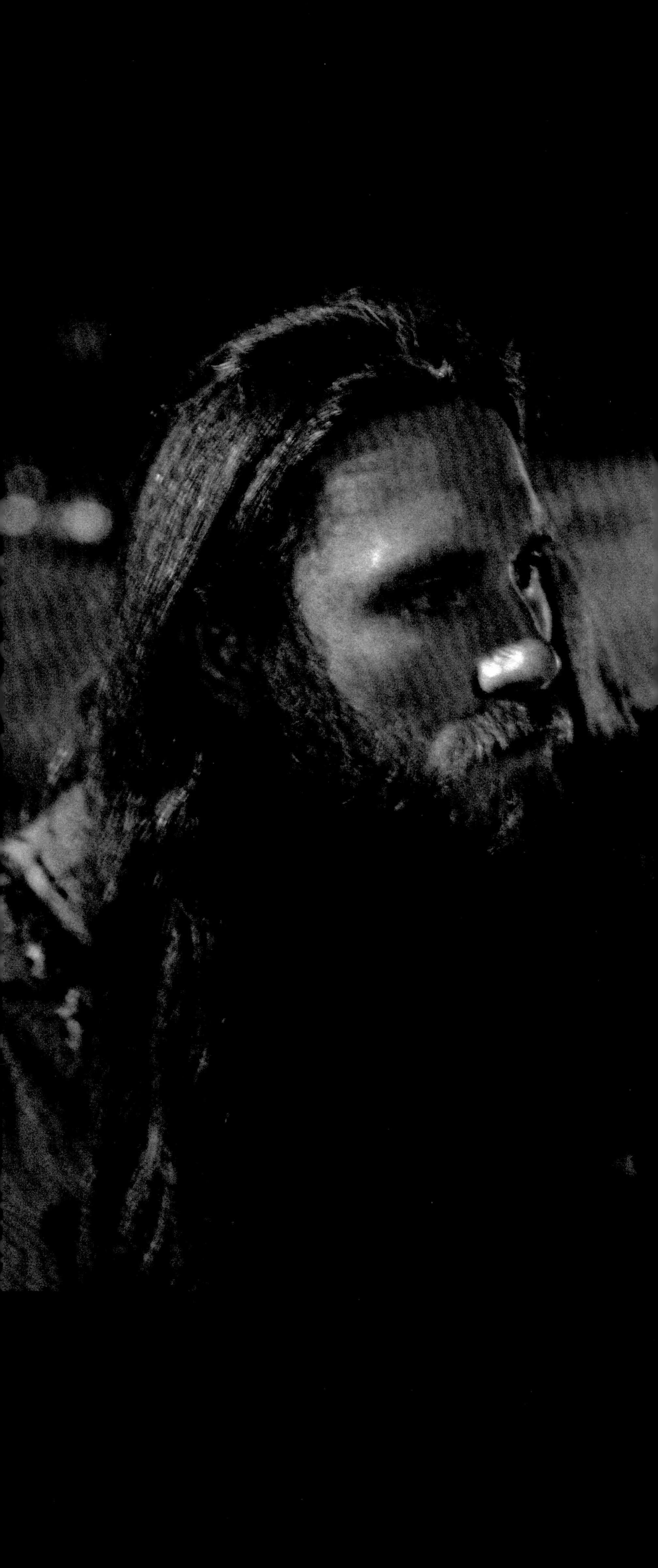

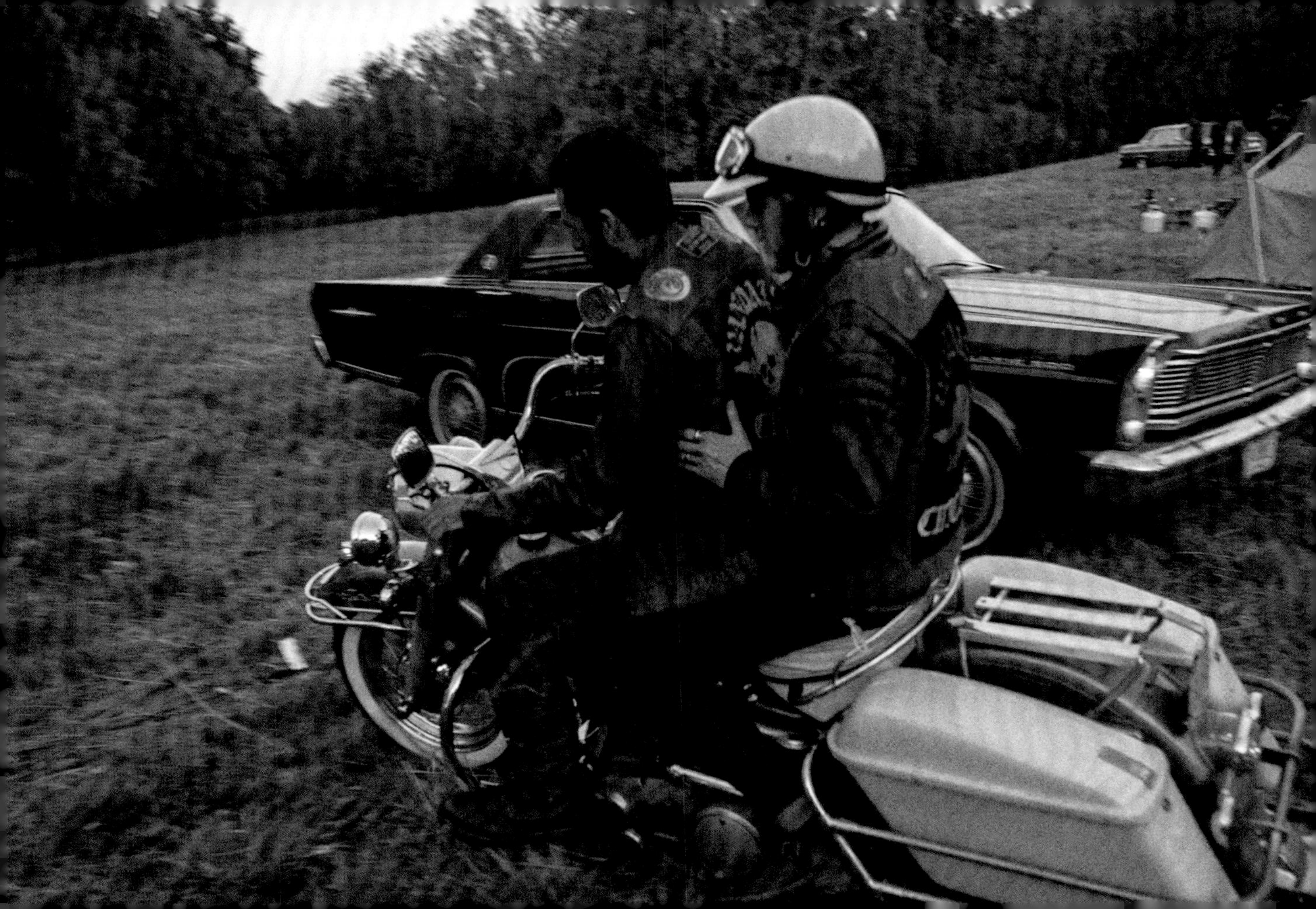

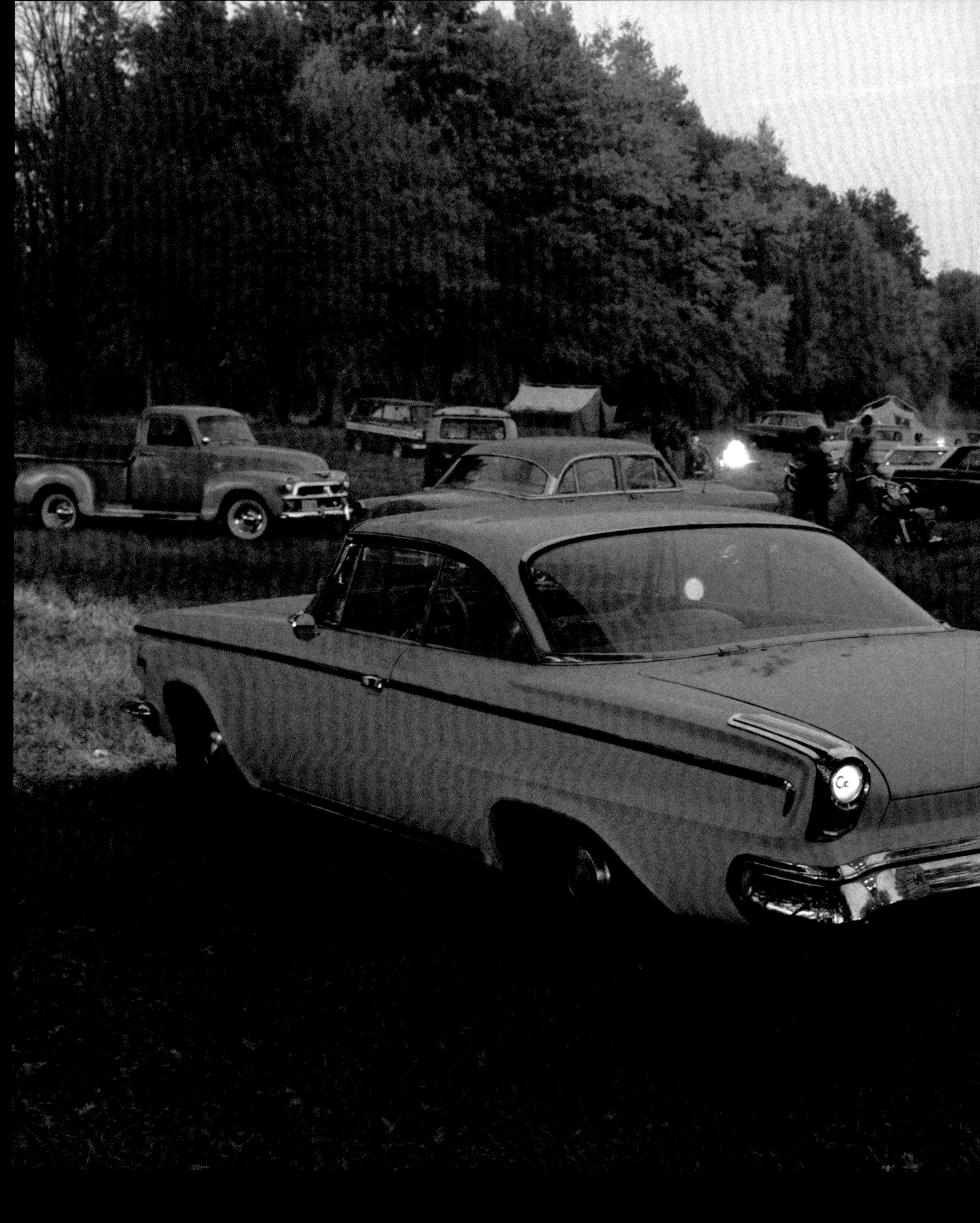

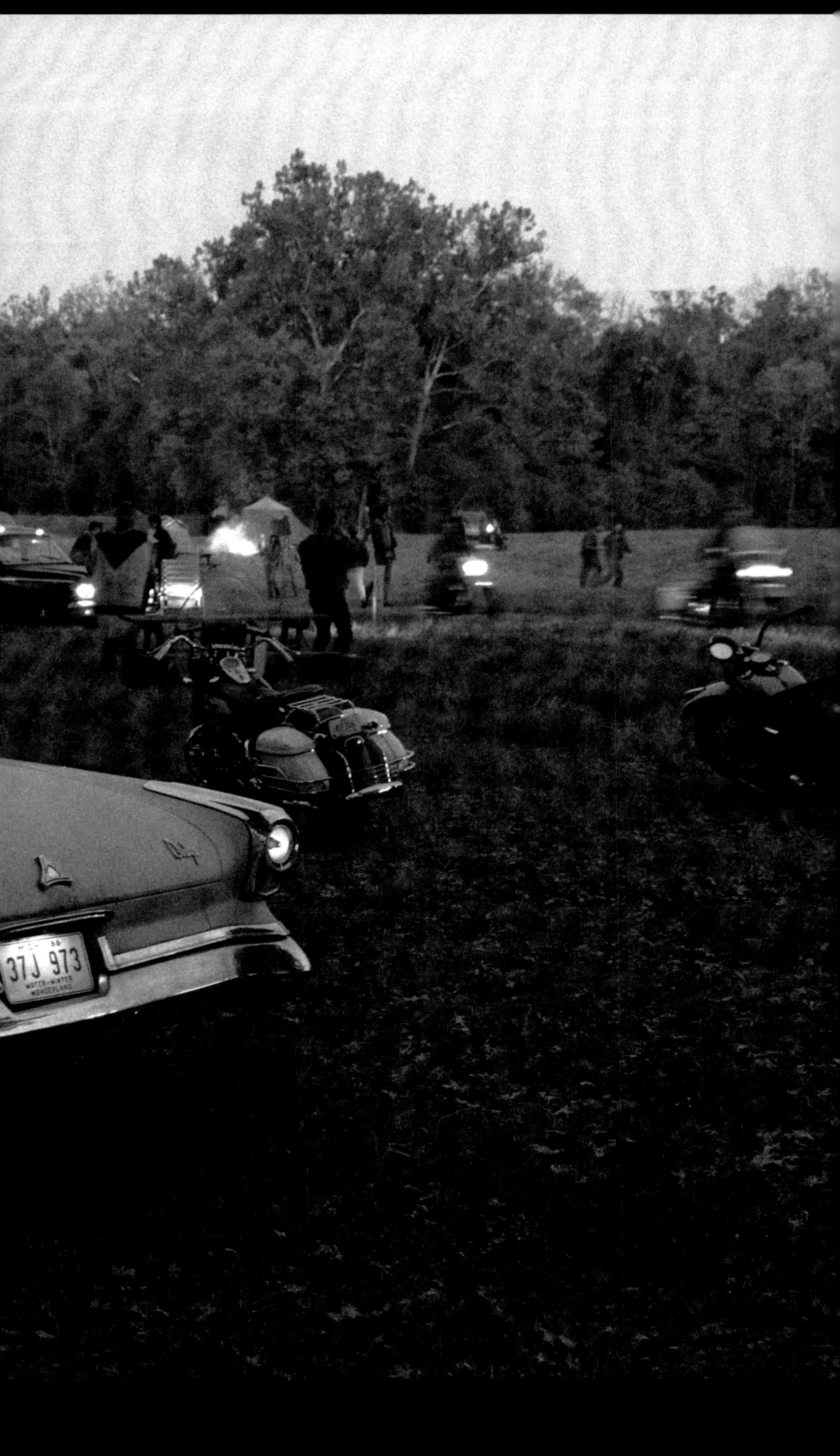
37J 973

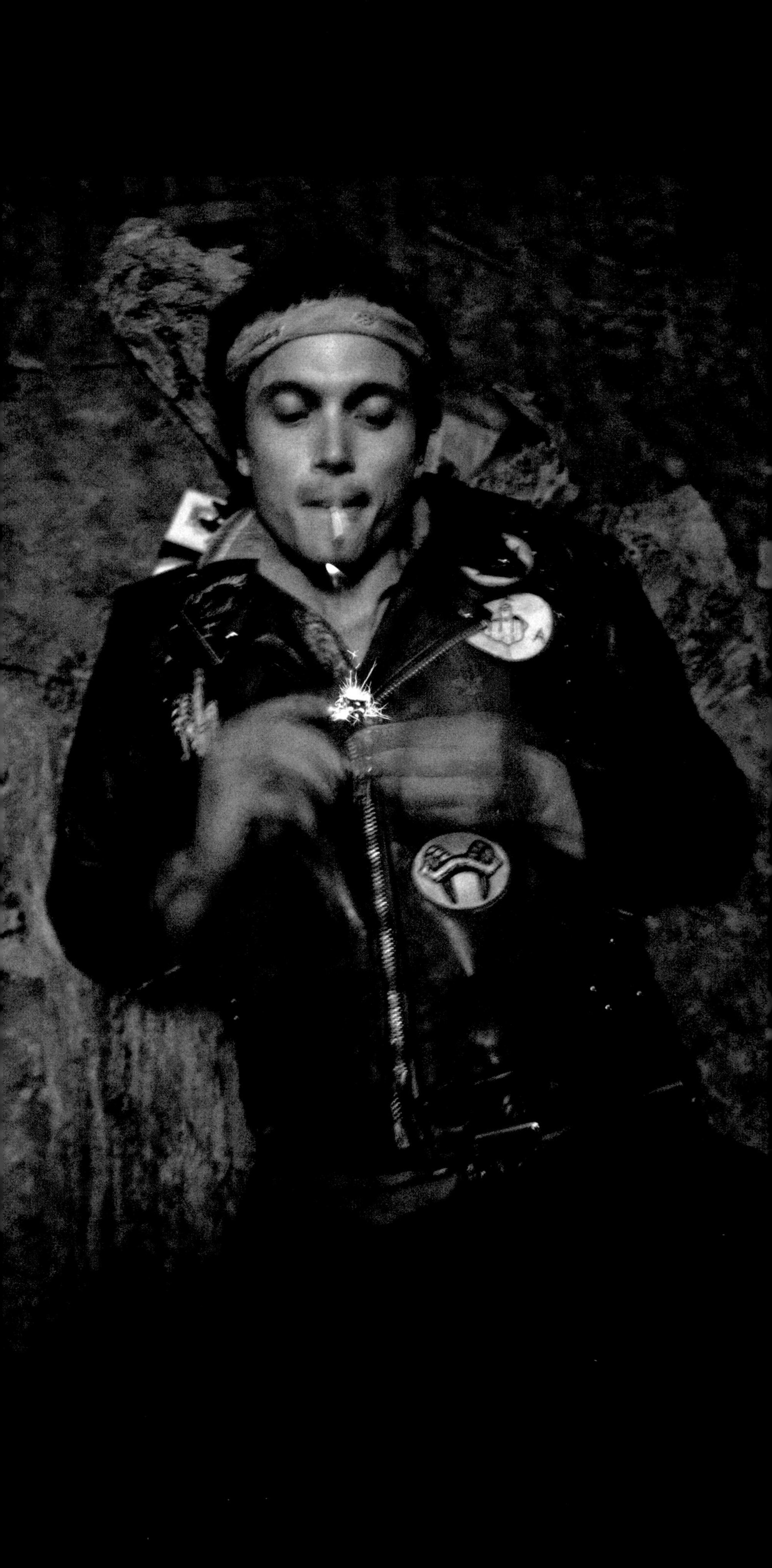

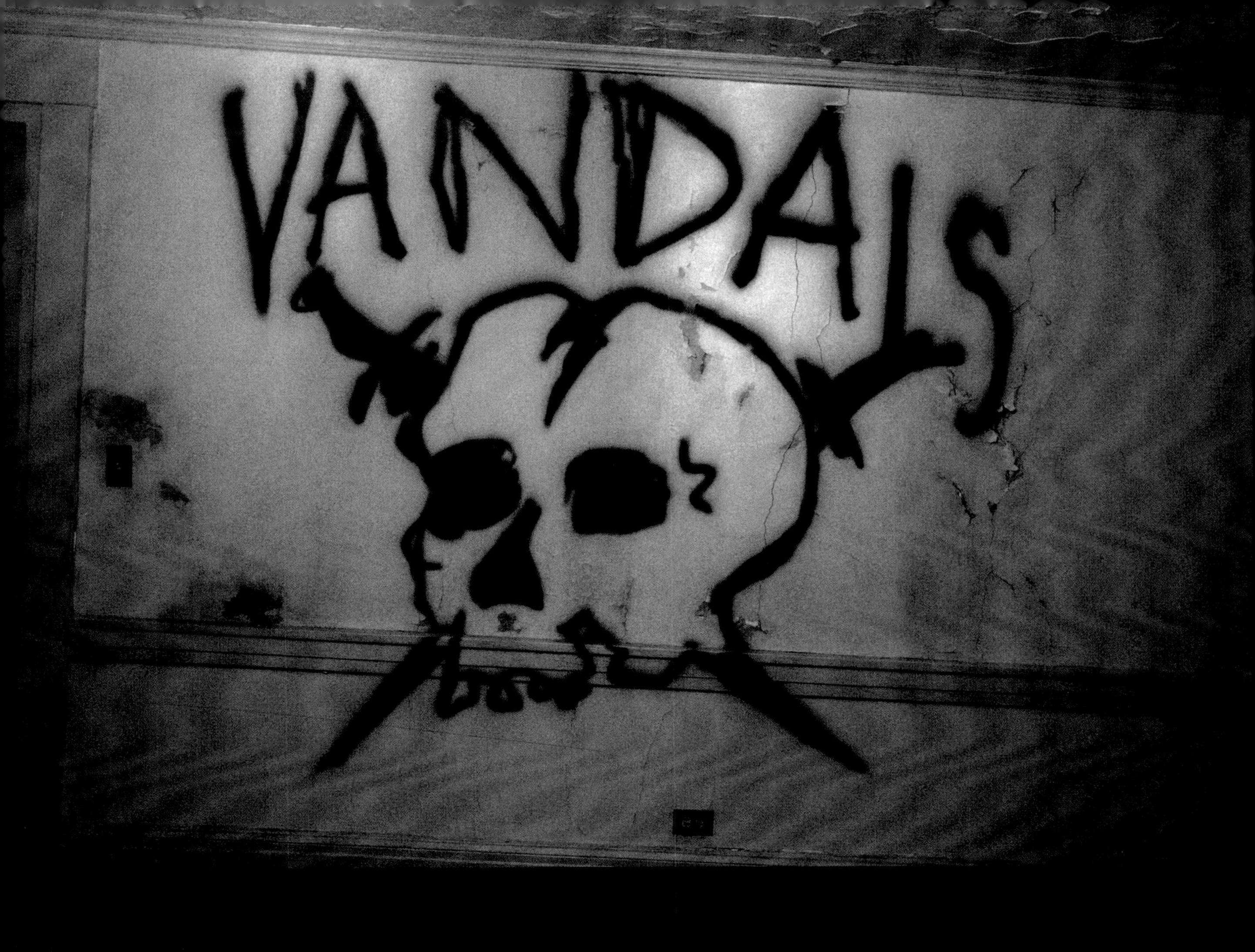
VANDALS

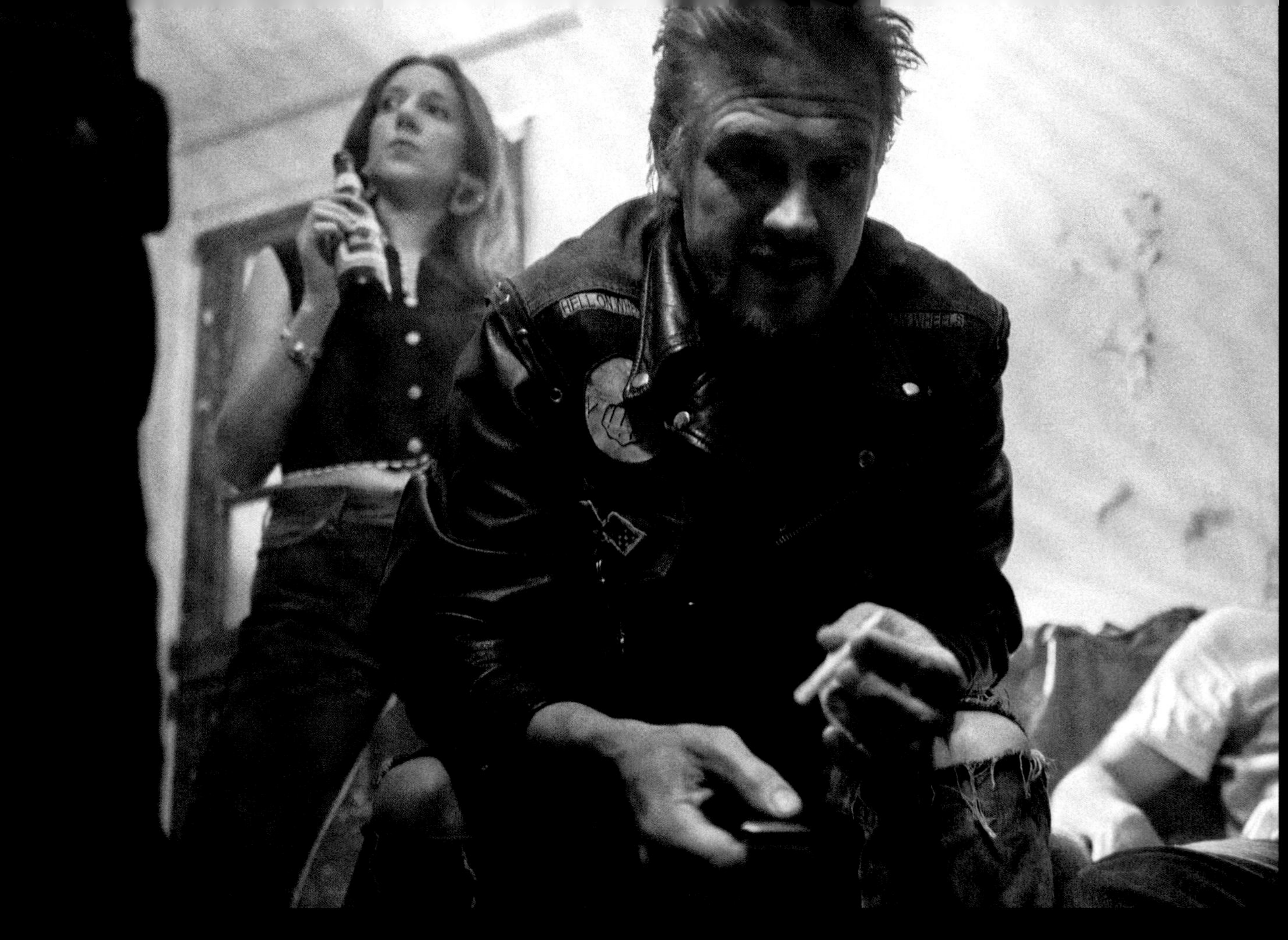

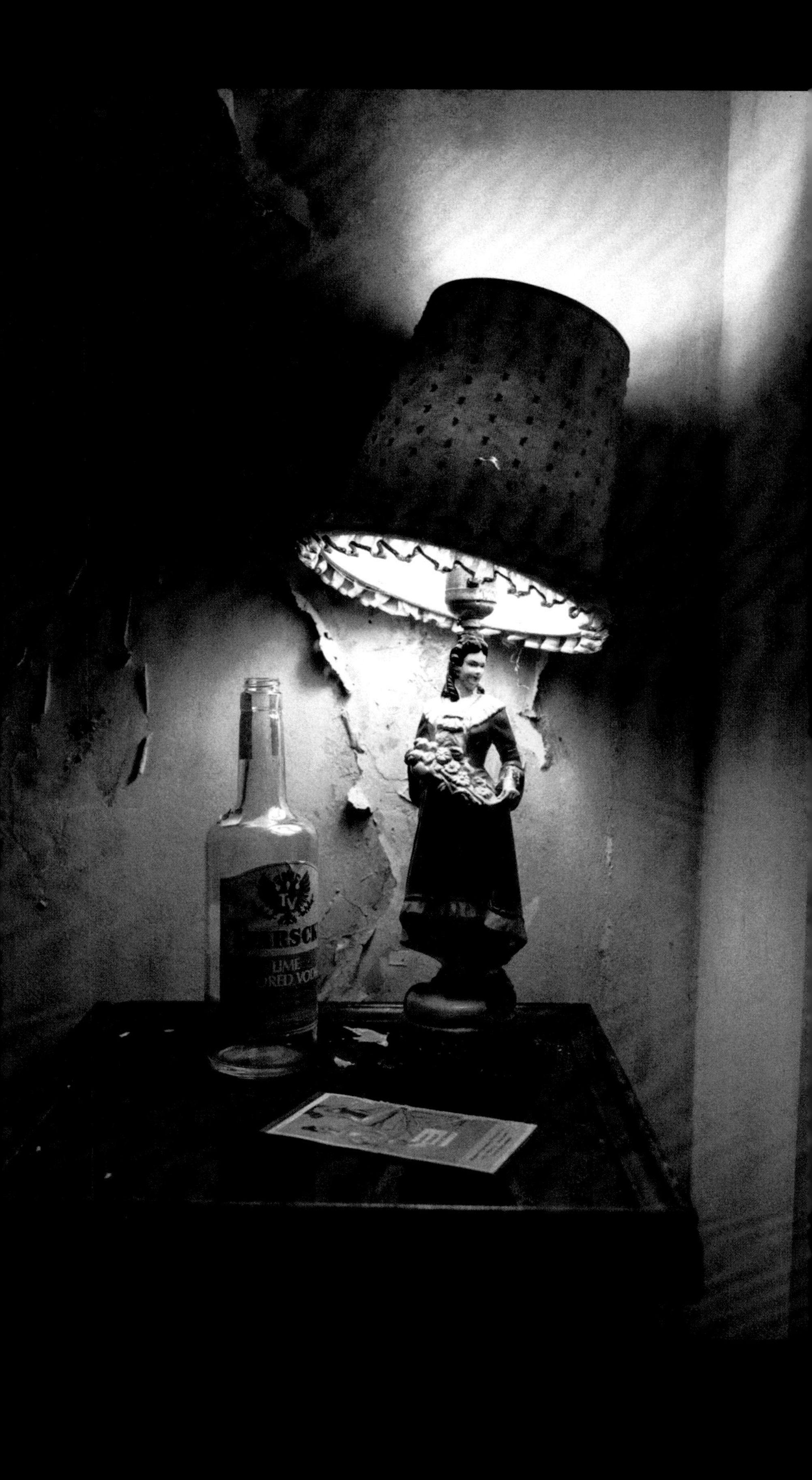
LIME

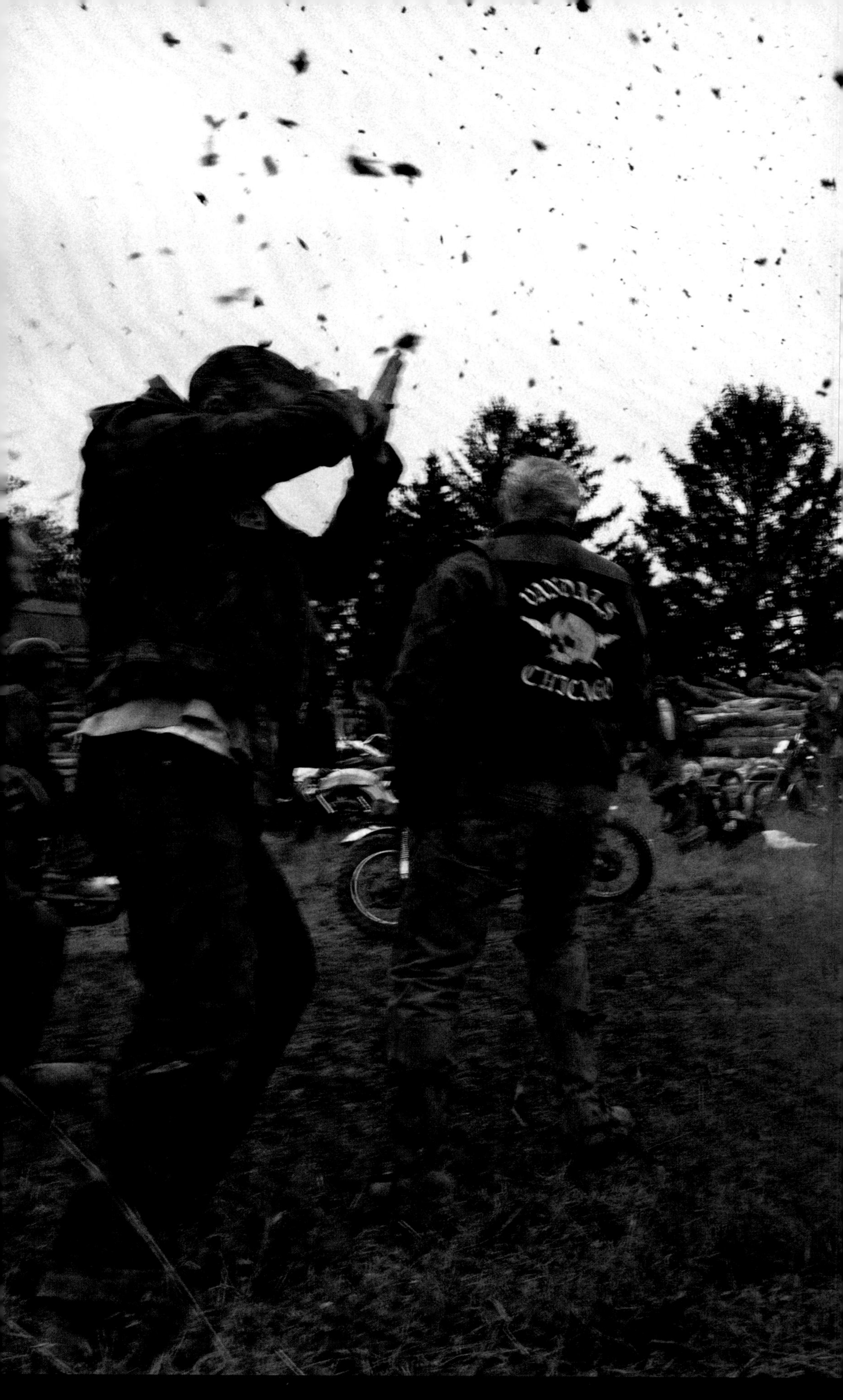
VANDALS
CHICAGO

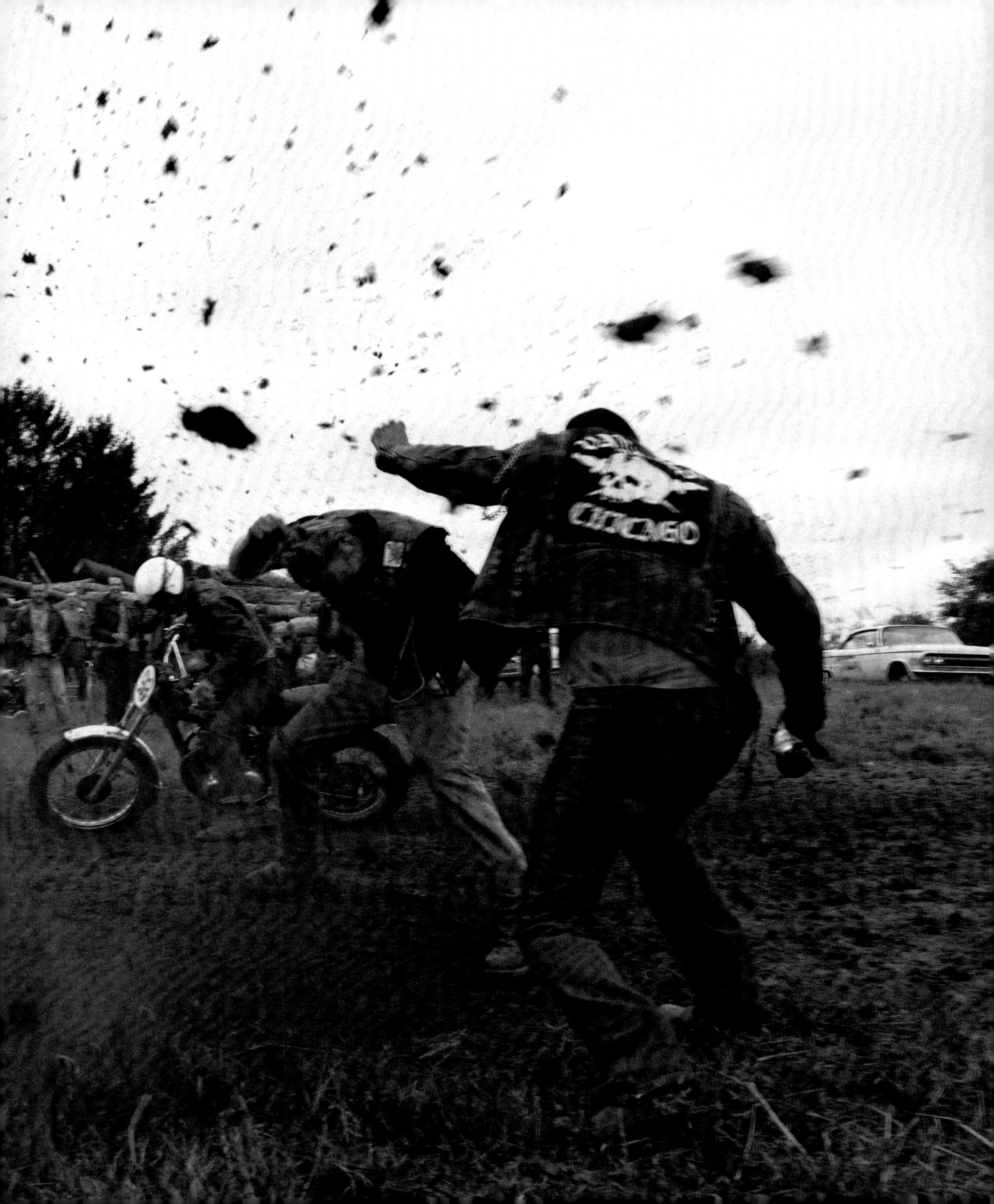
CHICAGO

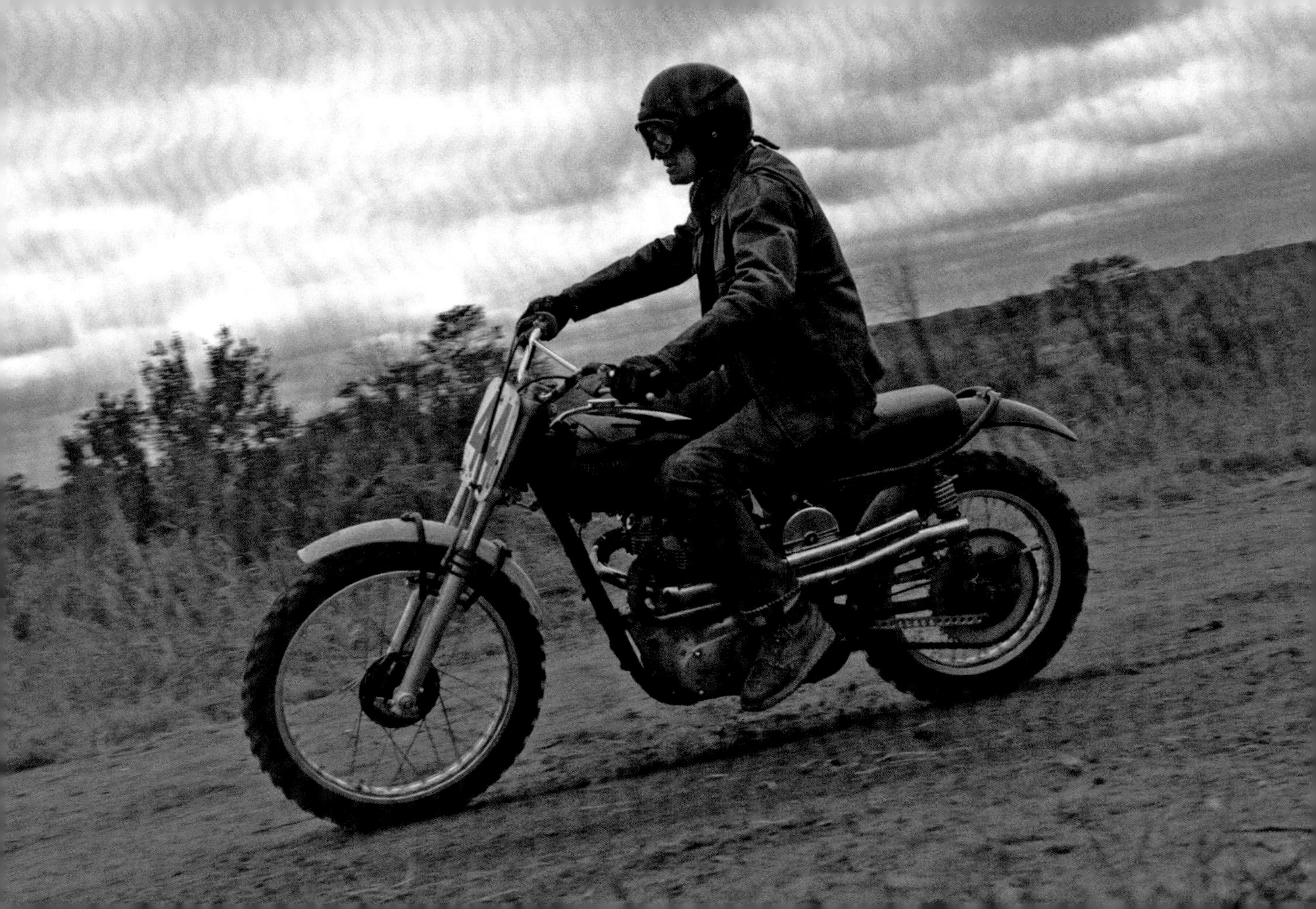

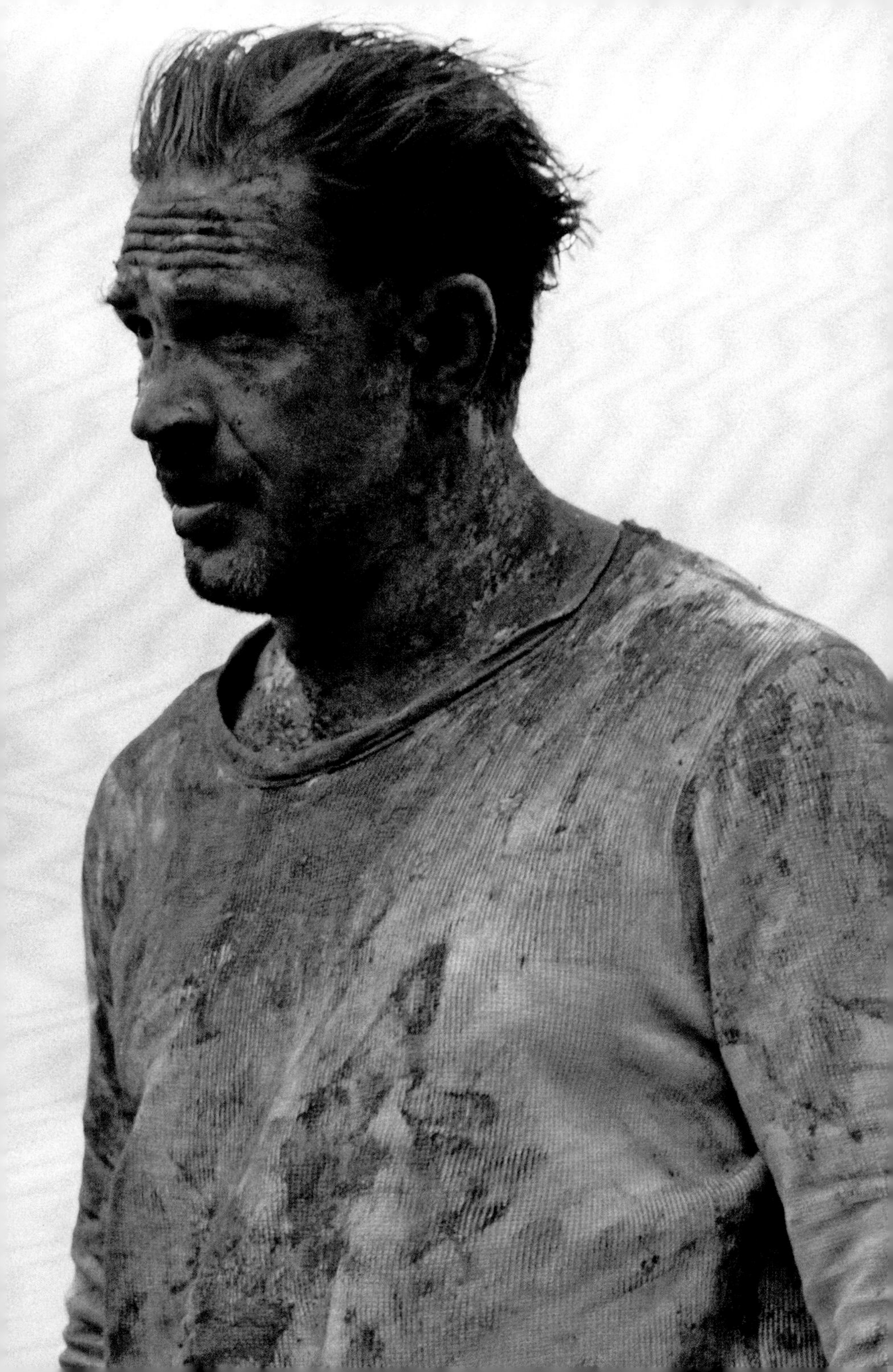

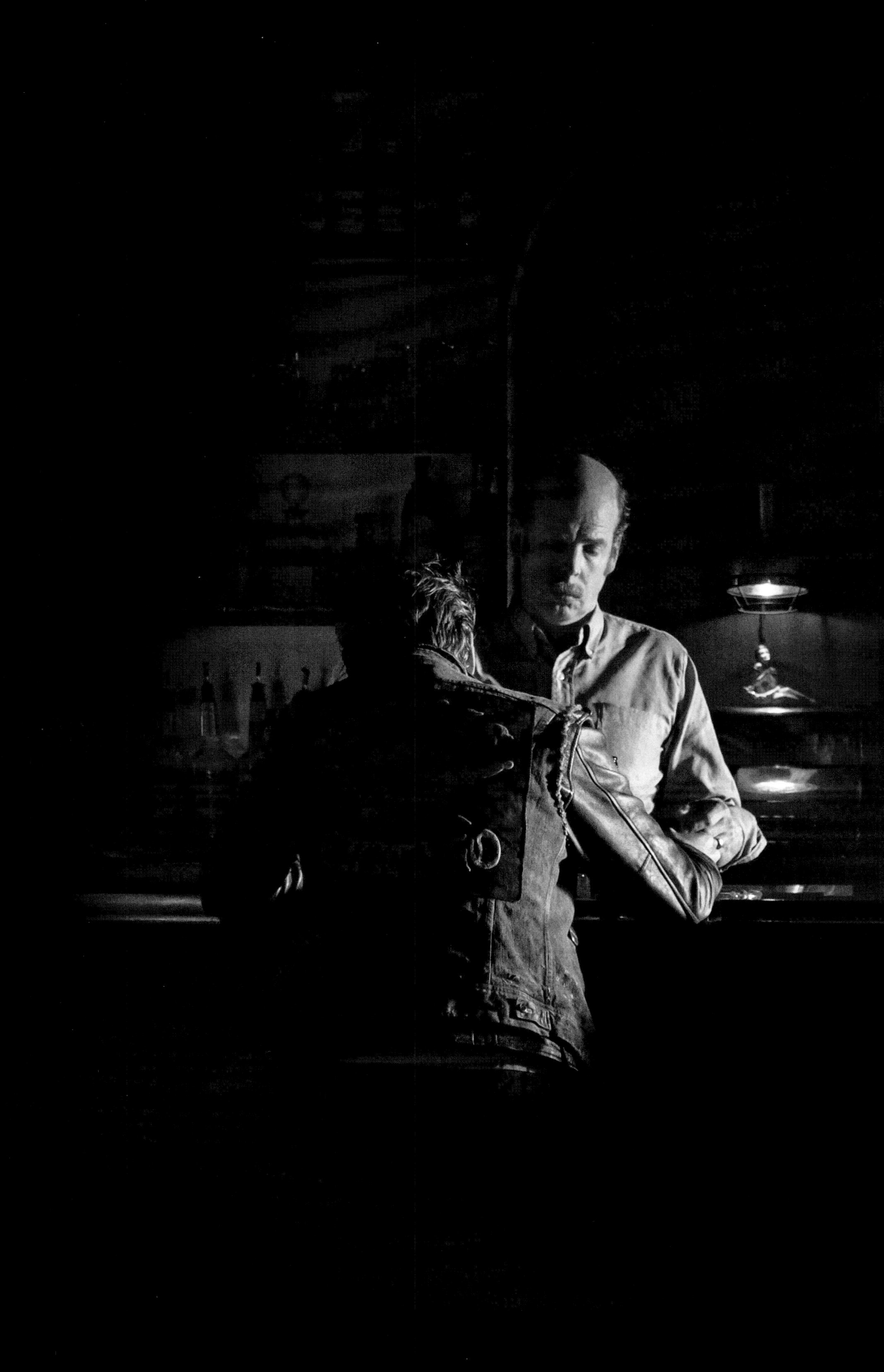

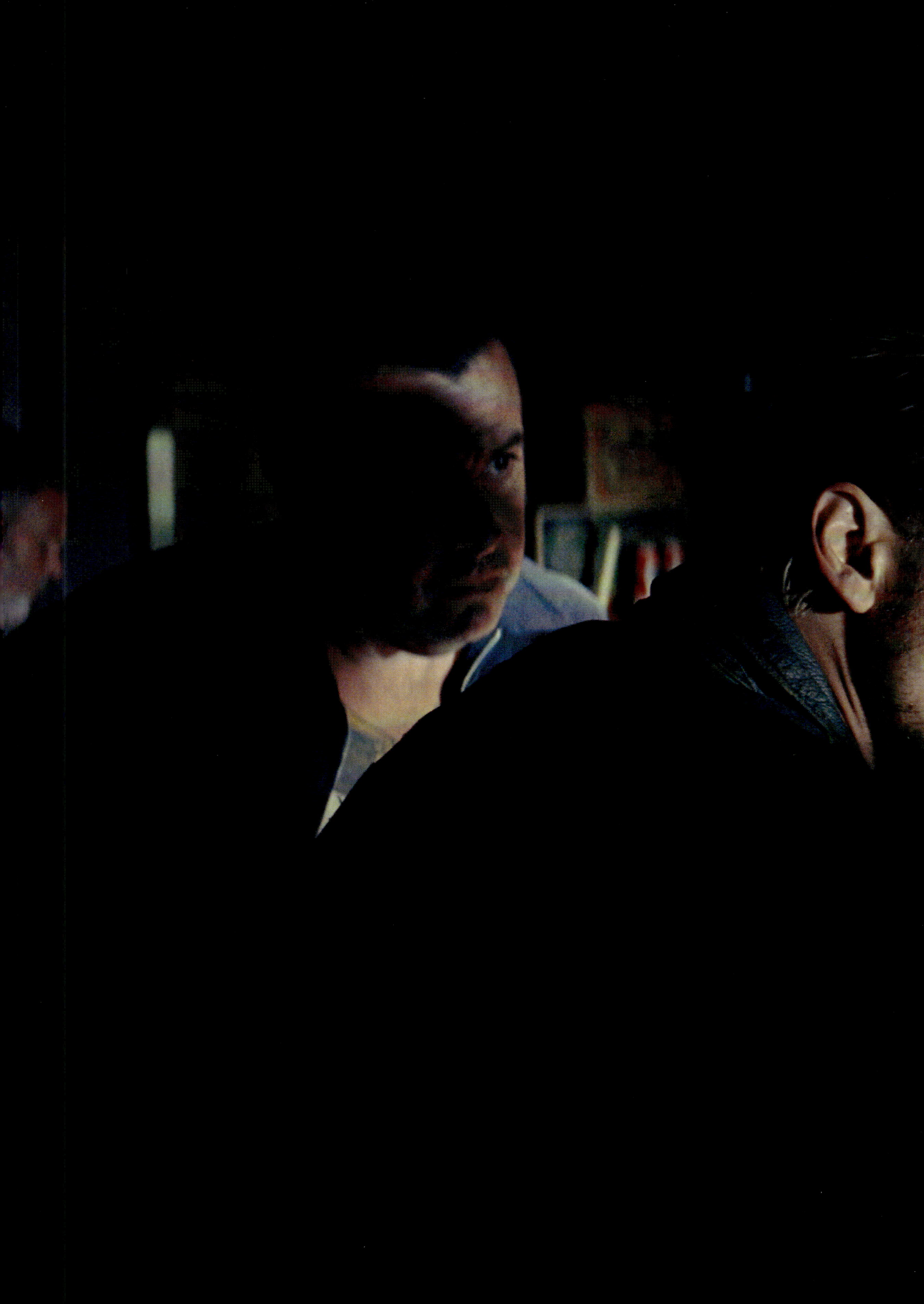

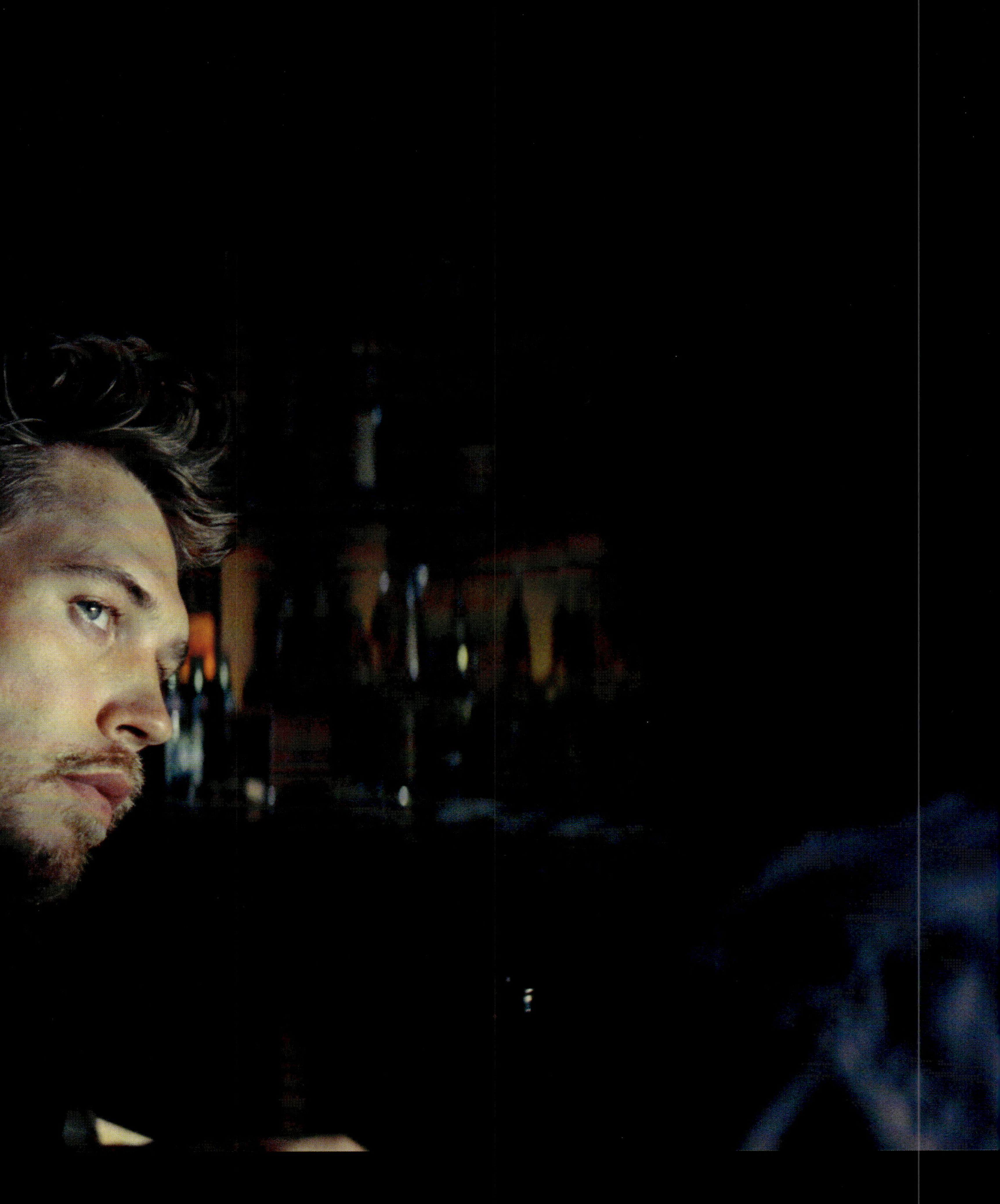

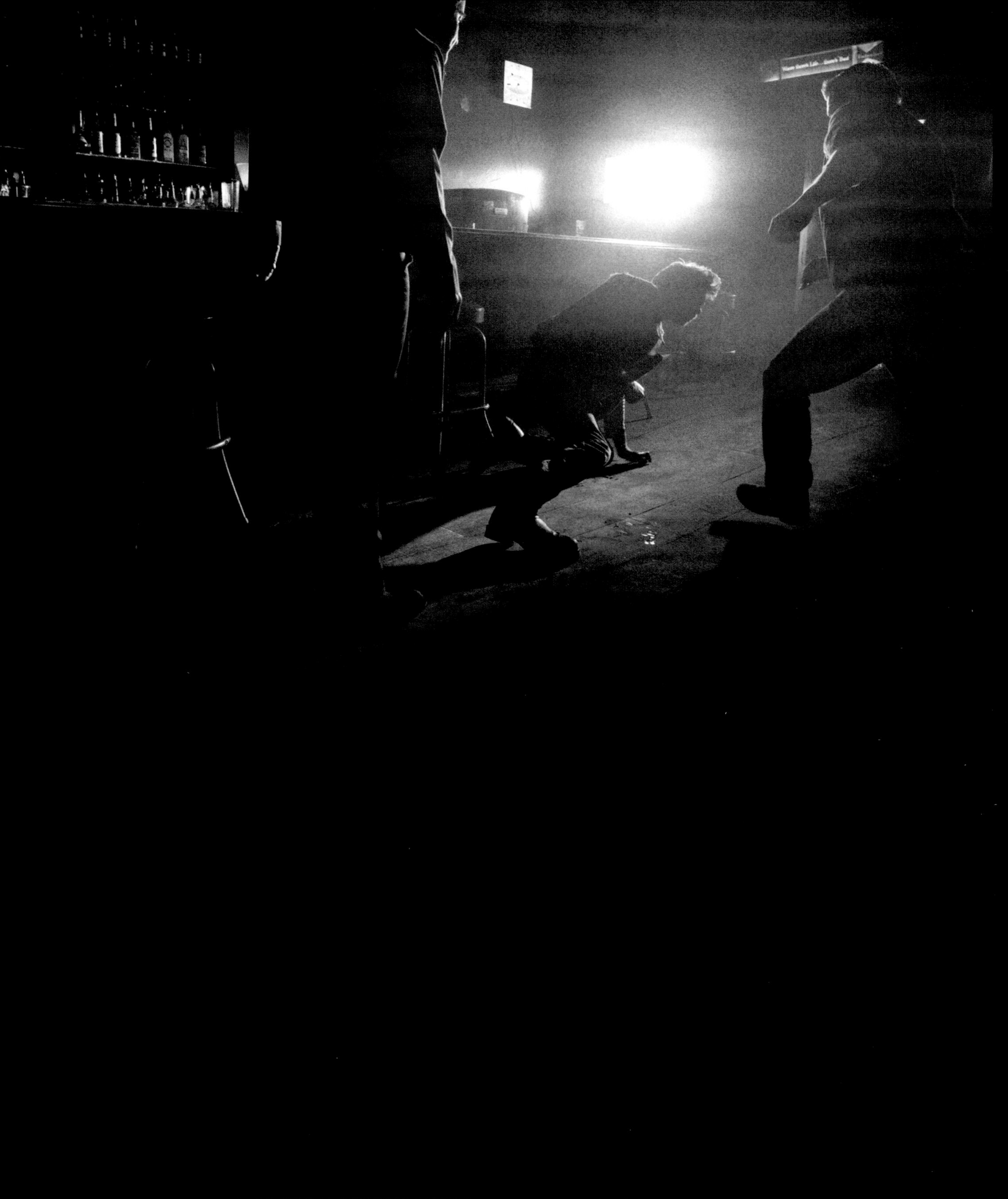

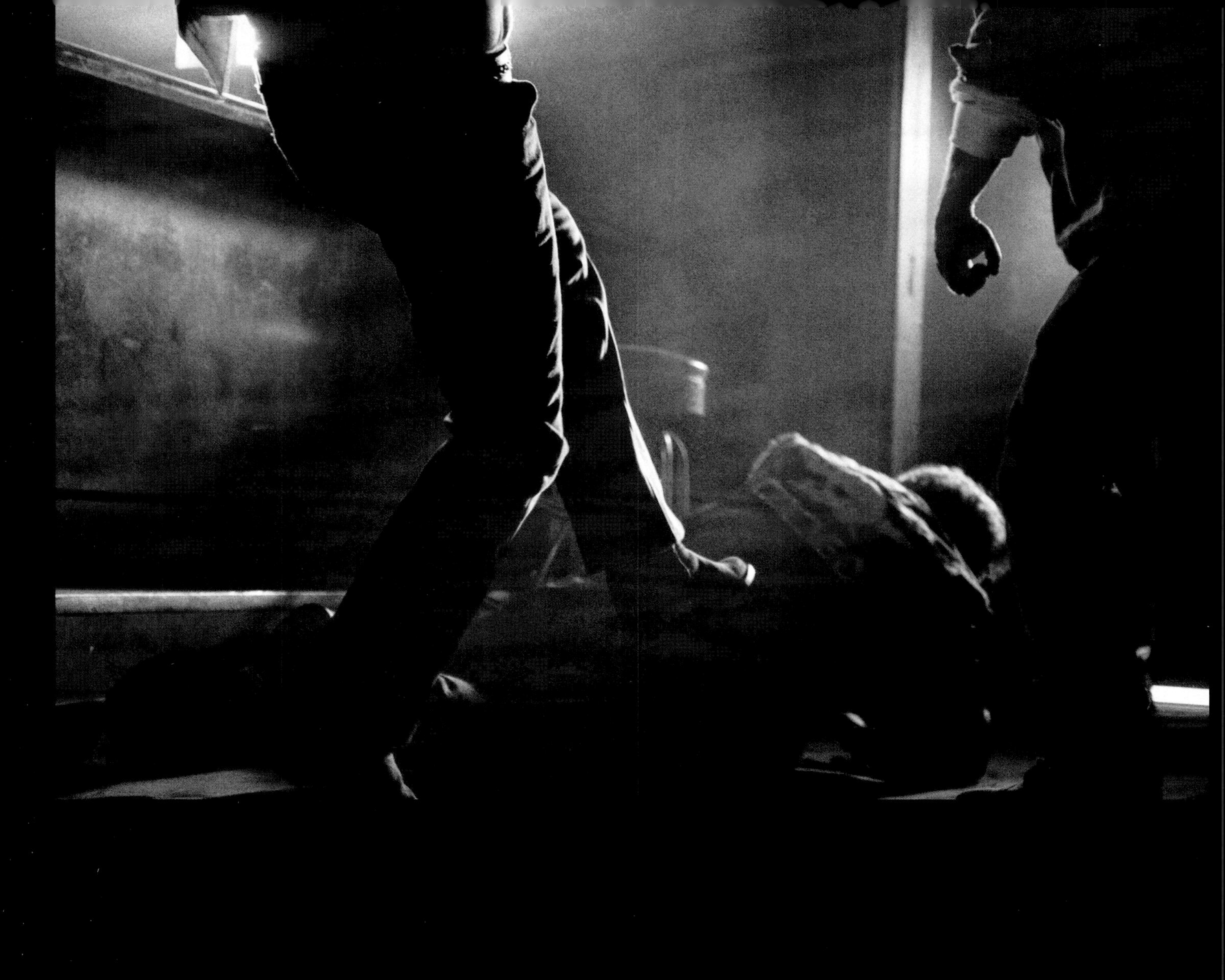

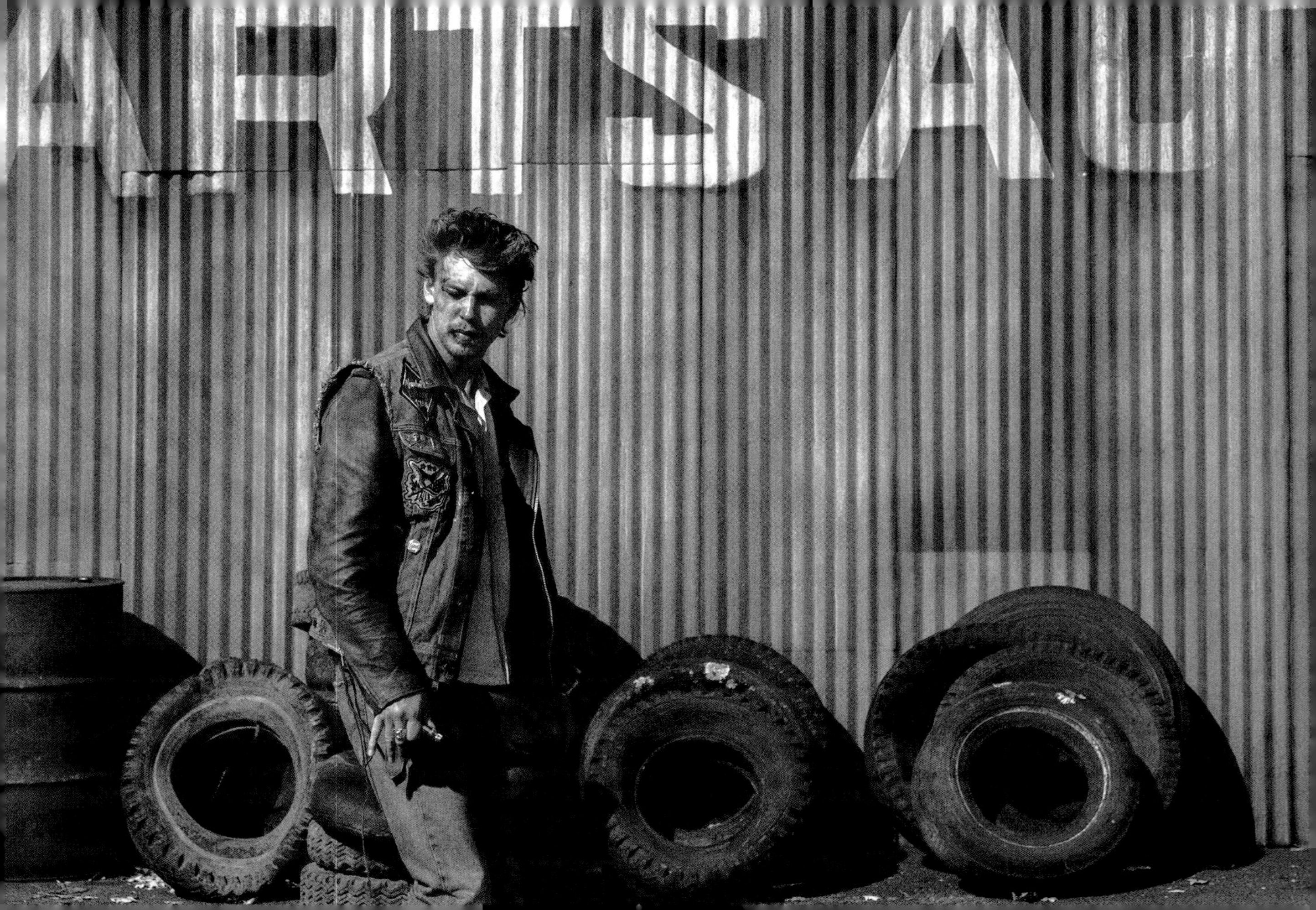

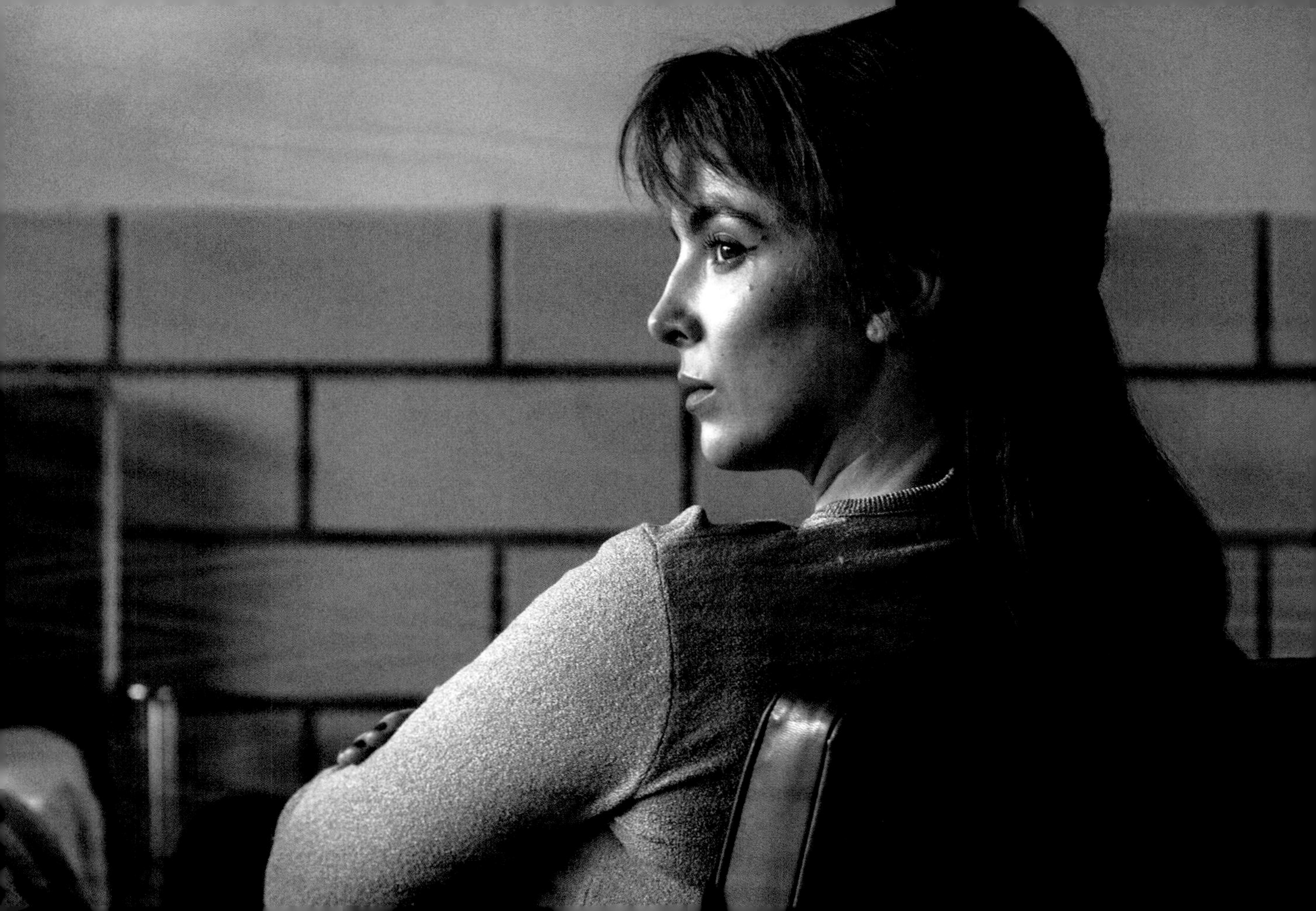

KATHY

He didn't want to lose his foot 'cause then he couldn't ride no more. Never mind that he'd got a concussion and this maniac nearly chopped his foot off for not taking his colors off, no. Never mind that he . . . He wasn't even supposed to be out ridin' 'cause his license was suspended from that one time the cops had chased him all over. I mean . . . No no no no, I mean all he could think about was ridin' his stupid motorcycle. I tell ya, you know. It'd be funny if it wasn't so tragic.

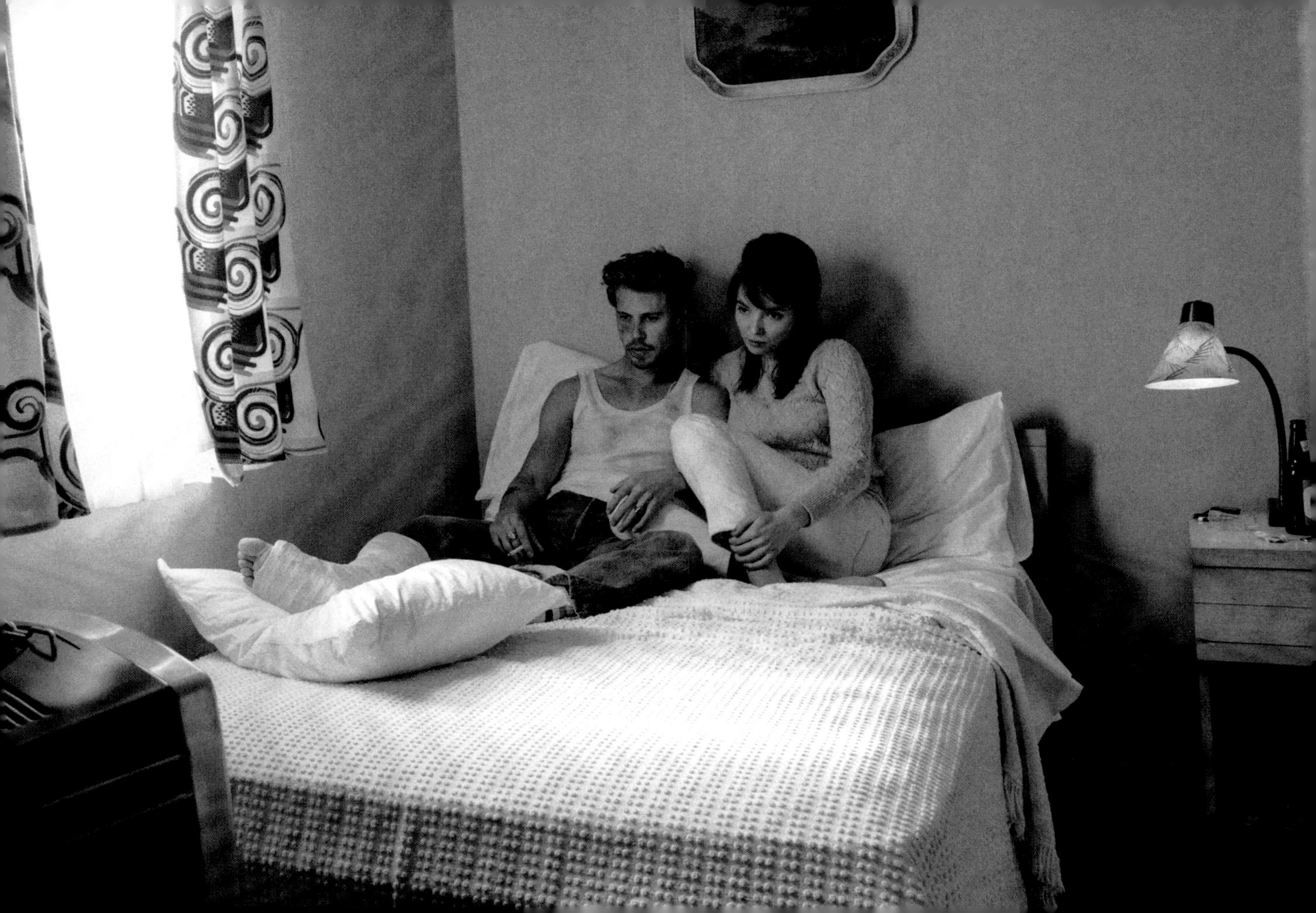

DANNY

And what about Johnny?

KATHY

Oh Johnny. Johnny went crazy.

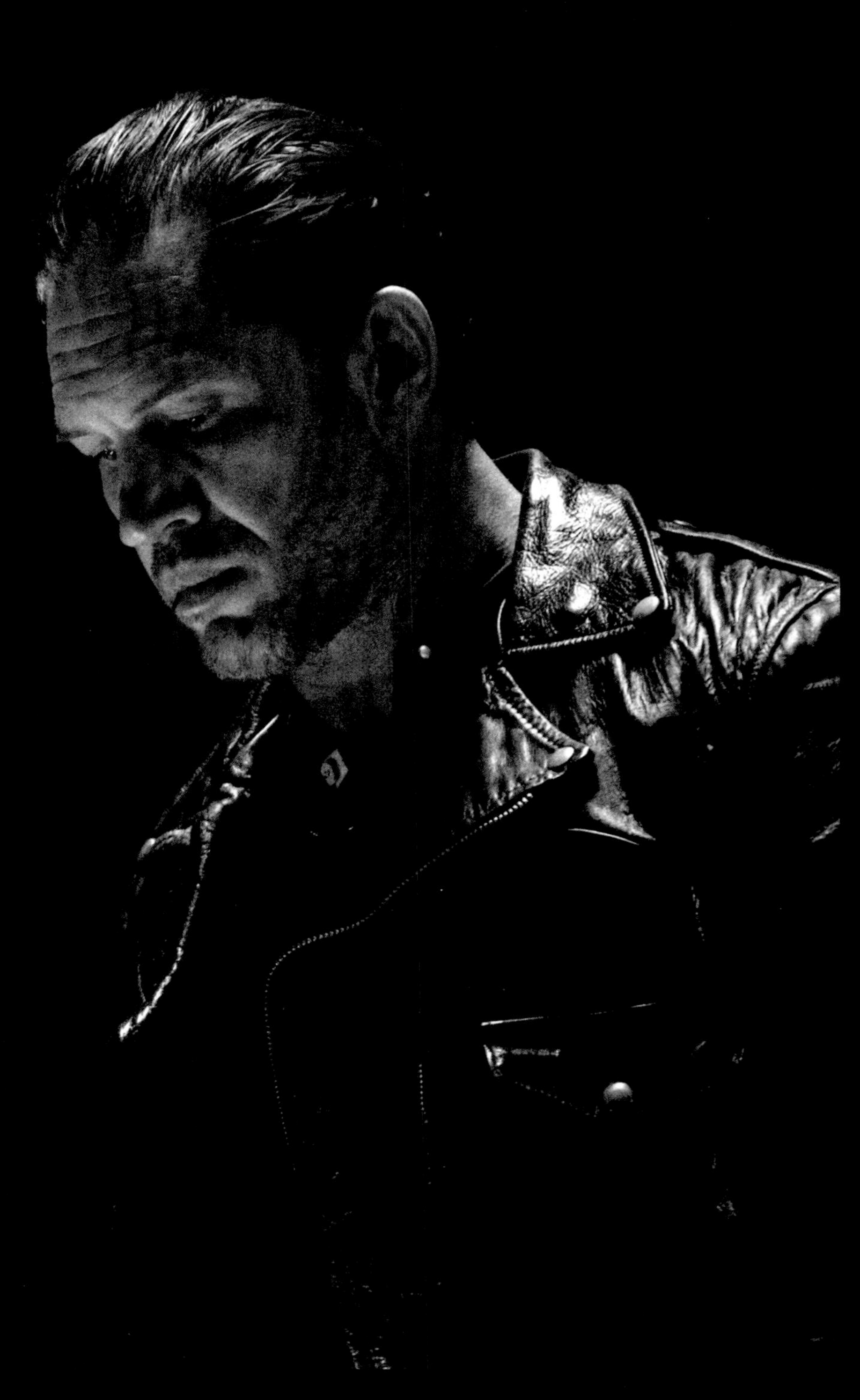

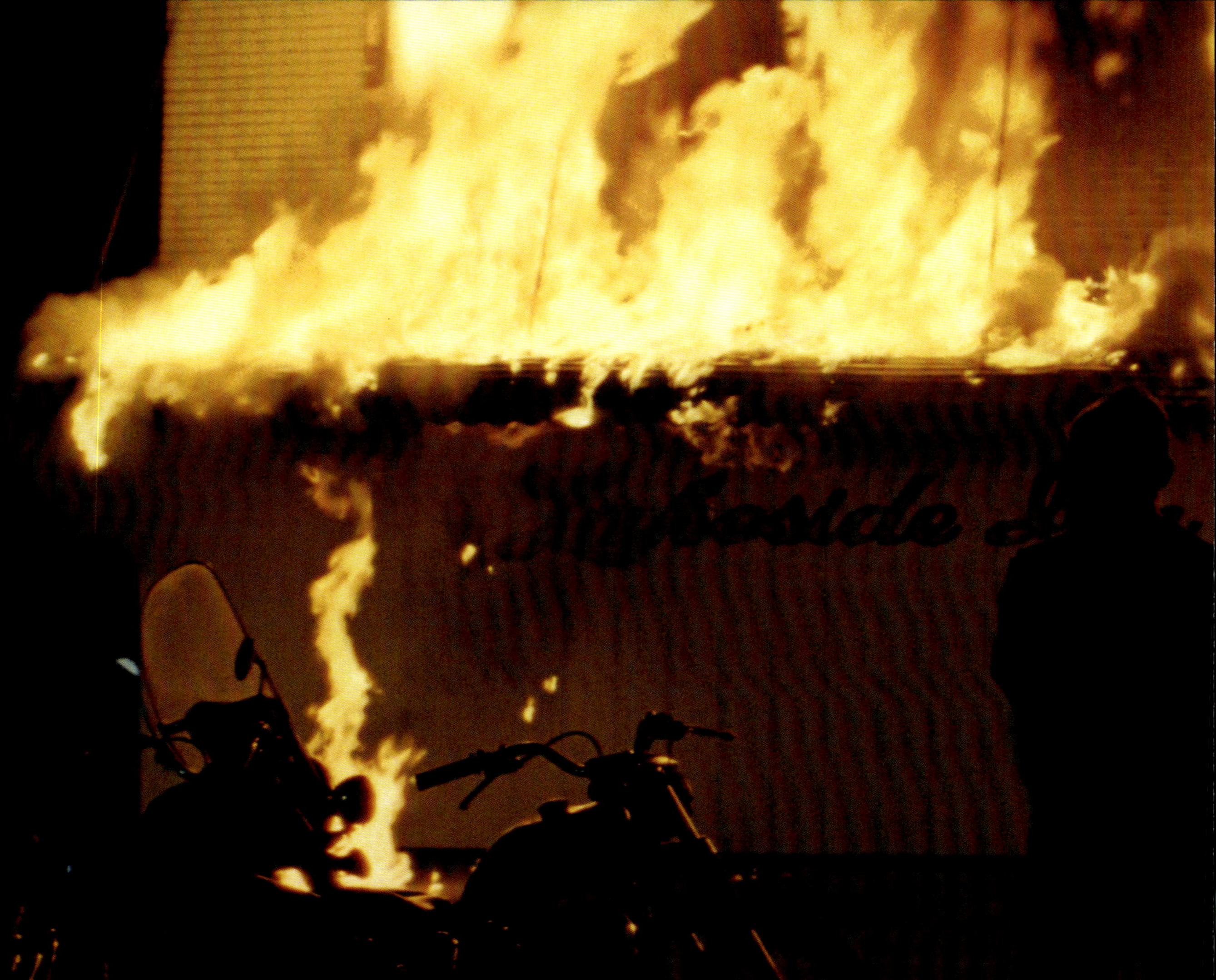

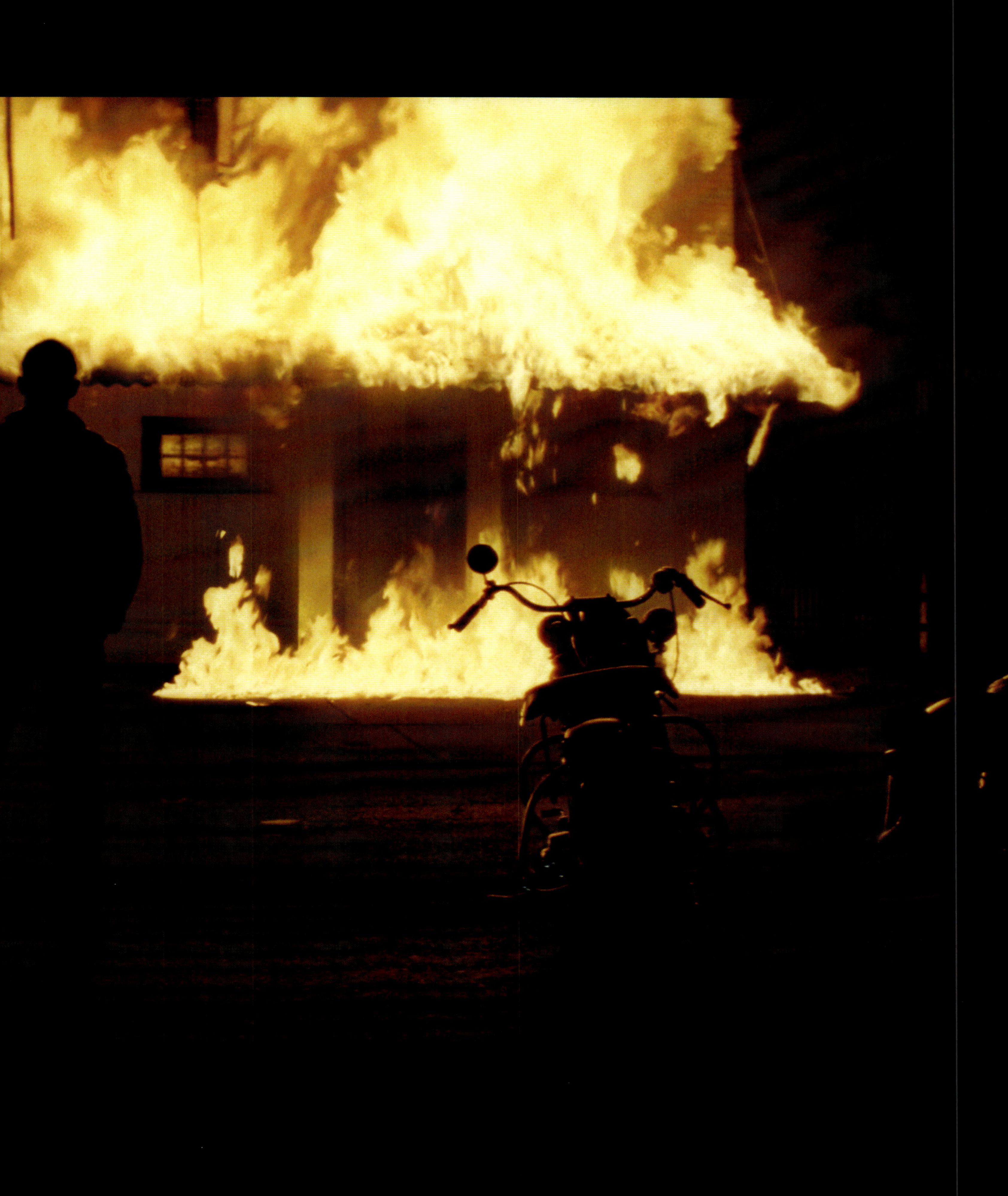

JOHNNY

You know these new guys. These young ones. Don't none of 'em listen.

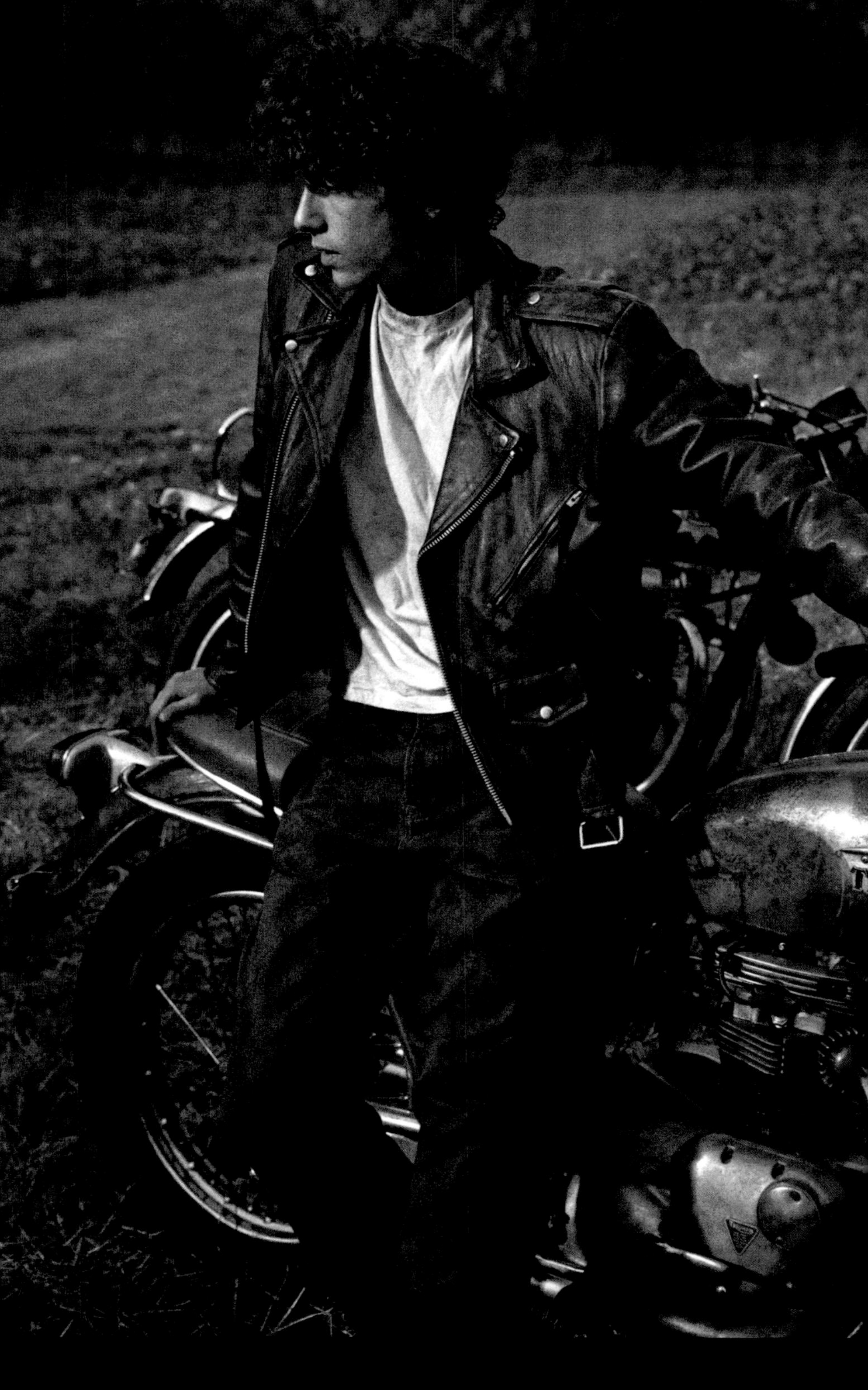

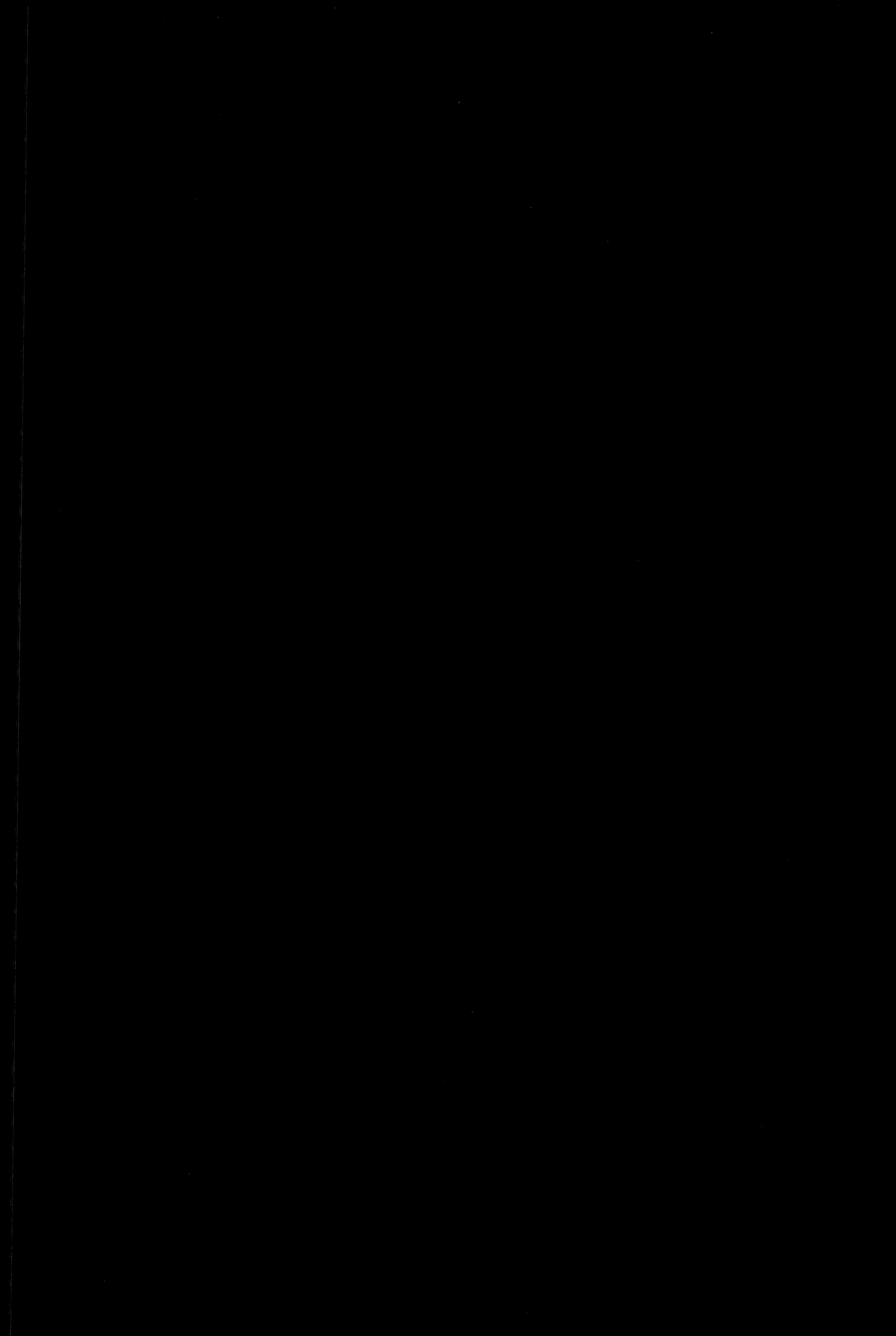

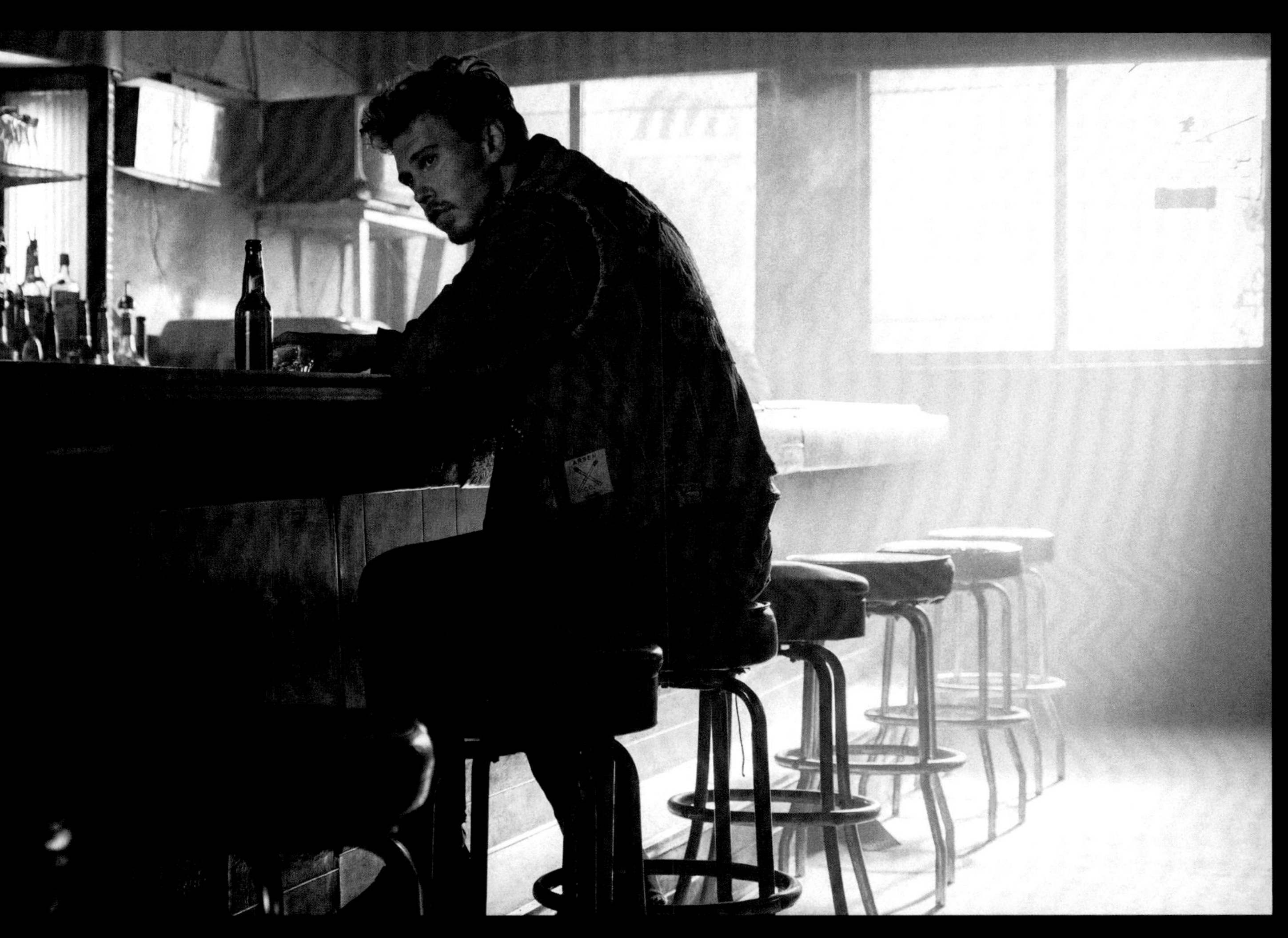

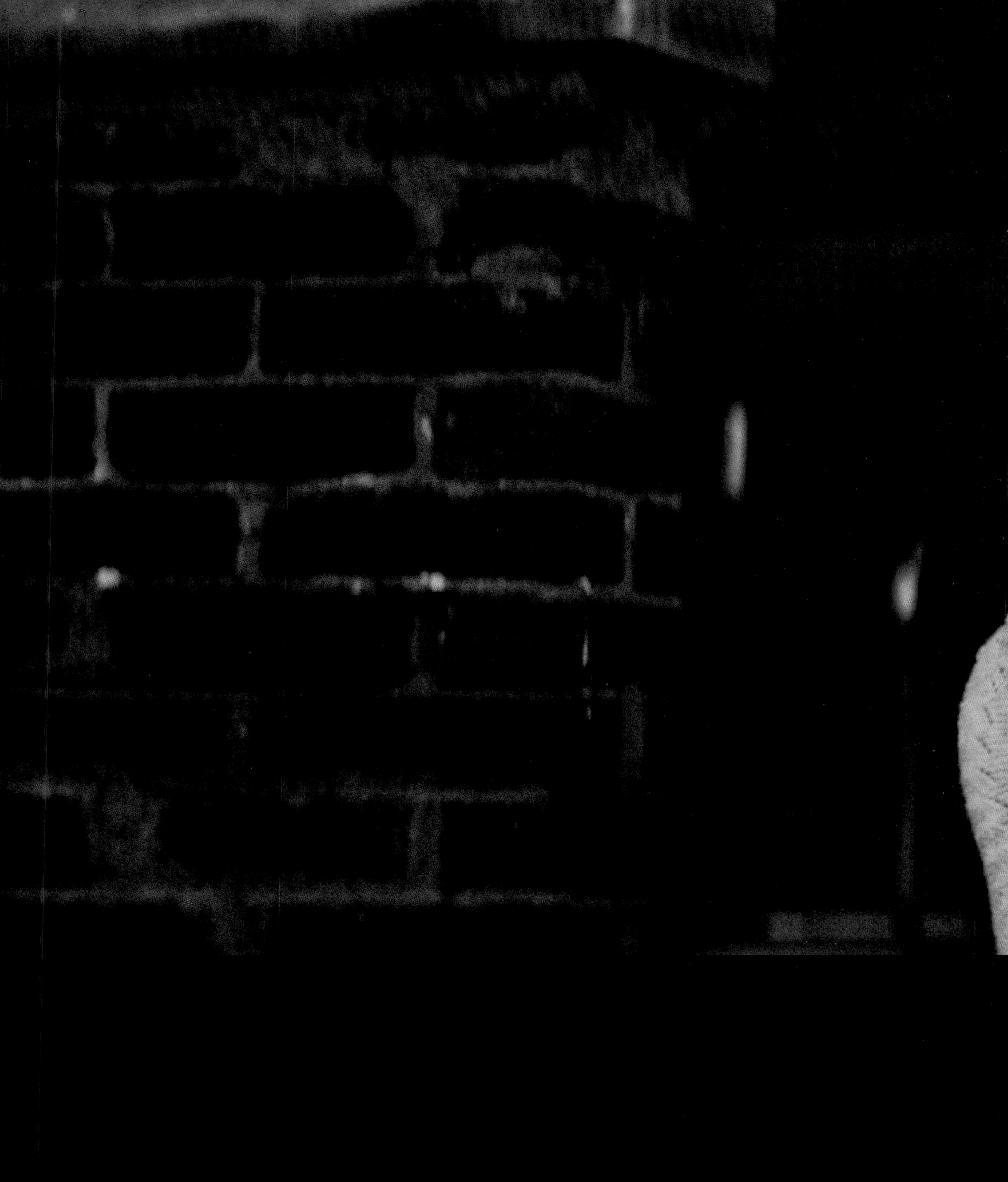

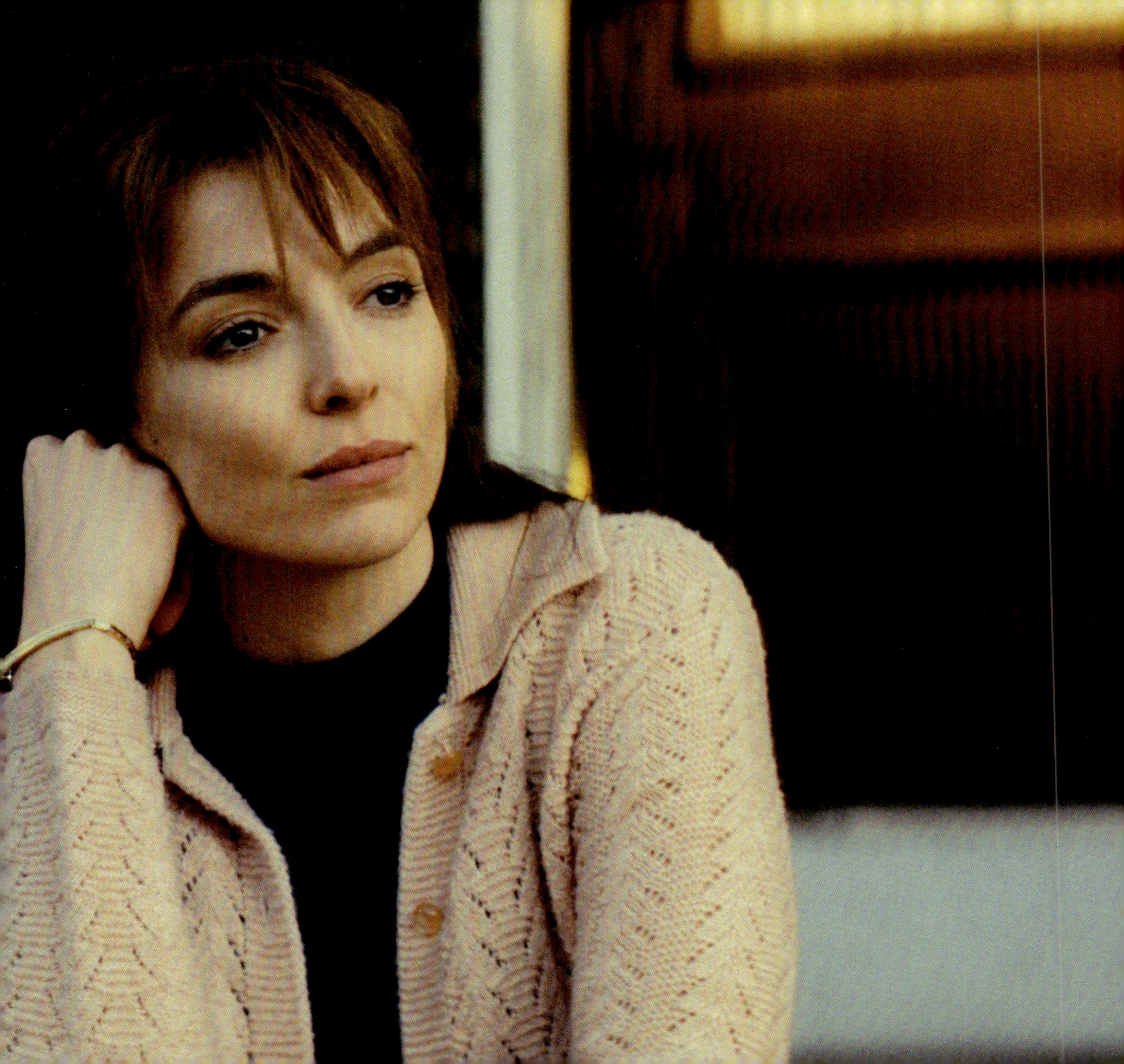

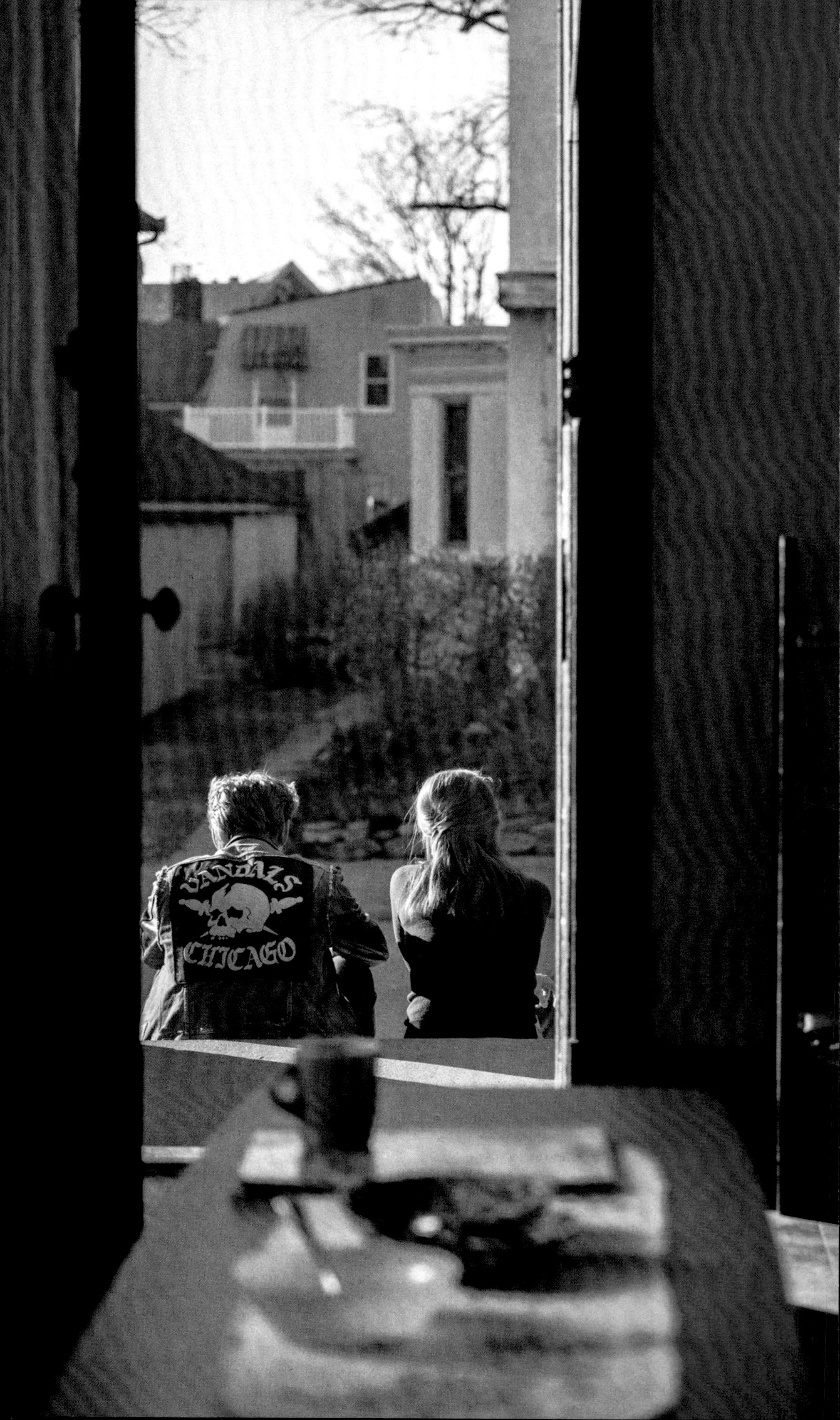
CHICAGO

JOHNNY

You know, you can give everything you got to a thing, you can give it all you got. And it's still just gonna do what it's gonna do.

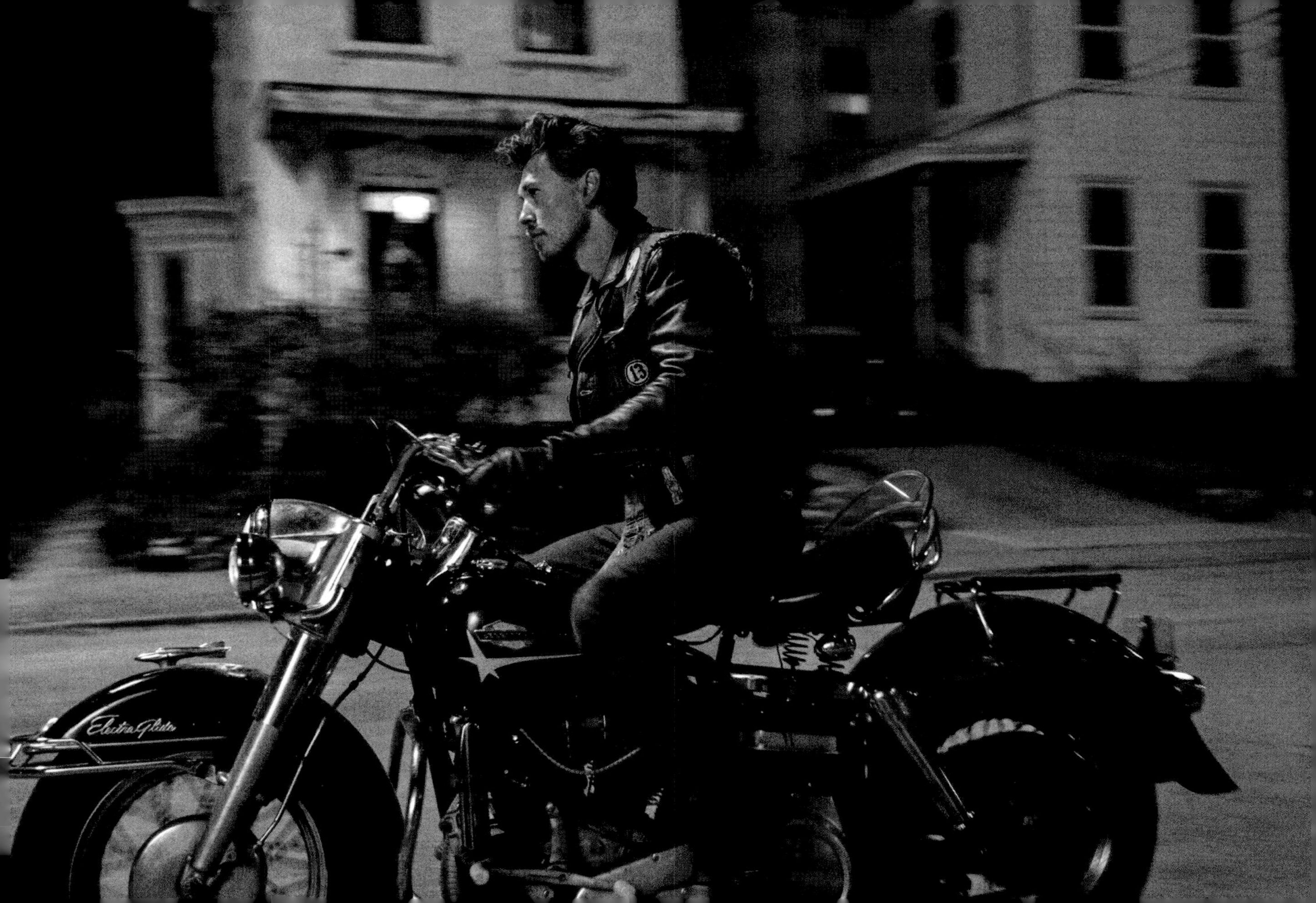
Electra Glide

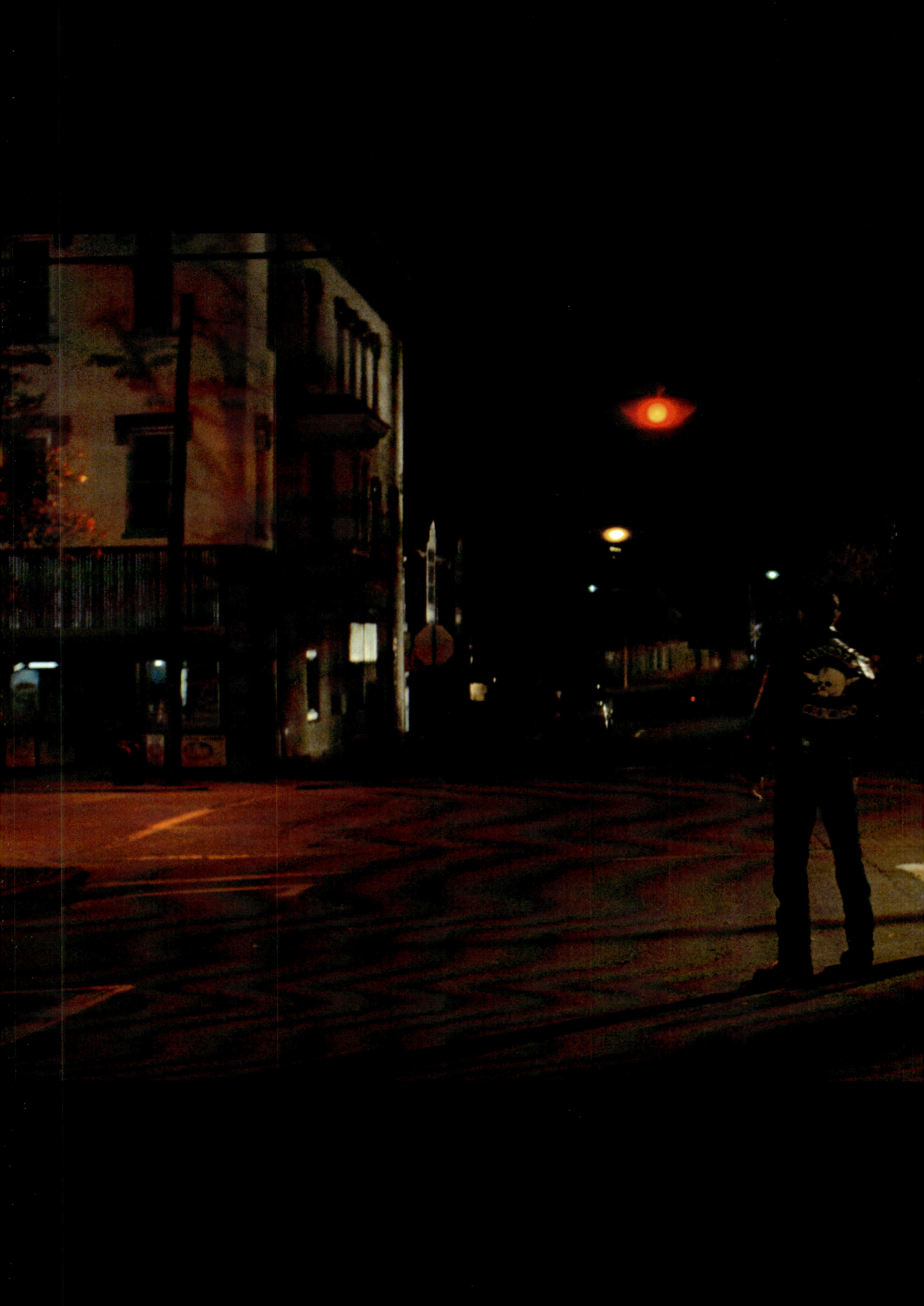

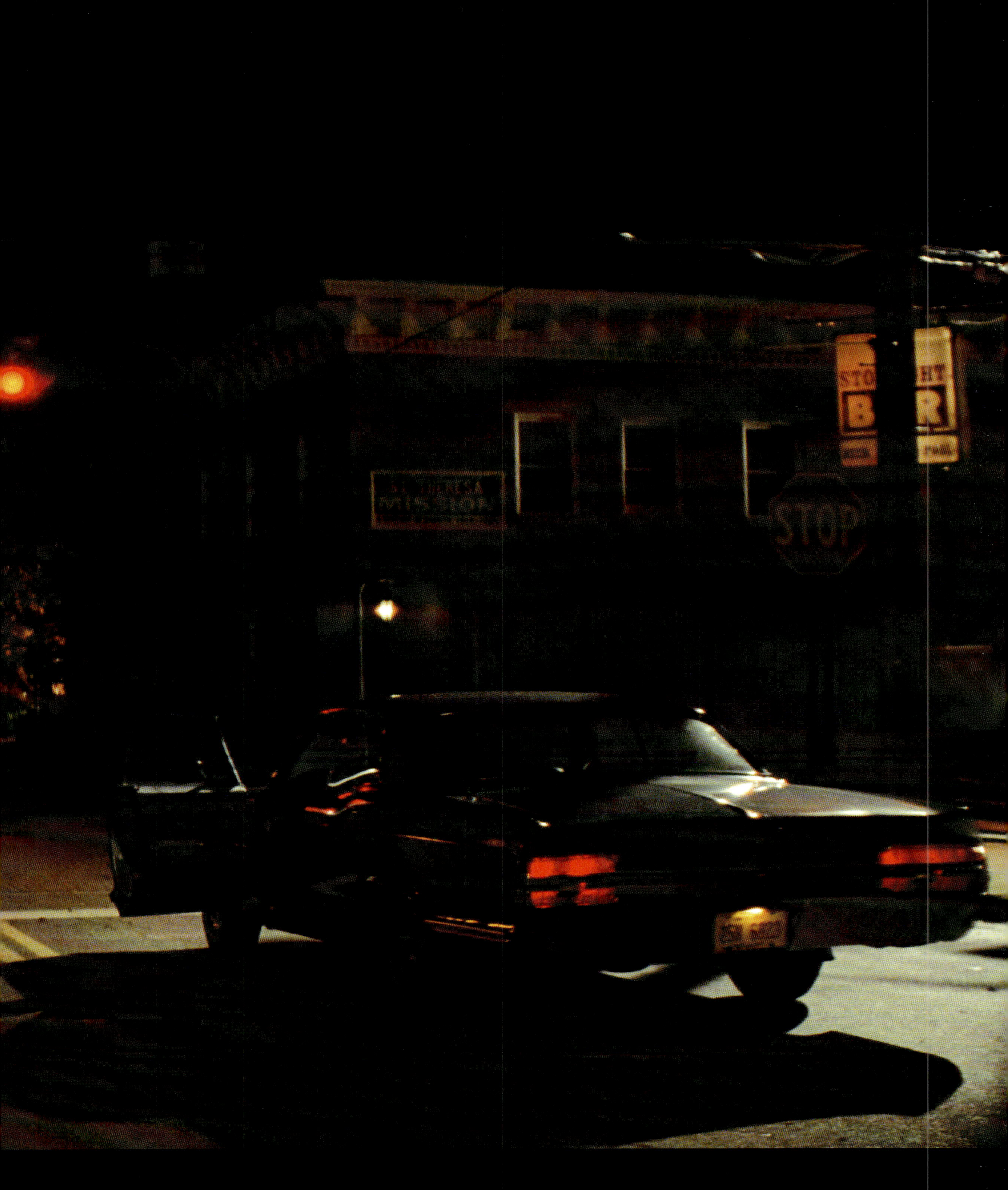
MISSION
STOP

NOTES ON PRODUCTION

Adam Stone, Cinematographer:

Over the past twenty years, I've been fortunate to collaborate with Jeff on all of his movies. Together, we worked with incredibly talented artisans, filmed in remote locations, and told compelling stories rooted in Americana. Each film was a unique learning experience, a stepping stone of sorts, culminating in: *The Bikeriders*.

Though the film took many years to evolve from concept to execution, shooting the forty-day film was fast paced. Lightning in a bottle. We had a superb cast, epic locations, and a truly historic blueprint to follow. Danny Lyon's photobook was our guide to a bygone era of hyper masculinity, unbridled youth, and counterculture. Just as Danny embedded himself in the middle of the bikers, our production crew did the same for our camera. From hand-embroidered vests, to period-correct sets and motorcycles, every possible facet of Lyon's book was studied to create a film that's authentic and tactile.

The same mantra went into shooting and lighting. We strove to get dirty and in the middle of things just as Danny did. Jeff and I wanted to create a film that felt timeless and slightly reckless. We opted to use celluloid over digital and shot all motorcycle scenes without the aid of CGI. The shoot was also entirely location-based, by choice. That imbued the lighting crew to build some truly stunning lighting setups not possible in a studio.

I am super proud of the film and accompanying book. Both are gorgeous, nuanced, and truly unique in an era of digital sprawl. I hope they inspire a new generation of artists to preserve their craft on celluloid like Danny and Jeff did.

Chad Keith, Production Designer:

Building worlds that are believable to the actors, the audience, and ourselves requires getting every detail right. We did some of our best work on this film to make that happen. Putting together the look of a period film always requires in-depth historical research, gathering inspirational photos and sourcing textural elements. Access to Danny Lyon's photographs and interviews proved to be integral in our pursuit to authentically re-create these environments. They were not only used as inspiration, but also as fully realized blueprints that we then felt challenged to fabricate accurately and honestly. Our collaborative efforts result in a wholly unique film that brings to life a bygone era and offers audiences a wild ride through a rare perspective of American history.

Erin Benach, Costume Designer:

Making the costumes for *The Bikeriders* was all about immersing myself into a world of grit, dirt, blood, and sweat. It was about finding the textures of grimy denim and well-worn leather that molded to the body the way it would have in 1967 after hours of hard riding.

The work had to be authentic, historically accurate, and, importantly, go unnoticed. My team of artisans consisted of pattern makers, metal workers, patch makers, and agers/dyers. We started with new denim jackets, then created our own versions of those patches and pieces of metal which we worked to feel appropriately road weary. We used methods of chainstitch embroidery that have become almost extinct.

The individuality of the riders was a huge focus for me; they all had details that mirror their psyches. I learned about the good luck charms, souvenir décor, and patchwork they used to decorate and define themselves. I considered the motivations of each character—what made them join up together, why do they love each other, when does being together make them feel stronger, and when does it make them fall apart?

Jodie Comer as KATHY

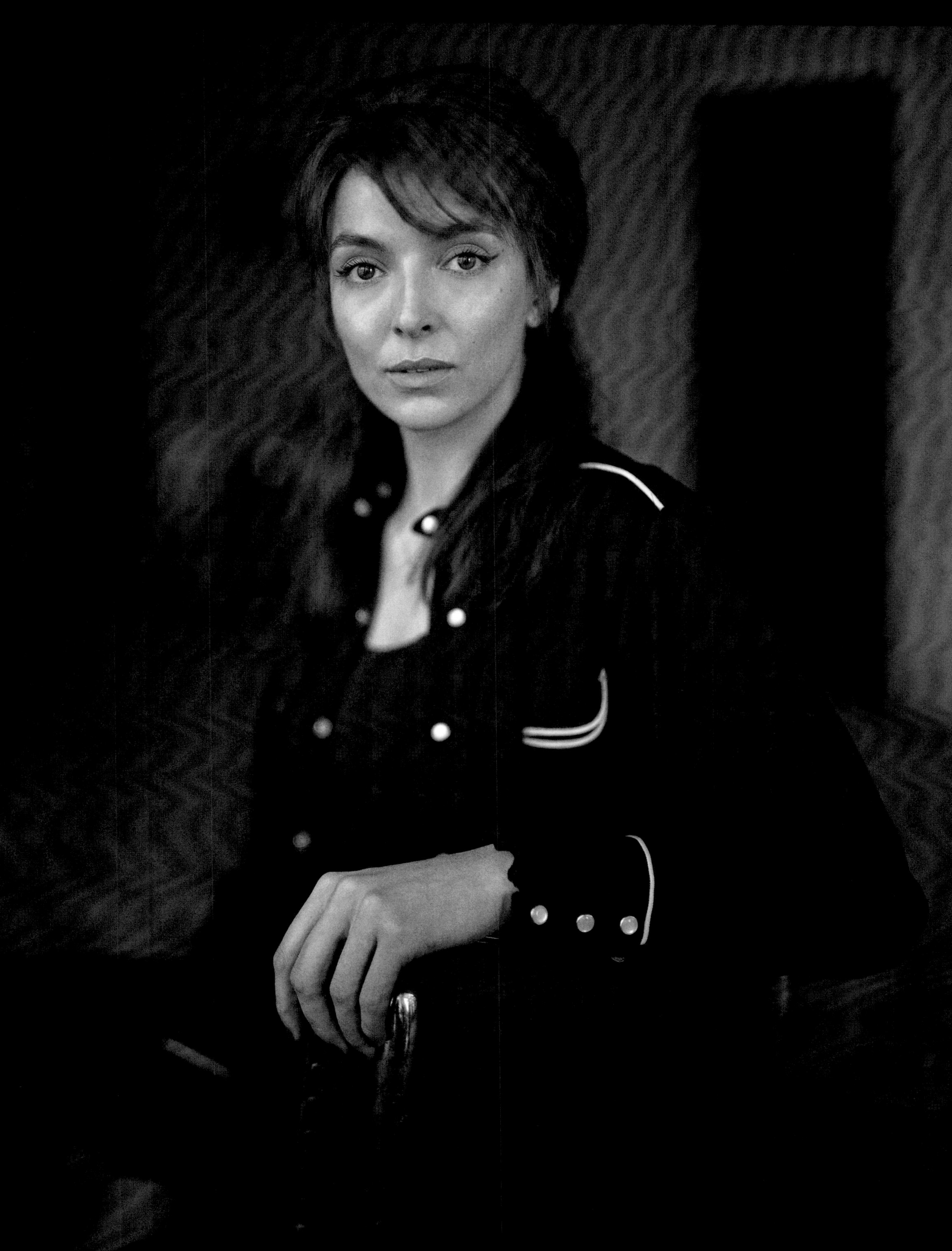

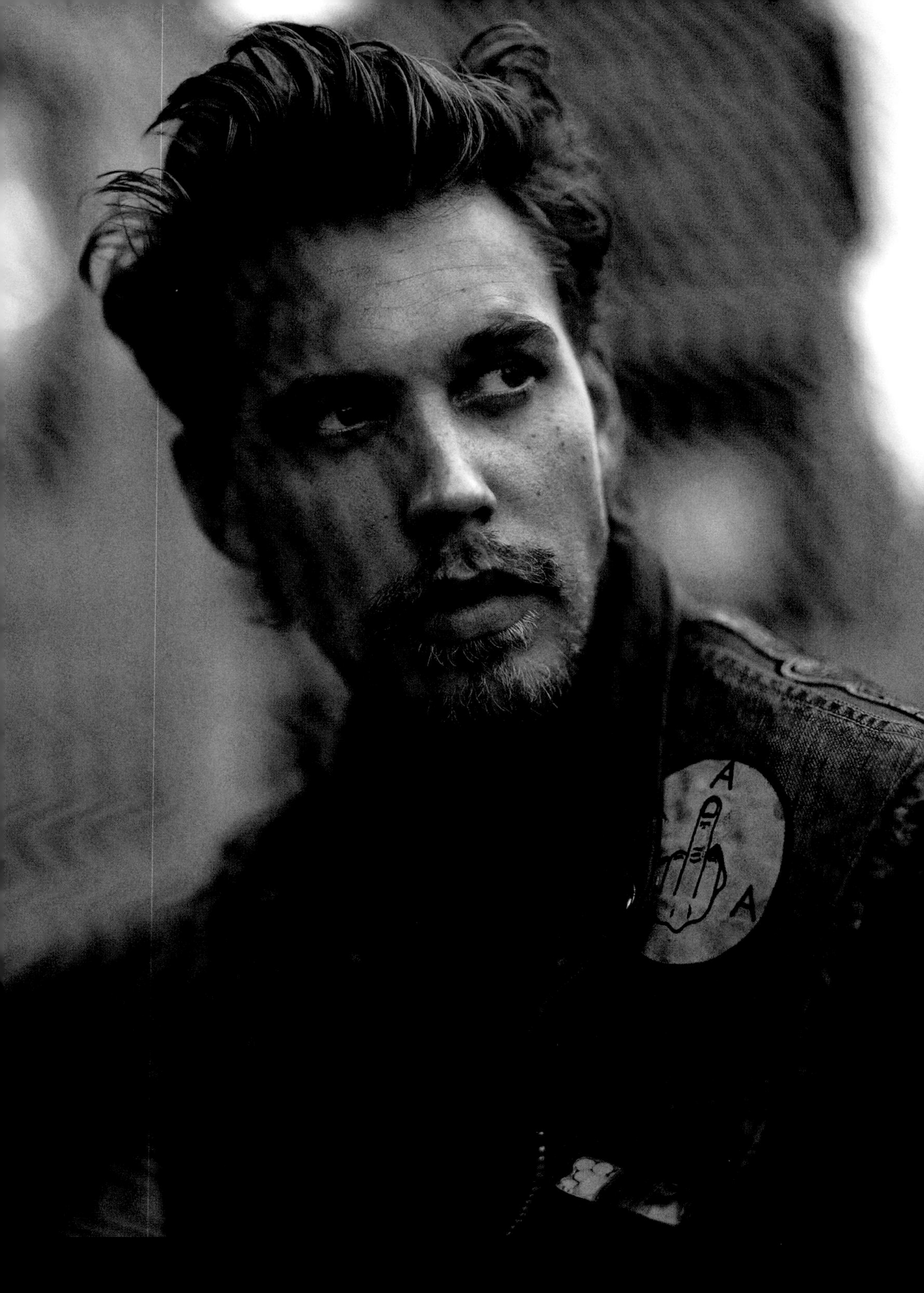

Austin Butler as BENNY

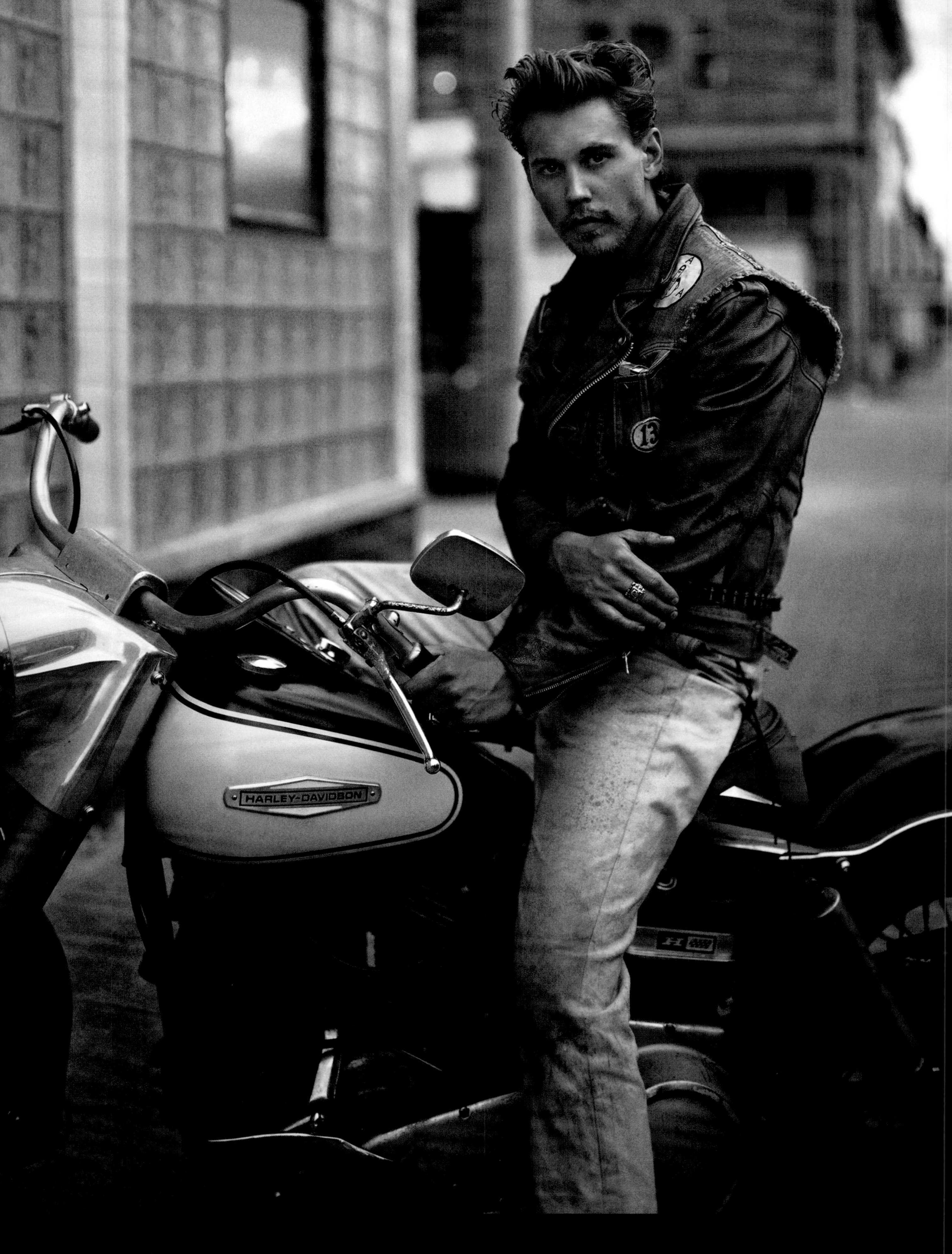
HARLEY-DAVIDSON

KATHY and BENNY

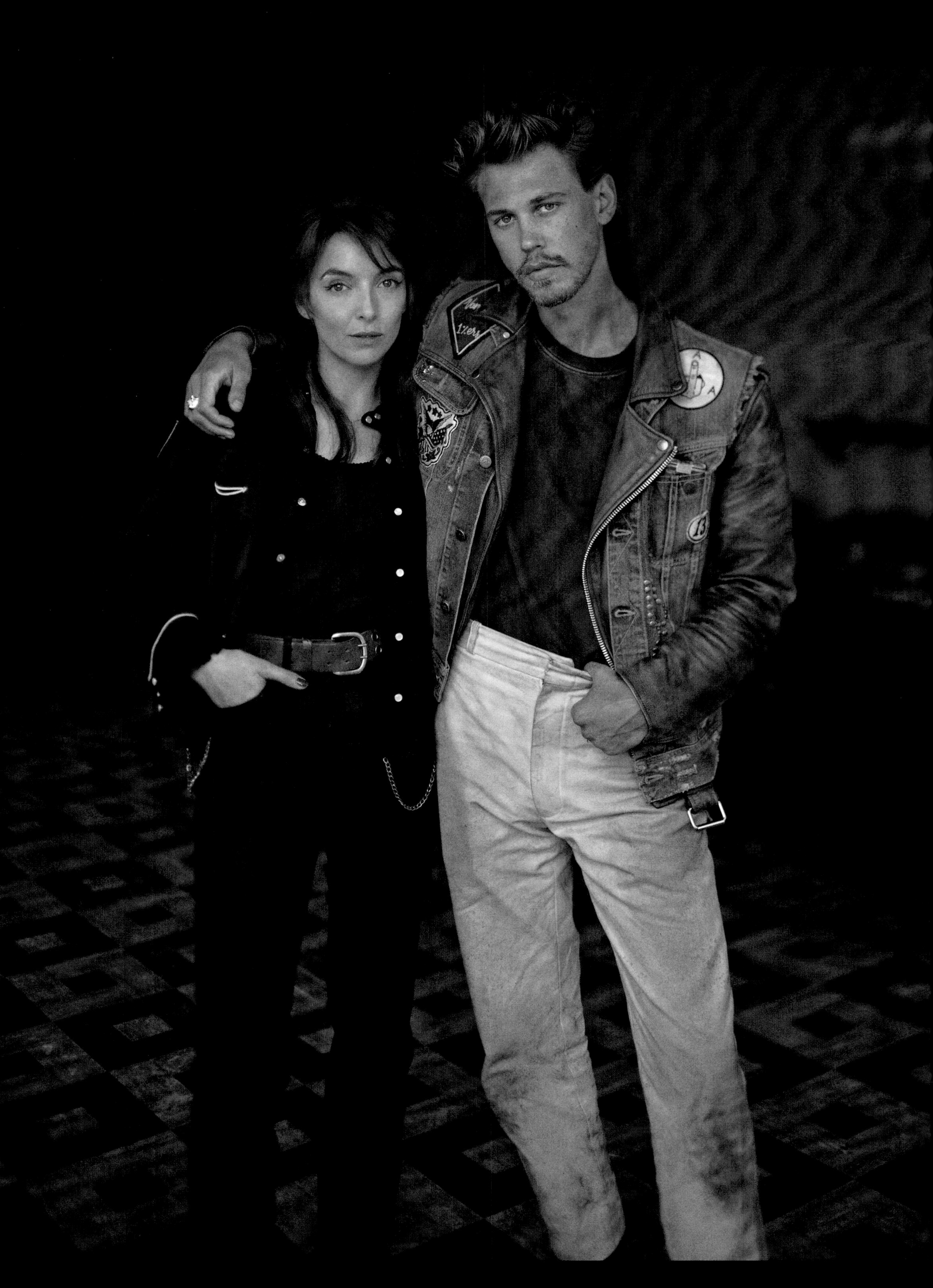

Tom Hardy as JOHNNY

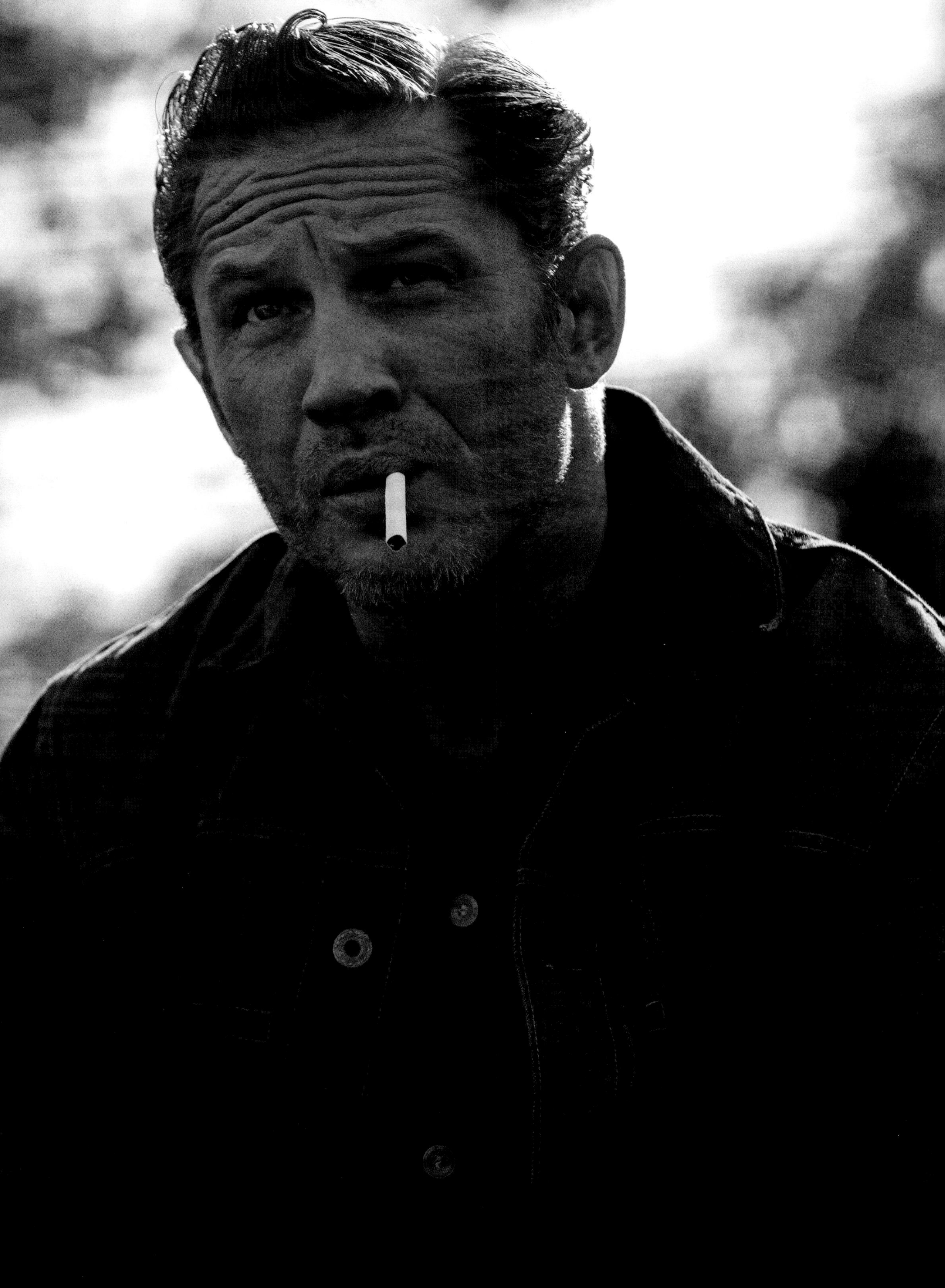

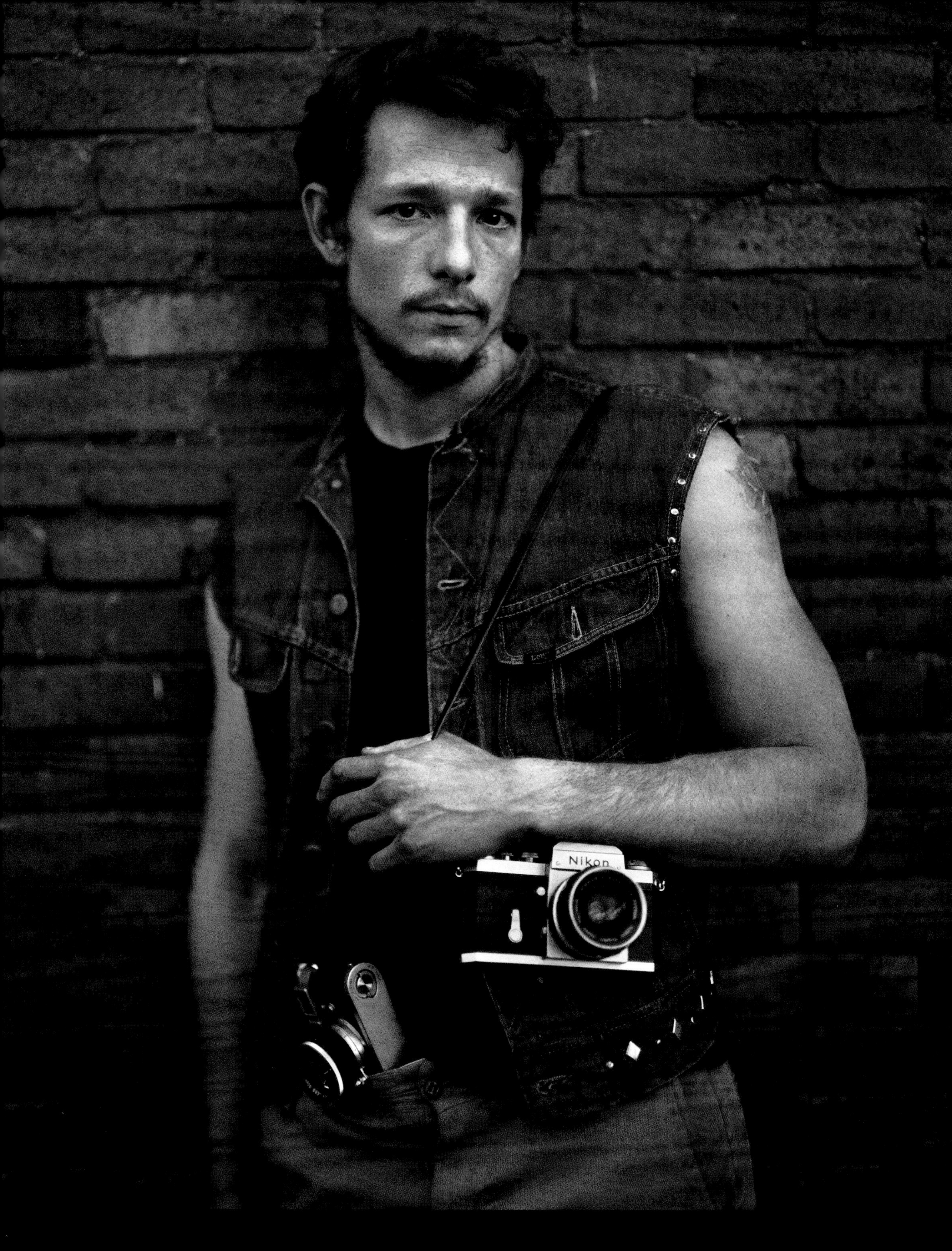
Nikon

Mike Faist as DANNY

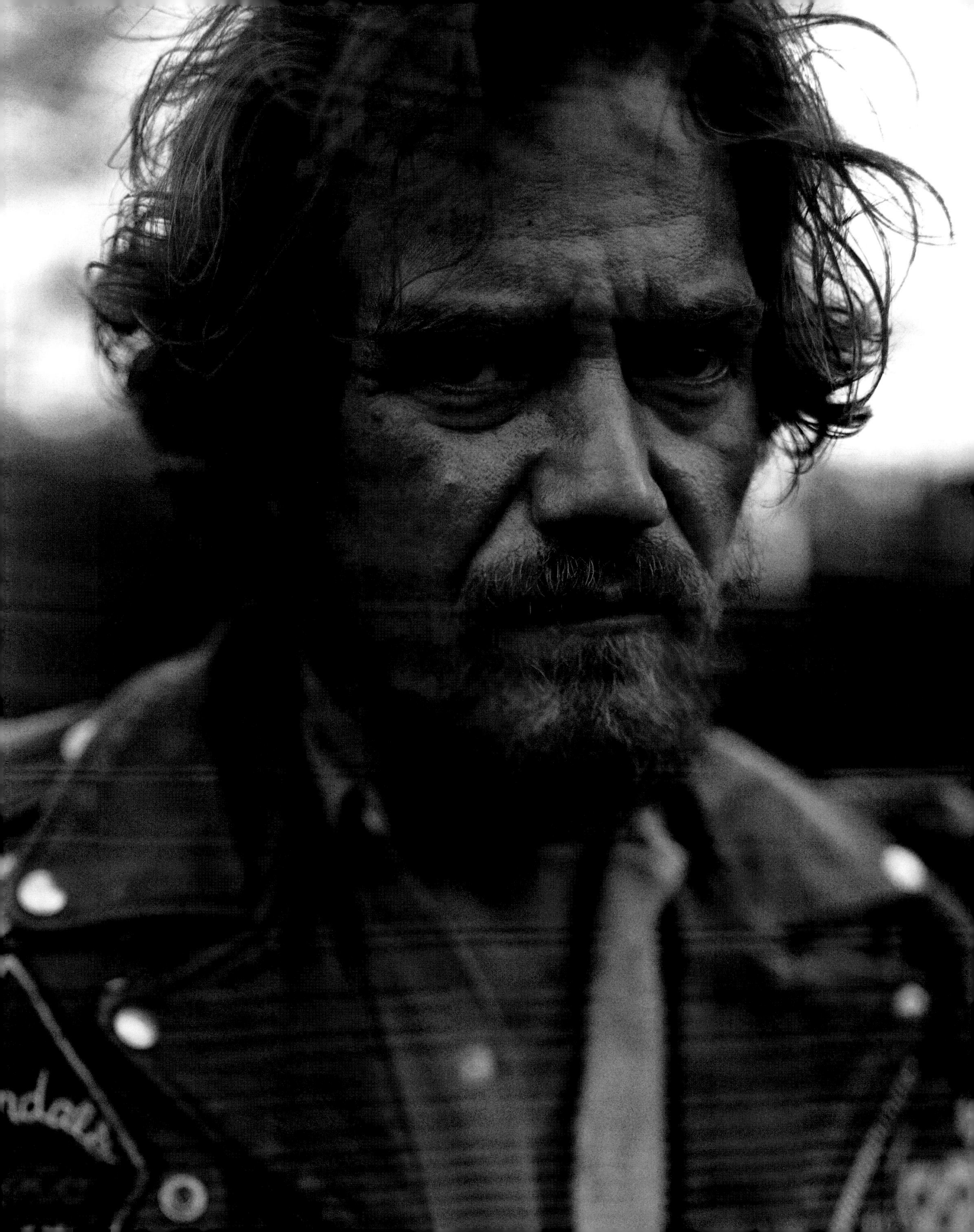

Michael Shannon as ZIPCO

Emory Cohen as COCKROACH

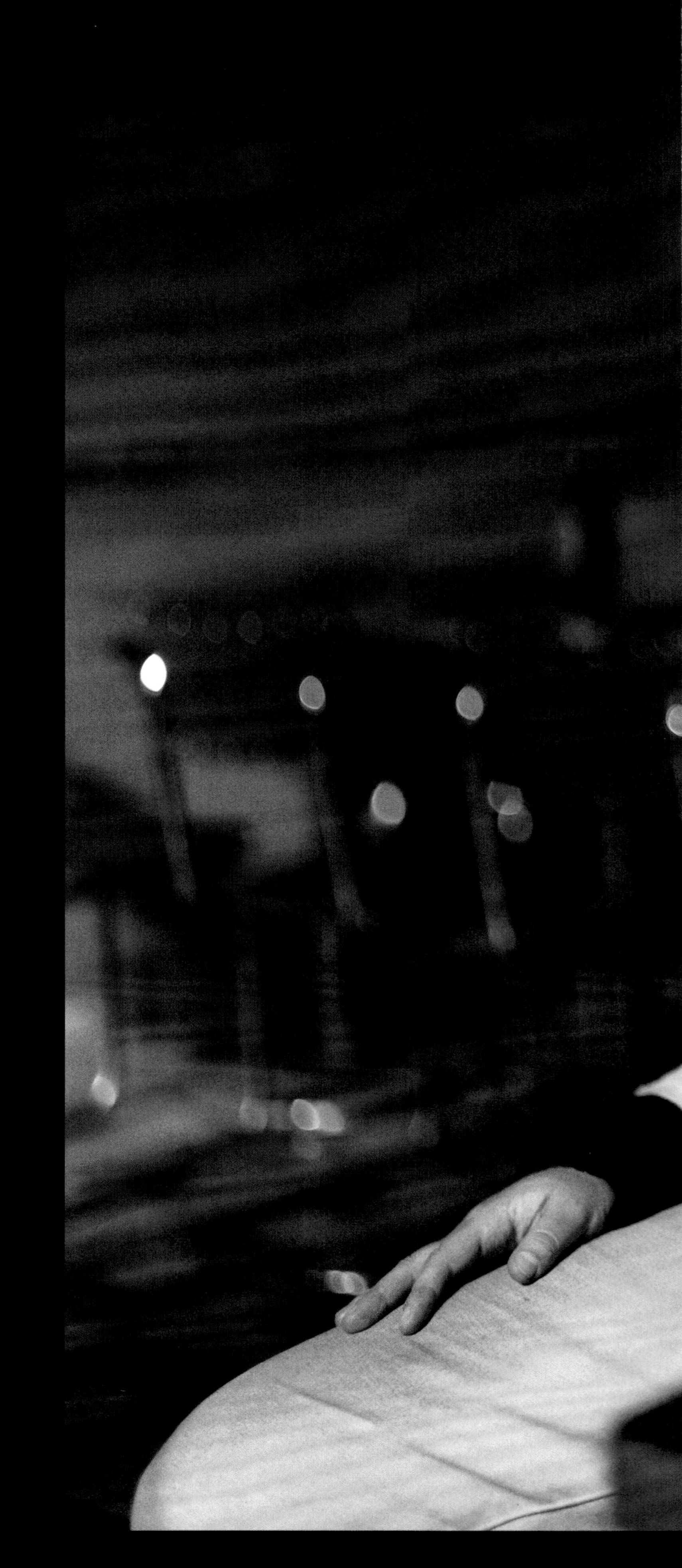

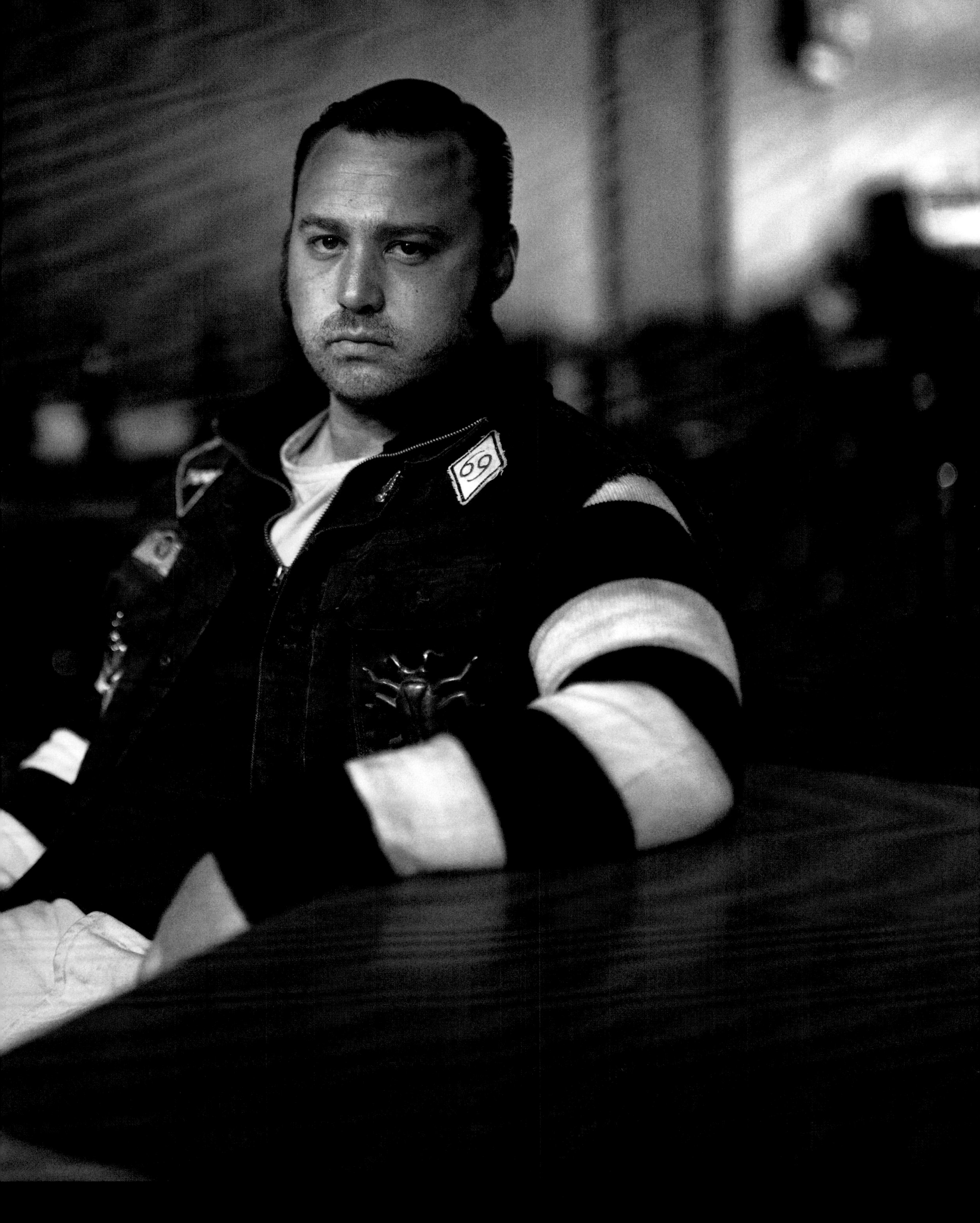

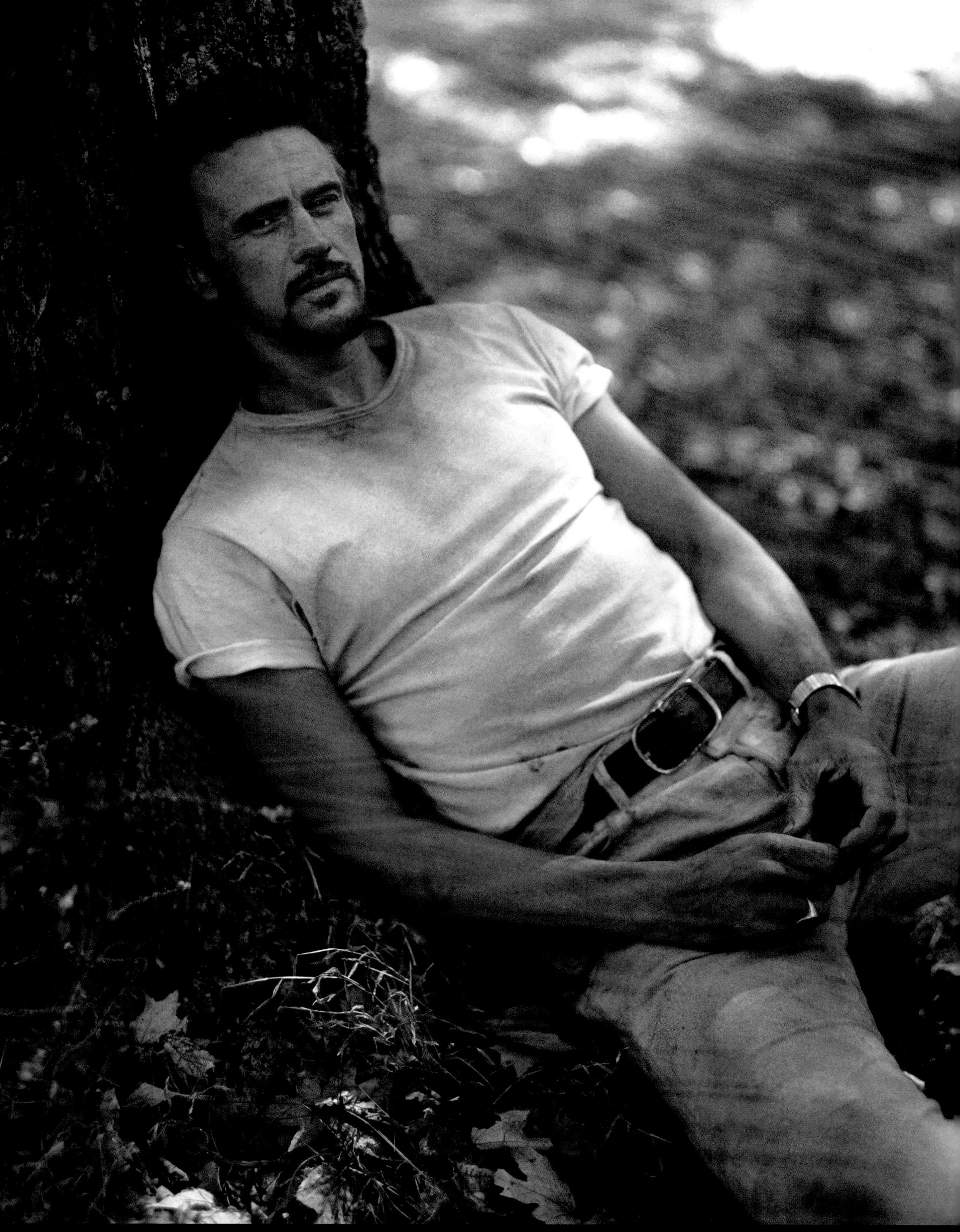

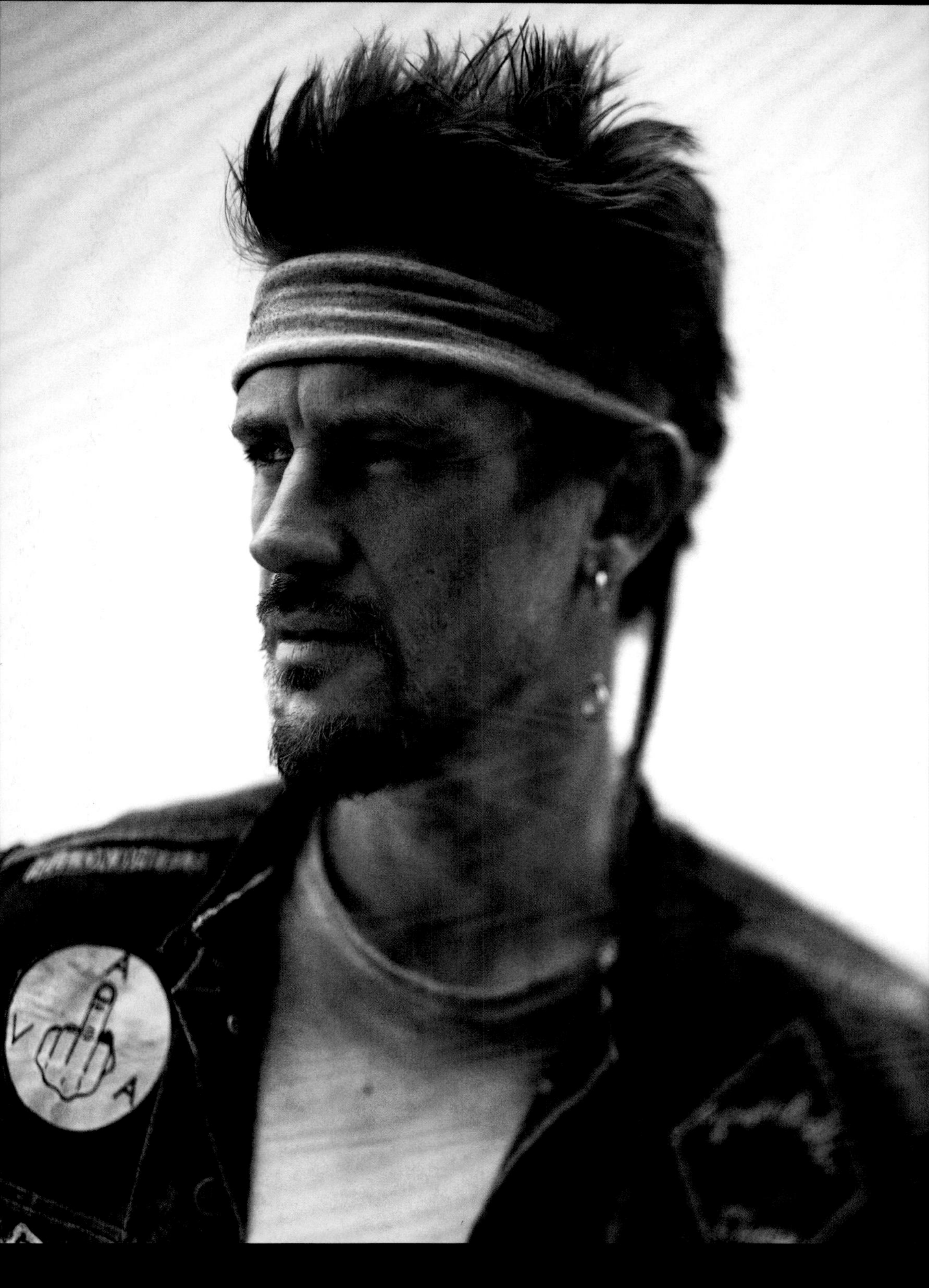

Boyd Holbrook as CAL

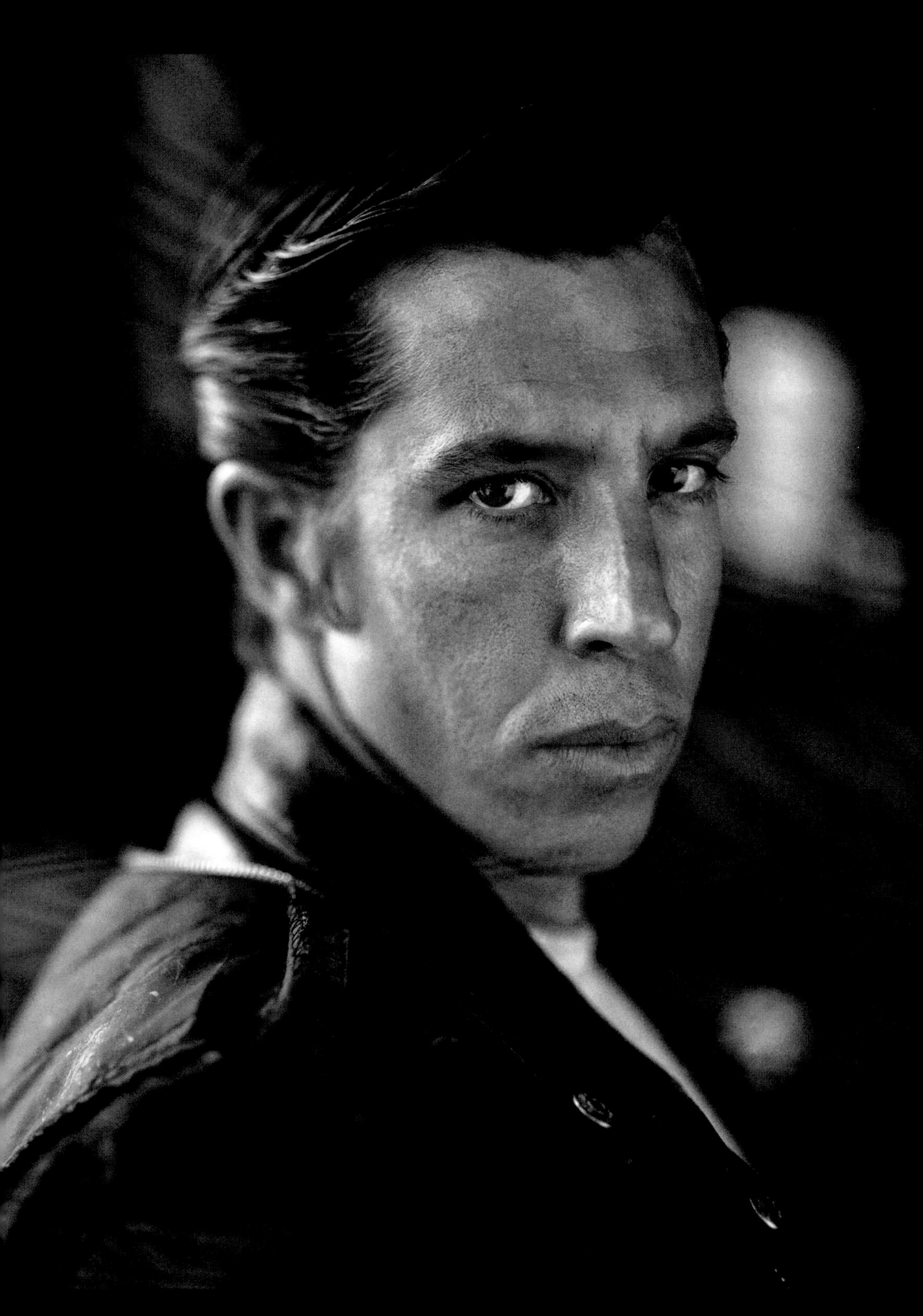

Beau Knapp as WAHOO

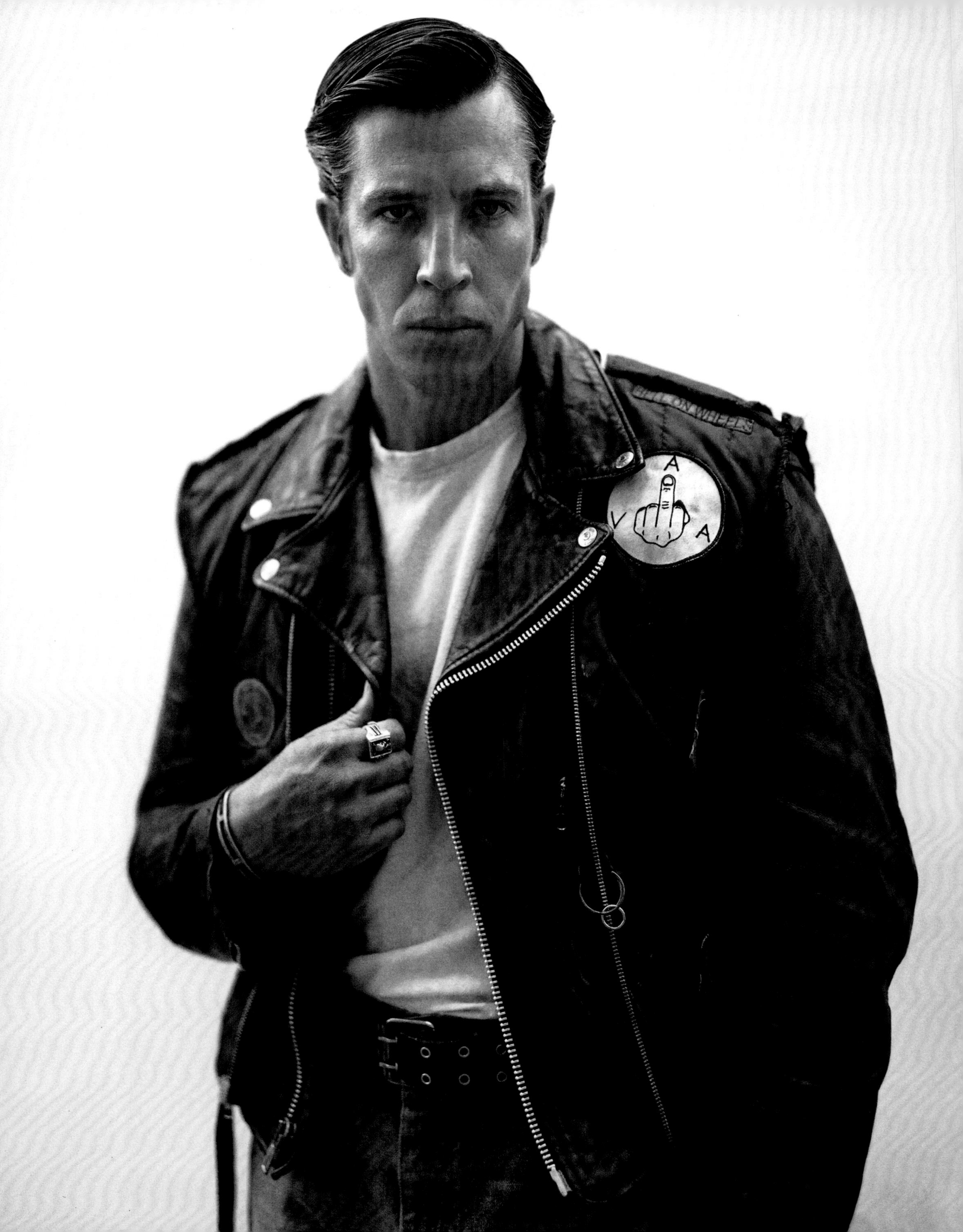
A
V
A

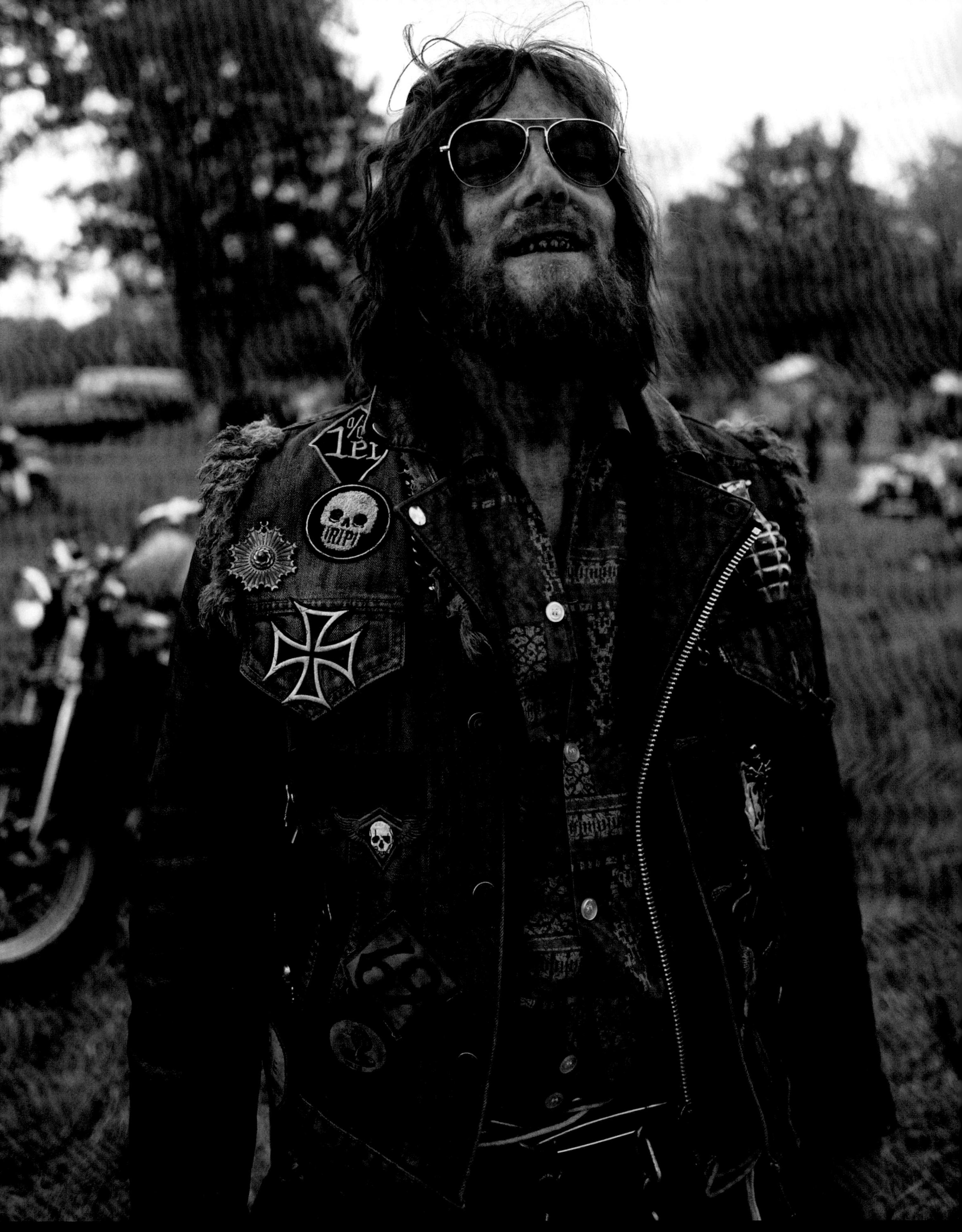
RIP

Norman Reedus as FUNNY SONNY

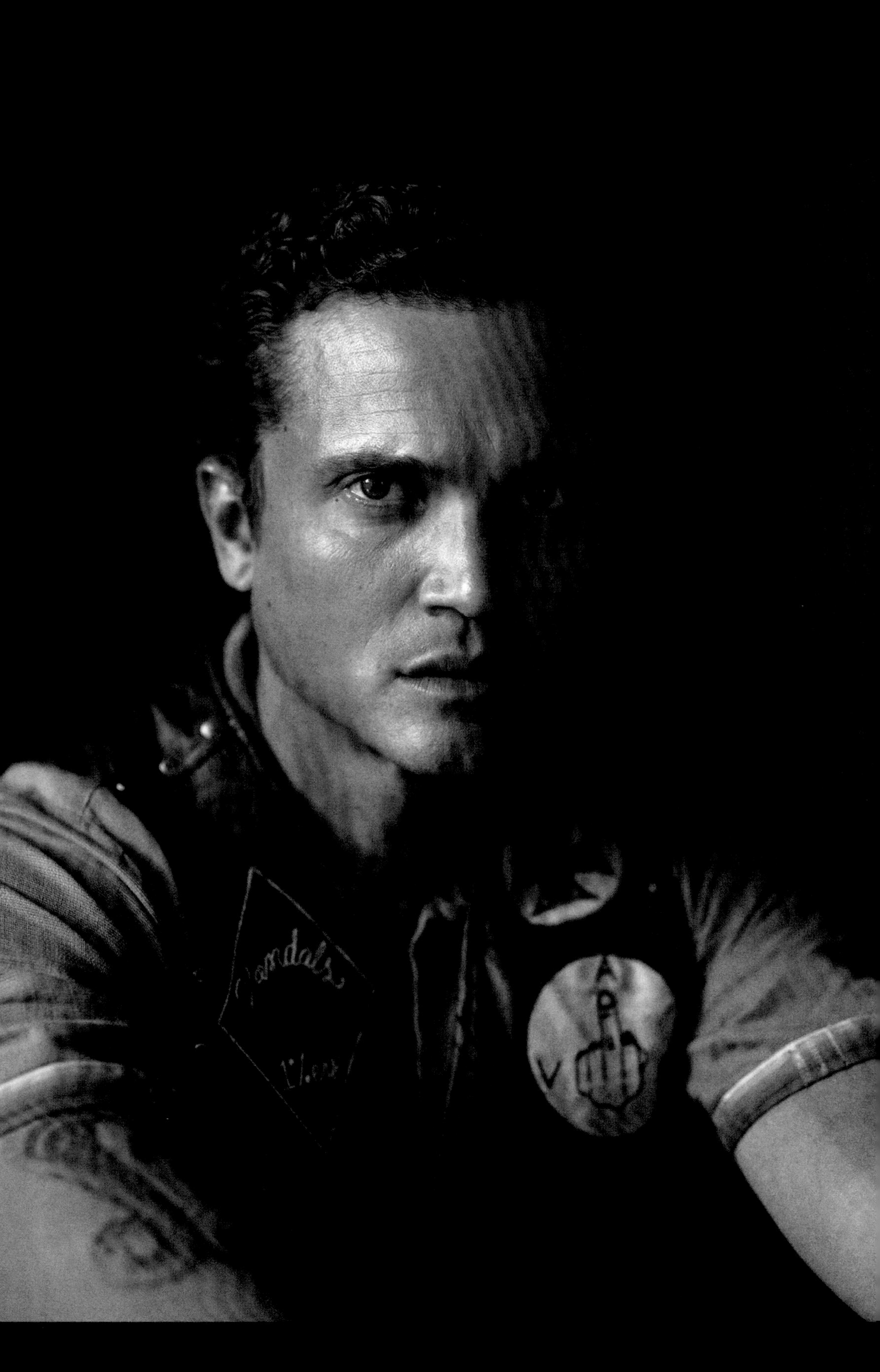

Karl Glusman as CORKY

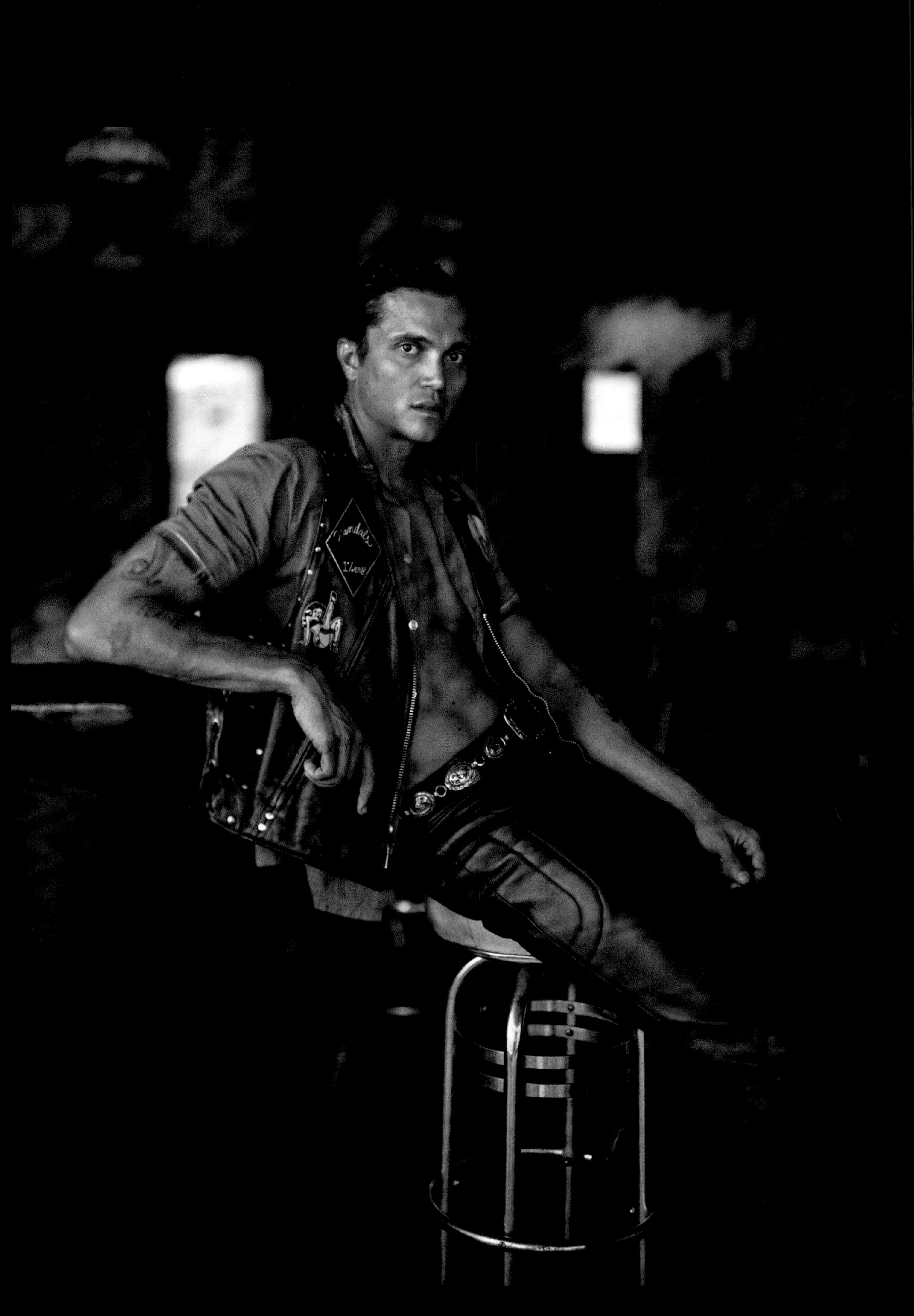

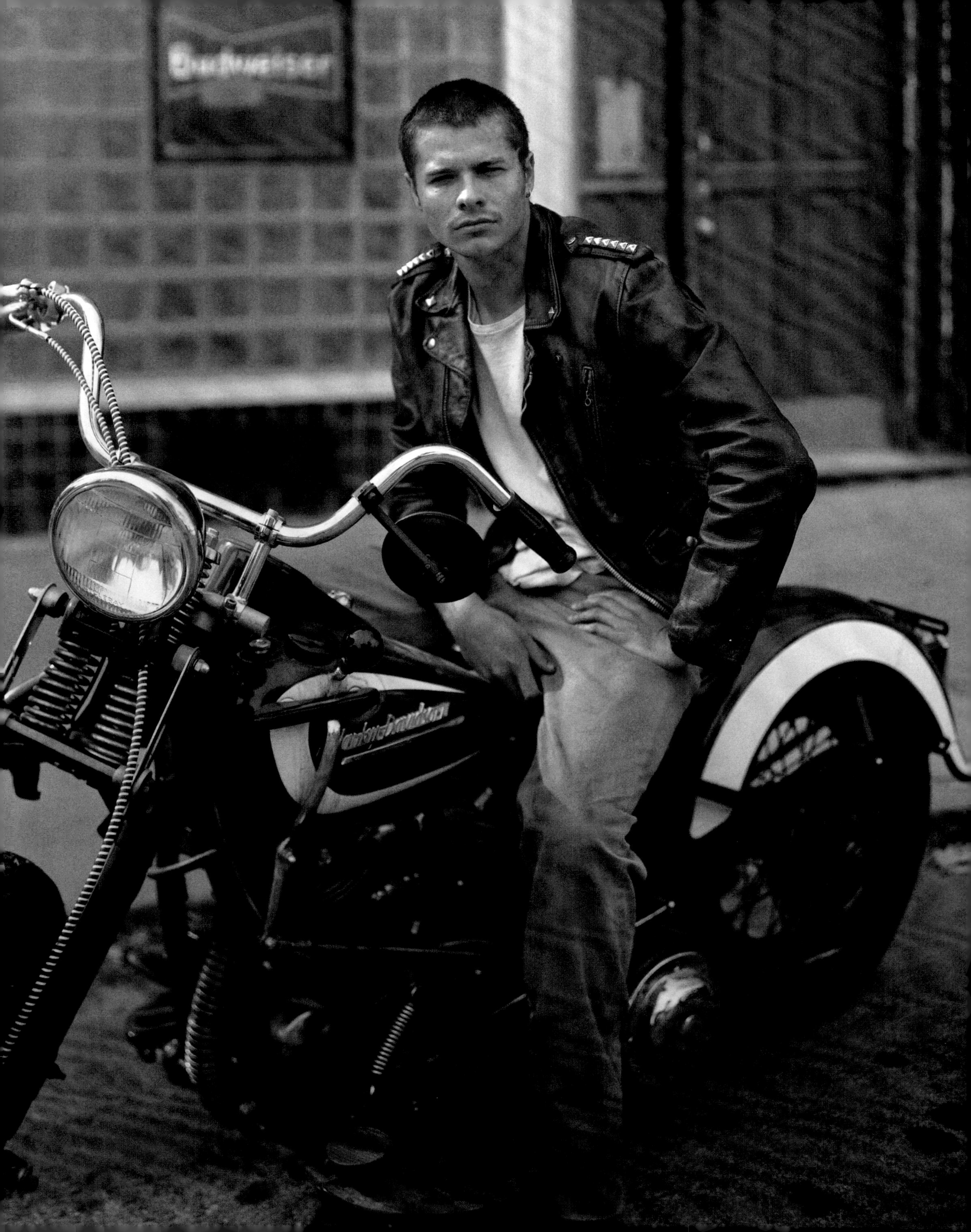

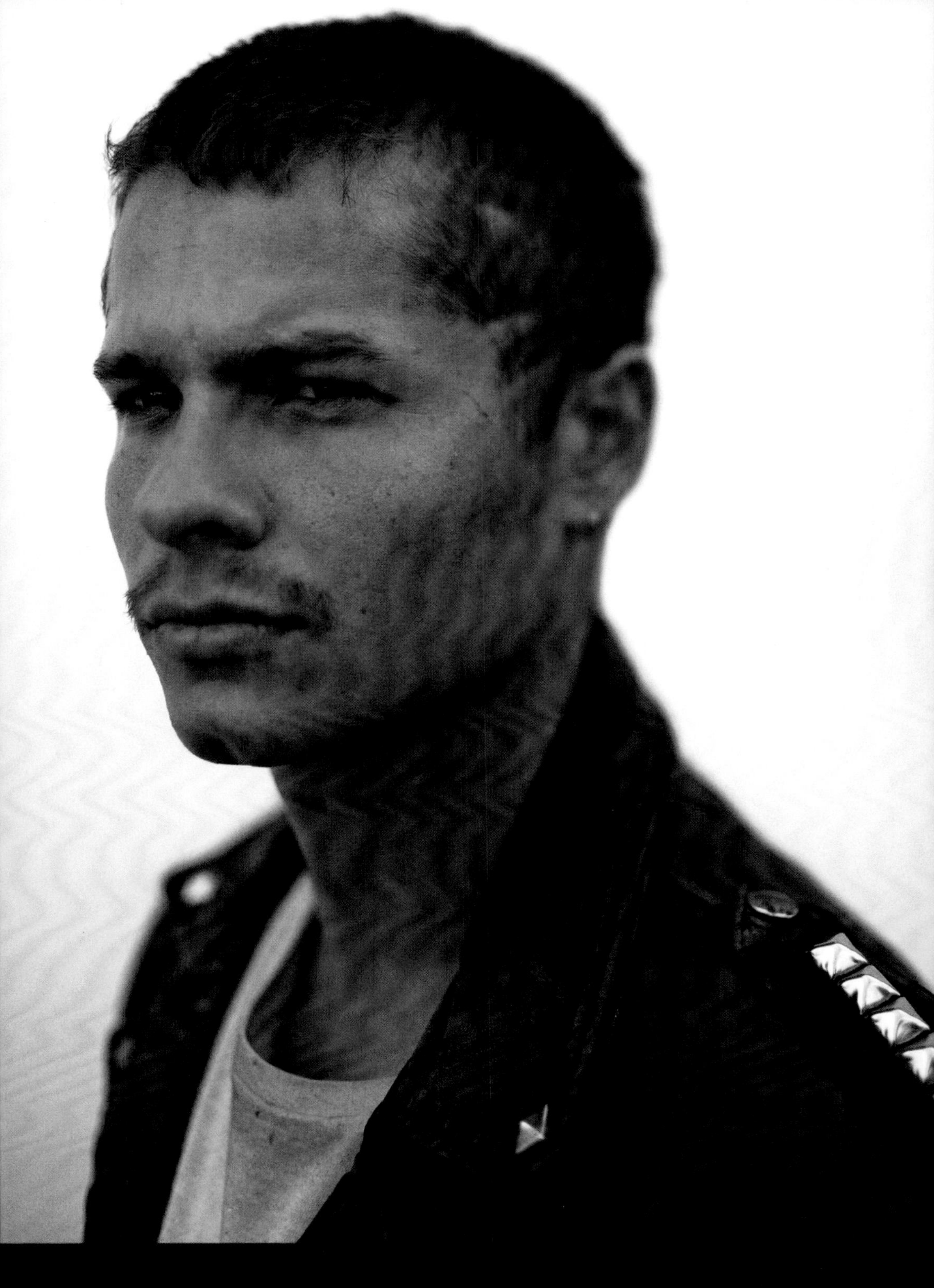

Toby Wallace as THE KID

Damon Herriman as BRUCIE
Phuong Kubacki as GAIL

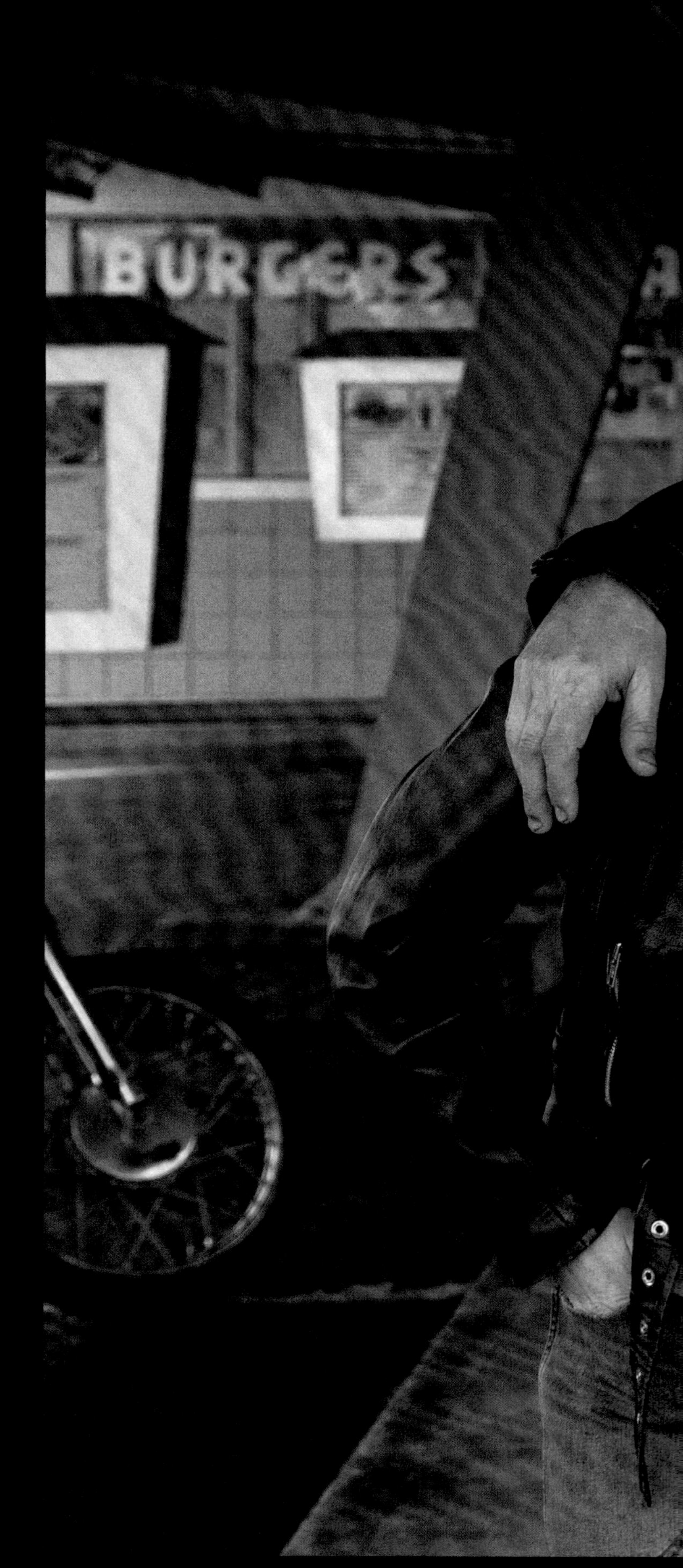

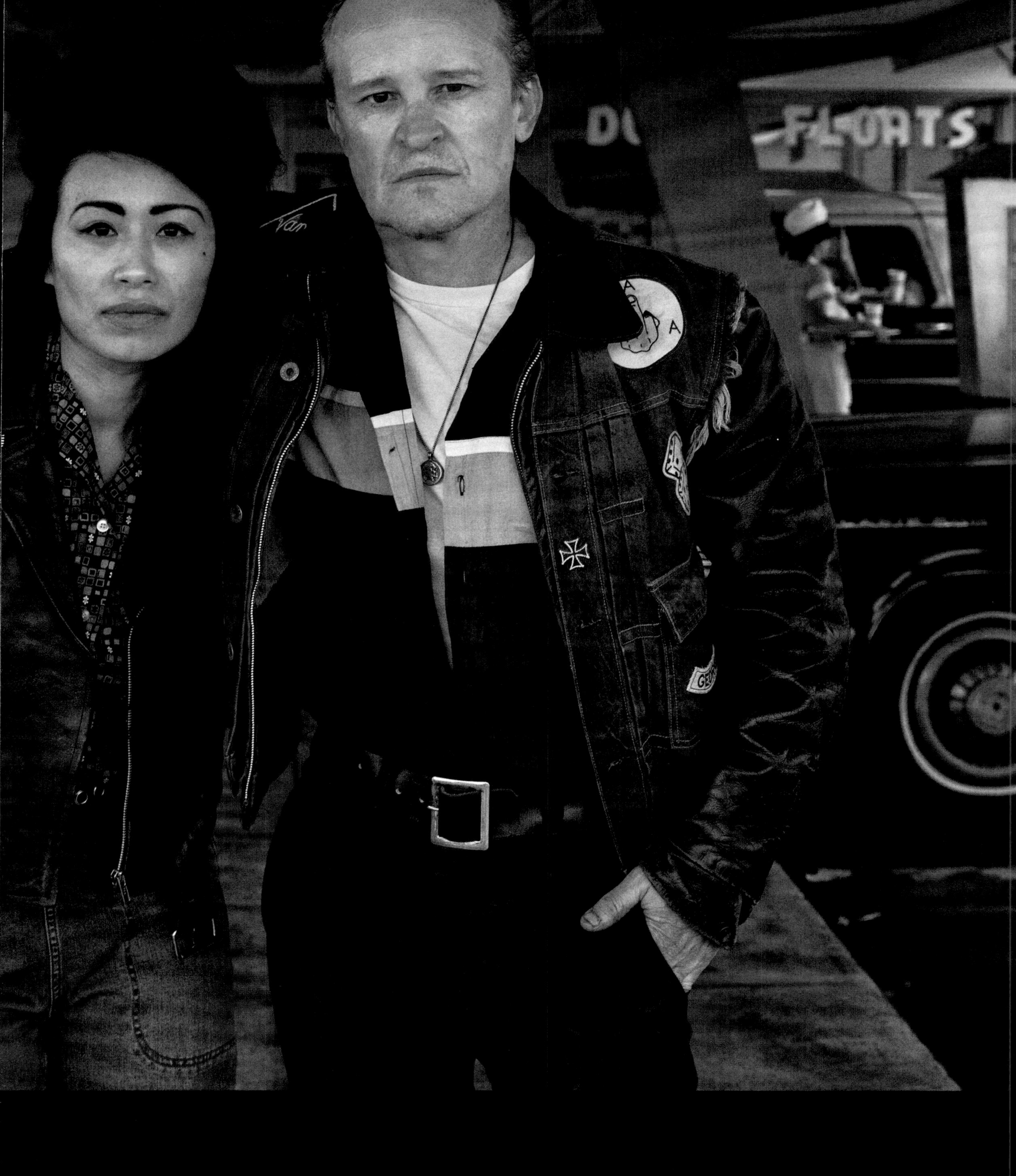
FLOATS

COCKROACH

There's a guy used to ride with us, took photos, he says he's ah . . . He says he's gonna make a book. So I says to him, all I ever want is to be photographed dressed up like a barbarian. Like a real barbarian you know, with fur and an axe or some shit.

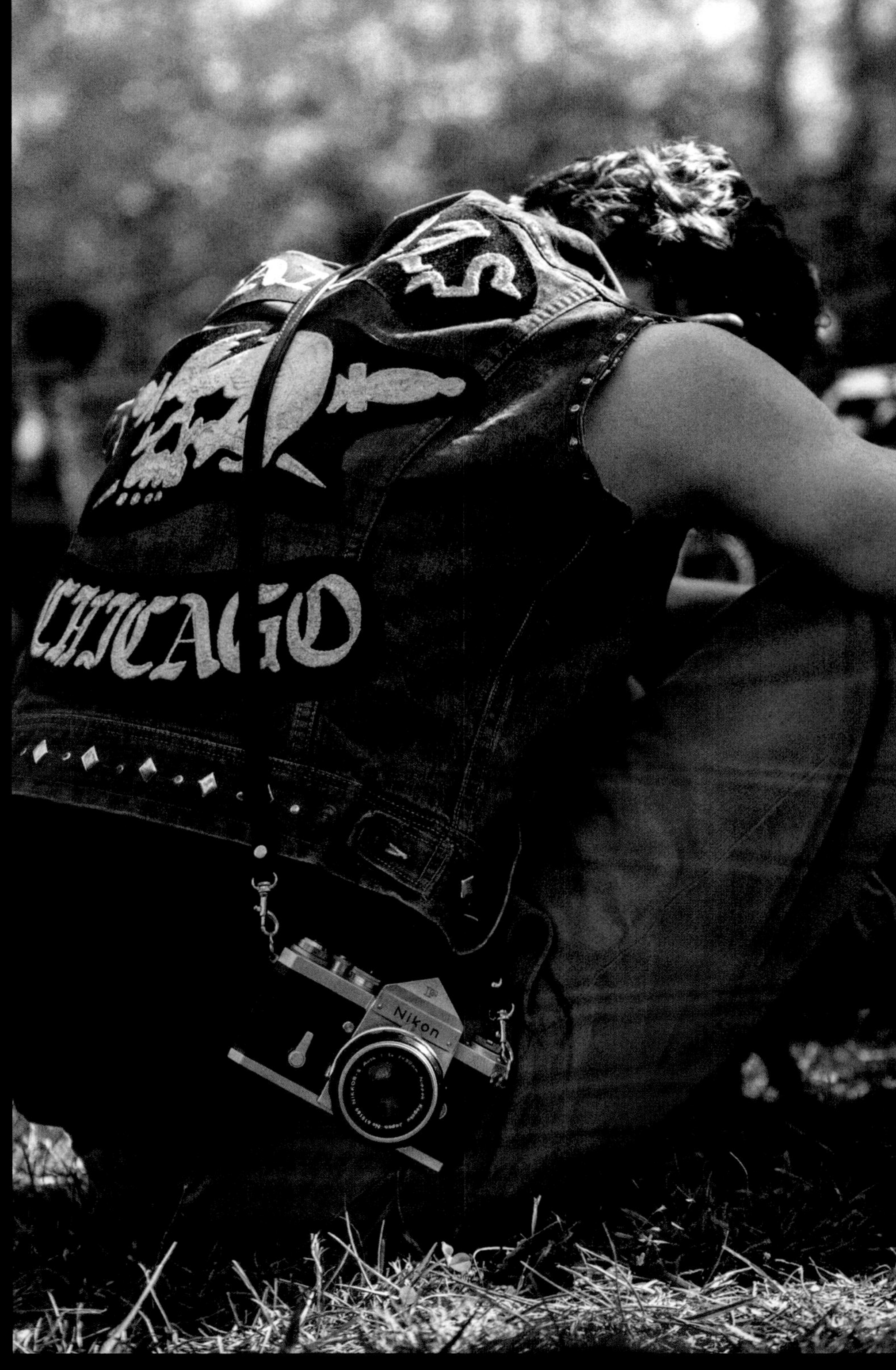
CHICAGO
Nikon

PHOTO CREDITS

The following images were reproduced from the 35mm feature film print, directed by Jeff Nichols, cinematography by Adam Stone.

8-9, 32-33, 58-59, 66-67, 78-79, 90-91, 118-119, 130-131, 136-137, 142-143

Kyle Bono Kaplan

2-3, 5, 10, 14-15, 20, 22, 23, 25, 31, 52, 57, 62, 63, 65, 68-69, 71, 73, 74, 75, 76, 77, 80-81, 83, 85, 86-87, 89, 98, 99, 108, 109, 110, 111, 112-113, 114, 115, 116-117, 120, 121, 122, 125, 127, 129, 135, 138-139, 141, 153, 173

Bryan Schutmaat

11, 12, 16, 17, 18-19, 27, 28-29, 30, 39, 40, 41, 42-43, 44, 45, 46, 48, 49, 51, 55, 60, 66-67, 92, 95, 96-97, 102, 103, 104, 105, 106-107, 133, 147, 148, 149, 151, 154, 156, 158-159, 160, 161, 162, 163, 166, 167, 168, 169

Adam Stone

35, 36-37, 101, 170-171

Boyd Holbrook

164

PHOTOGRAPHERS' ACKNOWLEDGMENTS

Bryan Schutmaat and Kyle Bono Kaplan give thanks to: Jeff Nichols for his remarkable vision and for keeping true cinema alive in this age; Adam Stone for his stunning imagery and for championing still photography alongside film production; Danny Lyon for a life's work that will always endure and inspire; Yariv Milchan, Michael Schaefer, Sam Hanson, Sarah Green, and Brian Kavanaugh-Jones for their passion and tireless work in bringing this project to life; Raoul Goff, Matt Girard, Ben Robinson, and Chris Prince for their publishing expertise and dedication to putting ink on paper in a digital era; all of the actors, from the leads to the background players, for their magnetism, generosity, and patience in front of the camera; Michael Roy and his team for mastery of light; the entire camera department for their achievements and for sharing space with still photographers; Erin Benach, Chad Keith, and their teams for invaluable work designing as well as written contributions to this book; Tony Ward, Patti Denahey, Ashleigh Chavis, Audrey Doyle, and their teams, who transformed the actors with indispensable skills; Rory Clark, for enthusiasm and support behind the scenes; Jeff Milburn, Nick Balibucci, and all the "Vandals" who kept the wheels turning; Tom Claxton, Kevin Messina, Cody Haltom, Matthew Genitempo, and Jake Knapp for friendship and feedback; Ben Rothstein for camaraderie and guidance; Anna Walker Skillman and Coco Conroy for inspiration; Zach Duckro for first-rate photo assisting; Chris Dawson and his team for technical proficiency and rigging; Travis Watkins whose Hasselblad was smashed up for the sake of night shots; April Chang and Penny Lin for helping out in a thousand different ways; and everyone on the film crew whose time went into conceiving, designing, producing, performing, lighting, crafting, and constructing nearly every detail that came before our camera lenses.

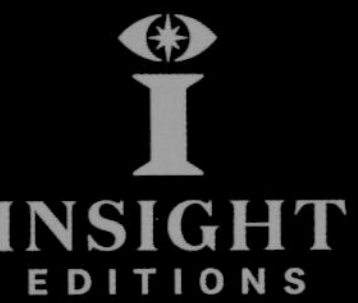

PO Box 3088
San Rafael, CA 94912
www.insighteditions.com

Find us on Facebook: www.facebook.com/InsightEditions
Follow us on Twitter: @insighteditions
Follow us on Instagram: @insighteditions

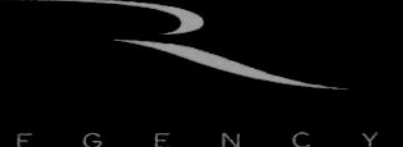

Trade ISBN: 979-8-88663-264-4
Collector's Edition ISBN: 979-8-88663-354-2

We would like to thank Arnon and Yariv Milchan for their partnership and vision; Sam Hanson, Sarah Green and Rory Clark for their tireless support; the cast and crew of *The Bikeriders* for their participation; and Bryan Schutmaat for his dedication, artistry, and passion, all of which have made this book what it is.

Publisher: Raoul Goff
VP, Co-Publisher: Vanessa Lopez
VP, Creative: Chrissy Kwasnik
VP, Manufacturing: Alix Nicholaeff
VP, Group Managing Editor: Vicki Jaeger
Publishing Director: Ben Robinson
Art Director: Matt Girard
Editorial Assistant: Emma Merwin
Managing Editor: Maria Spano
Senior Production Editor: Katie Rokakis
Senior Production Manager: Joshua Smith & Greg Steffen
Senior Production Manager, Subsidiary Rights: Lina s Palma-Temena

Edited by Bryan Schutmaat
Digital imaging by Bryan Schutmaat

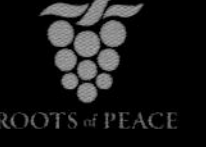

Replanted Paper

Insight Editions, in association with Roots of Peace, will plant two trees for each tree used in the manufacturing of this book.

Manufactured in China by Insight Editions

10 9 8 7 6 5 4 3 2